THE LAST TRUMPET

A HISTORY OF THE ENGLISH SLIDE TRUMPET

Thomas Harper Jr. in his Sergeant Trumpeter's regalia, holding a Köhler slide trumpet with heraldic banner. Photograph courtesy of John Webb.

THE LAST TRUMPET

A History of the English Slide Trumpet

by

Art Brownlow

The University of Texas at Brownsville

BUCINA: THE HISTORIC BRASS SOCIETY SERIES No. 1

Stewart Carter, *General Editor*

PENDRAGON PRESS
Stuyvesant, New York

Musicological Series by Pendragon Press

Aesthetics in Music
Annotated Reference Tools in Music
Bucina: The Historic Brass Society
  Series
The Complete Organ
The Croatian Musicological Society
  Series
Dance & Music
Dimensions & Diversity: Studies in
  20th-Century Music
The Festschrift Series
The Franz Liszt Studies Series
French Opera in the 17th and 18th
  Centuries

Harmonologia: Studies in Music Theory
Historical Harpsichord
Juilliard Performance Guides
Monographs in Musicology
Musical Life in 19th-Century France
The Complete Works of G. B. Pergolesi
Pergolesi Studies/Studi Pergolesiani
The Sociology of Music
Studies in Central European Music
Studies in Czech Music
Thematic Catalogues
Vox Musicae: The Voice, Vocal Peda-
  gogy, and Song

To Amy

Library of Congress Cataloging-in-Publication Data
Brownlow, Art.
    The last trumpet : a history of the English slide trumpet / by Art Brownlow.
        p. cm. — (Bucina ; no. 1)
    Includes bibliographical references (p.   ), discography, and index.
    ISBN 0-945193-81-5
    1. Trumpet—19th century. 2. Trumpet music—19th century—History and
criticism. I. Title. II. Series.
ML960.B76   1996
788.9'2'0942—dc20   96-28052
                                                                                CIP
                                                                                MN

Table of Contents

List of Figures

List of Musical Examples

Foreword

It is remarkable that upon any weekday one may stand outside Buckingham Palace in London and whilst witnessing the ceremony of "The Changing of the Guard" see a mounted Trumpeter of the Royal Household Cavalry fulfilling ceremonial duties that have been enacted in this way for over 300 years. Likewise, the flourishes sounded at "The Opening of Parliament" may well be those sounded at the time of the Coronation of Henry VII in 1483 when the Treasury submitted accounts for "betyng and gylding of forty trumpetts banners, beten with the kyng's armes." Banners bearing the present Queen's insignia cost £8000 (US $12,000) each, and few spectators realise that these emblems suspended from the trumpet gave their bearers heraldic if not diplomatic status in former centuries. Further evidence of immutable British conservatism may be found in the catalogues of musical instruments advertised by Hawkes and Son in 1906 and 1910, whereby it was still possible to buy a "slide" or tuneable "natural" trumpet whose sounds had traditionally graced performances of Handelian and Purcellian music long after and despite the invention of convenient contrivances such as valves.

Recently, the phenomenon of recorded sound has transformed our experience of music. Concert performances recreate the perfection of studio conditions with clinical accuracy, and undoubtedly in the thirty years of my own professional career, greater overall technical precision on most instruments has been achieved, arguably standardizing our perceptions and tastes. The drawbacks artistically have been the loss of national styles, and the equalization of instrumental tone in the quest for greater volume and security. The beautiful tone of wooden flutes played in the Philharmonia Orchestra, the sweetness of narrow-bore trombones, the incisive attack of Alexander horns and the springy bounce of the small Tuba have all been overwhelmed by the aggressive blare of the "Big Sound." Nowadays almost all Baroque trumpet music shrieks at us from the short-tubed "piccolo" trumpet, with shrill high frequencies, invariably smothered in spurious so-called "ornamentation" in the worst excesses of misplaced cornet style.

These changes have taken place in a little over a quarter of a century, so presumably the expectations of a late-seventeenth-century audience were markedly different from our own. Probably the greatest change is in regard to volume; this would explain the ability of performers to "bend" dissonant harmonics on "natural" brass instruments, and also why a century after Purcell's time when orchestras and choruses were much larger and louder that Charles Burney found the sound of specific notes insufferable. The practical invention of a half-tone tuning device—a slide—on the trumpet retained all the dignity of that "noble" instrument's tone and its surprising ability to balance with a single human voice, and therefore reproduced those qualities expected throughout Classical musical orchestration and in the ever-popular repertoire of the late Baroque period that had preceded it. Surely it must have been unthinkable to perform "The Trumpet Shall Sound" standing at the front of an orchestra with a Cornet—laughably so—and only the introduction of long valved trumpets in A and D in the 1880s provided a visually acceptable alternative.

In light of this observation, it should be recalled that when Mendelssohn invited Thomas Harper Senior to perform Bach's Magnificat, the latter reportedly asserted that "this music is not playable upon a modern trumpet" (his instrument was a conversion of one built by Harris in Handel's time, now exhibited in the Royal College of Music Museum, London), clearly emphasizing the different schools of playing in Leipzig and London during the same historical period.

The English Slide Trumpet (of which there are many excellent surviving examples) therefore not only retained the tonal concepts of Baroque times, but also sustained the same playing techniques almost into the twentieth century. The chapters that follow will greatly enhance all musicians' understanding of this subject, and hopefully will inspire those players interested in recreating historical-style performances to confront the challenges faced by our musical forebears. It may be timely to warn, however, that most of those employing us are more frequently concerned with the promotion of their own careers and reputations than in the exploration of genuine musical archeology; so great tenacity will be required of you as well as a strong lip and hard neck! I hope you will enjoy and learn as much from Dr. Brownlow's masterly treatise as I have.

Crispian Steele-Perkins
Abinger Hammer, Surrey

Preface

In the final two decades of the eighteenth century, trumpeters and brass instrument makers throughout Europe experimented with various ways of improving the intonation of the natural trumpet, and of creating a chromatic instrument. Late in the century an English instrument maker collaborated with a trumpeter to build a trumpet with a slide mechanism that essentially solved both problems. This instrument was the first of several generations of slide trumpets that came to dominate English orchestral playing in the nineteenth century.

Although several important French instrument makers, including Courtois and Sax, built slide trumpets, French players generally favored the *cornet à pistons* and the natural trumpet. German players also preferred the natural trumpet but gradually succumbed to the valved trumpet by the last quarter of the century. Thus, while the completely chromatic valved instruments were being developed and embraced by European orchestral trumpeters, the English continued to play slide trumpets until nearly the end of the century.

The slide trumpet has been previously addressed in a few scholarly works from several different viewpoints. To date, articles by Cynthia Hoover and John Webb are the most comprehensive studies of the subject. Hoover's 1963 *Brass Quarterly* article is entitled "The Slide Trumpet of the Nineteenth Century." This article focuses on physical descriptions of surviving instruments, particularly one housed at the Smithsonian Institution, and examines various nineteenth-century slide trumpet tutors. Webb's 1993 article "The English Slide Trumpet," in the *Historic Brass Society Journal*, is a good overview of the instrument and its history. Two studies of the Harpers, father and son performers who dominated nineteenth-century English trumpet playing, by Scott Sorenson (a 1987 Ph.D. thesis on Thomas Harper Sr.) and Sorenson and Webb (a 1986 *Galpin Society Journal* article entitled "The Harpers and the Trumpet"), are also important contributions to our knowledge of the slide trumpet.

None of these studies, however, deals with the literature of the instrument. While conventional wisdom has it that the slide trumpet was used almost exclusively as an orchestral instrument, the present study will demonstrate that it also was used as a solo instrument, and in a wide variety of ways. Sorenson, Webb, and Hoover mention performances of both Harpers, and some of the music they played, but this book represents the first attempt to examine in detail the music written for the slide trumpet.

The present study provides, in addition to a survey of repertory, a comprehensive history of the instrument and its predecessors. It further explores the reasons for the primacy of the slide trumpet over valved instruments in England, and offers some suggestions for modern use of the instrument. Supplementary material provided in appendices includes checklists of the important eighteenth- and nineteenth-century British trumpet players and makers, and nine cadenzas written for Handel's aria "Let the Bright Seraphim." As the early music movement increasingly focuses on nineteenth-century performance practice, it is hoped that the slide trumpet will again flourish as a valuable orchestral and solo instrument.

Art Brownlow
Brownsville, Texas

Acknowledgments

Many people have given freely and generously of their time, advice and knowledge to help me in the research and writing of this book. I cannot find words to express the depths of my gratitude to these people. I hope that these acknowledgments will in some small way show evidence of my appreciation. To Crispian Steele-Perkins and John Webb I offer my sincerest thanks for their invaluable assistance throughout the entire process. Without their help, this project would have never seen its completion.

The following librarians were extremely helpful in assisting in my research: David Hunter and others, University of Texas at Austin; Bob Parker, British Library; Peter Horton, Royal College of Music; Elizabeth Orton, Fitzwilliam Museum Library, Cambridge; Eva Heater, Yale; and Leslie Troutman, University of Illinois. The following curators and individuals took time to show and/or provide me with valuable information about surviving slide trumpets: Crispian Steele-Perkins; John Webb; Frank Tomes; G. Norman Eddy, Eddy Collection, Cambridge MA; Jeremy Montagu, Bate Collection, Oxford; Darcy Kuronen, Museum of Fine Arts, Boston; Franz Streitwieser and Ralph Dudgeon, Trumpet Museum, formerly of Pottstown PA; Albert R. Rice, Kenneth G. Fiske Museum, Claremont CA; Margaret Downie Banks and André P. Larson, Shrine to Music Museum, Vermillion SD; and Laurence Libin, Metropolitan Museum of Art, New York. To Oliver Davies, Department of Portraits and Performance History at the Royal College of Music, many thanks for showing me the Harper programs, photographs and lithographs.

Appreciation is gratefully extended to my editor, Stewart Carter, as well as to Jeffrey Nussbaum, Historic Brass Society, and Robert Kessler, Pendragon Press. Scott Sorenson, John Thiessen, Peter Barton, Frank Tomes, and Trevor Herbert provided detailed and prompt answers to my inquiries. Reine Dahlqvist sent me copies of several important manuscripts by Sigismund Neukomm and gave me many interesting points to ponder. Martin Lessen sent me a copy of

with information about the Scottish trumpeting family of Napier.
Thanks to Henry Meredith for sending me a copy of the J. H. Walch
solo for slide trumpet and military band.

Since this study originally began as a dissertation project at the
University of Texas at Austin, I would like to extend my appreciation
to the supervisors of my committee, Raymond Crisara and Michael
Tusa, for their leadership and encouragement. Likewise I am grate-
ful to my colleagues at the University of Texas at Brownsville, for
help in various aspects of the project: Terry Tomlin, Mary Jane
Garza, Eduardo Aguilar, Ronnie Zamora, and Arturo Lozano.

I would also like to acknowledge my trumpet teachers, past and
present, for their inspiration and guidance, and for instilling in me a
love for the instrument and its history: Larry Black, George Hitt,
Larry Cook, Michael Parkinson, Vincent Cichowicz, and Raymond
Crisara.

To my parents, Erma and Arthur Brownlow, I would like to offer
my enduring thanks for their support of my career in music. Finally,
I would like to thank my wife Amy, for her extraordinary patience
and unwavering support throughout the completion of this long—and
at times overwhelming—project.

List of Abbreviations

Standard library sigla are used; museum sigla appear as applied in
The New Langwill Index, by William Waterhouse.

A-Kremsmünster	Streitwieser Foundation, Schloss Kremsegg, Austria (formerly Trumpet Museum of Pottstown, PA)
B-Brussels	Musée Instrumental du Conservatoire de musique
F-Paris	Musée de la musique
GB-Brighton	Art Gallery and Museum
Cfm	Cambridge, UK, Fitzwilliam Museum Library
GB-Edinburgh	Edinburgh University Collection of Historical Musical Instruments
GB-Huddersfield	Tolson Memorial Museum
GB-Keighley	Cliffe Castle Museum
Lbl	London, British Library
GB-London-H	Horniman Museum
Lcm	London, Royal College of Music Library
GB-London-RCM	Royal College of Music Museum of Instruments
GB-Oxford	Bate Collection of Musical Instruments
US-CA-Claremont	Kenneth G. Fiske Museum, Claremont College
US-DC-Washington-S	Smithsonian Institution
US-MA-Boston	Museum of Fine Arts

US-MA-Cambridge   Eddy Collection of Musical Instruments

US-NY-New York   Metropolitan Museum of Art

US-SD-Vermillion   Shrine to Music Museum, University of
                         South Dakota

Behold, I tell you a mystery;
we shall not all sleep, but we shall all be chang'd,
in a moment, in the twinkling of an eye,
at the last trumpet....

I CORINTHIANS XV, 51, 52
Messiah by George Frideric Handel
No. 47, Recitative

Chapter One: Precursors

In late May and early June of 1784, five mammoth concerts were held in Westminster Abbey and the Pantheon[1] in London, to commemorate the 100th anniversary of Handel's birth, mistakenly one year early. The concerts consisted of selections from Handel's works; the secular in the Pantheon, and the sacred in the Abbey. All the concerts were impressive events, both in size and importance. Each Abbey concert featured more than 500 combined singers and instrumentalists, performing to an audience of nearly 3000, including King George III and most of the nobility. The celebration was such a success that it became an annual event, with the number of performers increasing yearly until interest began to decline in the 1790s. The event was documented by the music historian Charles Burney, among others.[2]

Burney had much to write about the performances, and his criticism of James Sarjant, the trumpet soloist in "The Trumpet Shall Sound" from the 29 May *Messiah* concert, has become legendary.

> The favourite Bass song, *"The Trumpet Shall Sound"* (I Cor. XV. 52) was very well performed by Signor Tasca and Mr. Sarjant, who accompanied him on the trumpet admirably. There are, however, some passages in the trumpet-part to this Air, which have always a bad effect, from the natural imperfection of the instrument. In HANDEL'S time, composers were not so delicate in writing for Trumpets and French-horns, as at present; it being now laid down as a rule, that the fourth and sixth of a key on both these instruments, being *naturally* so much out of tune that no player can make them perfect, should

---

[1]A building, built in 1772 on Oxford Street, which flourished as a large concert hall and opera house in the late eighteenth century. See *The New Grove Dictionary of Music and Musicians*, s. v. "London: Opera—Theatres," by Henry Raynor.

[2]Charles Burney, *An Account of the Musical Performances in Westminster Abbey and The Pantheon, May 26th, 27th, 29th; and June the 3d, and 5th, 1784 in Commemoration of Handel* (London: Printed for the Benefit of the Musical Fund, 1785).

never be used but in short passing notes, to which no base is given that can discover their false intonation. Mr. Sarjeant's [*sic*] tone is extremely sweet and clear, but every time that he was obliged to dwell upon G, the fourth of D, displeasure appeared in every countenance; for which I was extremely concerned, knowing how inevitable such an effect must be from such a cause.[3]

Burney refers, of course, to the eleventh note (f" in C; g" in D) of the harmonic series, the notes of which are the only ones available to the natural trumpet. As Burney indicates, this note is a special problem, being quite out-of-tune according to the tempered scale (see Example 1), and also because of its prominence as the subdominant of the fundamental pitch. It is much too high for an f, and yet not quite an f♯.

Example 1: Harmonic series with fundamental C (showing flat and
    sharp tendencies).

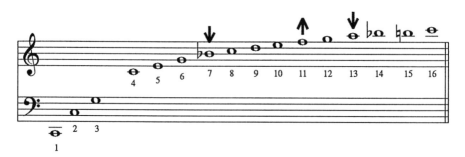

In an interesting footnote to the above, Burney writes of other places in Handel's works where the eleventh partial can be found (including the "Hallelujah" chorus and the *Dettingen Te Deum*) and remarks that the sustained sound of that note

perpetually deforms the fair face of harmony, and indeed the face of almost every one that hears it, with an expression of pain. It is very

---

[3]Ibid., 86–87.

much to be wished that this animating and brilliant instrument could have its defects removed by some ingenious mechanical contrivance.[4]

In the late eighteenth century there were many attempts made throughout Europe to "remove the defects;" that is, to improve the tuning of the trumpet and to make it chromatic. Some of these experiments included the use of hand stopping, and the addition of keys or valves. But in England, the "ingenious mechanical contrivance" was the slide. We know that slide trumpets had been in existence for at least 150 years before the Handel Commemoration, and probably since the early Renaissance. But a new type of slide trumpet, with an automatic slide return mechanism, was designed within perhaps five years of Burney's criticisms, and possibly *because* of them.

Eventually the valved trumpet prevailed in continental Europe, but in England the slide trumpet was used almost to the end of the nineteenth century. It was *the* standard orchestral trumpet, and evidence exists that it was a popular solo instrument as well. In fact, William Stone, in the first edition of Grove's *Dictionary*, published from 1878 to 1889, describes *this* instrument in the trumpet article.[5] Why was the slide trumpet used in England when valved trumpets had become standard elsewhere? What type of music was performed on this instrument? And how did this trumpet develop and evolve over the course of the nineteenth century? In order to understand fully the English slide trumpet, the instrument's history must first be considered.

EARLY SLIDE TRUMPETS

The concept of the slide trumpet was not new at the turn of the nineteenth century: the instrument was used during the seventeenth and eighteenth centuries. The Leipzig *Kantor* Johann Kuhnau and

---

[4]Ibid., 87.

[5]William H. Stone, "Trumpet," *A Dictionary of Music and Musicians*, ed. George Grove (London: Macmillan, 1878-1889), 4: 180–183.

his successor J. S. Bach wrote parts for *tromba da tirarsi* in their
cantatas, and the Leipzig trumpeter Gottfried Reiche had a
Zugtrompete among his possessions at his death.[6] The origin of the
slide trumpet, however, is not clear. No surviving instrument dates
from before the mid-seventeenth century, but even so, most scholars
believe that such trumpets were in use from the early Renaissance.
The evidence, found in documents, iconography, and music, is considerable, though mostly circumstantial.

The Slide Trumpet in the Renaissance

Several writers have documented the use of some type of slide
instrument in the shawm bands of Flanders throughout the fifteenth
century.[7] And although there is a lack of iconographic evidence of a
double-slide instrument before ca. 1450, there are many drawings
and illustrations of apparent single-slide trumpets from the early
fifteenth century. These instruments look much like contemporary
natural trumpets, either S-shaped or twice-folded loops, but it is the
manner in which they are depicted in the illustrations that has con-

---

[6]*The New Grove Dictionary of Musical Instruments*, s. v. "Slide Trumpet," by Edward H. Tarr.

[7]According to Reine Dahlqvist, the idea of a Renaissance slide trumpet was first
put forth by Curt Sachs in his *Handbuch der Musikinstrumentenkunde* (1920).
Later he developed the idea more thoroughly in "Chromatic Trumpets in the Renaissance," *Musical Quarterly* 36 (1950): 62–66. For other Renaissance slide trumpet arguments see Anthony Baines, *Brass Instruments: Their History and
Development* (London: Faber & Faber, 1976; repr., New York: Dover Publications,
1993), 94–107; Ross W. Duffin, "The *trompette des menestrels* in the 15th-century
alta capella," *Early Music* 17 (1989): 397–402; Herbert W. Myers, "Slide Trumpet
Madness: Fact or Fiction?" *Early Music* 17 (1989): 382–389; *New Grove Instruments*, s. v. "Slide Trumpet," by Tarr; Keith Polk, "The Trombone, the Slide
Trumpet and the Ensemble Tradition of the Early Renaissance," *Early Music* 17
(1989): 389–397; Don L. Smithers, *The Music and History of the Baroque Trumpet
before 1721*, 2nd. ed. (Carbondale: Southern Illinois University Press, 1988), 36–
39; and Edward H. Tarr, *The Trumpet*, trans. S. E. Plank and Edward Tarr
(Portland: Amadeus Press, 1988), 56–58.

vinced most writers. Both of these slide trumpet designs would have been played by moving the trumpet forward and backward with the right hand over a telescoping mouthpipe, while stabilizing the mouthpiece against the lips with the left hand.[8] In most of these illustrations, slide movement is suggested in either the configuration of the instrument or in the way that the trumpets are held.

This instrument would have been responsible for the largely improvised contratenor line of the polyphonic music played by shawm bands, which also would have included a *bombarde* playing a *cantus firmus* tenor line, and a shawm (or shawms) playing a florid treble part. Keith Polk, who has argued convincingly for the Renaissance slide trumpet, presents his chronology of the development of the instrument thusly:

> Soon after about 1350 a new concept evolved in the combination of a brass instrument with shawms. In the first stage this was quite likely a straight instrument, with, possibly, a simple slide mechanism. Around 1375 or so, the technology was available for the development of the 'S-shaped' instrument (with single slide), which would have come into more general use around 1400. Soon after the turn of the century, a 'folded form' emerged, also with a single slide, which became common by about 1430. Both of these last two seem to have been popular with musicians until near the end of the century. By shortly before 1450 the double slide principle was known, but performers seem not to have preferred this form until the last years of the century.[9]

In the sixteenth century, evidence for the existence of the slide trumpet becomes even more convincing. Anthony Baines has found a Kassel *Hofkapelle* inventory from 1573 that lists "three German

---

[8]This is opposed to the classic playing position for a natural trumpet in ceremonial playing; that is, holding the instrument perpendicular to the ground, or slightly upwards, with either both hands or one, gripping the trumpet near its center. See numerous examples in Tom L. Naylor, *The Trumpet and Trombone in Graphic Arts: 1500–1800* (Nashville: The Brass Press, 1979).

[9]Polk, "Ensemble Tradition," 395–396.

trumpets with their slides (*Zugen*) and mouthpieces," and another from the palace of Marburg dated 1601 that describes "2 *Zugk Trometten*."[10] Early in the century two important musical treatises, by Virdung (1511) and Agricola (1528), mention the *Tower horn*, an instrument that is generally regarded as a slide trumpet.[11] Identified as *Thurnerhorn*, or *Türmerhorn*, this instrument was used by tower musicians for sounding alarms in the event of enemies or fire, for calls at certain hours of the day, and for performing during civic celebrations and ceremonies. According to Edward H. Tarr the slide trumpet was used by tower musicians "until far into the Baroque period. They chose this instrument because during the course of the fifteenth and sixteenth centuries they had been assigned a new duty in addition to that of mere signaling: tower playing (*Abblasen* in German)."[12] *Abblasen* would have consisted of playing chorales and similar music, most of which would have been easily playable on a slide trumpet with four positions. Don L. Smithers suggests another reason for the use of slide trumpets on the towers.

> Some sources imply that a tower watchman's trumpet was drawn ('ziehen') in and out to execute various notes and that such an instrument was used to avoid difficulties with the knightly trumpet guilds. The guild looked upon such instruments with disdain, not regarding them as proper trumpets. It was not until the mid seventeenth century that the guild trumpeters realized that *Zugtrompeten* were actually a threat to their privileged position.[13]

Although some writers[14] do not believe in this scenario—

---

[10]Anthony Baines, "Two Cassel Inventories," *Galpin Society Journal* 4 (1951): 31–34.

[11] See Sebastian Virdung, *Musica Getutscht* (Basle: 1511; reprint, Kassel: Bärenreiter, 1970); and William Wood Holloway, "Martin Agricola's *Musica instrumentalis deudsch:* A Translation" (Ph.D. diss., North Texas State University, 1972).

[12] Tarr, *Trumpet*, 60.

[13]Smithers, *Baroque Trumpet*, 28.

[14]Most notably Peter Downey, "The Renaissance Slide Trumpet, Fact or Fiction," *Early Music* 12 (1984): 26–33.

whereby slide trumpets are found in shawm bands and on city towers from the early fifteenth century—the circumstantial evidence for an early slide trumpet is overwhelming. We know from archival documents that some type of slide brass instrument was used in the courtly shawm bands as early as the turn of the fifteenth century. And we also know that the trombone does not appear in iconography until the mid-fifteenth, and then with few examples. It seems unlikely that a double-slide trombone would have been developed without the intermediary step of the development of a single-slide trumpet.

The Baroque Zugtrompete

The seventeenth century has produced the first surviving slide trumpet, and the only one before the late eighteenth century. This instrument which is dated 1651, was made by Huns Veit of Naumburg, Saxony, and was housed as recently as the Second World War in a Berlin museum.[15] It was acquired in 1890 from the *Wenzelskirche* in Naumburg, which listed two new *Zugtrompeten* in its 1658 inventory.[16] The instrument is very much like the many iconographical representations of Renaissance slide trumpets, and would have been held and operated in the same manner. It is pitched in E♭, and built in the twice-folded shape. The mouthpiece shank is around twenty-two inches long, and telescopes inside the first yard of tubing. This type of trumpet would probably not have been widely used by trumpeters other than tower watchmen. Johann Ernst Altenburg writes about the slide trumpet in 1795:

The slide trumpet, which is commonly used by tower watchmen (*Thürmer*) and by city musicians (*Kunstpfeifer*) for playing chorales

---

[15]See description and photograph in Dieter Krickeberg and Wolfgang Rauch, *Katalog der Blechblasinstrumente: Polsterzungeninstrumente* (Berlin: Staatliches Institute für Musikforschung, 1976), 144; see also photograph in Baines, *Brass Instruments*, Plate VII.

[16]Baines, *Brass Instruments*, 178.

(*geistliche Lieder*), is constructed almost like a small alto trombone because it is pulled back and forth during playing, whereby [the player] can easily bring forth the missing tones [of the harmonic series].[17]

At Leipzig, however, a slide trumpet like the Huns Veit instrument might have been used in other situations. It was previously mentioned that a slide trumpet was left by Gottfried Reiche at his death in 1734. Reiche was one of Leipzig's *Kunst-* or *Stadtpfeifer*, and as such would have been proficient on the *Zugtrompete*, as well as the natural trumpet and several other types of instruments.[18] But he also regularly performed church music, and Bach wrote many of his most challenging trumpet parts for Reiche. Perhaps Reiche and other trumpeters played the *tromba da tirarsi* parts in Leipzig cantatas on this type of slide trumpet.[19]

The Flat Trumpet

The first documented evidence of a double-slide trumpet can be found in England, in the late seventeenth century. This instru-

---

[17]Johann Ernst Altenburg, *Essay on an Introduction to the Heroic and Musical Trumpeters' and Kettledrummers' Art, for the Sake of a Wider Acceptance of the Same, Described Historically, Theoretically, and Practically and Illustrated with Examples*, trans. Edward H. Tarr (Nashville: The Brass Press, 1974), 14.

[18]*New Grove*, s. v. "Reiche, Gottfried," by Edward H. Tarr.

[19]The reader should be aware of a book by Gisela and Jozsef Csiba, which claims that some Baroque trumpeters used short slides to help correct intonation on their natural trumpets. Photographs of mouthpipe interiors have revealed abrasions that were supposedly produced by these slides. According to Tarr's review of the book, this slide "was about one-third the length of the mouthpipe and is thus shorter than the true *tromba da tirarsi* slide, but of course permits intonation correction without 'lipping.' It is the Csibas' contention that the Leipzig (and other) *Stadtpfeifer* used the slide, whereas court trumpeters preferred 'lipping'." See Gisela and Jozsef Csiba, *Die Blechblasinstrumente in J. S. Bachs Werken* (Kassel: Merserburger, 1994); and Edward H. Tarr, review of same, in *Historic Brass Society Journal* 6 (1994): 380–381.

ment is the so-called "flat trumpet," the name of which is derived from its ability to play in "flat," or minor, keys, as opposed to the "sharp," or major, keys of the natural trumpet. The first probable evidence of the flat trumpet comes from a set of drawings made by Nicholas Yeates for Francis Sandford's *History of the Coronation of James II*, which was published in 1687, two years after the event. The extensive drawings include a depiction of the royal procession from Westminster, and include three instrumental groups: fifes and drums, trumpets and kettledrums, and The King's Music. The second group is obviously the royal trumpet corps, which consisted of natural trumpets only.

More important to this study, however, is the representation of The King's Music, which includes three wind instrumentalists.[20] The drawing is obviously of a cornetto player and two trumpeters, playing twice-folded trumpets. But the text labels these instruments as *sackbuts*. Eric Halfpenny believes that these instruments are slide trumpets, and prototypes of the flat trumpet, for which solid evidence appears as early as 1691. These trumpets are held in a downward position—like the many drawings of apparent Renaissance slide trumpets—as opposed to the more straightforward way that the corps trumpets are held. Also they are, as mentioned, grouped with a cornetto player and as such are characteristic of the city *waits*, or watchmen, which were the English equivalent of the German *Stadtpfeifer*.[21]

This use of the term *sackbut* as a generic slide instrument seems to be fairly consistent at this time, and has been documented by both John Webb and Trevor Herbert. Webb has examined drawings of the coronations of William and Mary in 1689, and Queen Anne in 1702, and has found depictions of trumpets similar to those

---

[20]See a reproduction of the drawing in John Webb, "The Flat Trumpet in Perspective," *Galpin Society Journal* 46 (March 1993): 157.

[21]Eric Halfpenny, "Musicians at James II's Coronation," *Music and Letters* 32 (1951): 103–112.

described above, and yet with the *sackbut* label.[22] Herbert mentions that "Elisha Coles's *English Dictionary*, published in 1695, defines 'sackbut' simply as 'a drawing trumpet'."[23] Thus Yeates' depictions of these instruments are compatible with slide trumpet iconography from the early fifteenth century, and the use of generic slide instrument terminology is also consistent throughout this period.

As was the case with the Renaissance slide trumpet, there are no surviving flat trumpets. But if the iconographical evidence is inconclusive, the musical and documentary information is not. James Talbot, a professor at Trinity College, Cambridge, from 1689 to 1704, left a manuscript that is now housed at Oxford. In this manuscript Talbot left detailed measurements and descriptions of various musical instruments, including a flat trumpet pitched in C. Talbot obtained his information about the instruments from consultation with leading London performers. We know this from a signed letter to John Shore, Purcell's friend and the premiere English trumpeter of the 1690s, in which Talbot thanks him for lending his instruments for study.[24] Part of Talbot's description of the flat trumpet is as follows:

> In a Flat Trumpet the mouthpiece stands oblique towards right. 2d Crook [bow] placed near left Ear & by it you draw out the Inward yards, whereof one reaches to the Boss of the Pavillion, the other to the 1st Crook: its size with the yards shutt the same with the common Trumpet.[25]

---

[22]Webb, "Flat Trumpet," 154–157.

[23]Trevor Herbert, "The Sackbut in England in the 17th and 18th Centuries," *Early Music* 18 (1990): 612.

[24]See Anthony Baines, "James Talbot's Manuscript (Christ Church Library Music MS 1187)," *Galpin Society Journal* 1 (March 1948): 9–26; for further information on Talbot see also Robert Unwin, " 'An English Writer on Music': James Talbot 1664-1708," *Galpin Society Journal* 40 (December 1987): 53–72.

[25]Baines, "James Talbot's Manuscript," 21.

This description, however, is at odds with the iconography of possible slide trumpets, in contemporary England and from continental sources. And it is very different from the continental slide trumpet by Huns Veit of some forty years earlier. Talbot describes a double-slide instrument, with the slide to be drawn *backwards* so that the "2d Crook [is] placed near [the] left Ear."

There is also musical evidence for the flat trumpet. Webb has mentioned five works written for the flat trumpet, all from the 1690s. They are: Gottfried Finger's *Tafelmusicke* for the St. Cecilia's Day celebration of 1691 (one part only for flat trumpet); a segment from Act V of Purcell's incidental music to the play *The Libertine* (1692); Purcell's *Funeral Music for Queen Mary* (1695);[26] the "Farewell for Henry Purcell" (1696) by Finger; and Daniel Purcell's "Symphony of Flat Trumpets" (1699) from the play *The Island Princess* (Figure 1, p. 12).[27] Finger's *Tafelmusicke* might have been the first music to feature this instrument, considering the comments made in the *Gentleman's Journal* about the St. Cecilia's Day festival.

Whilst the company is at table the hautboys and trumpets play successively. Mr. Showers [Shore] hath taught the latter of late years to sound with all the softness imaginable; they plaid us some flat tunes made by Mr. Finger with a general applause, it being a thing formerly thought impossible upon an instrument designed for a sharp key.[28]

Purcell's *Funeral Music for Queen Mary* consisted of a processional march and an anthem followed by a canzona, performed at the queen's funeral services and also for Purcell's own funeral later in 1695. All of these pieces were written for flat trumpets, as the

---

[26]The funeral march of which is the same music as that in *The Libertine*, but in a different arrangement.

[27]Webb has mistakenly identified the composer of the "Symphony of Flat Trumpets" as Jeremiah Clarke. See Webb, "Flat Trumpet," 156–158.

[28]*Gentleman's Journal* (January 1692); quoted in William H. Husk, "Shore, John," in *A Dictionary of Music and Musicians*, edited by George Grove (London: Macmillan, 1883), 3: 488.

Figure 1: Daniel Purcell, "Symphony of Flat Trumpets," from *The Island Princess* (f. 39). By permission of the British Library. [Add. 15318]

manuscript of the anthem, *Thou knowest Lord ye Secrets of our Hearts*, indicates:

> A Full Anthem sung at y[e] funerall Solemnity of Queen Mary 1694/5 accompanied wth flat Mournfull Trumpets. Compos'd by Mr. Henry Purcell; in Hon[r] to whose Memory the same Composition was perform'd y[e] year following at his own funerall, in Westminster Abbey.[29]

In considering aspects of the flat trumpet's design, Webb makes an interesting connection with the German-style *Zugtrompete*.[30] Of course the *Zugtrompete* and the flat trumpet embody com-

---

[29]See W. Barclay Squire, "Purcell's Music for the Funeral of Queen Mary II," *Sammelbände der Internationalen Musik-Gesellschaft* 4 (1903): 227.

[30]Webb, "Flat Trumpet," 158.

pletely different slide mechanisms, the former incorporating a mouthpipe slide over which the entire instrument moves, and the latter a backward moving double-slide. But it does invite interesting speculation about the origin of the flat trumpet: perhaps German immigrant musicians brought with them the principle of the *Zugtrompete*, and after some tinkering by English trumpeters and instrument makers, the flat trumpet resulted.[31] This scenario would explain the inconsistencies between the iconographical depictions of the flat trumpet and Talbot's description. Indeed, Webb thinks that there was not really a definitive flat trumpet, but rather several different designs.[32]

The role of the flat trumpet was most likely that of a specialty instrument. Although some writers have argued for a wider use of the instrument,[33] the lack of physical evidence and the limited musical and documentary evidence contradicts this argument. Indeed Crispian Steele-Perkins wonders why flat trumpets evolved at all. "An alto trombone is less cumbersome and plays fully chromatically, at speed. I should add that if tenor oboes and flutes were employed for only a few bars of an opera, the same apparently applied to the flat trumpet."[34]

---

[31]For an interesting discussion of Germanic and other continental influences on English trumpet style, see Peter Downey, "What Pepys Heard on 3 February 1661: English Trumpet Style under the Late Stuart Monarchs," *Early Music* 18 (1990): 417–428.

[32]Webb, "Flat Trumpet," 158.

[33]See Andrew Pinnock, "A Wider Role for the Flat Trumpet," *Galpin Society Journal* 42 (1989): 105–111; and Pinnock and Bruce Wood, "A Counterblast on English Trumpets," *Early Music* 19 (1991): 436–443.

[34]Crispian Steele-Perkins, "Practical Observations on Natural, Slide and Flat Trumpets," *Galpin Society Journal* 42 (1989): 126.

THE TRUMPET IN LATE-EIGHTEENTH-CENTURY ENGLAND

England in the second half of the eighteenth century witnessed a gradual decline of the *clarino* trumpet style of the Baroque.[35] This was the florid, vocally derived style of playing that made use of the very high fourth octave of the harmonic series. This register was necessary, of course, in order for trumpeters to be able to play diatonic melodies on their natural trumpets. The reasons for the decline were both social and musical. In the late eighteenth century there was a gradual change in the social order, due to the decline of court life in the wake of the French Revolution. The heroic court trumpet style and the related *clarino* style came to be considered outdated. But changes in musical style were even more significant. In the Baroque, one mood, or *Affekt*, was presented in a particular movement of a musical work. If that *Affekt* was heroic, then the trumpet, and its fundamental key, would have been featured throughout. But as sonata form evolved, so did the expression of several moods (and keys) in a movement. The instruments that were more adaptable to this change were the string instruments; thus, the dominant orchestral timbre of the late eighteenth century is a string timbre. Tarr explains the changing role of the trumpet in the orchestral ensemble:

> The new style made a tutti instrument of the once heroic trumpet, which formerly had led the melody. Sometimes a short fanfare which closed an allegro movement or a symphony called attention to the trumpeters' surviving court function. But heroic expression was not enough. The adaptable strings could better render the new range of expression, because in a musical work not one but several forms of emotion were now required.[36]

---

[35]This was true in most places as well, but there were isolated pockets of continuing *clarino* activity. Indeed, the *clarino* technique was brought to its most virtuosic levels in the music of late eighteenth-century Austrian composers such as Johann Matthias Sperger and Michael Haydn. See Tarr, *Trumpet*, 141–145.

[36]Tarr, *Trumpet*, 144.

Illustrations of this change can be found in Mozart's arrangements of Handel's oratorios, particularly in the rewriting and simplification of the trumpet parts. According to Smithers, Mozart "did not trust the trumpeters of his day to execute properly the difficult clarino parts of his predecessors."[37] But Reine Dahlqvist argues that the late-eighteenth-century Viennese trumpeters would have been quite up to the task, and that "Mozart changed much of Handel's orchestration in order to obtain a more up-to-date sound."[38]

In addition to control of the high register, trumpeters also lost the ability to "lip" or "bend" notes, and along with it control of the difficult eleventh partial. Lipping is the technique whereby naturally out-of-tune notes are corrected by relaxing or tightening lip muscles. In the Baroque period, notes outside the harmonic series were also produced by this technique, but it is doubtful that all trumpeters had this skill.[39] It is more likely that only the finest players mastered the technique of note-bending, and that much of Baroque trumpet playing was out-of-tune, especially when the eleventh partial was used. We have already observed that James Sarjant was criticized by Burney for his playing at the 1784 Handel Commemoration. But even Handel's great trumpeter Valentine Snow, who is fondly mentioned several times in Burney's *General History of Music*, did not escape criticism. In a discussion of Handel's overture to *Atalanta*, Burney writes:

> The fugue, different from most of Handel's other overture fugues…is light and airy; and the trumpet part, intended to display the tone and abilities of Snow…has fewer notes that are naturally and inevitably imperfect in the instrument, than common. The fourth of the key is, however, too much used even for vulgar ears to bear patiently.[40]

---

[37]Don L. Smithers, "Mozart's Orchestral Brass," *Early Music* 20 (1992): 259.

[38]Reine Dahlqvist, letter to the author, 24 September 1995.

[39]Smithers, *Baroque Trumpet*, 201.

[40]Charles Burney, *A General History of Music from the Earliest Ages to the Present Period* (London: 1776-1782; repr., New York: Harcourt, Brace and Co., 1935), 2: 801.

In a footnote, he lists several measures in which the note can be found, and adds, "Indeed, whenever the fourth or sixth of the key is otherwise used than as a passing-note, the ear is offended."[41]

In defense of Sarjant, the size of the ensemble with which he performed in 1784, as well as the cavernous environment of Westminster Abbey, must be considered. Steele-Perkins believes that because early-eighteenth-century orchestras were small, and the trumpet therefore was played at a relatively low volume, the large English mouthpieces allowed the players to lip the notes and correct faulty intonation. But the technical demands were different with the huge orchestras of the festivals of the 1780s and 90s. In Steele-Perkins' view, "It is not practicable to 'bend' notes at volume and by this time the subtlety of the trumpeting art was lost...."[42] Indeed, he believes that the increase in ensemble size, and the resulting increase in volume, was the most important factor in the decline of the clarino style, which "denotes 'clear, soft-blown' style."[43] Another possible reason for the decline in trumpeters' ability to bend notes is the gradual change to equal temperament during the last half of the eighteenth century. Perhaps the out-of-tune harmonics were not quite so out-of-tune, and therefore a bit easier to bend in meantone and related historical temperaments. According to Dahlqvist, "the natural trumpet sounds a 'little purer' [in meantone] than in equal temperament."[44]

John Thiessen suggests that it may have been Burney who, however indirectly, was the inspiration not only for the newly designed slide trumpet of the late eighteenth century, but for other trumpet designs as well.

> Even though Burney's main bone of contention, the eleventh partial f♯"/f♮", was rarely used in the late 18th-century English trumpet rep-

---

[41]Ibid.

[42]Crispian Steele-Perkins, letter to the author, 7 February 1992.

[43]Steele-Perkins, letter to the author, 13 February 1994.

[44]Dahlqvist, letter to the author, 24 September 1995.

ertory, comments from such a towering figure in London's musical circles did not go unheeded. ...[45]

One of these new designs was a primitive valved trumpet by Charles Clagget. In a pamphlet announcing his invention Clagget reproduces an endorsement that Burney evidently sent to Clagget, upon learning of his new trumpet:

> Not only science, but ignorance, is offended by the imperfections in particular notes of these instruments, which are false, as intervals, in themselves, and, as concords, are never in tune with any other instrument; the fourth and sixth, in particular, being detestably false in whatever key they are played. These imperfections are completely removed by Mr. Clagget's expedient.[46]

And in the earliest slide trumpet tutor, which was written by the self-proclaimed inventor of the slide trumpet, John Hyde, there is the following comment:

> Dr. Burney in his History of Music, has taken particular notice of the imperfect fourth and sixth, which imperfection is compleatly remedied by the Chromatic [slide] Trumpet. ...[47]

---

[45]John C. Thiessen, "The Late Eighteenth-Century Trumpet in England: A Reconstruction of Repertory" (M.M. thesis, King's College, University of London, 1990), 11.

[46]Charles Clagget, *Musical Phaenomena, founded on Unanswerable Facts; and a proof that Musical Instruments have been hitherto fabricated on the most uncertain, therefore the most improper materials: No. 1; The Aiuton, and the Chromatic Trumpets and the French Horns, capable of fine tune and regular harmony in all the keys in use, minor as well as major* (London: printed for the author and sold at the Musical Museum, 1793), 15–16.

[47]John Hyde, *A New and Compleat Preceptor for the Trumpet and Bugle Horn, With the Whole of the Cavalry Duty as approved of and ordered by his Royal Highness the Duke of York, Commander in Chief, To which is added a Selection of Airs, Marches & Quick Steps for Three Trumpets, A Scale of the Chromatic Trumpet, With Airs Adapted for it, And A Collection of Bugle Horn Duets, With The Light Infantry Duty* (London: Printed and to be had of the Author, [1799]), 51.

Crooking and Hand Stopping

Burney's comments notwithstanding, the fact remains that several experimental attempts to improve intonation and achieve at least a degree of chromaticism in the trumpet occurred in England within a few years of his writings. Further design changes and an increased use of crooking appeared in an effort to accommodate changing musical styles. In the late eighteenth century, trumpets and horns were being made in higher keys—usually F; other keys were attained by adding crooks, which were additional lengths of tubing. The tubing of a six-foot F trumpet was two feet shorter than eight-foot C, which along with D had been the standard pitches for trumpets throughout most of the eighteenth century in England.[48] No longer could the English trumpeter get by with natural trumpets pitched only in one or two keys, when the music demanded that they play in others.

One attempt at chromaticism that gained some popularity on the European continent was that of hand stopping. This technique was borrowed from late-eighteenth-century horn players, but because of the elongated form of the trumpet, some design changes were necessary in order to make hand stopping practical. The obvious solution was to make a trumpet with more than the normal two bows, thereby producing a tighter coil that reduced the overall

---

[48]It is interesting to speculate as to why the pitch of F became standard. Steele-Perkins thinks it is because so many players at the end of the eighteenth century played both trumpet and horn, and a standard F pitch for both made it easier to switch from one to the other (Steele-Perkins, conversation with the author, 2 June 1993). In fact, a look at The Royal Society of Musicians' membership list, which documents application information revealing the applicants' instruments, shows this to be so. Many of the trumpet players from the eighteenth and early nineteenth centuries also played horn, as well as other instruments such as violin and viola. See Betty Matthews, comp., *The Royal Society of Musicians of Great Britain List of Members 1738-1984* (London: Royal Society of Musicians, 1985). For a complete discussion of trumpet pitch, see Reine Dahlqvist, "Pitches of German, French, and English Trumpets in the 17th and 18th Centuries," *Historic Brass Society Journal* 5 (1993): 29–41.

length of the instrument. But crooking created an additional problem: each crook added to the mouthpipe made it more difficult for the trumpet (or horn) player to hold the instrument close to the body in order to facilitate hand stopping. One solution to the problem was the *Inventionstrompete*,[49] a design borrowed from the *Inventionshorn*, said to have been developed in the early 1750s by the hornist Hampel and originally built by Werner of Dresden.[50] Hampel's and Werner's *Invention* was "a curved sliding crook...inserted into the body of the horn or trumpet without disturbing the mouthpiece."[51] When applied to the middle of the trumpet or nestled in one of the bows, the *Invention* allowed the instrument to be short enough for the player's hand to reach into the bell, thereby facilitating hand stopping.[52]

According to Tarr, hand stopping was first applied to the trumpet by Michael Wöggel of Karlsruhe in the early 1770s.[53] His trumpet was bent slightly into a gentle curve in order to facilitate the insertion of the hand into the bell. A later design of this type was the *trompette demi-lune*, a "half-moon"-shaped instrument that became extremely popular at the end of the eighteenth century.[54] The popularity of hand stopping on the continent is evidenced by the fact that it was still in general use well into the nineteenth century. In 1830 the Prussian trumpeter Karl Bagans wrote an article that admitted the existence of keyed and valved trumpets, but dismissed them, "as

---

[49]See the photograph of a Roth *Inventionstrompete* in Tarr, *Trumpet*, 154.

[50]See *New Grove Instruments*, s. v. "Trumpet," by Tarr; and *New Grove*, s. v. "Invention," by Niall O'Loughlin.

[51]*New Grove*, s. v. "Invention," by O'Loughlin.

[52]For more information on hand stopping and the various uses of the term *Inventionstrompete*, see Edward H. Tarr, "The Romantic Trumpet," *Historic Brass Society Journal* 5 (1993): 218–223; and Reine Dahlqvist, "Gottfried Reiche's Instrument: A Problem of Classification," *Historic Brass Society Journal* 5 (1993): 180–181.

[53]Tarr, "Romantic Trumpet," 218.

[54]See the photograph of a *trompette demi-lune* by Sautermeister et Muller in Philip Bate, *The Trumpet and Trombone*, 2nd ed. (London: Ernest Benn, 1978), Plate 12.

they are not often used in the orchestra."[55] Bagans' instrument of choice was an improved *Inventionstrompete*, and in the article he gives scales, including stopped notes, for all keys, as well as three melodies playable on this trumpet. But the principal problem with hand-stopping technique was that the timbre of the stopped notes did not match that of the open tones. Bagans alludes to this in his article:

> With this improved state of the modern trumpet, the performer has principally to take care that he produce all his tones, whether natural or artificial, *equally*, so that there be no break or perceptible difference in force, between one note and another.[56]

Hand stopping achieved its greatest popularity in Germany and Italy, but never caught on in England, primarily because of this unevenness of timbre. Clagget, who admittedly had ulterior motives in advertising his new chromatic trumpet, nevertheless sums up the prevailing English attitude:

> Hitherto we could only hear certain notes, full and perfect, from them [the trumpet and horn]; and when tunes and melodies have been attempted, it was by a vile method of thrusting the hand into the bell of the Horn, which produced such heterogeneous sounds, some perfectly clear and charming, other buffed or muffled, as rendered it impossible almost to believe sounds, so unconnected, could be produced from the same instrument.[57]

The Keyed Trumpet

Another continental invention that had little success in England was the keyed trumpet. Although holes and keys were first ap-

---

[55]Karl Bargans [*sic*], "On the Trumpet, as at Present Employed in the Orchestra; with a Retrospective View of the Earlier Methods of Using it," *Harmonicon* (January 1830): 23.

[56]Ibid., 24.

[57]Clagget, *Musical Phaenomena*, 19.

plied to the trumpet in the early 1770s in Dresden, it was the five-key design by the Austrian court trumpeter Anton Weidinger that gained the widest acceptance.[58] This instrument, which Weidinger called the *organisirte Trompete*, was the one for which both Haydn and Hummel wrote their concertos. Jeremy Montagu claims that it became the standard orchestral trumpet in the early nineteenth century in Austria, Italy, and Bavaria.[59] But again the timbral inconsistencies from note to note seem to have prevented its acceptance in England, even though Weidinger himself performed on his instrument in London.[60] In 1829 the Gambatis, two Italian brothers and players of keyed trumpets, were engaged at the King's Theatre. The *Quarterly Musical Magazine* reviewed their performance in the orchestra: "Their execution is wonderful; but their instruments being furnished with keys, enable them to increase facility by means that take very much from the astonishment which they create at first hearing. Their tone is rough and raw...."[61]

---

[58]For the most complete discussion of the keyed trumpet and Weidinger, and photographs of surviving instruments, see Reine Dahlqvist, *The Keyed Trumpet and its Greatest Virtuoso, Anton Weidinger* (Nashville: Brass Press, 1975).

[59]Jeremy Montagu, *The World of Romantic and Modern Musical Instruments* (Woodstock, NY: The Overlook Press, 1981), 98.

[60]On 10 March and again on 28 March, 1803, Weidinger, "lately arrived from Vienna," played concertos on his "Organized Trumpet" for charity concerts at the King's Theatre, Haymarket. *The Times* announcement of the first concert mentions that Weidinger is the inventor of the trumpet, and that he "is particularly recommended to this country by Dr. Haydn." One can only wonder if Weidinger played Haydn's concerto on one or both of these occasions. See advertisement from *The Times* (London), 7 March 1803, 1.

[61]*Quarterly Musical Magazine* 8: 30, 134; quoted in Adam Carse, *The Orchestra from Beethoven to Berlioz: a History of the Orchestra in the First Half of the 19th Century, and of the Development of Orchestral Baton-Conducting* (New York: Broude Brothers, 1949), 167–168.

Charles Clagget's "Cromatic Trumpet"

Although hand stopping and keyed trumpets were imported from the continent with little success, there were several English attempts to improve the trumpet as well, and within only a few years of Burney's 1785 criticisms. Two of these, Clagget's "Cromatic Trumpet," and William Shaw's so-called "Harmonic Trumpet," also failed. Clagget's trumpet (Figure 2) was simply a combination of two natural trumpets a semitone apart (D and E♭), joined by means of a primitive box valve. This is believed to be the first use of a valve system to shift air flow from one tube to another, almost twenty-five years before the first continental experiments with valves. There is, however, no evidence that Clagget's valve was known on the continent. The system is described by Clagget in the patent specification dated 15 September 1788:

> My...new improvement...consists of uniting together two French horns or trumpets in such a manner that the same mouth-piece may be applied to either of them instantaneously during the time of per-

A CROMATIC TRUMPET.

ɪ'he Notes produced from the Patent Trumpets and Horns are always in the natural Tone of the Inſtruments, which are proved capable of regular Harmony and fine Tune, in all Keys, Mɪɴᴏʀ as well as Mᴀᴊᴏʀ ; and without the aſſiſtance of Crooks, or any change whatever·in the Inſtrument,

Figure 2: Charles Clagget, "Cromatic Trumpet," from *Musical Phaenomena*, p. 14. By permission of the British Library. [7890.bb.27.(1.)]

formance, as the music may require. These horns or trumpets are united together for a small length at their narrow ends, so that part of the two horns or trumpets may be parallel, and the circumference of their tubes in contact.... On the small ends of the two horns or trumpets, so united or brought near to one another, I fix a box of a cylindrical, oval, cubical, or other suitable form, fitted to the horns or trumpets so as to be air tight. In the cover of this box, what is commonly called the mouth-piece is fixed, by means of a joint, by means of a piece of elastic, gum, or leather, or otherwise, so that the point of the mouth-piece may be directed to the opening of either of the horns or trumpets at pleasure, at the same time that another piece of elastic, gum, or leather, or other proper material, stops the aperture of the horn or trumpet which is not in use.[62]

As previously mentioned, Clagget cites Burney's comments and the natural trumpet's limitations as inspiration for his invention. In his *Musical Phaenomena*, Clagget makes a strong case for his "Cromatic Trumpet" by criticizing not only the practice of hand stopping,[63] but also the natural trumpet itself:

It is true, the immortal Handel has said, "The Trumpet shall sound;" but he himself could never make it sound tolerably in tune, even in one key; but the Patentee will venture to say, the Trumpet shall sound, and with this valuable addition; it shall sound in tune; and this may be accomplished, in many keys, in a few mornings practice.[64]

As of the time of the writing of Clagget's pamphlet, there had been only two public performances using his new French horns, one in a concert in Bath and the other at the Hanover Square Concert Rooms in London. No performances using his trumpet have been

---

[62]*Clagget's Method of Constructing and Tuning Musical Instruments. A. D. 1788 ...No. 1664* (London: George Edward Eyre and William Spottiswoode, 1856), 3.

[63]See Clagget quote, p. 20.

[64]He further states his point in a footnote: "We are told that a gentleman at Salisbury, on hearing the celebrated song 'The Trumpet shall sound and the dead shall be raised,' exclaimed, with great emotion, 'Yes, yes; such horrid discordant sounds must raise the dead' " (Clagget, *Musical Phaenomena*, 19–20).

documented. Clagget unfortunately offers no details concerning the Hanover Square concert, but he does describe the Bath concert, at which Burney was present along with "several hundred auditors."[65] The result of this performance was Burney's endorsement, mentioned previously. But the instruments did not catch on, even after these successful public displays. Again citing Burney, Clagget alludes to this resistance in a footnote:

> Dr. Burney's compliments to Mr. Clagget, and is extremely concerned to find that Lord Macartney's Musicians cannot be prevailed on to make use of his Cromatic Horns.—Dr. B. assures Mr. C. that, having been long convinced of the excellence and utility of his improvements in the intonations in these instruments, he had proposed and heartily recommended them to Lord Macartney and his Musicians, a considerable time before he called to speak about them in Greek-street: for Dr. B. has constantly mentioned them with the highest praise.[66]

The reason for Clagget's failure is twofold. First, the instrument was not completely chromatic, despite the name. As there were only two tubes, there would have been gaps in the chromatic scale in the lower register (Example 2). But the most compelling reason may actually be found in Clagget's own argument for his trumpet. One of his criticisms of the natural trumpet is that "on account of its strength

Example 2: Scale of Clagget's "Cromatic Trumpet" (harmonic
    series of D and E♭).

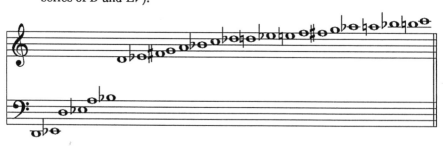

---

[65] Ibid., 20.

[66] Ibid., 16.

and power, it is difficult to moderate to the dimensions of ordinary rooms, [and] is present almost entirely confined to great orchestras, pompous processions, or military purposes."[67] By way of a solution, he offers his box valve, which, in addition to shifting the air flow from tube to tube, "also tempers the tune of that which sounds; by this means, the performers produce such harmonious proportions on their instruments, that must delight the most critical ear...."[68] Even at this early date, Clagget seems to have touched on the problem that was to provide ammunition for the detractors of the valve throughout the next century. This "tempering" of the trumpet's sound not only softened it but also changed its traditional noble character.

William Shaw's "Harmonic Trumpet"

The term "Harmonic Trumpet" was coined by Eric Halfpenny in an article on William Shaw's trumpet.[69] This is a silver trumpet in pristine condition that was discovered in St. James Palace in 1959, and is evidently the only one of its kind. The date 1787 is inscribed on the bell, along with the name of the maker and the coat of arms of George III; thus Halfpenny thinks that it was made for orchestral playing in the King's personal band. The unique feature of this instrument is that four small vent holes perforate the tubing of the middle yard. Metal sleeves rotate to cover three of the holes, while the fourth is covered by a key mechanism. The holes do not affect the instrument in the same manner as the larger holes found on keyed trumpets; that is, they do not change the pitch by semitones. Halfpenny calls the holes "nodal vents" because the opening of each vent effectively raises the fundamental pitch by a fifth. Each vent hole corresponds either to the uncrooked trumpet (in E♭), or one of the three crooks supplied (D, C and B♭).

---

[67]Ibid., 15.

[68]Ibid., 18.

[69]For a complete discussion and photograph, see Eric Halfpenny, "William Shaw's 'Harmonic Trumpet'," *Galpin Society Journal* 13 (1960): 7–13.

Example 3: Scale of Shaw's "Harmonic Trumpet" in E♭ (harmonic
series of B♭ achievable with fingerhole).

The reasons for the failure of this instrument are most likely the
same as for Clagget's. The traditional sound of the trumpet was compromised, and in addition there were gaps in its scale (Example 3).
Halfpenny has determined that use of the holes "adds very little to
the diatonic possibilities of the third…octave except the supertonic
and the leading note of the crook tonality; yet it is to the completion
of this octave that all other systems have been directed."[70] Steele-
Perkins has played the instrument, and thinks that "the notes requiring an open hole tend to lose the authentic 'gritty' tonal quality
(very aptly described by Roger North as the 'chirruping sound') and
this may have been the reason for the dismissal of the 'harmonic
trumpet' principle…."[71] Halfpenny suggests that the holes provided
quick shifts to the dominant tonality, thereby circumventing crook
changes.[72]

    Of all these late-eighteenth-century designs and experiments
produced in the wake of Burney's criticisms, only the slide trumpet
was successful in England. It was successful simply because, unlike
the other experimental trumpets, it allowed for the correction of the
tuning, and a chromatic scale with few gaps, without the loss of the
sound quality of the natural trumpet.

---

[70]Ibid., 10.

[71]Steele-Perkins, "Practical Observations," 125.

[72]Halfpenny, "Shaw's Trumpet," 10.

Chapter Two: The English Slide Trumpet

The circumstances of the initial development of the slide trumpet are somewhat mysterious. John Hyde, an English trumpeter, proclaimed himself the inventor of the instrument, but the date of its conception is not clear. In this chapter, following a description of the instrument itself, John Hyde's life and career and the circumstances surrounding the invention of the slide trumpet will be investigated. Also, the development of the slide trumpet throughout the nineteenth century, including several design modifications, will be explored. Finally, contemporary tutors will be used as a basis for the discussion of the technique of the instrument.

THE SLIDE TRUMPET DEFINED

The newly designed slide trumpet of late-eighteenth-century England was simply a natural trumpet pitched in F, to which was added a backward-moving double slide with an automatic return mechanism (Figures 13 and 14, p. 49). The prototype of this instrument was undoubtedly the flat trumpet of Baroque England; it is the only slide trumpet precursor with a backward-moving slide. Less than ninety years separates the last known documentary evidence of the flat trumpet—the 1699 play *The Island Princess*—from the development of the slide trumpet. Surely either some old flat trumpets were still around at the end of the eighteenth century, or perhaps tales of these instruments persisted among trumpet players. By the early years of the nineteenth century, instrument makers such as Clementi and Co. were manufacturing their own slide trumpets, rather than merely converting natural trumpets. During this century the automatic return mechanism went through several design changes, but the fundamental backward-pull slide concept remained the same, with few exceptions, until the last English slide trumpets were manufactured in the early years of the twentieth century.

The basic design featured a double slide at the rear bow of the trumpet, which telescoped inside the bell and middle yards. Because of the movement of the slide, it was necessary to stabilize the instrument, and this was done by means of three stays connecting the two lengths of tubing. To each outer stay was attached a central hollow tube, which was positioned between and parallel with the bell and middle yards. The tube extended through the middle stay. Inside the hollow tube was a device used to pull the slide back to its closed position—either a gut string, a coiled spring, or an elastic band. The player held the trumpet upside-down[1] and operated the slide by drawing a finger-pull, which was attached to the central tube, backward with the middle fingers of the right hand. The mouthpiece was inserted into a crooked shank, which required that the trumpet be held slightly to the left, and often slightly above or below the horizontal, rather than straight forward. This feature was necessary to avoid a collision of the backward moving slide (the extension could be as much as five to six inches) with the player's right cheek. The crooked shank was not necessary when the player was using several crooks, which increased the distance between the face and the trumpet.

According to Thomas John Harper Jr. (1816–1898), the most celebrated English trumpeter of the second half of the nineteenth century (Frontispiece and Figure 3), slide trumpets were made either of brass, copper, silver, or a brass-copper alloy, with the silver and alloy varieties being favored.[2] John Webb mentions the popularity of this brass-copper alloy with nineteenth-century instrument makers, and discusses the tradition of using copper in the production of English trumpets. He refers to late-seventeenth-century copper

---

[1]This was opposite the classic holding position of the natural trumpet, which was with bell yard on top. In ceremonial playing, banners would have been hung from the middle, or bottom, yard. See Figure 30, p. 84.

[2]Thomas Harper Jr., *Harper's School for the Trumpet: Containing (in addition to the usual Instructions) a Full Description of the Instrument, Observations on the Use of the Slide and on the Mode of Writing Music for the Trumpet, also Several Remarks Connected with the Art of Playing the Instrument, and 100 Progressive Exercises* (London: Rudall, Carte & Co., [1875]), 3.

Figure 3: Thomas Harper Jr., photograph. By permission of the Royal College of Music.

trumpets by William Bull, as well as the traditional English copper
field bugle, so made because of copper's supposed carrying power.
Quoting the late-nineteenth-century brass instrument maker William
Brown, Webb writes that "good brass was superior in 'musical quality' to copper and silver (pure metals), although the latter 'carried
farther'. So perhaps gold-brass [brass with a large amount of copper]
was a compromise, as it is on most modern trombones."[3]

Cynthia Hoover gives measurements for a typical slide trumpet
of the early part of the century (before 1828)—an instrument by an
unknown maker that is in the Smithsonian Institution,[4] and is the
subject of her article:

Length without crooks: 71-7/8 inches
Bell diameter: 4-5/8 inches
Cylindrical bore diameter: 7/16 inch
Length of flare to bell: 16-1/4 inches[5]

In his 1875 tutor, Harper Jr. gives the following measurements
for a late-century model:

Length without crooks: 66-3/4 inches
Bell diameter: 4 inches
Cylindrical bore diameter: 3/8 inch
Length of flare to bell: 15 inches[6]

Interestingly, perhaps the most significant difference between
the early- and late-century instruments (besides the return mechanism) is the overall length. The instrument described by Harper is
apparently a slide trumpet pitched in G. But he mentions that the

[3]John Webb, "The English Slide Trumpet," *Historic Brass Society Journal* 5 (1993): 272.

[4]*US-DC-Washington-S*, item no. 237,756.

[5]Cynthia Hoover, "The Slide Trumpet of the Nineteenth Century," *Brass Quarterly* 4 (1962–63): 162.

[6]Harper Jr., *School*, 3.

first crook, which is three inches long, "will make the length of the trumpet seventy-two inches [with mouthpiece], and give the key of F."[7] Actually, this first "crook" mentioned by Harper is none other than the bent shank which would always have been used to receive the mouthpiece when the trumpet was pitched in F (see Figure 19, p. 66). The mouthpiece would not otherwise fit properly into the first yard, and the slide would be inoperable anyway because of the obstacle of the player's face.[8]

Thus, the standard slide trumpet pitch was six-foot F, the same as that of late-eighteenth- and nineteenth-century natural trumpets. Along with the three-inch shank, the instrument came with four crooks, which lowered the pitch to E, E♭, D, and C, respectively. In addition, combinations of crooks provided for even lower keys—D♭, B, B♭, A, and A♭—but these were used less frequently. Since tuning slides do not seem to have been a standard feature of brass instruments until late in the century,[9] slide trumpets were supplied with tuning bits—usually two, of one-inch and one-and-a-half-inch lengths, respectively. These bits would have been inserted into the tubing between the mouthpiece and crook (or shank) to lower the pitch slightly. If the pitch needed to be raised slightly, the only option was to cut away part of the tubing; thus, the trumpets were "made quite up to...pitch."[10]

The mouthpieces used by Harper and other slide trumpet players were considerably larger than those in use today, with wide rim diameters and very deep cups. Figure 4 (p. 32) shows a drawing of a

---

[7]Ibid.

[8]The author has examined many slide trumpets in museums and private collections in and around London and Boston, has read many descriptions of museum instruments, and yet has not seen or read about a surviving slide trumpet pitched in G.

[9]Tuning slides for trumpets and horns were apparently invented in the late eighteenth century by Haltenhof, but there are few nineteenth-century survivors with them. See *New Grove*, s. v. "Tuning-slide," by Howard Mayer Brown.

[10]Harper Jr., *School*, 4.

The Mouthpiece

The Mouthpiece is of greater importance to the performer than is generally supposed, as the quality of tone and facility of execution depend principally on its construction. The following is a Drawing of the exact size and form of that I have used for twenty years past.

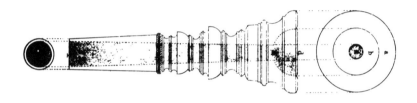

Explanation of the Mouthpiece

a. *Width of the rim or lip of the Mouthpiece.*
b. *Circumference of the cup.*
c. *Circumference or entrance of the tube.*
d to e. *Depth of the cup.*
e to f. *Length of the tube.*
f. *Circumference of the end of the tube.*
   The shade down the centre of the Mouthpiece shews the exact size of the cup and tube. The above-described Mouthpiece may be used for Trumpets of every description. A heavy Mouthpiece is recommended as laying steady on the lips and not requiring so much pressure as a light one.

Figure 4: Thomas Harper Sr., mouthpiece, from *Instructions for the Trumpet*, p. 10. By permission of Spring Tree Enterprises.

typical slide trumpet mouthpiece, from the tutor of Thomas Harper Sr. (1786–1853), the most important London trumpeter in the first half of the nineteenth century and father of Harper Jr. (Figure 5, p. 34). Also, like natural trumpet mouthpieces of the previous centuries, the rims were flat, and "not less than one-eighth of an inch in width...[with] the outer and inner edges slightly rounded, in order that pressure may not cut the lips...." The overall lengths of the mouthpieces were about three-and-one-half inches, and they were generally made of brass or silver.[11]

THE EARLY DEVELOPMENT OF THE SLIDE TRUMPET

The slide trumpet was apparently invented by John Hyde, an important trumpeter of late-eighteenth- and early-nineteenth-century London. In 1799 Hyde published a tutor for natural trumpet, bugle, and his new slide trumpet, which he called the "Chromatic Trumpet" (Figure 6, p. 35). The following is Hyde's account of the instrument's conception, which is found under the heading "Observations on the Chromatic Trumpet":

Invented by J. Hyde, and made by Woodham.

The plain Trumpet being so imperfect, and so confined in its scale, I found it necessar [sic] to invent something to make it perfect and more universal before I could feel any satisfaction in playing it, Dr Burney in his History of Music, has taken particular notice of the imperfect fourth and sixth, which imperfection is compleatly remedied by the Chromatic Trumpet; which besides makes a number of notes never thought [sic] of on that Instrument as will appear from the Scale;

Before the learner makes use of the chromatic Trumpet he should make himself Master of the plain one; he may then adopt any air to his own playing that lies within the compas [sic] of the Scale [Figure 7, p. 35] which is as follows.[12]

---

[11]Ibid.

[12]Hyde, *Preceptor*, 51.

Figure 5: Thomas Harper Sr., lithograph. By permission of the Royal College of Music.

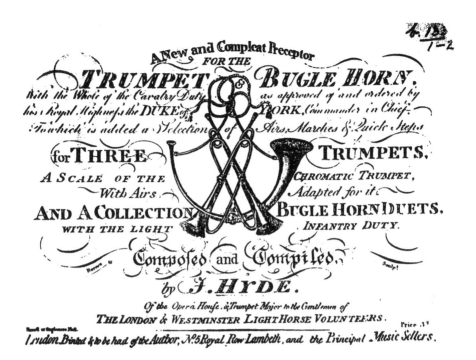

Figure 6: John Hyde, *A New and Compleat Preceptor for the Trumpet and Bugle Horn*, title page. By permission of the British Library. [b.133.1]

Figure 7: John Hyde, "Chromatic Trumpet" scale, from *A New and Compleat Preceptor for the Trumpet and Bugle Horn*, p. 51. By permission of the British Library. [b.133.1]

His tutor is not the only existing evidence that Hyde was the inventor of the slide trumpet. Several references to the slide trumpet and its origins can be found throughout the nineteenth century. William Parke, the celebrated oboist, writes about the 1784 Handel Commemoration, "partly derived from my own reminiscences, (having been engaged in it) and partly from Dr. Burney's book on the subject,"[13] in his memoirs of 1830:

> The favourite bass trumpet song, "The trumpet shall sound," was uncommonly well sung by Signor Tasca, and was finely accompanied on the trumpet by Mr. Sarjant. The imperfect note on the fourth of the key on the trumpet has since been rendered perfect by Mr. Hydes' [*sic*] ingenious invention of a slide.[14]

Although he does not mention Hyde by name, Thomas Busby also writes about the early slide trumpet in his 1823 *Dictionary of Music*:

> Solo performers can also produce B♭ (the third above the treble-cleff note): and by the aid of a newly-invented *slide*, many other notes, which the common *trumpet* cannot sound, are now produced.[15]

Later writers who acknowledge Hyde as the inventor of the slide trumpet include the French trumpeter and pedagogue F. G. A. Dauverné in 1857[16] and the English trumpeter Walter Morrow in 1894–5.[17]

---

[13]William Thomas Parke, *Musical Memoirs; Comprising an Account of the General State of Music in England from the First Commemoration of Handel, in 1784, to the Year 1830* (London: 1830; repr., New York: Da Capo Press, 1970), 36–37.

[14]Ibid., 41.

[15]Thomas Busby, *A Dictionary of Music, Theoretical and Practical*, 5th ed. (London: Sir Richard Phillips and Co., 1823), 314–315.

[16]François Georges Auguste Dauverné, *Méthode pour la trompette* (Paris: Brandus, Dufour et Cie, 1857; trans. Gaetan Chenier, Ruby Miller Orval, Rebecca Pike, and Jeffrey Snedeker, *Historic Brass Society Journal* 3 [1991]): 207 (page reference is to translation).

[17]Walter Morrow, "The Trumpet as an Orchestral Instrument," *Proceedings of the Musical Association* 21 (1894–95): 137.

John Hyde

Hyde's birth and death dates are unknown, but it can be established that his career flourished from the 1780s to the second decade of the nineteenth century. The earliest mention of professional activity by Hyde, albeit on a part-time basis, can be found in personnel lists for the orchestra of Drury Lane Theatre from the years 1789 to 1799. His name is also found in band personnel lists for several Handel memorial concerts in the 1790s;[18] and Parke mentions Hyde as being a performer at the 1793 Canterbury Festival.[19] After the death of James Sarjant in 1798, Hyde seems to have become much more active as a soloist. Concert announcements for the 1800 season in *The Times* mention him as a principal performer and as a soloist several times. On Monday, 26 May 1800, a benefit concert was held for Hyde, at which he performed Handel's "Let the Bright Seraphim," a trumpet concerto, and a "Finale with the Buglehorn obligato."[20] It is also known that John Hyde was the proprietor and owner of a concert venue eventually known as Hyde's Rooms, on Tottenham Street, from 1800. It may be that Hyde's 26 May benefit was the premiere event at his newly purchased Tottenham Street Rooms (Figure 8, p. 38).

Adam Carse claims that Hyde was the foremost English trumpeter during the first two decades of the nineteenth century;[21] but in truth, Hyde was not quite the dominant player that either Sarjant was before him or Thomas Harper Sr. after him. Following his banner year of 1800, Hyde's name is completely missing from *Times* concert announcements of 1801: other trumpeters are mentioned and trumpet solos are listed for that season, but Hyde's name is nowhere to be

---

[18]*A Biographical Dictionary of Actors, Actresses, Musicians, Dancers, Managers & Other Stage Personnel in London, 1660–1800*, s. v. "Hyde, John," by Philip H. Highfill Jr., K. A. Burnim, and E. A. Langhans.

[19]Parke, *Musical Memoirs*, 179–180.

[20]Advertisement from *The Times* (London), 24 May 1800, 1.

[21]Carse, *Orchestra*, 179.

found. In 1802 and 1803 two foreign trumpeters, Johann Georg Schmidt and Anton Weidinger, had successful debuts in London, with Schmidt eventually settling there and becoming the most important London trumpeter by around 1810. Hyde became more active as a soloist again in 1803 and 1804, almost as if in response to the increased activity of Schmidt, and his name is mentioned in orchestra lists well into the 1810s. But there is no doubt that Schmidt

For the BENEFIT of Mr. HYDE.

AT the ROOMS in TOTTENHAM-STREET, (lately occupied for the KING'S CONCERT of ANCIENT MUSIC).—On MONDAY NEXT will be performed a Grand CONCERT of VOCAL and INSTRUMENTAL MUSIC. The principal Vocal Parts by Madame Mara (being the last time of her performing in London this Season); Miss Jackson; Miss Richardson, and Mr. Leete. Leader of the Band, Mr. Cramer. Amongst the principal Instrumental, are Messrs. Holmes, Leander, Lindley, Dragonetti, Monzani, Mahon, Gresbach, &c.

Part I. Overture, Haydn, M.S. Song, Miss Richardson; Concertante Bassoon and Clarinet, Messrs. Holmes and Mahon. Song, "Let the bright Seraphims," Madame Mara, accompanied on the Trumpet by Mr. Hyde. Glee, "O Strike the Harp," Stevens; Miss Jackson, Miss Richardson, Mr. Leete, accompanied on the Harp by Miss Hoffman; and the Piano Forte, by Master Field.

Part II. Concerto Trumpet, Mr. Hyde; Song, Miss Jackson; Concerto Piano Forte, Master Field. Glee; Scena, Madame Mara: Finale, with the Bugle-horn obligato.——To begin precisely at 8 o'clock. Tickets, 10s. 6d. each, to be had of Mr. Hyde, at the Rooms in Tottenham-street, and at the Music-shops. The Concert Room has undergone a complete and thorough repair. The Decorations designed and executed by Mr. Desmaria.

Figure 8: John Hyde, advertisement of benefit concert, from *The Times* (24 May 1800).

became the leading player of that time: Carse even claims that "he was reputed to be the best trumpeter in Europe."[22]

Another contemporary source casts still further doubt on Hyde's dominance as a player. Michael Kelly, writing in his memoirs (1826), recalls hearing an Irish trumpeter while singing in a theatre in Limerick, around the turn of the century:

> The finest trumpet player I ever heard in any country played in our orchestra; his execution on the instrument almost baffled belief;—his name was Willman, and he is the brother of Mr. Willman, the principal clarionet,...at the King's Theatre.[23]

As one of the principal English singers of the time, Kelly certainly would have come in contact with Hyde in London during the first two decades of the century.

Hyde may have been active as late as the 1820s. He is reported to have been a member of the band at the King's Theatre in 1817,[24] and to have played in a provincial music festival with Thomas Harper Sr. in that same year.[25] In 1823, a Hyde of London played as principal trumpeter (along with Harper) in the Yorkshire Festival; but another Hyde, of Manchester, was also listed as a section player at the same festival.[26] Thus Hyde's career may have been a long one

---

[22]Ibid., 179.

[23]Michael Kelly, *Reminiscences of Michael Kelly, of the King's Theatre, and Theatre Royal Drury Lane, Including a Period of Nearly Half a Century; with Original Anecdotes of Many Distinguished Persons, Political, Literary, and Musical* (London: Henry Colburn, 1826), 275.

[24]*Biographical Dictionary*, "Hyde," by Highfill, et. al.

[25]John Edmunds Cox, *Musical Recollections of the Last Half-Century* (London: Tinsley Brothers, 1872), 1: 37–38.

[26]"Yorkshire Grand Musical Festival," *Harmonicon* 1, no. 10 (October 1823): 152–153.

but perhaps not unusually so; if he began playing professionally in the late 1780s, when he was fifteen to twenty years of age, he would have been in his fifties at the time of the Yorkshire Festival of 1823.

It is not really clear, though, if these references are to Hyde, or to one or more of his offspring. Documents of the Royal Society of Musicians suggest that Hyde had at least one son who was active as a trumpeter in London. The Society application documents mention one Henry Hyde (ca. 1792–ca. 1853), who

> has served an apprenticeship to his Father for Seven Years and has practiced Music for a Maintenance ever since, is a Single Man...performs on the Trumpet Piano Forte & Violin, is engaged at the Ancient Vocal & Philharmonic Concerts & the Royalty Theatre.[27]

But Carse describes a William Hyde as having succeeded his father as principal trumpeter in the late 1810s,[28] and the *British Musical Biography* dictionary of 1897 lists the patriarch's son as James Hyde, who was also a "clever performer on the trumpet," and who settled in Manchester as a composer and performer of popular ballads.[29] Thus there may have been as many as three trumpeter Hydes working in London in the 1810s and 20s, and at least one also in Manchester.

Of the fifty-four pages in Hyde's tutor, only the last four deal with the slide trumpet. In addition to the explanation and scale mentioned above, there are seven compositions for the instrument: including five for one trumpet and one each for two and three trum-

---

[27]Betty Matthews, comp., "Henry Hyde," *The Royal Society of Musicians of Great Britain List of Members 1738–1984* (London: The Royal Society of Musicians, 1985).

[28]Carse, *Orchestra*, 179.

[29]James D. Brown and Stephen S. Stratton, "Hyde," in *British Musical Biography: A Dictionary of Musical Artists, Authors and Composers, born in Britain and its Colonies* (London: William Reeves, 1897; repr. New York: Da Capo Press, 1971).

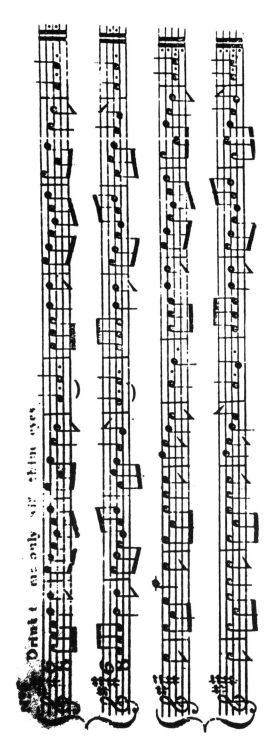

Figure 9: John Hyde, arrangement of "Drink to me only with thine eyes," from *A New and Compleat Preceptor for the Trumpet and Bugle Horn*, p. 54. By permission of the British Library. [b.133.1]

pets. Several are settings of popular melodies, including "Drink to me only with thine eyes" (Figure 9, p. 41) and "How great is the Pleasure." Some are in the key of A, contrasting with the exercises in the key of C for natural trumpet and bugle in C and D from the first fifty pages of the tutor. All the slide trumpet compositions use numerous notes outside the harmonic series; most often b' and a', and both the natural and sharp versions of the eleventh partial (f" and f♯") appear. The only other non-harmonic-series note is f♯', but it is found only in the second trumpet part of the duet, and appears only seven times. It is evident from these first printed exercises by the inventor of the slide trumpet that the instrument's main purpose was to correct the intonation of both high and low versions of the eleventh partial, and to provide notes outside the harmonic series, most often b' and a', in diatonic passages.

Although Hyde called his invention the "Chromatic Trumpet," not all saw it in the same light. In an orchestration treatise from 1806, John Marsh writes about the possible uses of the new slide trumpet:

> By a sliding tube also, attached to the trumpet, some additional notes may be gained; which may be of use in solos, or concertos for the trumpet. But in orchestra music I cannot help thinking the present natural compass fully sufficient. For the trumpet and kettle-drums form, as it were, a corps de reserve, to augment the band and produce a grand fortissimo by way of contrast now and then; and therefore it is enough, if they are brought into action at those times, when the original key, or that next related to it is preserved, there being plenty of instruments without them for the purpose of modulating into others. The sliding tube may yet however be of material use in correcting the otherwise imperfect fourth in the upper octave.[30]

---

[30]John Marsh, *Hints to Young Composers of Instrumental Music* (London: [ca. 1806]; repr., with an introduction by Charles Cudworth, *Galpin Society Journal* 18 [March 1965]), 66 (page reference is to reprint edition).

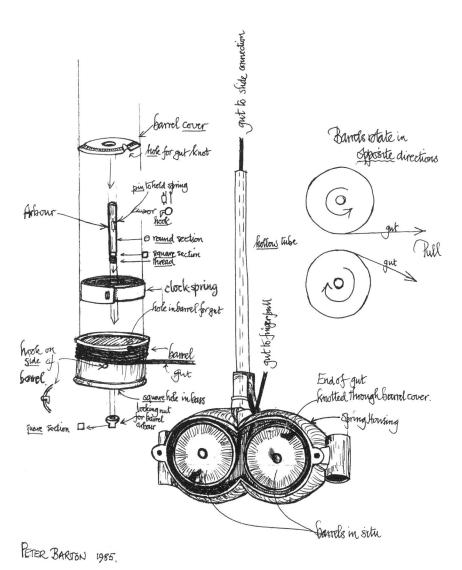

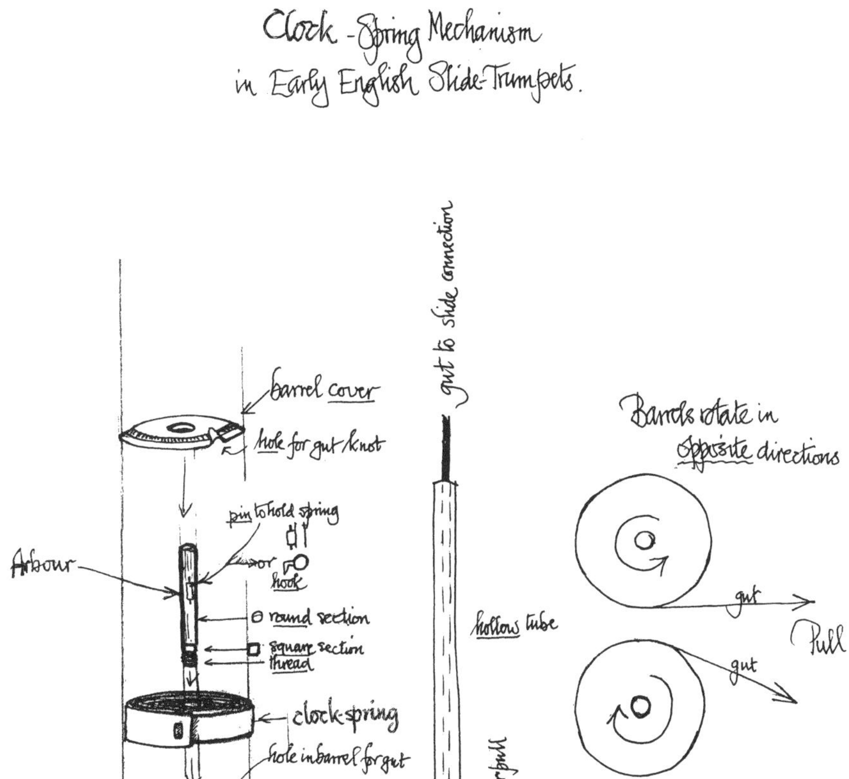
Clock-Spring Mechanism
in Early English Slide-Trumpets.
gut to slide connection
barrel cover
hole for gut knot
Barrels rotate in
opposite directions
pin to hold spring
or
hook
Arbour
round section
square section
thread
hollow tube
gut
Pull
gut
clock-spring
hole in barrel for gut
gut to finger pull
hook on
side of
barrel
barrel
gut
End of gut
knotted through barrel cover.
square hole in base
locking nut
for barrel
arbour
Spring Housing
square section
barrels in situ
PETER BARTON 1985.

Figure 10: Clock-spring mechanism. Courtesy of Peter Barton.

Clock-Spring Conversions

The earliest slide trumpets, including presumably the Hyde trumpet, were converted natural trumpets in F. The slide, as previously mentioned, was attached at the second bow, and the return of the slide was effected by one or two gut strings and a double clock-spring mechanism (Figure 10, p. 43, and Figure 11, p. 45). Each clock-spring was placed inside a barrel, which in turn was placed inside a double casing attached to the central tube. One end of a gut string was wound around the barrel closest to the bell yard, with the string then being passed through the hollow central tube and fastened at the other end to a washer on the rear bow-stay. When the slide was pulled back, the tension of the spring increased; when released the spring unwound and the slide was drawn back to the closed position (Figure 12, p. 46).

Another gut string was wound around the second clock-spring barrel, and emerged from the clock-spring casing through an open slot at the point where the casing was attached to the central tube. There has been some disagreement over the function of this second clock-spring and gut string. Most writers think that the additional mechanism was intended as a spare, in case the first were to malfunction with little time available to reset the spring—during a performance, for example.[31] In this scenario the second gut string would function like the internal string, but rather outside the central tube. A small crossbar or bead attached to the end of the second string would be slipped into a V-shaped notch in the finger-pull arm closest to the middle yard of the instrument. This notch is present in all slide trumpets with clock-spring mechanisms.[32] The slide mechanism would function just as before, but the player would have to be careful not to let the spare gut string slip from the finger-pull notch when drawing the slide backwards.

---

[31]See Hoover, "Slide Trumpet," 161; Baines, *Brass Instruments*, 182; Carse, *Musical Wind Instruments*, 238; and Bate, *Trumpet and Trombone*, 123–124.

[32]Webb, "Slide Trumpet," 267.

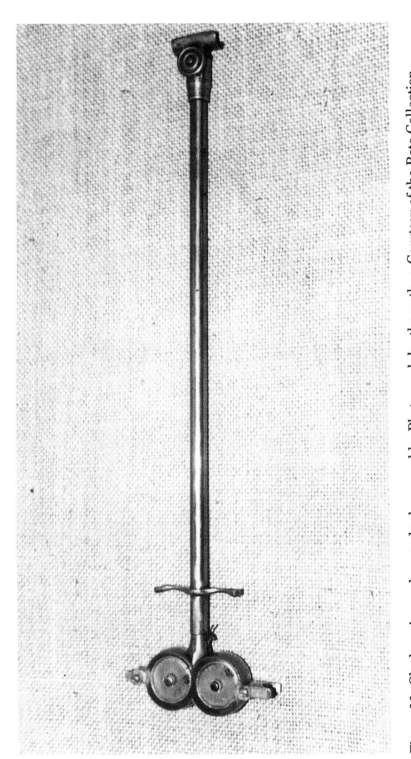

Figure 11: Clock-spring and central tube assembly. Photograph by the author. Courtesy of the Bate Collection of Musical Instruments, Oxford.

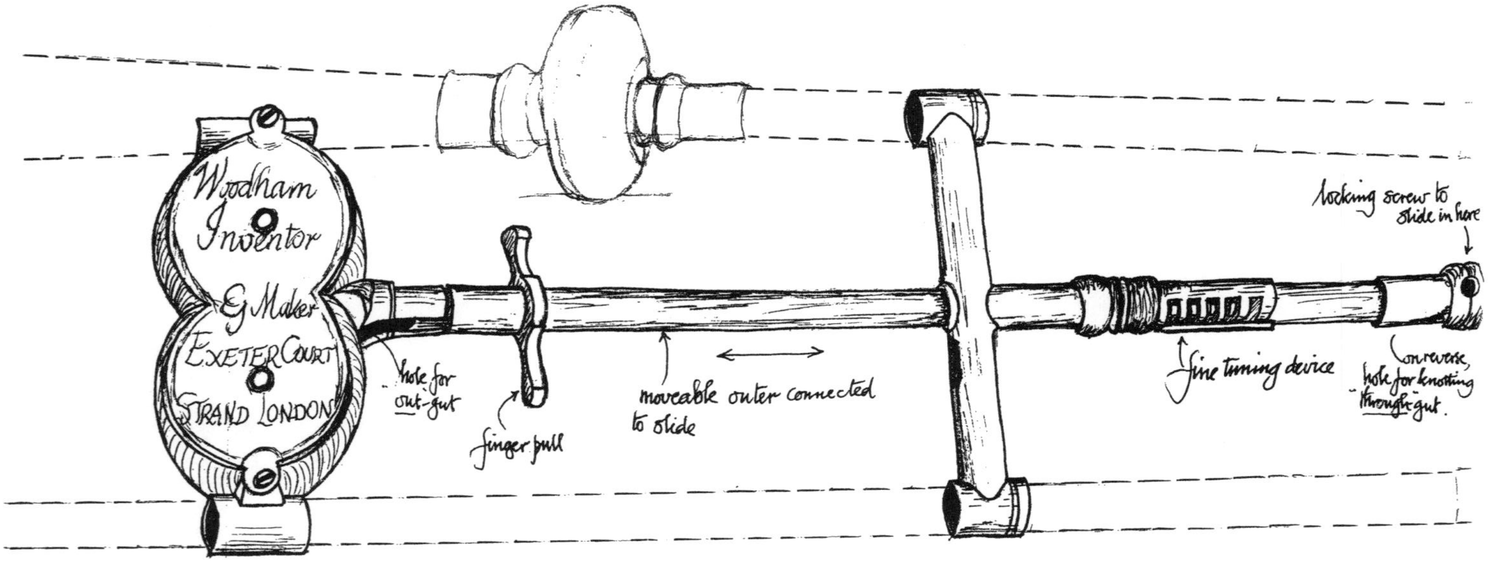
Woodham
Inventor
G Maker
EXETER COURT
STRAND LONDON
hole for
out-gut
finger pull
moveable outer connected
to slide
fine tuning device
locking screw to
slide in here
on reverse,
hole for knotting
through-gut.

Figure 12: Slide mechanism. Courtesy of Peter Barton.

Brass-instrument-maker Peter Barton, however, has argued that both springs were used in tandem, allowing the player to "adjust the tension on either or both springs to increase or diminish the power in the return of the slide...."[33] Having worked with these mechanisms during the process of restoring several clock-spring models, he thinks that switching to a spare spring would not be an easy task.

> First the lid of the spring-box has to be removed, by undoing two tiny screws which are very liable to escape if not carefully guarded; then, the barrels have to be set up, with the guts threaded correctly and wound round the barrels with the springs under tension. If one spring is relaxed, and the free end of the gut cannot be secured, this gut will foul the one in use. Both guts have to be secured, with their springs under tension, before playing can begin. Nor is there any way whereby, if both are secured, the player can change over from one spring to the other.[34]

But Steele-Perkins has demonstrated to the present writer that it is indeed possible to secure both springs, and yet attach the cross-bar on the end of the spare string to the finger-pull in a matter of seconds, thereby easily switching to the alternate gut-string/clock-spring mechanism. Furthermore, Steele-Perkins has found through practical experience that the tension of only one clock-spring at a time is sufficient to provide a smooth slide pull and equally smooth return.[35] Considering the possibility of a gut string break, or primary spring failure, and the extraordinary amount of time required for re-setting,[36] it does not seem peculiar that a spare mechanism would

---

[33]Peter Barton, "The Woodham-Rodenbostel Slide Trumpet and Others, Employing the 'Clock-Spring' Mechanism," *Galpin Society Journal* 42 (1989): 117.

[34]Ibid., 117.

[35]Steele-Perkins, conversation with the author, 2 June 1993.

[36]During a demonstration by John Webb of the clock-spring mechanism on his 1835 Köhler slide trumpet, the author observed a gut string break and subsequent unwinding of the clock-spring, for which there was no solution except to hire a watch repairer to reset the mechanism, at considerable expense and time according to Webb. (Webb, conversation with the author, 31 May 1993)

have been provided. Indeed, Barton now agrees with Steele-Perkins and is convinced that the resulting tension from the use of both springs at once is too much.[37]

Several of the early slide trumpet conversion models can be found in museums and private collections. One of the most famous of these is a Harris trumpet (see Appendix C) from the first or second decade of the eighteenth century. Originally a natural trumpet in D, it was later cut down to the key of F and then converted to a slide trumpet with a clock-spring return mechanism (Figure 13). This reddish-brass trumpet is now in the Bate Collection of Historical Instruments in Oxford, but was formerly in the possession of Thomas Harper Jr., Walter Morrow, W. H. F. Blandford and Anthony Baines.[38] Another Harris trumpet apparently converted in the mid-nineteenth century and also owned by Thomas Harper Jr., can be found in the Museum of Instruments at the Royal College of Music in London. The original instrument was a natural trumpet pitched in D, made in the early eighteenth century.[39] In the United States, representative examples of converted clock-spring slide trumpets can be found at the Kenneth G. Fiske Museum in Claremont, California,[40] and at the Boston Museum of Fine Arts.[41]

---

[37]Steele-Perkins, letter to the author, 8 September 1993.

[38]*GB-Oxford*, item no. x70.

[39]*GB-London-RCM*, item no. 189. See also E. A. K. Ridley, *The Royal College of Music Museum of Instruments Catalogue Part I: European Wind Instruments* (London: The Royal College of Music, 1982), 55–57.

[40]A natural trumpet, possibly by Ulyate, converted by Ulyate in the first third of the nineteenth century. *US-CA-Claremont*, item no. B66.

[41]The maker was once thought to be Astor, because of initials engraved on the instrument, but the initials are now thought to be those of an owner, and the maker is considered anonymous. *US-MA-Boston*, item no. 210. See also Nicholas Bessaraboff, *Ancient European Musical Instruments: An Organological Study of the Musical Instruments in the Leslie Lindsey Mason Collection at the Museum of Fine Arts, Boston* (Cambridge, MA: Harvard Univ. Press, 1941), 196.

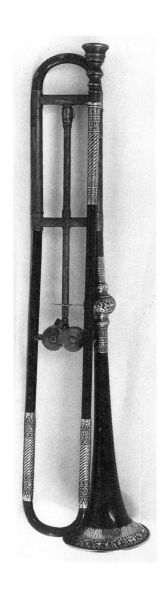 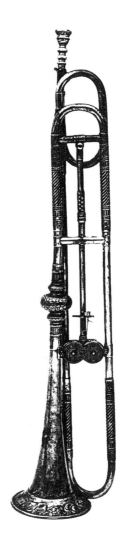

Figure 13 *(left):* Harris, natural trumpet (ca. 1716) converted to clock-spring slide trumpet. Courtesy of the Bate Collection of Musical Instruments, Oxford.

Figure 14 *(right):* The Woodham-Rodenbostel slide trumpet. Courtesy of Peter Barton.

49

The most famous of the converted clock-spring models is the Woodham-Rodenbostel slide trumpet (Figure 14, p. 49), now owned by Brian Galpin.[42] The connection with Woodham suggests that this instrument may have been one of Hyde's early slide trumpets, if not the original model. Richard Woodham (d. 1797) was a watchmaker who is said to have opened a workshop for making brass and copper instruments in 1780.[43] His name is inscribed on the clock-spring barrels of the trumpet (Figure 12, p. 46), but on the bell is the inscription: "Geo. Henry Rodenbostel, maker, Piccadily, London." Peter Barton, who has examined the trumpet and made minor repairs to it, thinks that Rodenbostel built it during the time he worked in Piccadilly (from 1764 to 1769), after which it was used professionally as a natural trumpet before Woodham added the slide mechanism between 1780 and 1797.[44] Perhaps Hyde gave the idea to Woodham, or was even more directly involved in the trumpet's conversion, thus taking credit in his tutor.

Musical Evidence

We know, of course, that the new slide trumpet design was created by the time of the publication of Hyde's tutor in 1799, but there is strong musical evidence that the instrument was being used well before this date. A manuscript with annotated listings of music performed during the summers of 1790 and 1791 at Vauxhall Gardens has been analyzed by Charles Cudworth.[45] This document, which is entitled *Lists of the Songs and Instrumental Music perform'd at Vaux-Hall, 1790–1791*, indicates that trumpet solos with notes outside the harmonic series were being performed there.

---

[42]The instrument and its clock-spring mechanism are described in detail in Barton, "Woodham-Rodenbostel," 112–120.

[43]Algernon S. Rose, *Talks with Bandsmen: a Popular Handbook for Brass Instrumentalists* (London: William Rider and Son, [1895]), 347.

[44]Barton, "Woodham-Rodenbostel," 113.

[45]Charles Cudworth, "The Vauxhall 'Lists'," *Galpin Society Journal* 20 (1967): 24–42.

Vauxhall Gardens was one of the so-called pleasure gardens where Londoners could escape the rapidly growing metropolis, and go to stroll or relax in nature.[46] Orchestra concerts of a decidedly popular nature were presented in these outdoor settings. There are references to James Sarjant throughout the two seasons, indicating that he was the principal trumpeter of the orchestra. For example, an entry for 14 July 1790 reveals that Sarjant was ill, resulting in the cancellation of a scheduled orchestral piece and substitution of an oboe concerto. On 4 August of that same year, Sarjant was scheduled to play a solo, but it had to be withdrawn because "Mr. Sarjant had lost his D crook." In the 1791 season, Sarjant is mentioned as having gone to Oxford on 5 July, "...to assist in that famous occasion when Haydn received his doctorate." It was noted in the entry for the ninth of July that Sarjant had returned from Oxford.[47]

On 19 July 1790 a violin concerto was removed from the program because of the illness of the soloist. In its place Sarjant performed two adaptations of music of Handel: "Se l'arco," an aria from Act I of the opera *Admeto*, and *March in Scipio*, a march from Act I of the opera *Scipione*.[48] A cursory look at an excerpt from the melody line of "Se l'arco" reveals that it could not have been played on a natural trumpet (Example 4, p. 52).[49] Even if transposed up a fifth to the trumpet key of C, the "Se l'arco" melody would have required Sarjant to play b' repeatedly throughout. Similarly, a contemporary Vauxhall arrangement of the march shows that it too would have

---

[46]For an excellent introduction to the Pleasure Gardens see Christopher Hogwood, "The London Pleasure Gardens," article in *Johann Christian Bach: Favourite Songs Sung at Vauxhall Gardens*, Music for London Entertainment: 1600–1800, ser. F, vol. I (Tunbridge Wells: Richard Macnutt, 1985), ix–xv.

[47]Cudworth, "Vauxhall 'Lists'," 31–36.

[48]Ibid., 31.

[49]George Frideric Handel, *Admeto*, Kalmus Miniature Scores #1253 (Leipzig: Kalmus, 1877; repr. Melville, NY: Belwin Mills, n. d.), 38–39.

Example 4: G. F. Handel, "Se l'arco," from *Admeto*.

been impossible on a natural trumpet (Figure 15).[50] A slide trumpet, however, like the Woodham-Rodenbostel or the one Hyde describes in his tutor, would have been able to manage either melody without any problem.[51] Anthony Baines believes that a skillful arrangement of the march from *Scipione* would have allowed Sarjant to play the essential notes of the melody on his natural trumpet, but not "Se l'arco," "which would be musically futile without playing the vocal line."[52] We know that Sarjant and Hyde were both active professionally in London in the 1780s and 90s, so they must have known each other. Could Sarjant have used Hyde's new slide trumpet to play this music?[53]

---

[50]George Frideric Handel, *A Song to the March in Scipio*, arr. unknown (London: [1730]), BL cat. no. G.305.(39.).

[51]The full-tone shift to f' in the untransposed "Se l'arco" melody would have been difficult to lip down to pitch, but the likely C transposition would have made this tune easy and idiomatic for early slide trumpets in F.

[52]Baines, *Brass Instruments*, 182.

[53]Crispian Steele-Perkins has recorded both "Se l'arco" and the *Scipione* march, along with other Handel arias and the overture from *Atalanta*, on a slide trumpet by Wyatt. See *Music for Trumpet and Orchestra*, Crispian Steele-Perkins, trumpet, and *Tafelmusik*, conducted by Jeanne Lamon, compact disc Sony Classical SK 53 365, 1993.

Figure 15: G. F. Handel, *A Song to the March in Scipio* (1730). By permission of the British Library. [G.305.(39.)]

John Thiessen has attempted to reconstruct the trumpet parts of thirty-one late-eighteenth-century English operas, mostly by William Shield (1748–1829). He has concluded from the use of notes outside the harmonic series in these trumpet parts that some type of chromatic trumpet—most likely the slide trumpet—was in use in the London theatres from the early 1780s.[54] Thiessen, however, had neither full scores nor orchestral parts at his disposal, and had to use reduced conductor's scores for his analysis. For several of the works,

---

[54]Thiessen, "Late Eighteenth-Century Trumpet," 9–17.

Example 5: William Shield, *Siege of Gibraltar,* excerpts from
    Overture.[55]

therefore, more convincing evidence for the use of the slide trumpet
is needed. Thiessen, for example, believes that the slide trumpet
first appeared in the overture to Shield's opera *The Siege of Gibraltar*
(1780). The musical material on the treble staff of the score is written in duet fashion, and the lower part contains many b' naturals
(Example 5). But trumpets are not designated in the score, and Thiessen admits that the use of the trumpet is only a possibility, "given
that much of the undesignated material in the treble staff is me-
lodically and rhythmically stylistic to the trumpet."[56] He acknowledges that either oboes or violins could have played the parts.

The next work that might contain parts for a chromatic trumpet
is Shield's opera *Robin Hood,* which premiered on 17 April 1784.
Here a case is made for the second act aria entitled "As burns the
charger," for bass voice and trumpet obbligato. According to Thies-

[55]Ibid.

[56]Ibid., 27.

sen this piece is an example of "the first imaginative trumpet writing" by Shield, and "also the first significant collaboration between Shield and Covent Garden's first trumpeter, James Sarjant."[57] Clearly the part was meant for Sarjant: William Parke mentions the fact in his memoirs[58] and a 1784 edition of the opera names Sarjant as a performer of the song.[59] But the song's only two non-harmonic-series notes are "two quaver f' naturals on beats 2 and 3 of m. 54."[60] Roger Fiske writes that this part and others were played on Charles Clagget's "Cromatic Trumpet,"[61] but Thiessen correctly points out that the f' naturals would be impossible on this instrument (see Example 2, p. 24). Another point mentioned by Thiessen is that Clagget's *Musical Phaenomena*, published in 1793, specifies only two previous public performances of his "Cromatic Horns" and none of his trumpets.[62] These notes would have been playable on the E♭ crook of William Shaw's "Harmonic Trumpet" (see Example 3, p. 26), but the Shaw trumpet was not made until three years after the premiere of *Robin Hood*.

Thiessen therefore concludes that the slide trumpet must have been involved in the performance of this "trumpet song." The f' naturals, however, were notes that would have been difficult to sound on a slide trumpet of the Hyde/Woodham/Rodenbostel design. Besides having shorter slides than later models, many of the early converted slide trumpets, including the Woodham-Rodenbostel, made use of a notched tuning device, "a means whereby the slide is

---

[57]Ibid., 30.

[58]Parke, *Musical Memoirs*, 33.

[59]Thiessen, "Late Eighteenth-Century Trumpet," 31.

[60]Ibid., 31.

[61]Roger Fiske, *English Theatre Music in the Eighteenth Century*, 2nd ed. (Oxford: Oxford University Press, 1986), 463.

[62]See discussion in Chapter One.

pushed incrementally out to flatten the instrument."[63] This contrivance (see Figure 12, p. 46) was attached to the central tube, and restricted slide movement to half-step shifts at most.[64] The f♮' requires a downward shift of a full tone from the sixth partial. Although Hyde did not describe such a device in his tutor, the scale that he provided does not include the f♮' (see Figure 7, p. 35). Thus there is no clear proof that this part was written for or played on a slide trumpet. One thing that can be said with certainty, though, is that it would have been much easier for Sarjant to lip down to these notes with a slide trumpet than with a natural trumpet.

The first clear proof for the use of a slide trumpet comes from another Shield opera from 1784, *The Magic Cavern*, which had its premiere late in the year, on 27 December.[65] In the song "The noble mind," Thiessen has found a clearly cued trumpet solo line (Example 6) that includes the concert pitch c♯" (b' for trumpet in D). The use of a slide trumpet to play this note seems likely. In fact, throughout the nineteenth-century solo literature for the slide trumpet, b' and a' are the two pitches outside the harmonic series used most often. Similarly definitive evidence for the slide trumpet can be found in Shield's operas *The Crusade* (1788) and *The Woodman* (1791).[66] The non-harmonic-series notes used in these works are b' and a'. The only other appearances of the non-series tone f', which would have required a slide shift of a full tone, were found by Thiessen in operas by James Hook (*Diamond Cut Diamond*, 1798) and John Morehead (*The Naval Pillar*, 1799).[67] Perhaps by this time longer slides were in use, or the notched tuning devices abandoned, in order to facilitate the production of this note.

---

[63] Webb, "Slide Trumpet," 267.

[64] See Barton, "Woodham-Rodenbostel," 115 and 119; and Hoover, "Slide Trumpet," 163.

[65] Thiessen, "Late Eighteenth-Century Trumpet," 40.

[66] Ibid., 48–52.

[67] Ibid., 62–69.

Example 6: Shield, *The Magic Cavern.*

Musical evidence for use of the slide trumpet prior to 1784 is inconclusive. Moreover, if the instrument had been developed before that year and Sarjant had access to a reasonably well-perfected slide trumpet for the Handel Commemoration concerts, surely he would have used it to improve his performance. It is entirely possible, however, that the trumpet was being developed at that time, but it was too new and untested for Sarjant to use it at such an important event. He could, however, have experimented with it in the opera house to play the b' in *The Magic Cavern.*[68] It is worth remembering that this opera premiered in late December of 1784, almost seven months after the Handel performances in Westminster Abbey. Considering the many references to Burney's criticism of Sarjant, the former's com-

_____

[68]For an explanation of the importance of the Handel Commemoration, relative to an opera performance, see above, p. 1.

ment was very possibly the primary motivating force behind the development of the slide trumpet.

At any rate, we know that composers included certain notes outside the harmonic series in the trumpet parts of English operas of the late 1780s and 90s, and that those parts were intended for James Sarjant. We also know that he played diatonic solos at Vauxhall Gardens in 1790 and 91. This evidence suggests that some type of chromatic trumpet was in use, and for the reasons cited here, that instrument was probably a slide trumpet. As Thiessen suggests, further examination of trumpet parts in late-eighteenth-century English opera might provide additional clues as to the development and early use of the slide trumpet.

NINETEENTH-CENTURY MODIFICATIONS

By the second decade of the nineteenth century, some instrument makers were manufacturing slide trumpets and making certain improvements over the conversion models. Both the Woodham-Rodenbostel and the Harris instrument in the Bate Collection, for example, are notable for the difficulties encountered while operating the slide mechanism. According to Barton, "the finger-pull tends to jam the player's finger against the bell-boss, since the latter lies between the finger-pull in the closed position and its position when the slide is fully extended."[69] To alleviate this problem the bosses were moved closer to the bell so that the player's fingers never touch the boss. Another refinement in the design was the abandonment of the notched tuning device in favor of tuning bits. This adjustment allowed the slide to be extended further, thus adding a full-tone shift, at least in the higher keys. But the advantages of this improvement did not come without a price. Using tuning bits on late-eighteenth-century trumpets, with their many crooks, must have been awkward and imprecise, while the notched tuning device is,

---

[69]Barton, "Woodham-Rodenbostel," 114.

according to Steele-Perkins, a "refined tuning system which works quickly and well...."[70]

"Harper's Improved" Model

The earliest known company to make clock-spring slide trumpets with the above-mentioned modifications was Clementi and Co., the musical instrument and music publishing enterprise founded by the composer Muzio Clementi (1752–1832). This firm, which made many different types of brass and woodwind instruments, manufactured slide trumpets in collaboration with Thomas Harper Sr., and inscribed "Harper's Improved" on their bells. The Bate Collection possesses a Clementi and Co. clock-spring model (Figure 16, p. 60) with the inscription "Harper's Improved No. 9."[71] According to Webb it is one of the earliest survivors of this type, having been manufactured before 1821.[72] It is pitched in F, made of brass, and compared with the Harris conversion model in the same museum, has a longer slide extension and a boss that does not interfere with the finger-pull movement.

After the retirement and subsequent death of Clementi in 1831 and 1832, respectively, Thomas Harper switched his allegiance to the brass instrument maker John Köhler. A contract dated 21 February 1833 proves that Köhler had an exclusive agreement with Harper to manufacture "Harper's Improved" models.[73] Figure 17 (p. 60) shows an 1835 Köhler "Harper's Improved" model from the private collection of John Webb. According to the agreement, Harper was to receive thirty shillings for each slide trumpet "so made and sold." It is an exclusive contract for both parties: the penalty for breaking it was to have been twenty pounds per trumpet. It is not clear, however, which John Köhler signed the contract. The patriarch of the

---

[70]Steele-Perkins, letter to the author, 7 February 1992.

[71]*GB-Oxford*, item no. x7.

[72]Webb, "Slide Trumpet," 270.

[73]Thomas Harper Sr. and John Köhler, Contract, 1833, *Lcm*, MS 4071.

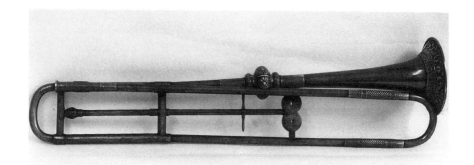

Figure 16: Clementi and Co., "Harper's Improved" clock-spring slide trumpet (before 1821). Courtesy of the Bate Collection of Musical Instruments.

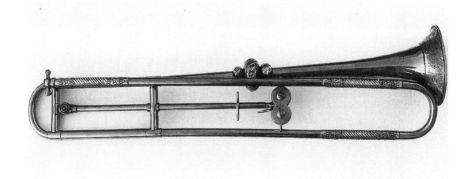

Figure 17: Köhler, "Harper's Improved" clock-spring slide trumpet (1835). Courtesy of John Webb.

Figure 18: Pace, compression-spring slide trumpet (ca. 1840). Photography by S. R. H. Spicer, the Shrine to Music Museum, University of South Dakota.

firm—from Volkenrode, a town near Kassel—was a John Köhler who emigrated to England about 1775 as a Hessian mercenary. His business was established in 1780, and in 1790 he set up shop first at 9 Charing Cross Road and then on Whitcomb Street as a "French Horn Maker."[74] A nephew, also John Köhler, followed his uncle to England, and inherited the business in 1801. According to William Waterhouse, this Köhler was followed by his son John Augustus Köhler (ca. 1810–1878) who entered his silver hallmark at Goldsmith's Hall in 1835.[75] So most likely it was Köhler the father who signed the Harper contract, but it could have been either John or John Augustus who fulfilled the obligations of the contract, depending upon the date of retirement of the former. The business was moved in 1834 to 35 Henrietta Street and it continued there until 1881. In 1863 the name of the firm was changed to Köhler and Son, and remained so until 1904. After Harper's death in 1853, the Köhler relationship persisted with his son, Thomas Harper Jr.

The nature of the improvements implied by the "Harper's Improved" inscription is a mystery. As mentioned above, moving the boss closer to the bell and removing the notched tuning device are refinements found on the Clementi and Co. "Harper's Improved" trumpet in the Bate Collection. Certainly the addition of a whole-tone shift would have been regarded as an improvement, but these refinements were probably already being applied to slide trumpets by the turn of the century anyway. Webb and Sorenson are not sure that there was any major "improvement" inherent in the trumpets, and suggest that perhaps "the legend 'Harper's Improved' was... merely a marketing device...."[76] Webb explains:

---

[74]William Waterhouse, *The New Langwill Index: A Dictionary of Musical Wind-Instrument Makers and Inventors* (London: Tony Bingham, 1993), 210.

[75]Ibid.

[76]John Webb and Scott Sorenson, commentary to *Instructions for the Trumpet, With the Use of the Chromatic Slide, Also the Russian Valve Trumpet, the Cornet à Pistons or Small Stop Trumpet, and the Keyed Bugle, In which the Rudiments of Music and the Various Scales, Are Clearly Explained in a Series of Examples,* [cont.]

There is no evidence that either of the Harpers initiated any significant design features on the slide trumpet. Nothing was ever patented
or registered, and instruments similar in every respect were produced
by other makers throughout the whole of the 19th century....the arrangement with Kohler seems to have been purely commercial, a
merchandising endorsement, although both father and son 'no doubt
contributed general guidance about bores and bell profiles, etc.[77]

Although Clementi and Köhler were the only firms contracted
to produce "Harper's Improved" trumpets, they were not the only
firms to manufacture slide trumpets with the clock-spring mechanism. The Edinburgh University Collection of Historic Musical Instruments has a Goodison clock-spring model, with the notched
tuning device, from about 1830.[78] The Smithsonian Institution in
Washington, DC, has a Pace clock-spring model that is assumed to
have been made between 1834 and 1849.[79] In addition, a "short
model" by Power is described below (see "Short Model"). Other
clock-spring models are listed in Appendix C.

Compression-Spring Model

The next modification of the slide trumpet involved the abandonment of the clock-spring return mechanism for a relatively uncomplicated spiral-spring system. Several writers have wondered
why the clock-spring mechanism was developed in the first place,
and also why it persisted as long as it did. Of course, Richard
Woodham was a watchmaker, and although the original inspiration
for the slide was perhaps Hyde's, the return mechanism could have

---

Preludes, Lessons, Solos, Duets, etc., for Each Instrument, 2nd ed., by Thomas Harper (London: Thomas Harper, 1837; repr., Homer, NY: Spring Tree Enterprises,
1988), vii.

[77]Webb, "Slide Trumpet," 270.

[78]*GB-Edinburgh*, item no. 3288. See Arnold Myers, ed., *Historic Musical Instruments in the Edinburgh University Collection*, Vol. 2, Part H, Fascicle iii: *Trumpets
and Trombones* (Edinburgh: Edinburgh University Collection of Historic Musical
Instruments, 1993), 18–19.

[79]*US-DC-Washington-S*, item no. 76.25.

been Woodham's responsibility. At any rate, Webb thinks that the clock-spring was "an unnecessarily complex device for such a simple function. It is expensive to make, and very difficult to assemble and service."[80] The spiral-spring models that were developed were certainly simpler, although the earliest spring mechanism, the compression spring, also had its complications. It is described as follows:

> Here a spring is enclosed in a cylinder between the bell- and bow-stays. The finger-pull rod passes through the center, and a fixed disc on it, inside the cylinder, squeezes the spring when the rod (and slide) is drawn back. Released, the spring returns the rod (and slide) to closed position.[81]

This device works reasonably well, but disassembly of the spring mechanism evidently proved to be a needlessly complicated procedure, which involved dismantling the soldered finger-pull.[82] Most likely this hindrance was the reason that very few of these models were made. Webb describes two survivors: one by T. Lloyd of Handsworth[83] and a "short model" from about 1840 by Pace.[84] In addition, the author has seen a painting of a Pace compression-spring model in The Eddy Collection of Musical Instruments in Cambridge, Massachusetts. The bell inscription, which was carefully reproduced by G. Norman Eddy, reads "PACE, Maker / 49 King St., West." Charles Pace's shop was at this address in Westminster from 1834 to 1849. The Pace firm continued at the King Street address until 1858, but under the designation Charles Pace and Sons.[85]

---

[80]Webb, "Slide Trumpet," 267.

[81]Ibid., 268.

[82]Ibid.

[83]The instrument is not dated. From the private collection of John Webb. See Webb, "Slide Trumpet," 265.

[84]*GB-Huddersfield*, item no. 3684–1984. For a description see Webb, "Slide Trumpet," 271.

[85]Waterhouse, *New Langwill*, 289.

The Shrine to Music Museum in Vermillion, South Dakota, has two compression-spring models that were catalogued in December of 1992 by Herbert Heyde.[86] According to Heyde's notes, a Pace slide trumpet (Figure 18, p. 60) was procured by Arne B. Larson from Philip Bate in 1945, and acquired by the Shrine to Music Museum in 1979 as part of the Arne B. Larson Collection.[87] The instrument's inscription is similar but not identical to that of the Eddy painting. It was also made at the King Street address, and can thus be dated between 1834 and 1849. The Shrine to Music also has a "short model" made by William Grayson (Figure 22, p. 68) between 1840 and 1842 at his Cooper Street address, indicating a fairly early date for this compression-spring slide trumpet (see Appendix C).[88]

Expansion-Spring/Elastic-Cord Model

By around mid-century, the clock-springs and the few compression springs gradually gave way to the last and simplest of the slide-return mechanisms. This system features either an expansion spring or elastic cord inside the hollow central tube. The spring or cord is stretched as the slide is pulled out and then contracts, drawing the slide back to the rest position. The change from clock-spring to expansion spring/elastic cord was gradual, and no doubt some players continued to prefer their old clock-spring models to the new mechanism. Steele-Perkins writes that Köhler "maintained the option during the 1850's of clock-spring or elasticated spring at the choice of the buyer."[89]

---

[86]Herbert Heyde, catalogue notes, December 1992, *US-SD-Vermillion.*

[87]*US-SD-Vermillion*, item no. 418.

[88]*US-SD-Vermillion*, item no. 423.

[89]Steele-Perkins' information comes from a matching pair of contemporary trumpets in the collection of Arnold Myers of Edinburgh. "They were ordered by the same player, having the 'traditional' and 'new' mechanisms." Steele-Perkins, letter to the author, 3 October 1995.

There are many slide trumpets of this type on display at museums. One of the earliest examples is a Köhler "T. Harper's Improved" model in the Bate Collection.[90] This instrument must have been made before 1863, when the name of the firm, and thus the bell inscription, was changed to Köhler and Son. Another example is a Köhler and Son "T. Harper's Improved" model in the Royal College of Music.[91] This trumpet would have been made sometime between 1863 and 1881, when the Köhler and Son firm was doing business on Henrietta Street.[92] The Carse Collection at the Horniman Museum in London contains a Köhler and Son, with the bell inscription "Harper's Improved 196."[93] That this is a fairly late instrument can be deduced from the address inscription "61 Victoria Street, Westminster, London": the Köhler and Son shop was at this address only between the years 1890 and 1896.[94] The Edinburgh University Collection of Historic Musical Instruments has two slide trumpets of this type: a Köhler and Son from about 1870; and one made by Joseph Higham of Manchester in the 1860s.[95]

Several interesting expansion-spring/elastic-cord slide trumpets can be found in private collections, including Webb's silver Köhler from 1860 (Figure 19, p. 66), which was owned by Harper Jr. and is likely the trumpet featured in the photograph of Harper as Sergeant Trumpeter (see Frontispiece).[96] Frank Tomes' Köhler, originally a

---

[90]*GB-Oxford*, item no. 76.

[91]*GB-London-RCM*, item no. 252. See also Ridley, *Royal College Museum*, 57.

[92]Waterhouse, *New Langwill*, 210.

[93]The Carse Collection, *GB-London-H*, item no. 71. For a description see Adam Carse, *Catalogue of the Adam Carse Collection of Old Musical Wind Instruments* (London: London County Council, 1951), 56–57.

[94]Waterhouse, *New Langwill*, 210.

[95]*GB-Edinburgh*, items no. 2977 (Köhler) and no. 3215 (Higham). See Myers, ed., *Edinburgh Collection*, 18–19.

[96]The original sepia photograph of Harper Jr. was found in the case with the Köhler trumpet along with two silk City of London trumpet banners. Webb, conversation with the author, 31 May 1993.

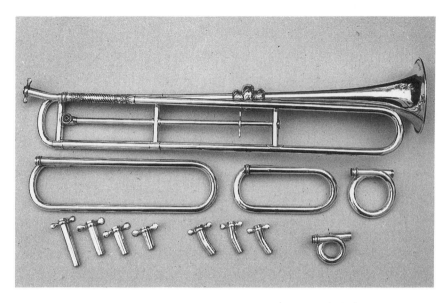

Figure 19: Köhler, "Harper's Improved" elastic-cord slide trumpet (1860). Courtesy of John Webb.

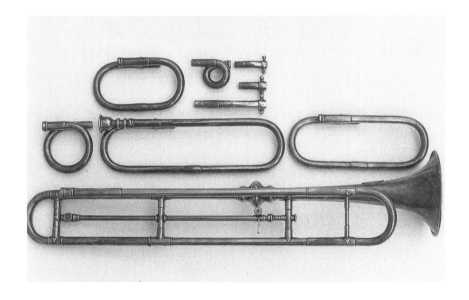

Figure 20: Besson, elastic-cord slide trumpet (ca. 1880). Courtesy of John Webb.

clock-spring model from the 1840s or 1850s, was later converted to the elastic-cord design.[97] Webb also owns a Besson from about 1880, which features a tuning slide on the front bow (Figure 20).[98]

In the United States, a Köhler and Son expansion-spring/elastic-cord model can be found at The Metropolitan Museum of Art in New York.[99] This instrument was made between 1881 and 1890, when the Köhler firm was at 116 Victoria Street in Westminster. Another Köhler and Son, numbered 185 and made at 35 Henrietta Street between 1863 and 1881, is housed in the Kenneth G. Fiske Museum.[100] The Shrine to Music Museum has a Köhler, which was made at the same address, probably between 1834 and 1863, the years in which the firm was located at Henrietta Street, before the change of name to Köhler and Son.[101] A late elastic-cord model (Figure 21, p. 68) can be found in the Eddy Collection.[102] This instrument, from about 1900, was made by Hawkes and Son. The address engraved on the bell is "Denman Street, Piccadilly Circus": the Hawkes and Son firm was located at this address from 1895 to 1930.[103]

Short Model

The so-called "short model" or "military" slide trumpet is folded four times rather than the conventional two, thereby shortening the distance between mouthpiece and bell. In addition, some models have a somewhat larger bell with a more conical flare. This

---

[97]Frank Tomes, conversation with the author, Wimbledon, England, 4 June 1993.

[98]Webb, "Slide Trumpet," 270.

[99]The Crosby Brown Collection of Musical Instruments, *US-NY-New York*, item no. 89.4.2533.

[100]*US-CA-Claremont*, item no. B67.

[101]*US-SD-Vermillion*, item no. 420.

[102]*US-MA-Cambridge*, item no. 258.

[103]Waterhouse, *New Langwill*, 165.

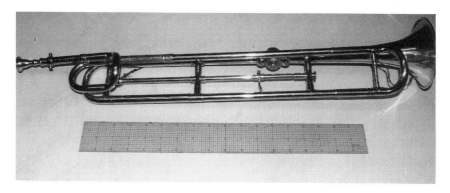

Figure 21: Hawkes and Son, elastic-cord slide trumpet (ca. 1900). Photograph by the author. Courtesy of G. Norman Eddy and the Eddy Collection of Musical Instruments.

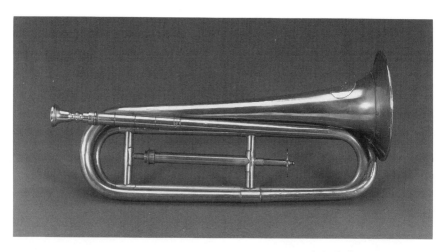

Figure 22: Grayson, compression-spring short model slide trumpet (ca. 1840). Photography by S. R. H. Spicer, the Shrine to Music Museum, University of South Dakota.

design made use of all the various slide return mechanisms described above. A late example, with the expansion-spring/elastic-cord mechanism and a six-inch slide pull, can be found in the Cliffe Castle Museum in Yorkshire.[104] A Pace compression-spring short model was mentioned above. In the United States, a Grayson compression-spring short model (Figure 22), also previously mentioned, can be found in the Shrine to Music Museum.

Two clock-spring short models are described in a 1925 *Musical Times* article by W. F. H. Blandford: one by Clementi and Co., dated 1832, and another by James Power, dated 1819–1820 and with only a two-and-one-half-inch slide pull.[105] The Power trumpet was owned in 1966 by Joseph Wheeler, and is described by him in an article in the *Galpin Society Journal*.[106] Philip Bate calls this type the "military" slide trumpet, because "in general size it resembled the 'short' duty trumpet of the British army, [thus] it may have been designed primarily for military use." Bate has owned one of these instruments, which "had an established military provenance and was reputed to have been used up to the turn of the present century."[107]

Earlier in this century, the short model slide trumpet seems to have been confused with the so-called "Regent's Bugle," an instrument described as having been made by Percival of London and introduced by Schmidt in 1815.[108] Blandford, in his 1925 article, assumes that the Clementi and Co. and Power short models he examined are examples of the Regent's Bugle, described in an article

---

[104]Bradford Art Galleries and Museums, *GB-Keighley*, item no. 68:28:1. For a description see Webb, "Slide Trumpet," 270–271.

[105]See W. F. H. Blandford, "The Regent's Bugle," *The Musical Times* (1 May 1925), 442–443; and Anthony Baines, *European and American Musical Instruments* (New York: The Viking Press, 1966), 137.

[106]Joseph Wheeler, "New Light on the 'Regent's Bugle'; with Some Notes on the Keyed Bugle," *Galpin Society Journal* 19 (April 1966): 65–70.

[107]Bate, *Trumpet and Trombone*, 124.

[108]See Blandford, "Regent's Bugle," 442; and Bate, *Trumpet and Trombone*, 124.

by Curt Sachs in the *Real Lexicon der Musikinstrumente*.[109] Reginald Morley-Pegge perpetuates this assumption, and suggests a motive for its development involving a supposed rivalry between Schmidt and John Distin, then a player of the keyed bugle.[110] Wheeler in 1966 and Bate in 1978 conclude that the real Regent's Bugle is a five-keyed trumpet with a slide used only for changing keys in the manner of crooks, made by Richard Curtis of Glasgow and now housed in the Brighton Museum.[111]

Since there are very few survivors, it seems likely that few short models were made. But because they "...seem to have occurred from time to time throughout the life of the slide trumpet," as evidenced by the use of all the various slide return mechanisms, Webb believes that they were not "just experimental anomalies."[112] Indeed, Webb, in his description of the two short models he examined, writes of a distinct advantage of these models: their bells were longer than the standard long-model slide trumpet. "On the short models the slide is fitted to the second loop so that the tapered bell tubing can be bent to form the main back-bow. The two instruments...have bells of twenty-three inches and twenty-five inches, much closer to the conical/cylindrical ratios associated with natural trumpets."[113] This feature, then, presumably made the sound of the short model even closer to that of the natural trumpet. But a final problem involves the apparently original mouthpieces found with many of the surviving short models. They have deep, funnel cups, which would have given the instruments a mellow sound, less like natural trumpets and more like keyed bugles. "The general format of these instruments resem-

---

[109]Blandford, "Regent's Bugle," 442–443.

[110]Reginald Morley-Pegge, "The Regent's Bugle," *Galpin Society Journal* 9 (June 1956): 94–95.

[111]The Albert Spencer Collection, *GB-Brighton*, item no. 37. See Wheeler, "New Light," 66–67; and Bate, *Trumpet and Trombone*, 125.

[112]Webb, "Slide Trumpet," 268.

[113]Ibid.

bles that of keyed bugles. Were they perhaps meant to sound like them, too?"[114] This inevitable comparison with the keyed bugle was perhaps what led earlier writers to associate these short-model types with the Regent's Bugle. So the mystery of the short model slide trumpet remains. Were they made for military use, as Bate suggests, or were they intended as slide versions of the keyed bugle?

Wyatt's Design

William Wyatt, whose patent specification was dated 1890,[115] finally produced a completely chromatic slide trumpet one hundred years after its initial development. This instrument (Figure 23, p. 72) is folded four times and features two double slides that are connected, thereby permitting the player to move the slides half the normal distance for each position and, at the same time, allowing for shifts of up to a major third. The patent specification describes the mechanism as follows:

> An additional slide…is added and is secured to the ordinary slide…and moves with it. This makes an extra length of tube available so that any note down to E♭ (in the third space of the bass clef), can be obtained.[116]

One of the most interesting features of this design is the false tubing added to take the place of the missing first bow of the standard slide trumpet. Most writers have suggested that this is a decorative addition intended to make the instrument look like a traditional slide trumpet, but the patent specification claims that it "serves as a support for the bell &c."[117] The slide return mechanism was of the expansion-spring/elastic-cord type, but the Wyatt model in Webb's

---

[114]Ibid.

[115]William Wyatt, Patent No. 9157, 13 June 1890; reproduced in Webb, "Slide Trumpet," 277.

[116]Ibid.

[117]Ibid.

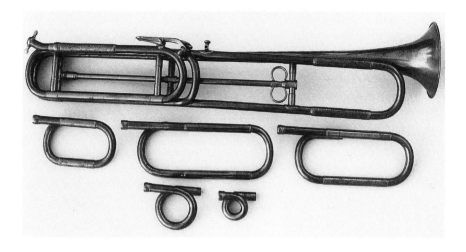

Figure 23: Wyatt, slide trumpet (1890). Courtesy of John Webb.

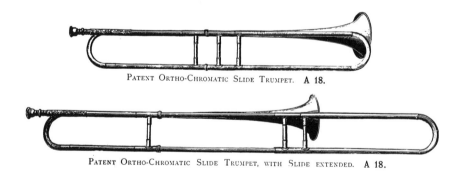

PATENT ORTHO-CHROMATIC SLIDE TRUMPET. A 18.

PATENT ORTHO-CHROMATIC SLIDE TRUMPET, WITH SLIDE EXTENDED. A 18.

Figure 24: Boosey, "Ortho-Chromatic" slide trumpet (ca. 1892). Courtesy of John Webb and the Historic Brass Society.

private collection makes use of the spring rather than the quieter rubber cord. According to Webb, "the spring was no doubt deemed necessary to return the weight of the double slide."[118]

From a practical standpoint, the Wyatt design has drawbacks as well as the obvious advantage of full chromaticism. Steele-Perkins finds that the return mechanism works "rather clumsily,"[119] which Webb attributes to "the friction caused by 4 sets of slide legs...."[120] Also, the small slide movements must have caused problems for players accustomed to conventional slide trumpets. According to Steele-Perkins, "...the half-tone shift is so small that it became troublesome."[121] On the other hand, Wyatt was apparently one of the first of the slide trumpet makers to develop crooks with tuning slides. Steele-Perkins finds this idea "is *so* simple and obvious," that he cannot understand "why they were not used from the earliest of times."[122]

Both Webb and Steele-Perkins think that only ten or so of the Wyatt models were made; Webb owns one in mint condition that is numbered seven,[123] and Steele-Perkins owns number eight, which "was mistakenly re-converted to a single slide."[124] The reason for the instrument's poor sales was that the final "perfection" of the slide trumpet came too late; by the 1890s the orchestral trumpet of choice was the valved trumpet in F. It was not, however, because of a lack of promotion: Carse claims that the trumpet was on display at the Royal Aquarium Exhibition of 1892,[125] and an anonymous editorial announcement from that same year in *The Musical Times* suggests

---

[118]Ibid., 270–272.

[119]Steele-Perkins, letter to the author, 7 February 1992.

[120]Webb, "Slide Trumpet," 272.

[121]Steele-Perkins, letter to the author, 23 September 1993.

[122]Steele-Perkins, letter to the author, 7 February 1992.

[123]Webb, "Slide Trumpet," 269–272.

[124]Steele-Perkins, letter to the author, 7 February 1992.

[125]Carse, *Musical Wind Instruments*, 238–239.

that the instrument "should, if it comes anywhere near its maker's estimate, be a real boon to trumpet players."[126]

Designs with Forward-Moving Slides

A final English slide trumpet design, by Boosey and Co., was also patented in the early 1890s, and appears in Boosey's 1892 catalog.[127] Called the "Patent Ortho-Chromatic Slide Trumpet," this instrument had a forward-moving slide with no return mechanism, and was really nothing more than an alto trombone with the bore and bell configurations of a trumpet (Figure 24, p. 72). The instrument allowed a shift of two whole tones, and "looked just like a State trumpet except for some additional cross stays."[128] Bate believes that the slide was not used as a chromatic device, as on the standard slide trumpet models, but only as an apparatus for quick crook changes. This model must have also been short-lived, with few being made, "for ten years later it had disappeared from the maker's literature altogether."[129]

Interestingly, a Frenchman designed a slide trumpet with a forward-moving slide in the 1830s, but this instrument was mostly ignored by the French, who preferred the use of the natural trumpet and *cornet à pistons* in the orchestra.[130] The trumpet was designed by François Georges Auguste Dauverné, who, as we have seen above, acknowledged Hyde as the originator of the slide trumpet, but then adapted and attempted to improve the English model.[131] The result was an instrument that offered a shift of a tone-and-a-half, and thus

---

[126]*The Musical Times* 33 (1 January 1892): 17.

[127]Webb, "Slide Trumpet," 272–273.

[128]Bate, *Trumpet and Trombone*, 126.

[129]Ibid.

[130]Tarr, *Trumpet*, 153.

[131]Dauverné, *Méthode*, 207 (page reference is to translation).

was more completely chromatic than the English design.[132] The instrument (Figure 25, p. 76) was manufactured by Courtois and Sax,[133] and Baines writes that it was sold as late as "after the mid-century, but with little success."[134] The forward-moving slide did not utilize a return mechanism, and in some models, according to Bate,

> the slide could be locked in any position by the turn of a knurled thumbscrew bearing on a rod. Thus, when free, this slide could be employed for the same purpose as the English model, but when the lock was used, it represented an alternative to the shorter crooks with the benefit of quicker changing.[135]

There was, however, an earlier French design with a forward-moving slide that may have provided more of a model for Dauverné than the English design. This instrument was designed by Legram, a French military bandsman, who took out a patent for it in 1821[136] and also provided a one-page tutor, complete with an illustration of the instrument.[137] This trumpet also had a tone-and-a-half downward shift and was made by François Riedlocker of Paris.[138] Sibyl Marcuse acknowledges that Legram brought out a trumpet with a slide extension of up to six-and-one-half inches, but claims, however, that the Parisian Smittschneider patented the *trompette-trombone* in 1821,

---

[132]See the photograph of a French-system slide trumpet by Sax in Martin Lessen and André M. Smith, "A New Compensating Valve System for Brass Instruments," *Journal of the International Trumpet Guild* 19 (May 1995): 51.

[133]*New Grove Instruments*, s. v. "Slide Trumpet," by Tarr.

[134]Baines, *Brass Instruments*, 184.

[135]Bate, *Trumpet and Trombone*, 124.

[136]Baines, *Brass Instruments*, 184.

[137]For a discussion of Legram and a reproduction of the tutor, see Friedrich Anzenberger, "The Earliest French Tutor for Slide Trumpet," *Historic Brass Society Journal* 4 (1992): 106–111.

[138]See Ibid., 108; and Victor Charles Mahillon, "The Trumpet—its History—its Theory—its Construction," trans. Major F. A. Mahan, *Dominant* 16 (October 1908): 15.

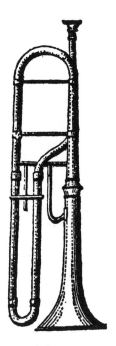

Figure 25: French-system slide trumpet, from F. G. A. Dauverné, *Méthode pour la trompette*, xxv.

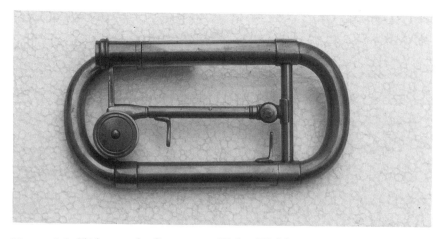

Figure 26: Slide-crook. Courtesy of John Webb.

which was "a trumpet with slide pushed forward like that of a trombone."[139]

Other Designs

There were other continental slide trumpet designs, but none of them were widely used. Tarr mentions a trumpet developed by Michael Saurle of Munich around 1820, with a tuning slide and a pitch slide, and one by Haltenhof of Hanau, which was played in France by J. D. Buhl but discarded because of its "cumbersome slide mechanism."[140] Friedrich Anzenberger has found a report in *Revue Musicale* of 1833 that claims Buhl (1781–1860) as the inventor of this instrument.[141]

One of the most interesting and mysterious designs inspired by the slide trumpet is the slide crook (Figure 26), an example of which was found in the case of an 1835 Köhler in the collection of John Webb.[142] This D crook includes a forward-moving slide operated by its own single clock-spring return mechanism. Like the slide trumpet mechanism in miniature, the crook also has two stays and a central tube with a finger pull extending from the tube at a right angle.

A portrait of a young trumpeter, found in an antique store near Worcester by the English trumpeter Stephen Keavy, shows what appears to be a slide crook.[143] In the portrait, the trumpeter is holding his instrument so that only the mouthpiece and rear bow can be seen. A crook with a clock-spring, however, is also clearly shown behind the rear bow. Unfortunately, the identity of the portrait's

---

[139]Sibyl Marcuse, *A Survey of Musical Instruments* (London: David & Charles, Ltd., 1975), 808.

[140]Tarr, "Slide Trumpet," 405.

[141]Anzenberger, "French Tutor," 106.

[142]See Webb, "Slide Trumpet," 267.

[143]Ibid., 266. For a better reproduction of the photograph, see "Errata for Volume 5," *Historic Brass Society Journal* 6 (1994): viii.

subject is not known, but Webb makes an interesting supposition that it might actually be a "youthful Harper Sr."[144]

From the evidence of the painting and the surviving slide crook, it is apparent that the only way the crook slide could have been operated was by pushing forward with the left hand. What were the uses of this device? Webb speculates that the slide crook might have been made for a natural trumpet in F,[145] for which it would have been effective for fine tuning, but not as effective as using an actual slide trumpet. Perhaps the crook could have been used early in the century to correct the intonation of out-of-tune harmonics—by trumpeters who were wary of having their expensive natural trumpets converted to slide trumpets. Or perhaps it allowed the player in the painting to achieve a whole-tone downward shift on the early slide trumpets with short slides. But the simultaneous forward and backward motion must have been awkward in practice. At any rate, the slide crook was probably not widely used. In fact, the survivor owned by Webb and the painting are the only known evidence of this accessory.

Henry Bassett's "Teleophonic, or Perfect-Sounding, Trumpet" was an experimental design that was undoubtedly rarely played. In the 1870s Bassett designed trumpets with the intention of correcting the intonation problems inherent in valved instruments, and yet retaining the tone quality of the slide trumpet. His experiments resulted in a regular slide trumpet to which a single valve was attached. The trumpet was evidently held in the ordinary manner, and the valve was manipulated by the first finger of the left hand. The extra tubing engaged by the working of the valve had the effect of lowering the pitches of the harmonic series by a tone-and-a-half.

Bassett's invention was introduced at the meetings of the Musical Association,[146] and subsequently championed by William Stone

---

[144]Ibid., 267.

[145]Ibid.

[146]See Henry Bassett, "On Improvements in the Trumpet," *Proceedings of the Musical Association* 3 (1877), 140–144.

in the first edition of the Grove *Dictionary*. Stone devotes a substantial final paragraph in his article on the trumpet to Bassett's instrument, which he calls the "Univalve Trumpet."[147] Stone's paragraph, which is basically an advertisement for the trumpet, describes it in the following way:

> This valve...does not injure in the slightest degree the pure tone of the old Trumpet, the bore of the main tube remaining perfectly straight. By use of this single valve and the slide, it is possible to produce a complete scale, major or minor, with a perfection of intonation only limited by the skill of the player, as it is essentially a slide instrument.[148]

But the problem with this instrument is that it is a hybrid, without the complete facility of the valved trumpet and little advantage over the slide trumpet. When asked in the Musical Association discussion if the instrument was chromatic, Bassett replied that it was, but that "it was not suitable for very rapid passages...."[149] It is no surprise that English trumpeters ignored this instrument: composers were regularly writing rapid passages for the trumpet by the 1880s.

SLIDE TRUMPET TECHNIQUE

The basic technique of the slide trumpet is the same as that of the natural trumpet, since the essential elements—such as metal, bore, shape, and mouthpiece—are all similar. Therefore the modern player who wishes to learn the slide trumpet must first learn the technique of the natural trumpet.[150] Beyond this, however, there are certain techniques that are unique to the slide trumpet, and must be

---

[147]Stone, "Trumpet," 182–183.

[148]Ibid.

[149]Bassett, "Improvements," 142.

[150]For a discussion of natural trumpet technique see Tarr, *Trumpet*, 85–90.

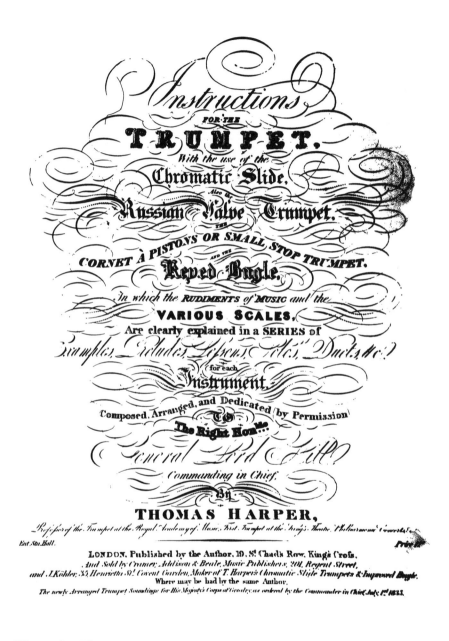

Figure 27: Thomas Harper Sr., *Instructions for the Trumpet*, title page. By permission of Spring Tree Enterprises.

considered. Detailed explanations of slide trumpet technique can be found in the 1875 tutor of Thomas Harper Jr. For the modern slide trumpet player this tutor, and that of Thomas Harper Sr. (Figure 27), are indispensable for playing instructions and study material.[151] Since the Harper Jr. tutor (Figure 28, p. 82) is not widely available today, the information will be summarized here, and compared with the information from his father's tutor and a later tutor[152] published by Hawkes and Son (Figure 29, p. 83).[153]

Playing Position

The way the slide trumpet is held depends on the slide return mechanism. The clock-spring models from the first half of the nineteenth century were supported more with the right hand than the left (Figure 30, p. 84). According to Thomas Harper Sr., the instrument

> is held horizontally in the right hand, with the Mouthpiece and Crook to the left side of the Performer. The second and third fingers are placed on the lower end of the small cross in the middle of the Trumpet to move the slide up when required. The thumb is on the upper part of the middle cross (or stay) The first and fourth fingers are placed nearly opposite each other on the outside of the Trumpet but are not to move.[154]

As for the left hand, Harper suggests that the fingers "be placed on any part of the Trumpet most convenient, the thumb resting on the side of the Mouthpiece, so as to keep the Trumpet in a steady position."[155]

---

[151] A facsimile edition of the Harper Sr. tutor can be obtained from Spring Tree Enterprises, 5745 U.S. Route 11, Homer, NY, 13077. The Harper Jr. tutor is not currently available, but nineteenth-century editions can be found in some libraries.

[152] *The Trumpet: Valve and Slide*, Hawkes and Son's Simplicity Instruction Books (London: Hawkes and Son, 1906).

[153] For information on another tutor, see Addendum, p. 214.

[154] Harper Sr., *Instructions*, 12.

[155] Ibid.

Figure 28: Thomas Harper Jr., *Harper's School for the Trumpet*, title page.

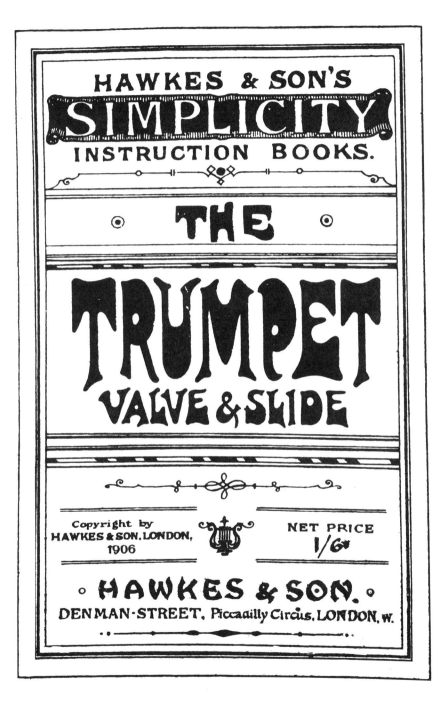

Figure 29: Hawkes and Son's trumpet tutor, title page.

Figure 30: Thomas Harper Sr., lithograph, showing slide trumpet playing position. By permission of the Royal College of Music.

In holding the later expansion-spring/elastic-cord models, the left hand takes on more of the responsibilities of support and balance. The change is evident in the slightly different description of the holding position given by Thomas Harper Jr.:

> The Trumpet is held horizontally with the left hand; the crook, bit, and mouthpiece being to the left of the instrument. The first, second, and third fingers of the left hand must be placed on, or round the crook; the thumb and fourth finger supporting the instrument.[156]

His description of the right-hand finger position is identical to his father's.

In the 1906 Hawkes and Son tutor, the latest slide trumpet tutor known to this author, the description of left-hand responsibilities even more closely resembles that of valved trumpets: "The instrument is held firmly by the Left hand grasping the crook and the main tube; the pressure of the mouthpiece is regulated by this hand."[157]

Thus, with the clock-spring models the right hand not only operates the slide but also provides the support and balance, while the left hand is responsible for steadying the mouthpiece. In the later models, balance and support are more equally provided by both hands. The reason probably lies in the fact that the clock-spring mechanism caused more of a jolt upon the return of the slide than did the later designs.[158] Indeed, Harper Sr. warns of this in his tutor:

> When using the Slide, the first and fourth fingers and thumb of the right hand remain stationary, while the second and third fingers move the Slide up, As the Slide returns the fingers must guide it, or it will jerk the mouth piece from the lips.[159]

Another possible reason for the change has to do with the earlier shorter slides compared with the slides used by Harper Jr. The use

---

[156]Harper Jr., *School*, Preface p. 5.

[157]*Trumpet: Valve and Slide*, 8.

[158]Hoover, "Slide Trumpet," 170.

[159]Harper Sr., *Instructions*, 20.

of the left hand to help support the trumpet leaves the right hand freer to move, and more movement would be required to draw back the longer slides of the last half of the century.

Slide Movement

As we have seen, both Harpers instruct the player to leave the thumb and first and fourth fingers of the right hand immobile. In practice, however, full extension of the later, longer slides demands that these fingers move with the backward pull of the slide. But, as mentioned above, this is not a problem as long as the left hand assists with the support of the instrument.

The scale that Harper Sr. provides in his tutor (Figure 31) indicates that most of the slide movement was used to correct the eleventh and thirteenth partials, and to achieve half-step downward shifts from all partials. To correct the out-of-tune partials, Harper instructs that the slide be drawn out about an inch-and-a-half. For the half-step shifts he instructs that the slide be pulled out about half way for the higher keys of F, E, E♭, and D, and two-thirds for the lower keys of D♭, C, B, B♭, A, and A♭. He allows that only "two or three whole tones may be obtained by the full length of the Slide, but as they incline to be sharp they are generally used as passing notes."[160] These whole-tone-shift, passing notes include b♭, d', and a♭'.

Interestingly, Harper Sr. does not allude to the fact that the thirteenth partial (a") is naturally a bit flat, and that the suggested inch-and-a-half shift would lower the pitch even further. Harper Jr. mentions that the thirteenth partial is "too flat for A [natural]" in a footnote explaining the shift necessary to achieve G♯", but is vague in the text when referring to the correction of the a": "The slide perfects the *fourth* and *sixth* (F and A) of the fourth octave, (or more strictly speaking the 11th and 13th) for which purpose it must be

---

[160]Ibid., 11.

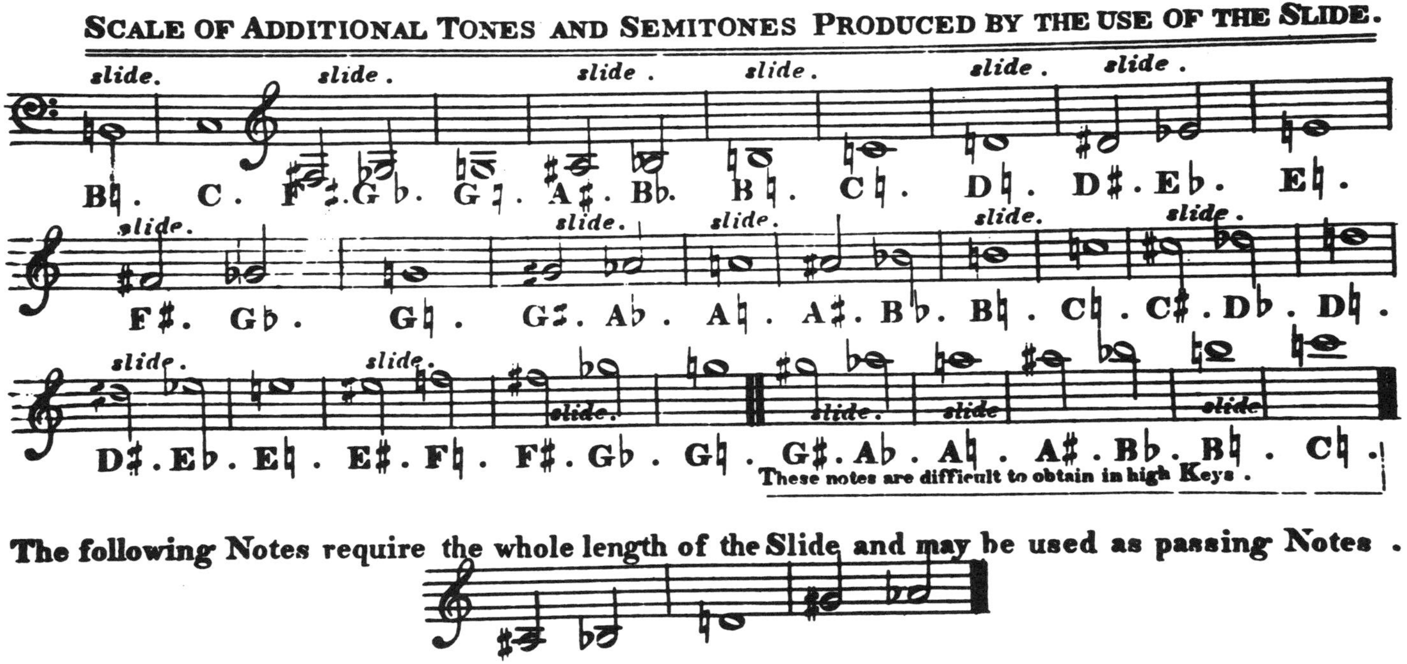

Figure 31: Thomas Harper Sr., slide trumpet scale, from *Instructions for the Trumpet*, p. 11. By permission of Spring Tree Enterprises.

extended about one inch and a half."[161] But neither father nor son mention that in order to produce the a'' in tune, the player must actually play the fourteenth partial (b♭''), and draw out the slide the necessary distance. Steele-Perkins has found that "a touch more than 1-1/2 inches is best but this may vary from one player to another or one instrument to another."[162]

Harper Jr. allows for a whole-tone extension of the slide to produce f', in addition to the whole-tone shifts that his father used. Also, Harper Jr. does not restrict the use of these whole-tone shifts to passing notes, no doubt because of the longer slide he was using. But he does confine the whole-tone shifts to the key of D and higher, and instructs that "a little less than the whole slide will be found sufficient" for the keys of F and E.[163] Harper then gives specific instructions on the playing of certain notes which are summarized in the following chart:[164]

f'   available with full slide extension in F, E, and E♭;
        may be used as e♯ in key of D;
        not to be used in keys lower than D.

b♭'   in some keys this note will be flat;
        if so play c'' (8th partial) with full slide extension.

a♭''   will be more secure if played as b♭''
        (14th partial) with one-and-a-half-inch extension.

b♭''   alternate positions to improve intonation:
        play as b'' (15th partial) with two-inch extension;
        or, play as c''' (16th partial) with full extension.

b''   play as c''' (16th partial);
        use approximately a one-and-a-half-inch extension.

---

[161]Harper Jr., *School*, 1.

[162]Steele-Perkins, letter to the author, 23 September 1993.

[163]Harper Jr., *School*, 1.

[164]Ibid., 3–4.

Harper Jr., however, cautions the player that these recommended slide extensions are for the key of D only, and must be modified with each crook change. Somewhat less than the distances given will be proportionately required for the keys higher than D. And as for the lower keys:

> When the Trumpet is crooked below D, a greater proportionate length will be found necessary; even the addition of an extra tuning bit will necessitate a slight change. It will therefore be seen that the required length of slide for certain notes, varies with each change of crook, consequently when it is necessary to extend the slide, the "Ear" must assist the fingers.[165]

The 1906 Hawkes and Son tutor allows for a fully chromatic instrument above d'. But the lowest crook provided for the Hawkes and Son slide trumpet is the C crook, and the tutor recommends the distances for the various slide positions based on use of this lowest crook; "when the *D, E* or *F* crook is in use the extension must be lessened with each change of crook."[166]

Articulation

The prescribed method of tonguing on the slide trumpet is no different from that for English natural trumpets, although it is quite different from traditional, continental practices. Harper Sr. instructs the player to "introduce the tongue between the teeth, (the tip just touching the upper lip)...."[167] Later, Harper writes that the player should

> then draw the breath at each side of the mouth, press the breath a little forward (but it must not escape) untill [*sic*] the tongue is with-

---

[165]Ibid., 4.

[166]*Trumpet: Valve and Slide*, 9.

[167]Harper Sr., *Instructions*, 12.

drawn from the lips with a slight jerk (similar to that of dislodging something from the lips that is offensive)....[168]

Harper Jr.'s description of the tonguing process is almost identical to his father's.[169]

The practice of unequal tonguing in passages of short note values, the so-called "ti-ri-ti-ri" *cantabile* tonguing advocated by Altenburg and described by Fantini in his *Modo per imparare a sonare di tromba* of 1638,[170] was apparently not used in England. English trumpet music from the late seventeenth through the eighteenth century was very different from continental trumpet music, without the very high floridity that is found in Molter, Richter, or even J. S. Bach. Steele-Perkins argues this point, and as an example relates a relevant story: "When Harper Senior was invited by Mendelssohn to play Bach's 'Magnificat' he replied that it 'was unplayable on the modern trumpet'; his trumpet was in fact a Harris from the early 18th Century converted to a 'slide' mechanism...."[171] In addition, English mouthpieces were larger than those used by continental trumpeters, and the resulting sound quality was different. Steele-Perkins writes: "John Shore's playing is described by Roger North as like 'the chirruping' of a bird and this is a remarkably descriptive account of the effect by striking and stroking the notes with the tip of the tongue on a large English mouthpiece."[172] Because of the different musical style and the different mouthpiece construction, it is not surprising that a different approach to articulation was developed in England.

The later Hawkes and Son tutor, however, describes a more modern approach to tonguing: "...the breath is forced between the lips

---

[168]Ibid., 13.

[169]Harper Jr., *School*, Preface p. 5.

[170]For a discussion of natural trumpet articulation, see Tarr, *Trumpet*, 91–93.

[171]Steele-Perkins, letter to the author, 29 January 1992.

[172]Ibid.

into the mouthpiece and through the instrument by the action of the tongue, in a manner somewhat like pronouncing the letter T!"[173]

For double- and triple-tonguing, Harper Jr. recommends an approach that would be more recognizable to modern players. He suggests that the player use the syllables "tick ca" for double tonguing, and either "tick ca ta" or "ta ga da" for triple tonguing.[174] Harper Sr. also suggests the syllables "ta da ga" for triple tonguing.[175]

Interestingly, neither of the Harpers addresses the problem of the articulation of slurred passages that include notes requiring a slide shift. Both mention slurring, but describe only what would be called "lip slurring" today; that is, slurring between notes of the harmonic series.[176] For slurred passages involving slide shifts, slide trumpeters must borrow the *legato* tonguing technique of trombonists.

Transposition

With the use of trumpets that were almost fully chromatic, nineteenth-century players of the slide trumpet must have begun thinking about keys and pitch in a different way. Harper Jr. touches briefly, and not at all clearly, on the concept of transposition, but does not use the term; instead, he tries to explain the phenomenon through examples. On pages eight and nine of his tutor, Harper gives examples of several different chords: how they would be written in the various trumpet keys (crooks), and how they would sound in concert pitch. But he tends to make it more confusing than it need be. For example, he writes that the chord of D♭ can be written c', e', g', c" for a trumpet in D♭, which will sound d♭', f', a♭', d♭"; or it can be written b, d♯', f♯', b' for trumpet in D, which will sound d♭', f', a♭',

---

[173]*Trumpet: Valve and Slide*, 8.

[174]Harper Jr., *School*, 5.

[175]Harper Sr., *Instructions*, 5.

[176]Ibid., 4; and Harper Jr., *School*, 6.

d♭".[177] But, theoretically, the trumpet in D should sound c#', e#', g#', c#".

Finally, Harper Jr. provides a chart that seems to be intended more for the composer than the player. This chart recommends the different trumpet keys (crooks) to use when writing in all possible keys.[178] Perhaps he included it with the thought that composers wishing to learn the technical possibilities of the trumpet might consult his tutor. The chart is reproduced in Figure 32.

George Hogarth,[179] writing in *The Musical World* in the same year as the publication of the Harper Sr. tutor, makes an early comment on the emerging practice of transposition:

> Before the modern improvements on the trumpet, it could be played only in the single key on which it was pitched. Thus a C trumpet could only be played in the key of C, a D trumpet in the key of D, &c; but upon one and the same, of the same trumpets now in use, not only the major key in which it is pitched, but also several other keys may be produced. Taking the C trumpet, for example, besides the key of C, it may be played upon in the keys of G, F, B♭, E, C minor, E minor, G minor, and A minor. By the occasional use of the slide, the principal notes of all these keys may be produced on the C trumpet; and hence it is no longer necessary to change the crooks at every modulation that may occur in a composition.[180]

The technique of the slide trumpet allowed the players, especially virtuosos like the Harpers, an extraordinary amount of facility. We know this from the exercises and study material included in the tutors. But there were limits to that facility, especially with regard to slide movement and the important gaps in the scale. In order to un-

---

[177]Ibid., 9.

[178]Ibid., 12.

[179]Hogarth was an important music critic and father-in-law of Charles Dickens. See Norman Lebrecht, *Music in London* (London: Aurum Press, 1992), 118.

[180]George Hogarth, "Musical Instruments: The Trumpet, Trombone, Serpent and Ophicleide," *The Musical World* 4 (17 February 1837): 131.

When writing Music for the Trumpet the following method is recommended.

For the key of		write in		Trumpet in
{	C	C		C.
	A minor	G minor _ _ _ _		D.
{	G	G _ _ _ _ _		C.
	E minor	C minor _ _ _ _		E.
{	D	C		D.
	B minor	A minor { _ _ _ _		D.
{	A	G		
	F♯ minor	E minor { _ _ _ _		D.
{	E	C		E.
	C♯ minor	B minor _ _ _		D.
{	B	G		E.
	G♯ minor	see A♭ minor		
{	F♯	E _ _ _ _ _		D.
	D♯ minor	see E♭ minor		
{	C♯	see D♭		
	A♯ minor	see B♭ minor		
{	F	C _ _ _ _		F.
	D minor	C minor		D.
{	B♭	G		
	G minor	E minor { _ _ _		E♭.
{	E♭	C		E♭.
	C minor	C minor		C.
{	A♭	G		D♭.
	F minor	C minor		F.
{	D♭	C _ _ _ _		D♭.
	B♭ minor	G minor _ _ _ _		E♭.
{	G♭	see F♯		
	E♭ minor	C _ _ _ _		E♭.
{	C♭	see B♮		
	A♭ minor	G minor _ _ _		D♭.

In order to facilitate certain passages, a little change in the above arrangement may_ with advantage_ be sometimes made, but it is better if possible to avoid Crooks below C.

Harper's chool for the Trumpet.

Figure 32: Thomas Harper Jr., trumpet key chart, from *Harper's School for the Trumpet*, p. 12.

derstand how this instrument was used, in both orchestral and solo playing, and to what degree the trumpeters' technique was challenged, we must consider the literature for the slide trumpet.

Chapter Three: The Literature of the Slide Trumpet

Thanks to the efforts of Hyde and Harper Sr., the slide trumpet was adopted by English orchestral trumpeters in the first decades of the nineteenth century. Just how widespread was its use depended, of course, on the availability of converted natural trumpets, and, by the 1820s, newly manufactured slide trumpets. An examination of the trumpet parts of English operatic and orchestral scores, however, reveals that use of the slide trumpet was not exclusive. Rather, the slide trumpet existed in an environment, much like today, in which players were required to use a variety of instruments in order to perform adequately all the music written for them. The nineteenth-century players, though, had to be even more versatile than today's players. Although modern B♭ trumpet playing requires a slightly different approach than that of, say, piccolo trumpet playing, the basic mechanism and finger technique remain the same. The successful nineteenth-century London players, however, would have been obligated to master the various mechanisms and playing styles of instruments as diverse as the natural trumpet, slide trumpet, keyed bugle, valved cornet, and valved trumpet.

In addition to orchestral playing, the slide trumpet was used in solo playing by all the prominent trumpeters of the slide trumpet's heyday—from Sarjant to Hyde to the Harpers to Walter Morrow. An examination of the sources reveals that there was much solo literature written for and performed on the slide trumpet for about one hundred years—from the late eighteenth to the late nineteenth century. There probably was more solo literature for the slide trumpet than there was for the instrument that was developed at about the same time—the keyed trumpet. But unlike the keyed trumpet, the slide trumpet did not have the good fortune to have two outstanding concertos written for it by composers such as Haydn and Hummel. For the most part, the solos performed on the slide trumpet were either natural trumpet solos, such as Handel's arias with trumpet obbligato, that continued to be played into the nineteenth century, or solos written or arranged by trumpeters for themselves to play. Unfortunately, since most of the slide trumpet solos were performed only by the players who wrote them, and never published, much of that material is now presumably lost.

In this chapter, the literature of the slide trumpet will be studied in depth; some 200 works, including operatic and orchestral trumpet parts, chamber works, solos, and songs with trumpet obbligato, have been examined (see Bibliography for complete listing). The following discussion will focus on this music in an attempt to form a better understanding of the role and scope of the slide trumpet and other soprano brass instruments in the nineteenth-century English orchestra.

ORCHESTRAL LITERATURE

Sources examined for this study include trumpet parts of operatic and orchestral works, for the most part by nineteenth-century British composers. The rationale for this is, of course, that native composers would likely have written trumpet parts for the trumpets being used in the local orchestras. Several non-British composers are represented in the study because their works, such as Weber's *Oberon* and Mendelssohn's "Italian" Symphony, were written for British ensembles. Most of the music played by the London concert orchestras during the nineteenth century, however, was by continental composers, and these works will also be considered because they tell us much about the demands on the players. It is not on the concert stage, however, but in the opera house where the slide trumpet first appears with regularity.

The Opera Orchestra

As we have seen earlier, John Thiessen's study of William Shields' late-eighteenth-century operas proves that tones not found in the harmonic series were being written in the trumpet parts, and offers substantial evidence that the slide trumpet was used to play those parts. By the turn of the nineteenth century, we can assume that the slide trumpet had become common in the opera house, since John Hyde was one of the principal trumpeters playing in the opera orchestras, including the most important, the King's Theatre. This is not surprising, considering that the more experimental and progressive orchestration, throughout the nineteenth century, was to be found in the opera house rather than on the concert stage. According to Ralph Dudgeon:

> Composers who wrote for the opera, military bands or various types of popular music were wildly experimental in comparison with the composers of concert music. One need only to compare the orchestration of a Rossini opera with a contemporary symphony of Schubert to see the gap between the concert hall and the theatre.[1]

Thus, trumpeters in the English opera orchestras in the early years of the century were not only playing slide trumpets but also experimenting with other soprano brass instruments, such as the keyed bugle and cornet.

The principal theaters for opera production in nineteenth-century London were the King's Theatre, the Covent Garden Theatre, and the Drury Lane Theatre. The King's Theatre, which was renamed Her Majesty's Theatre at Queen Victoria's accession in 1837, was the most exclusive venue for opera during the first half of the century. The theater, which was also called the Italian Opera House, featured the latest Italian opera, and occasionally English opera sung in Italian. It had the best opera orchestra of the city, and it regularly engaged the top singers, both foreign and domestic. In 1847 most of the singers and orchestra members moved, along with conductor Michael Costa, to the Covent Garden Theatre, where the new Royal Italian Opera was established; it soon began to replace Her Majesty's as the best operatic theater in town. Before 1847,

---

[1]Ralph T. Dudgeon, "The Keyed Bugle, Its History, Literature and Technique" (Ph.D. diss., University of California, San Diego, 1980), 97.

Covent Garden featured English opera performances and occasionally foreign opera in English translations. The Drury Lane Theatre was also used for opera in English. Some of the theaters of lesser importance included the Lyceum Theatre (also known as The English Opera House) and The Little Theatre, Haymarket, which was used for operatic productions only occasionally.

There are no published listings of orchestral personnel for these theaters, but information from various sources can give us the names of some of the players engaged in the opera orchestras at various times.[2] Thomas Harper was principal trumpet at the King's/Her Majesty's Theatre at least by 1823, and remained in this post even after the move to Covent Garden in 1847. Shortly thereafter, Harper began to limit his engagements and before his death in 1853, Harper Jr. had taken over as principal, and was still there through the 1850s. We can assume, then, that the slide trumpet was in regular use at these theaters during the time the Harpers were there. But their presence, and therefore that of the slide trumpet, was felt at the other theaters as well. Harper Sr. began his career as principal trumpet at both the Drury Lane and Lyceum Theatres in 1806, and was still principal at the former in 1815, and the latter in 1823. He was also engaged at the Little Theatre, Haymarket, at least from 1814 to 1817.

In order to determine the extent of the use of the slide trumpet in the opera house, one must consult full orchestral scores for the operas performed. Unfortunately, full scores of late-eighteenth- and early-nineteenth-century English operas are hard to find. Thiessen complains specifically about late-eighteenth-century scores:

> The orchestral parts to much of the best trumpet music of the period
> have been lost, including the repertories at Covent Garden and other

[2]Sources consulted include Carse, *Orchestra*; Cox, *Recollections*; Highfill, et. al., *Biographical Dictionary*; Matthews, comp., *Royal Society*; Scott Paul Sorenson, "Thomas Harper, Sr. (1786–1853): Trumpet Virtuoso and Pedagogue" (Ph.D. diss., University of Minnesota, 1987); and *New Grove*, s. v. "Harper," by William H. Husk and Edward H. Tarr.

London theatres. This often leaves the published vocal/pianoforte scores which appeared around the time of a work's first production, as the only musical source materials.[3]

Indeed, full scores of operas by British composers throughout the nineteenth century are similarly difficult to obtain. Even as published scores became more common after the mid-century point, operas tended to be published as piano-vocal arrangements. It is therefore fortunate that the works of two of the most successful British opera composers of the first two-thirds of the nineteenth century, Henry Bishop (1786–1855) and Michael Balfe (1808–1870), are well represented by numerous manuscript full scores in the British Library. In addition to these works, manuscript full scores by George Macfarren (1813–1887), another important mid-century composer for the theater, can be found in the Fitzwilliam Museum Library in Cambridge.

Early Nineteenth Century: Henry Bishop

Though little regarded today, Sir Henry Rowley Bishop was one of the most important and influential musicians of early-nineteenth-century England.[4] He was a founding member and sometime conductor of the Philharmonic Society, musical director of all the major London theaters at various times, and a prolific composer of theater music. His lasting legacy, however, is the sentimental ballad "Home, Sweet Home," from his 1823 opera *Clari, or The Maid of Milan*.

Bishop's trumpet writing is, for the most part, very conservative. The challenging trumpet parts, songs with trumpet obbligato, and notes outside the harmonic series that permeate the operas of Shield are nowhere to be found in Bishop's music. This is in part due to the general decline in the clarino style (see Chapter One), of which James Sarjant seems to have been the last English practitioner. Bishop often gives the trumpeters much to do, including military-

---

[3]Thiessen, "Late Eighteenth-Century Trumpet," 3–4.

[4]*New Grove*, s. v. "Bishop, Sir Henry Rowley," by Nicholas Temperley.

style solos and stage-band playing, but the parts are not challenging with regard to either non-harmonic-series notes or range. With a few notable exceptions, Bishop stays within the harmonic series, and only rarely writes notes outside the tonic triad. Thus the out-of-tune seventh and eleventh partials (b♭' and f"), are almost entirely missing from his trumpet parts. Also, Bishop rarely gives the first trumpeter the sixteenth partial (c'"), and when he does it is usually in the lower crookings, or he instructs the player to use a bugle.

One of Bishop's early works, however, stands above the rest of his entire repertory for its adventurous writing for the trumpet, and shows us how the slide trumpet might have been used to its full potential. *The Miller and his Men*, "a Melo Drama, with Choruses etc.," was premiered on 25 October 1813 at The Theatre Royal, Covent Garden, and became one of Bishop's most popular works.[5] In the overture, Bishop writes for two trumpets in C, and the first trumpeter is instructed to double on keyed bugle. The keyed bugle was simply an ordinary military bugle with tone-holes drilled into the tubing, which were opened and closed with a system of keys and pads.[6] It is remarkable that Bishop would write a part for this instrument, which had been invented only three years earlier by the English bandmaster Joseph Haliday.[7] Nonetheless, in the middle of the overture are an "Arietta" and a "Bohemian Waltz," both with keyed bugle as the solo melody instrument. Seven measures before the solo in the arietta, the instruction "change to keyed bugle" appears in the score above the trumpet staff (f. 16). This direction is clearly meant for the first trumpeter because at the same place in the score, but below the

[5]Henry R. Bishop, *The Miller and his Men*, autograph score (1813) *Lbl*, Add. 27703; see also Henry Rowley Bishop, "Overture to *The Miller and his Men*," ed. Nicholas Temperley with assist. of Matthew Greenbaum, facsimile repr. of autograph score, *The Symphony, 1720–1840*, ed. Barry S. Brook, Series E, Vol. VI: *The Overture in England, 1800–1840* (New York: Garland, 1984), 1–28.

[6]For an excellent discussion of the history, literature, and technique of the keyed bugle see Ralph T. Dudgeon, *The Keyed Bugle* (Metuchen, NJ: Scarecrow Press, 1993).

[7]Dudgeon, "Keyed Bugle," 1.

trumpet staff, appears the instruction "2nd Solo" and the second trumpet part continues with downward-stemmed notes. Immediately after the keyed bugle solo, and at the beginning of the "Bohemian Waltz," the instruments indicated on the trumpet staff are "Keyed Bugle & Trombe 2ndo" (f. 18).

The first trumpeter evidently continues to play keyed bugle to the end of the overture, as there are no instructions to return to the trumpet. After the waltz solo, however, there is a twenty-nine measure rest for both trumpets, followed by a reprise of the waltz melody in the first part, transposed up a fourth (f. 20). The second trumpeter now joins in for the first time since the arietta, playing natural tones of the harmonic series in the low register. This reprise of the waltz melody would have been playable on a slide trumpet (Example 7, p. 102); moreover, this version is less ornamental than the earlier keyed bugle solo (Example 8, p. 103) and therefore more idiomatic to the slide trumpet. At the coda the first part abandons the melody and both parts resume with fanfare-like figures to the end. It seems unlikely that the blending of keyed bugle and natural trumpet colors would have been satisfactory for the traditional trumpet scoring at the end of this overture, especially considering the English resistance to the uneven sound of keyed brass. It is entirely possible that, to achieve a more balanced tone quality, the trumpeter would have picked up a slide trumpet during the twenty-nine measure rest—or returned to the one he might have been playing from the opening of the overture—to play the transposed waltz melody and the rest of the overture.

Of course, much of this is speculation, and is intended only as a suggestion as to how the slide trumpet might have been used at this time. Dudgeon has found a piano edition of the opera in the British Library that indicates the arietta was performed by "Mr. Wallis" on a "Patent Keyed Bugle."[8] We know that Thomas Wallis (see Appendix B) was first trumpeter at the Theatre Royal, Covent Garden, at the

---

[8]Ibid., 137.

Example 7: Henry Bishop, *The Miller and His Men* (ff. 23–25v).

time of his admittance to the Royal Society of Musicians in 1808,[9] and according to Carse, still the first trumpeter there in 1818.[10] Whether the keyed bugle was used to perform all of the overture's melodic material, or alternated with the slide trumpet, it is clear that the latter would have come in handy for this music. In addition to providing a more homogeneous trumpet sound, use of the slide trumpet would have greatly improved the intonation of the eleventh harmonic, the numerous examples of which include an extended f'' held over parts of three measures (f. 16v).

---

[9]Matthews, comp., *Royal Society*, "Thomas Wallis, Jr.," 150.

[10]Carse, *Orchestra*, 489.

Example 8: Bishop, *The Miller and His Men* (ff. 18–19v).

The only other example of notes outside the harmonic series for trumpet in Bishop's operas occurs in *Yelva, or The Orphan of Russia*, premiered in 1829 at Covent Garden.[11] The overture to this opera, like that for *The Miller and his Men*, has a contrasting middle section (*Andante grazioso*) with the first trumpet playing the melody line. But unlike the earlier opera, the melody here is shared with the first clarinet, flute, and piccolo, while the horn plays a countermelody. But the melody includes unmistakable non-harmonic-series notes; b' appears four times (Example 9).

Example 9: Bishop, *Yelva* (ff. 26v–27).

---

[11]Henry Rowley Bishop, "Overture to *Yelva*," ed. Nicholas Temperley with assist. of Matthew Greenbaum, facsimile repr. of autograph score, *The Symphony, 1720–1840*, ed. Barry S. Brook, Series E, Vol. VI: *The Overture in England, 1800–1840* (New York: Garland, 1984), 29–55.

Of course, this part could easily have been played on a keyed bugle as well as a slide trumpet. It is, however, similar to the melodies in Hyde's tutor. Indeed, the preponderance of notes of the harmonic series, combined with a few non-series tones, usually b' and a', is typical of the music written for slide trumpet in tutors and solos of this time. This melody from *Yelva* would have most likely been played on a slide trumpet.

Two final observations regarding Bishop's trumpet scoring concern trumpet pitch and the similarity of trumpet and horn parts. Bishop's early works usually feature trumpet parts pitched in E, E♭, D, and C, while later works may be written in all possible keys. Consider the "Romantic Fairy Opera" *Aladdin*, premiered at the Theatre Royal, Drury Lane, in 1826.[12] At various times during the opera, trumpets must play in the keys of F, E, E♭, D, D♭, C and B♭; A is added in *The Romance of a Day!* (1831).[13] Thus, all the keys available to a slide trumpet with a full set of crooks are represented in Bishop's later operas.

Finally, in several of his operas Bishop makes virtually no distinction between trumpet and horn parts. An example is the 1821 pastiche *Henry the Fourth*,[14] in which many of Bishop's arrangements feature trumpet and horn parts on the same staff, with the parts labeled "Tromba Corni 1" and "Tromba Corni 2do" (see f. 100). This is more evidence that many early-nineteenth-century horn and trumpet players doubled on these instruments.[15] Indeed, Thomas Wallis, mentioned above as first trumpeter at Covent Garden, is listed as playing both trumpet and horn in his Royal Society of Musicians application documents.[16]

---

[12]Henry R. Bishop, *Aladdin*, autograph score (1826) *Lbl*, Add. 36957.

[13]Henry R. Bishop, *The Romance of a Day!*, autograph score (1831) *Lbl*, Add. 36959.

[14]Henry R. Bishop, arr., *Henry the Fourth*, autograph score (1821) *Lbl*, Add. 33570.

[15]See n. 48.

[16]Matthews, comp., *Royal Society*, "Wallis, Jr.," 150.

Mid-Nineteenth Century: George Macfarren and Michael Balfe

English opera of the middle third of the century is dominated by two composers who are on opposite ends of the spectrum with regard to orchestration. A conservative orchestrator, Sir George Alexander Macfarren was a pedagogue as well as a composer who taught at Cambridge University and the Royal Academy of Music, where he became principal in 1876.[17] He composed symphonies and other orchestral music, but he is best known for his operas and oratorios. Macfarren's trumpet writing is conventional, and although he does make liberal use of the out-of-tune harmonics, especially b♭', he rarely uses notes outside the harmonic series and rarely writes the first trumpet part above the treble staff.

Of the Macfarren opera scores examined by this writer, only the late work *She Stoops to Conquer*, premiered at Covent Garden in 1864,[18] contains non-harmonic-series notes for trumpet. In the overture to this opera, both trumpets must play b' and a' in a descending passage (Example 10) that is immediately repeated (ff. 22v and 23).

Example 10: G. A. Macfarren, *She Stoops to Conquer* (f. 22v).

In F

In the entire opera, these are the only notes outside the harmonic series. Cornets in E♭ appear later (e.g., Act I; Number 3), and while they play series notes only, their parts are a bit more active than the trumpet parts in the rest of the opera. Macfarren's conser-

---

[17]*Baker's Biographical Dictionary of Musicians*, 6th ed., s. v. "Macfarren, Sir George Alexander."

[18]George A. Macfarren, *She Stoops to Conquer*, autograph score (1864) *Cfm*, MS 1087.

vative scoring in *She Stoops to Conquer* is remarkable, especially since there is little doubt, as we shall see, that use of the cornet was extensive in the London opera houses by the 1860s.

Michael William Balfe, an Irishman by birth, was one of the best-loved British opera composers before Arthur Sullivan, as evidenced by the enduring popularity of *The Bohemian Girl* (1843), which was successfully performed on the continent in German, French, and Italian translations, and enjoyed regular revivals in London.[19] His writing for trumpet, while at times confusing, is nonetheless progressive. Balfe regularly wrote parts for the cornet, beginning with *The Maid of Artois* in 1836, which was just five short years after Jean-Louis Antoine Halary invented the instrument by attaching valves to a posthorn.[20] Indeed, Balfe may be the composer who led the way toward the acceptance of the cornet in English opera orchestras. Carse thinks that *The Maid of Artois* was the first English opera score to feature the cornet.[21] He also suggests that the instrument was enjoying its first widespread use at this time, pointing out that the 1836 tutor of Harper Sr. "included some instructions for playing the cornet…, and in 1837 appeared the first published book of airs arranged for the 'cornopean' and piano by Macfarlane [a military bandsman]."[22]

The two-act opera *The Maid of Artois* premiered on 26 May 1836 at the Drury Lane Theatre.[23] The work is scored for two trumpets in various keys from A♭ up to E, as well as a *cornet à pistons* in A and A♭. That the cornet was to have been played by the first trumpeter is clear; it is never heard simultaneously with the two trumpets, but several times the scoring calls for one cornet, pitched high,

---

[19]*Baker's*, 6th ed., s. v. "Balfe, Michael William."

[20]Tarr, *The Trumpet*, 168.

[21]Carse, *Orchestra*, 420.

[22]Ibid.

[23]Michael W. Balfe, *The Maid of Artois*, autograph score (1836) *Lbl*, Add. 29327–8.

and one trumpet, often pitched low. The first act features a "Trio and Chorus" which is written for a cornet in A and a trumpet in D, while in the second act there is a march for *Cornette à Pistons* in A♭ and *Tromba 2nd* in A♭ *basso*. In addition, Balfe writes several parts for two stage trumpets, with two cornets in A required on at least one occasion.

Notes outside the harmonic series are written throughout the opera for both trumpets and cornet; but, interestingly, in the overture the trumpets are required to produce octave d♭. The second trumpet's d♭' requires a downward shift of a tone-and-a-half from the fifth partial on a slide trumpet, which is impossible. This is an early example of a composer writing non-harmonic-series notes for the trumpet, but writing those that even the slide trumpet could not play. Presumably the valved cornet would have played that note, even though it is not so indicated. Balfe's only previous opera for the London stage, *The Siege of Rochelle* (1835),[24] requires no notes outside the harmonic series for the trumpet.[25]

A representative example of Balfe's trumpet scoring of the 1830s is found in *Falstaff* (with an Italian text),[26] premiered at Her Majesty's Theatre on 19 July 1838.[27] The overture to this opera is scored for two trumpets in A, but there is little doubt that many of the passages were played by cornets. Example 11 (p. 108) shows a melody written for the trumpets.

---

[24]Michael W. Balfe, *The Siege of Rochelle*, autograph score (1835) *Lbl*, Add. 29325.

[25]Balfe wrote two earlier Italian operas that were premiered in Pavia and Milan in 1831 and 1833, respectively. See Eric Walter White, comp., *A Register of First Performances of English Operas and Semi-Operas from the 16th Century to 1980* (London: The Society for Theatre Research, 1983), 70–71. *Baker's Biographical Dictionary*, 6th ed., 91, informs us that he also wrote two operas for the French stage in the early 1840s.

[26]Michael W. Balfe, "Overture to *Falstaff*," autograph score (1838) *Lbl*, Egerton 2740, ff. 40–73v; and *Falstaff*, autograph score (1838) *Lbl*, Add. 29334.

[27]White, *Register*, 74.

Example 11: Michael Balfe, *Falstaff*, overture (ff. 42v–43).

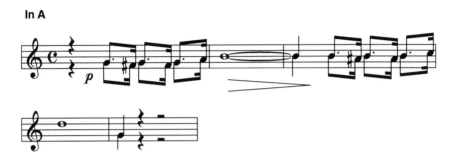

This passage is perfect for the slide trumpet; it is martial and trumpet-like with its dotted rhythms, and the notes outside the harmonic series are easily attainable. Throughout the overture there are additional non-harmonic-series notes, many of them in quick-tongued chromatic passages and active, florid sections, which seem more characteristic of the cornet. There are even whole-tone shifts, which would have been impossible on a slide trumpet in the low pitch of A—another clue that cornets played some of these passages: early cornets were supplied with shanks for B♭ and A.

The remainder of the opera is similar: while much of the music would have necessitated a cornet, the slide trumpet would have probably been used equally. In the introduction to Act I, the trumpets in A♭ play another typically martial melody (Example 12), with notes not found in the harmonic series, that would show off the diatonic possibilities of the slide trumpet, but yet without sacrifice of

Example 12: Balfe, *Falstaff* (ff. 8v–9v).

Example 13: Balfe, *Falstaff* (ff. 302v–304v).

the classic trumpet tone quality. Example 13, on the other hand, shows a typical passage for cornets, from an aria for the Falstaff character near the beginning of Act II.

Unfortunately, the contrast between trumpet and cornet parts is not always so clear as in these examples. There are many passages designated for trumpet which would have been difficult, if not impossible, on the slide trumpet. In several instances, for example, the slide trumpet would be required to produce full-tone shifts while using the C crook (see Example 14, from the finale to Act I).

Both Harpers, in their tutors, warn against playing whole-tone shifts in keys lower than D (see discussion in Chapter Two); even

Example 14: Balfe, *Falstaff* (ff. 260v–261).

with the slightly longer slide pulls available in the latter part of the century, Harper Jr. still cautioned against this. In a manuscript draft of a reply to an unknown correspondent, Harper warns that the f' and a♭' (both whole-tone shifts), "are possible in D but better in E♭, E[natural] & F."[28] In lower keys, Harper continues, the f' "is an imperfect note & should be avoided as it is too sharp." We must assume, therefore, that cornets were used for passages in low keys that included whole-tone shifts.

In *Falstaff* Balfe generally distinguishes between trumpet and cornet. Cornet parts tend to be more active, technical, and sometimes more lyrical as well; they also tend to be written in a higher register (the first cornet ascends to c''' on f. 289). Trumpet parts often feature melodies that are built around the harmonic series, although there are many notes outside the harmonic series—as many as, or perhaps even more than, in the parts designated for cornet. The trumpet parts also feature martial melodies and punctuate the harmony with chord tones in octaves and unisons.

Harper Sr. was principal trumpet at Her Majesty's Theatre in 1838 and would likely have played this opera. Considering his preference for the slide trumpet over the cornet, it can be assumed that he would have played the former instrument in every possible passage, substituting the cornet only when necessary. Interestingly, the designated cornet parts in this opera probably would have been played by his son. Harper Jr., then twenty-two years of age and just beginning his professional career, was engaged at Her Majesty's Theatre to play violin and first cornet.[29]

Balfe's *The Bohemian Girl*, which premiered on 27 November 1843 at Drury Lane,[30] is similarly scored for both trumpets and cornets, and illustrates the same confusion as to the type of instrument

---

[28]Thomas Harper Jr., to unknown addressee, 1 March 1894, *Lcm*, MS 4071.

[29]Thomas Harper Jr., Engagement Book, 1838–1897, entry for 1838, *Lcm*, MS 4073.

[30]Michael W. Balfe, *The Bohemian Girl*, autograph score (1843) *Lbl*, Add. 29335.

required to play the trumpet parts. Cornet is designated less frequently than trumpet, but when the former is specified it is often in a
solo role. Again, however, the trumpet part often includes notes requiring whole-tone shifts in low keys, such as f' for the trumpet in A
in Act II, no. 2 (f. 377v). Surely cornets in A were meant to play
these parts; but, if so, why did the composer use the "trumpet" designation in the score? Could it be that the two instruments were by
this time interchangeable, at least in the mind of Balfe?

In the late 1840s Balfe specifies the cornet with decreasing frequency. An example is *The Maid of Honour*, a three-act opera produced 20 December 1847 at Drury Lane.[31] In the overture, Balfe has
written a rising scale passage that includes several notes outside the
harmonic series and requiring whole-tone shifts (f. 9). Just before
this passage, the designation "Cornet à Piston in C" has been inked
in, but then marked through. It is interesting to speculate as to why
Balfe changed his mind. Perhaps he felt the trumpets could not play
the passage and added the cornet designation, only to be told (or
discover in rehearsal) that the players were using cornets throughout
anyway. Conceivably, he could have then decided to score all the
parts for trumpet, leaving the players to decide which instruments to
play. Indeed, the principal player in the Drury Lane Theatre orchestra in 1847 according to Carse was Koenig, one of the most celebrated cornet players in all of Europe.[32]

Later in the opera is another indication that Balfe was inclined
to leave the choice of instrument to the players. In the scene numbered 17 (Add. 29349, f. 221) near the beginning of Act III, Balfe
has marked "Trombe (on Stage)" and then directly underneath
added "or Cornetti in B♭". The melodic passage that follows is the
same material from the overture—the aforementioned scale passage
with the confusing inscription.

---

[31]Michael W. Balfe, *The Maid of Honour*, autograph score (1847) *Lbl*, Add.
29348–9.

[32]Carse, *Orchestra*, 490.

A final Balfe opera to be considered is *The Sicilian Bride*, first performed on 6 March 1852 at the Drury Lane Theatre.[33] The entire opera is scored for trumpets—cornets not are specifically mentioned—and while portions of the opera could be played on slide trumpet, there is much material that would have necessitated switching to cornet. Many passages, such as those in the overture (Add. 29350; f. 39v) and Act I (Add. 29350; ff. 85v–86), include low a, which could not have been played on any slide trumpet of the time. In the "Ritornello and Chorus" of Act II (Number 19) is the passage in Example 15, written for trumpets in C and including whole-tone shifts of the slide. This passage does not lie well on a slide trumpet, especially at the *Allegro vivace* tempo; it most likely would have been played on a cornet.

Example 15: Balfe, *The Sicilian Bride* (f. 255).

Tromba C

In general Balfe, in *The Sicilian Bride*, writes the more active and melodic cornet-like parts in lower keys, especially A and A♭. The more common style of writing, however, is more martial, or with octave/unison scoring and less solo material; and this style is for higher-pitched parts, especially D, E, and E♭. The predominance of this "trumpet" style of writing might be taken as an indication of the type of instrument to be used—the cornet for the former and the slide trumpet for the latter. But unfortunately this theory cannot be sustained because there are many examples of notes that are not available on the slide trumpet, such as the low a, that appear even in the higher keys.

---

[33]Michael W. Balfe, *The Sicilian Bride*, autograph score (1852) *Lbl*, Add. 29350–1.

It is more likely that by the time of *The Sicilian Bride* there was no need for Balfe to distinguish between trumpet and cornet. He continued to score parts for trumpet in various keys and write as many non-harmonic-series notes as he desired. He may simply have left the choice of instrument to the players, or they simply played all of the music on cornets anyway. Six subsequent operas by Balfe[34] support this hypothesis; there are very few passages for which cornets are specifically designated, and the trumpet parts continue to be written with many notes not in the harmonic series and in all keys.

Of course, one might assume that these trumpet parts with non-harmonic-series notes were played by valved trumpets, rather than cornets, thereby confirming the trumpet designation. Several sources, however, suggest that the valved trumpet in F (with crooks to lower the pitch) came into general use in England much later than on the continent, and that the cornet, because it was easier to play, was used when the music could not be played on the slide trumpet. Walter Morrow, the most important London trumpeter after Harper Jr. and an advocate for the valved F trumpet, writes in 1894–5: "The valve trumpet was generally adopted in Germany, but not in England; the tone of the slide trumpet being considered superior."[35] However, as we shall see, the valved trumpet probably was used to some extent by mid- and late-century trumpeters.

Late Nineteenth Century: Arthur Sullivan

Further confirmation of late-century use of the cornet in the opera pit can be found in operettas by Sir Arthur Seymour Sullivan

---

[34]*The Rose of Castille*, autograph score (1857) *Lbl*, Add. 29352–3; *Satanella, or, The Power of Love*, autograph score (1858) *Lbl*, Add. 29354; *Bianca, the Bravo's Bride*, autograph score (1860) *Lbl*, Egerton 2740, ff. 224–257v (overture), and Add. 29356; *The Puritan's Daughter*, autograph score (1861) *Lbl*, Add. 29358; *Blanche de Nevers*, autograph score (1862) *Lbl*, Add. 29361; and *The Armourer of Nantes*, autograph score (1863) *Lbl*, Add. 29363–4.

[35]Morrow, "Trumpet," 138.

(1842–1900). The four works consulted, with premieres from 1878 to 1889, are scored for cornets in B♭ and A.[36] Gordon Jacob, in the introduction to the 1968 publication of *The Mikado*, writes about the use of cornets in the late nineteenth century:

> We have noted that cornets, not trumpets, are written for in this score. In 1885 trumpets in F and E and other keys were still commonly used in symphonic and operatic scores. The trumpets in B♭ and C which superseded them owed their success to their greater ease of execution and brilliance, qualities which were being increasingly demanded by composers. The sonority of the old trumpets with their low fundamentals and consequently greater range of open notes is said to have been extremely impressive and some nobility of sound seems to have been sacrificed in favour of greater flexibility. At the time *The Mikado* was written, cornets had the agility and lightness that trumpets lacked, and as cornets did not exist in the pre-valve era, there were no inhibitions about writing freely for them in all keys, their transpositions being the same as for clarinets—B♭ for flat keys and A for sharp keys.[37]

This principle is followed in all four of the Sullivan operettas examined: Sullivan consistently writes for the B♭ cornet in flat keys, and designates the A cornet when using sharp keys. The nature of the writing also indicates use of cornets over slide trumpets; the musical material is written with total disregard for the harmonic series.

---

[36]Unfortunately, full scores of Sullivan's early stage works, such as the 1867 operettas *Cox and Box* and *The Contrabandista*, are extremely rare, and were not available to this author. Operettas consulted include: Arthur S. Sullivan, *H.M.S. Pinafore*, libretto by W. S. Gilbert (Braunschweig: Henry Litolff's Verlag, [ca. 1890]), prem. 1878; *Patience*, libretto by W. S. Gilbert, autograph score, n. d., *Lbl*, Add. 53778, prem. 1881; *The Mikado*, libretto by W. S. Gilbert (Farnborough: Gregg International Publishers, 1968), prem. 1885; and *The Gondoliers*, libretto by W. S. Gilbert, autograph score, n. d., *Lbl*, Add. 53779, prem. 1889.

[37]Gordon Jacob, introduction to *Mikado* by Sullivan, *vii*.

Interestingly, Sullivan's 1891 serious opera *Ivanhoe* is scored for trumpets rather than cornets.[38] A cursory examination of the score reveals that Sullivan had valved trumpets in mind, and was most likely influenced by Wagner. The parts are for trumpets in F, E, E♭ and D, and include quick technical passages unplayable on the slide trumpet. Wagner's influence is revealed in the constant shift of trumpet pitch as keys change, even within a number; there is a small part for bass trumpets in F, and there are parts for an on-stage trumpet band as well. There is no doubt that at this date late in the century valved trumpets in F were used for this opera. What is significant is that Sullivan wrote for trumpets in his opera, and for cornets in his operettas, further proof that the cornet was never truly accepted for performance of "serious" music.

The Trumpet in the Opera House

How much, then, was the slide trumpet used in the opera pits, as opposed to keyed bugles, then cornets and finally valved trumpets? It seems that much depended upon the predilection of both conductor and trumpeter. Judging from many of the complaints by purists from the last half of the century, it is clear that most conductors cared little about the relative differences between the sound of the cornet and trumpet. Much of the time, it seems the choice of instrument was left to the individual trumpeter, and many took the easy route, opting for use of the cornet. We can assume from their writings, however, that both Harpers condescended to use the cornet only when it was absolutely necessary, and thus many of the suggested uses of the slide trumpet proposed above can be assumed as valid, at least in situations where the Harpers were playing; and often in other circumstances as well, considering the significant influence of the Harpers.

It is probable that the slide trumpet was used in all London opera houses until the introduction of the cornet in 1836. The latter

---

[38]Arthur S. Sullivan, *Ivanhoe*, libretto by Julian Sturgis (London: Chappell and Co., [1891]).

then coexisted with the slide trumpet until after mid-century it gradually became the dominant soprano brass instrument, at least in the London theaters specializing in English opera. In the theaters that featured Italian opera, where Thomas Harper and subsequently his son were principal trumpeters, the slide trumpet was dominant and the cornet was used only when necessary. Because of the influence of Walter Morrow after 1885, we can assume that the slide trumpet/cornet tandem in the serious opera houses gradually gave way to the valved trumpet in F.

Steele-Perkins brings up a valid point about the practicality of this scenario.[39] One might envisage a trumpet section surrounded by instruments and crooks in an already overcrowded opera pit. Is this notion of trumpeters using multiple instruments realistic? Apparently so, at least in the Paris Opéra. Tarr has related the following telling story:

> Merri Franquin (1848–1934), trumpet professor at the Paris Conservatory from 1894 to 1925 and an eye-witness, reminisces that the natural trumpet remained in use at the Paris Opéra even until 1891, well into the valve era. According to him, the players had a box under their music stands, containing both a natural trumpet and a valved trumpet, together with crooks fitting both; the choice of instrument depended on whether the passage in question was chromatic or used natural notes only.[40]

If the trumpeters at the Paris Opéra could manage their natural and valved trumpets, then perhaps the London trumpeters could have juggled their slide trumpets with other instruments, too. Indeed, changing instruments must have been necessary for second (and third) players, whose parts would have involved more low-register tones outside the harmonic series than players of first parts, and yet could have required notes beyond the low range limit of the cornet.

---

[39]Steele-Perkins, letter to the author, 27 September 1995.

[40]Tarr, "Romantic Trumpet," 219.

The Concert Orchestra

We have already made an argument for the slide trumpet as a solo instrument in orchestra concerts at Vauxhall Gardens in the 1790s. We can assume its use as an orchestral instrument as well; and considering the activity and influence of, subsequently, Sarjant in the 1790s, Hyde in the first decade of the century, and Harper in the 1810s and beyond, we can also assume that it became the standard orchestral trumpet of London orchestras during this time.

At the turn of the nineteenth century, however, there were few established concert organizations in England. Probably the most important was the Concert of Ancient Music, which originated in 1776 and would continue until 1848, when competition finally caused its demise. This organization dedicated its concerts to the performance of music not less than twenty years old, and featured mostly choral/orchestral works of Handel, with orchestral music by Mozart and Haydn added in the late 1820s and 30s. An orchestra of about fifty players was maintained for the Ancient Concerts, as well as a professional chorus of over sixty singers.[41] However, the organization performed only twelve concerts per year.[42] From 1804 the Ancient Concerts were given at the Hanover Square Rooms, a 900-seat hall that was London's most important concert venue in the first half of the nineteenth century.[43]

The Vocal Concerts was an organization that also featured Handel's oratorios and various other choral/orchestral works, but performances were not as regular as those of the Ancient Concerts. These concerts were held haphazardly from 1792 to the 1830s; they were very popular in the first two decades of the century, but then began to decline in importance. The orchestra was not as large as

---

[41]Carse, *Orchestra*, 204.

[42]Joel Sachs, "London: the Professionalization of Music," in *The Early Romantic Era Between Revolutions: 1789 and 1848*, ed. Alexander Ringer (Englewood Cliffs: Prentice Hall, 1991), 206.

[43]*New Grove*, s. v. "London: Concert Life—Choirs and Choral Societies, Concert Organizations and Concert Rooms and Halls," by Henry Raynor.

that of the Ancient Concerts (thirty-eight players in 1819), but the concert venue, the Hanover Square Rooms, was the same.[44] Subscription oratorio performances could also be heard at theaters such as King's/Her Majesty's, Covent Garden, and Drury Lane, especially during Lent.[45]

Purely orchestral concerts were not given by any established organization until the formation of the Philharmonic Society in 1813. Before that time, orchestral concerts existed in the form of subscription series, such as the Haydn concerts organized by J. P. Salomon in the 1790s, and benefit concerts, with the latter being the most important and numerous. These benefit concerts were the only opportunities for solo artists before the time of the solo recital,[46] and an early example—John Hyde's benefit of 1800—has been mentioned previously. Nicholas Temperley further explains:

> Benefit concerts...were the real bulwark of the concert season. Leading musicians were each allowed one annual benefit. They took the entire profits, which were substantial, because other musicians gave their services for nothing. The result was that a very similar group of musicians would perform some twenty or thirty concerts in the season, so an informal "London symphony orchestra" came into existence. The programs generally mixed orchestral, vocal, and chamber music.... Most of Beethoven's symphonies and overtures were given in London at such concerts, very shortly after their first performance in Vienna; Paris, the only comparable capital, fared much worse in this respect.[47]

For orchestral music of a more popular nature, one could still go to Vauxhall Gardens in the summer; it was the only survivor of the numerous eighteenth-century pleasure gardens. According to

[44]Carse, *Orchestra*, 206–207.

[45]J. Sachs, "London," 206.

[46]Ibid., 219.

[47]Nicholas Temperley, intro. to *The Symphony, 1720–1840*, ed. Barry S. Brook, Series E, Vol. VI: *The Overture in England, 1800–1840* (New York: Garland, 1984), ix–x.

Carse, though, the 1820s saw a long, slow decline "in the quality of music and entertainments" which "gradually brought the once-fashionable gardens into the lowest repute."[48] But Thomas Harper Jr., according to his engagement book, was working there for the entire summer of 1844.[49] Vauxhall finally closed its gates forever in 1859.

The numerous provincial music festivals also provided an opportunity for late-summer and fall employment for orchestral musicians. The earliest of these was the famous Three Choirs Festival, which began in 1715 and was held alternately at Gloucester, Worcester, and Hereford.[50] Other important festival towns included Birmingham, Norwich, York, and Manchester. The principal players in the festival orchestras were the same London musicians who played in the major theaters, and later the Philharmonic concerts; the rest of the sections were often filled out by local musicians and amateurs.[51] The three- to four-day festivals were held in successive weeks so that the same players could perform at many festivals during the season. As railroad lines connected more and more British towns during the course of the century, it became easier for the top orchestral musicians to appear at a greater number of festivals. The engagement book of Harper Jr. reveals that, toward the end of his career, he spent virtually the entire months of September through November traveling from festival to festival.[52] The musical fare, though mostly the standard Handel oratorios and symphonies of Mozart and Beethoven, occasionally included more adventurous offerings; for example, the world premiere of Mendelssohn's *Elijah* took place at the Birmingham Festival of 1846.[53]

---

[48]Carse, *Orchestra*, 228.

[49]Harper Jr., Engagement Book, entries for 1844.

[50]*New Grove*, s. v. "England: Art Music," by Jack Westrup.

[51]Carse, *Orchestra*, 245.

[52]Harper Jr., Engagement Book.

[53]*New Grove*, s. v. "England," by Westrup.

The most important orchestral organization during the entire century was the Philharmonic Society, begun in 1813 by a group of musicians intending to institutionalize the existing series of subscription and benefit concerts.[54] The Society was never associated with a permanent orchestra during the nineteenth century, but rather hired the leading musicians from the theater orchestras for concerts.[55] It was not an opportunity for full-time employment; the Society's season consisted of only eight concerts per year until 1897. The concerts took place during London's high social season, between February and June, and were held first at the Argyll Rooms,[56] then at the Hanover Square Rooms from 1833 to 1868,[57] and finally at St. James Hall.[58] The last few years of the century, from 1894, saw the Philharmonic concerts performed at the new Queen's Hall, acclaimed as one of the most acoustically perfect halls in Europe.[59]

---

[54]For histories of the Philharmonic Society, see Robert Elkin, *Royal Philharmonic: the Annals of the Royal Philharmonic Society* (London: Rider and Co., 1946); and Myles Birket Foster, *History of the Philharmonic Society of London 1813–1912: a Record of a Hundred Years' Work in the Cause of Music* (London: John Lane, 1912).

[55]The first orchestra to provide concerts under agreement with the Society was the London Philharmonic Orchestra, upon its creation in 1932. Later other orchestras, such as the BBC Symphony Orchestra, the London Symphony Orchestra, and the Royal Philharmonic Orchestra, were contracted to provide concerts for the Society. See *New Grove*, s. v. "London: Concert Organizations," by Raynor.

[56]Originally a mansion converted to a concert hall, but leveled and rebuilt into an 800-seat concert hall in 1820. It burned down in 1830. See *New Grove*, s. v. "London: Concert Organizations," by Raynor.

[57]Ibid.

[58]It could seat over 2000, and was thus a much larger hall than Hanover Square. See Elkin, *Royal Philharmonic*, 67.

[59]This 2500-seat auditorium quickly became the center of musical activity for London and Britain, and remained so until its destruction by Nazi bombs in 1941. See *New Grove*, s. v. "London: Concert Organizations," by Raynor; and Elkin, *Royal Philharmonic*, 88.

Information about members of the London concert orchestras, like that of the opera orchestra personnel, comes from various sources.[60] We know that the top players from the opera orchestras were the principal concert orchestra members as well, at least in the first half of the century. Thomas Harper sat in the principal trumpet chair of the Philharmonic Society orchestra concerts from its inception until he began to limit his performing several years before his death. We know from the engagement book of Harper Jr. that he took over the post of principal trumpet in March of 1848, and retained that position until his retirement in 1885 (Figure 33, pp. 122-123). Following Harper Jr. was Walter Morrow, who held the position until his retirement in 1902. The Harpers held principal positions in most of the other concert orchestras as well, including the Ancient Concerts and Vocal Concerts, the early-century oratorio subscription concerts; and later the Sacred Harmonic Society,[61] the New Philharmonic Society,[62] and all the provincial festivals. They were less dominant in the concert orchestras that featured more popular music, although both of them were regularly engaged for the various

---

[60]Sources consulted include *New Grove*, s. v. "Morrow, Walter," by Anthony Baines and Edward Tarr; Richard P. Birkemeier, "The F Trumpet and its Last Virtuoso, Walter Morrow," *Brass Bulletin* 65 (1989); Brown and Stratton, *British Musical Biography*; Carse, *Orchestra*; Cox, *Recollections*; Foster, *Philharmonic Society*; Harper Jr., Engagement Book; Highfill, et. al., *Biographical Dictionary*; *New Grove*, s. v. "Harper," by Husk and Tarr; Matthews, comp., *Royal Society*; Parke, *Musical Memoirs*; Sorenson, "Harper, Sr."; Scott Sorenson and John Webb, "The Harpers and the Trumpet," *Galpin Society Journal* 39 (1986); and Tarr, *The Trumpet*.

[61]A successful mid-century challenge to the Ancient Concerts; the organization existed from 1832 to 1880. See Carse, *Orchestra*, 207–208.

[62]A mid-century challenge to the Philharmonic Society; the organization existed from 1852 to 1879. See *New Grove*, s. v. "London: Concert Organizations," by Raynor.

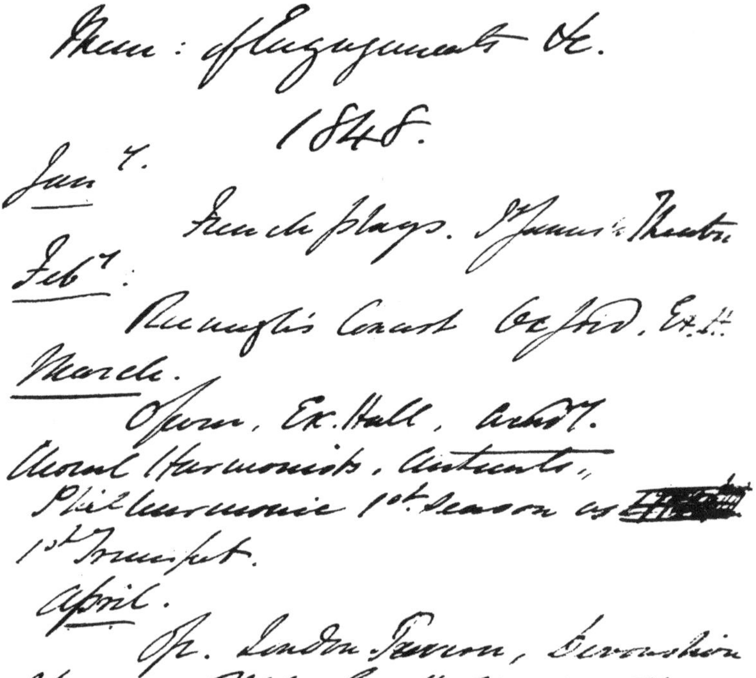

Figure 33: Thomas Harper Jr., pages from engagement book. Note entry for March 1848: "Philharmonic 1st season as 1st Trumpet." By permission of the Royal College of Music.

July.
Op. Oxford Commemoration, Acadᵗ Concert, R. for Worcester and Norwich Festivals.

August.
Op. R. Norwich Festival.

Sepᵗʳ.
Worcester Festival, Norwich Festival — to Brighton.

October
Beaumont Inst: Acadᵗ Rˢ

Novʳ.
D.H.S. L.S.H.S. Acadᵗ Rˢ

Decʳ.
D.H.S. L.S.H.S. Eastern Har. Society. Cecilian Society, Acadᵗ.

Pupils. Bradbury, Frazer.

D. Do. A.   D. A. F.

123

promenade orchestra concerts,[63] and concerts at the Crystal Palace[64] and Royal Albert Hall.[65] These orchestra concerts often featured cornet solos by such virtuosos as Koenig and Arban, but both Harpers regularly played trumpet solos as well.

Nineteenth-century British orchestral scores are much easier to obtain than full scores of operas. Orchestral music from the early part of the century can be found in manuscript in various British museums and libraries, and printed orchestral scores begin to appear in abundance in the late 1860s. But it is difficult to find scores from mid-century, a time when demand for orchestral music by British composers was low and hence less music was written. The scores of the few prominent British composers of the mid-century are often inaccessible. Most of Sterndale Bennett's manuscripts, for example, are still in the possession of his descendants. More and more of this music, however, is being made available in modern editions and facsimile reprints. Trumpet parts to over one hundred scores of overtures, symphonies, incidental music, and choral/orchestral works by British composers have been analyzed for this study. They reveal an approach to the trumpet very different from that in operas.

---

[63]For information on Jullien Concerts and other popular concert organizations see Carse, *Orchestra*, 230–242; and *The Life of Jullien: Adventurer, Showman-Conductor and Establisher of the Promenade Concerts in England, Together with a History of those Concerts up to 1895* (Cambridge: W. Heffer & Sons, 1951).

[64]Built in Hyde Park for the Great Exhibition in 1851, but dismantled and rebuilt in Sydenham in southeast London in 1852. See *New Grove*, s. v. "London: Concert Organizations," by Raynor; John Ella, *Musical Sketches, Abroad, and at Home* (London: Longmans & Co., 1869), 323–324; and Ernest Walker, "An Orchestra of Fifty Years Ago," *Monthly Musical Record* 61 (January 1951): 11–12.

[65]Built in 1871 in honor of Queen Victoria's consort. See *New Grove*, s. v. "London: Concert Organizations," by Raynor.

Early Nineteenth Century: Crotch, Clementi, Potter, and Wesley

It is interesting that while English orchestral composers had the slide trumpet at their disposal in the first third of the century, they did not use the instrument to its full advantage. Composers generally avoided not only notes outside the harmonic series, but also the out-of-tune eleventh partial, even though the correction of this note was one of the principal reasons for the development of the instrument. The conservative orchestration practices of these early-nineteenth-century English composers reflect their traditional approach to music in general; many aspects, particularly form and harmony, are underdeveloped when compared with contemporary orchestral music from Austria, Germany, or France.

The decline in the clarino technique can be seen in orchestral scores, as in opera scores. The challenging eleventh partial appears frequently in scores before and at the turn of the century, but seldom after that, with a few exceptions. This trend can be seen in the scores of William Crotch (1775–1847), the respected organist, composer, teacher, and first principal of the Royal Academy of Music.[66] An overture by him from 1795 contains no notes outside the harmonic series, but several examples of the eleventh partial.[67] In a symphony from 1814, Crotch writes the eleventh partial only once, and in the next year, in another overture, f" is not used at all.[68] Trumpet parts in Henry Bishop's orchestral works are similarly confined to notes in the harmonic series, and contain no examples of the eleventh partial. An exception is the Italian immigrant Muzio Clementi, whose orchestral trumpet parts include no notes outside the harmonic series, but make liberal use of the eleventh partial, beginning with his first

---

[66]*Baker's*, 6th ed., s. v. "Crotch, William."

[67]William Crotch, *Overture (in A)*, autograph score (1795) *Lbl*, Add. 30393, ff. 1–30.

[68]William Crotch, *Symphony (in F)*, autograph score (1814) *Lbl*, Add. 30393, ff. 31–63b; and *Overture (in G)*, autograph score (1815) *Lbl*, Add. 30393, ff. 64–94.

symphony, which was performed during the first season of the Philharmonic Society.[69] It is probably no coincidence that his company was involved in making the earliest "Harper's Improved"-model slide trumpets.

Another of the conservative, but influential, British composers of this time was Cipriani Potter (1792–1871), also a reputable pianist and teacher, who succeeded Crotch as principal of the Royal Academy of Music.[70] Of the symphonies and overtures by Potter to 1833, only one, from 1826, includes the eleventh partial, though this note appears numerous times in the final two movements.[71] In general, though, Potter's trumpet writing is even more conservative than the others of this period. He does not stray outside the harmonic series, rarely writes either the eleventh or the slightly flat seventh partial, and never requires the player to ascend beyond e" when writing for trumpets crooked above B♭. And Potter, like Bishop in his opera scores, often writes identical parts for trumpets and horns. The trumpet writing in George Macfarren's early scores likewise follows this conservative pattern and, although his trumpet and horn parts are differentiated, he writes only harmonic-series notes for the trumpet.

Crookings for trumpet also tend to be very traditional in Potter's music, with most parts pitched in the standard late-eighteenth-century keys of C, D, E♭ and E. Some composers begin to use other keys, such as B♭ and F in the 1820s and 30s. Potter even uses the crooking of B for the B-Minor Scherzo of his D-Major Symphony of 1833.[72] It is surprising that the standard F pitch of the slide and natural trumpet was not used more often until the 1820s. Crotch's F

---

[69]Muzio Clementi, *Sinfonia N. 1 in Do maggiore* (Milan: Edizioni Suvini Zerboni, 1976).

[70]*Baker's*, 6th ed., s. v. "Potter, Philip Cipriani Hambly."

[71]Cipriani Potter, *Sinfonia (in C minor)*, autograph score (1826) *Lbl*, Add. 31783, ff. 1–55.

[72]Cipriani Potter, *Sinfonia (in D)*, autograph score (1833) *Lbl*, LOAN 4/379.

major symphony of 1814 requires trumpets in three of its four movements, but all for trumpets crooked in C!

The first break with conventional practices came in the 1830s. An early symphony by Samuel Sebastian Wesley (1810–1876), the illegitimate son of the eccentric composer Samuel Wesley,[73] features trumpet parts with several notes outside the harmonic series and a range that is slightly more expanded (up to g″ in the crooking of C). The one-movement Symphony in C Minor was written about 1832; it was rehearsed in 1833 by the Philharmonic Society orchestra, but not performed in concert by that ensemble.[74] A revised version of the work was first performed at the 1834 Three Choirs Festival. Non-harmonic-series notes include a′ (p. 295), and octave f♯ (Example 16).

Example 16: S. S. Wesley, Symphony in C Minor (p. 300).

A more intriguing use of notes not in the harmonic series can be found later in the work. Example 17 (p. 128) shows a rising unison passage for C trumpets that even includes an a♭′, which, though requiring a full-tone shift on the slide trumpet, was probably playable because of the fact that the b♭′ is by nature slightly low in pitch.

Wesley continues to write non-harmonic-series notes for the trumpet in subsequent works. It seems apparent from his trumpet

[73]Frederick George Edwards, "Wesley, Samuel (1766–1837)," *The Compact Edition of the Dictionary of National Biography* (London: Oxford University Press, 1975), 2: 2234.

[74]Samuel Sebastian Wesley, Symphony in C Minor, ed. John I. Schwartz, *The Symphony, 1720–1840*, ed. Barry S. Brook, Series E, Vol. III (New York: Garland, 1983), 275–328.

Example 17: S. S. Wesley, Symphony in C Minor (pp. 310–312).

writing that Wesley was aware of Harper and the potential of his instrument. Although Wesley's works were not performed by the Philharmonic Society during the nineteenth century, many of them were
played at provincial festivals; thus, the principal trumpet part to his
1834 symphony was undoubtedly played on slide trumpet by Harper,
who would have been involved in such an important festival as the
Three Choirs. Wesley's break with the standard English approach to
trumpet writing in the early 1830s opens the door for a more adventurous approach in the hands of mid-century English composers.

Of the early-century continental composers who were writing
notes outside the harmonic series for either stopped trumpet, keyed
trumpet, or valved trumpet, very few had works performed by the
Philharmonic Society at this time. In the early 1830s Mendelssohn's
orchestral music was just beginning to be heard in England, and the
Melusine Overture, with notes for trumpet not in the harmonic series,
was performed at a Philharmonic Society concert in 1834; Rossini's
Semiramide overture, also with non-harmonic-series notes, had already been performed in 1831. Though they were most likely written
for other types of chromatic trumpets, both of these pieces could and
would have been played on the slide trumpet in England.

While music by continental composers played in London during the first third of the century, like that of English composers, did
not allow Harper and others to take full advantage of their slide instruments, these players at least had the capability of playing the
music better in tune than their continental counterparts. Consider

the example of Mendelssohn's *Hebrides* Overture, written for and premiered by the Philharmonic Society in 1832: beginning in measure 249, the trumpeters are required to play the eleventh partial in a sustained, fanfare figure over the better part of three measures.[75] Played on the D crook, this concert pitch g'' is in unison with the entire woodwind section as well as with the horns, and it is crucial that it be played in tune. Harper, of course, would have had no difficulty placing the correct pitch of this note with his slide trumpet, but one wonders what Mendelssohn heard at that point in the music when his overture was played in Germany on natural trumpets. It is easy to understand why the Belgian music historian and critic Fétis admitted that French and German trumpeters compared unfavorably to Harper: he claimed that Harper was "the greatest performer of the day."[76] There is no doubt that Harper was one of the most talented trumpeters of the nineteenth century, but the instrument he played certainly helped to place him at an advantage over continental players of the natural trumpet, keyed trumpet, and early valved trumpet.

Mid-Nineteenth Century: Potter, Macfarren, Wesley, and Bennett

The full potential of the slide trumpet begins to be realized in the orchestral music of British composers of the mid-century, although several composers continue their conservative manner of writing. Cipriani Potter's scores still feature simple trumpet parts restricted to harmonic-series notes, limited range (rarely rising above e''), limited use of out-of-tune harmonics, and considerable doubling of trumpet and horn. Indeed, Potter apparently tries to simplify the trumpet parts whenever possible. Much of his D-major

---

[75]Felix Mendelssohn, *The Hebrides Overture (Fingal's Cave)*, from *Felix Mendelssohn, Major Orchestral Works*, ed. Julius Rietz (New York: Dover Publications, 1975), 214.

[76]François-Joseph Fétis, cited in George Hogarth, "Musical Instruments: The Trumpet, Trombone, Serpent and Ophicleide," *The Musical World* 4 (17 February 1837): 131.

Symphony of 1834, for example, features identical trumpet and horn parts.[77] But when the horns are required to play notes at the top of the staff, such as f'' and g'', the trumpets cease their doubling and rest. In the late 1830s and 1840s, Potter makes greater use of the seventh partial, but his trumpet writing is never more progressive than this.

George Macfarren, however, seems to become aware of the slide trumpet, and begins to make use of it, in the 1830s. Macfarren's first use of trumpet notes outside the harmonic series can be found in his 1835 Symphony No. 5 in A Minor.[78] Although used only once in the entire symphony, the a' is written for both trumpets in a rising scale (Example 18).

Example 18: Macfarren, Symphony No. 5 in A Minor (f. 38v).

In D

Macfarren began teaching at the Royal Academy of Music in 1834.[79] Harper, who was employed there at the same time,[80] published the first edition of his slide trumpet tutor in 1835.[81] Surely it is no coincidence that this is when Macfarren began to write notes not in the harmonic series that are playable on the slide trumpet. Although he returns to a more conservative approach to trumpet writing in his Symphony No. 6 (1836), the fourth movement of his Symphony No. 7 in C♯ Minor (1839-40) makes frequent use of the

---

[77]Cipriani Potter, *Sinfonia (in D)*, autograph score (1834) *Lbl*, LOAN 4/376.

[78]George A. Macfarren, Symphony No. 5 in A Minor, autograph score (1835) *Cfm*, MS 1020.

[79]*Baker's*, 6th ed., s. v. "Macfarren."

[80]Harper began teaching at the RAM about 1829, and continued there until 1845. See Webb and Sorenson, commentary to *Instructions, v.*

[81]Ibid., *xii.*

non-harmonic-series d♭", as well as the raised eleventh partial (f♯").[82] In contrast to most other composers Macfarren wrote more challenging trumpet parts in his orchestral music than he did in his operas.

S. S. Wesley continued to write notes outside the harmonic series for the trumpet in his works into the 1850s and 1860s. His anthem *The Wilderness*, composed for the Birmingham Festival and premiered there in 1852, features four trumpets (two pitched in E, and two in C) in the final "Quartet and Chorus."[83] Wesley often designates the trumpets as *Clarini* in the manuscript score, and while he writes many non-harmonic-series notes, the parts are idiomatic for the slide trumpet. He avoids one-and-a-half-tone shifts, and he restricts the trumpets pitched in C to half-tone shifts, save the g♯'/a♭', which probably would have been playable in the key of C because the whole-tone shift is from the slightly flat b♭'. Example 19 (below) and Example 20 (p. 132) show examples of Wesley's progressive scoring from *The Wilderness*.

Example 19: S. S. Wesley, *The Wilderness* (f. 11).

"Clarini" 1/2 in E

"Clarini" 3/4 in C

---

[82]George A. Macfarren, Symphony No. 7 in C♯ Minor, autograph score (1839–40) *Cfm*, MS 1022.

[83]Samuel Sebastian Wesley, *The Wilderness* (1852) *Lcm*, MS 4030. This anthem has recently been edited by Peter Horton, and published by Stainer and Bell in volume 63 of the *Musica Britannica* series.

Example 20: S. S. Wesley, *The Wilderness* (f. 18).

Wesley perhaps had the valved trumpet in F in mind when writing his *Ode for the North London Working Mens' Industrial Exhibition* in the 1860s.[84] Among the notes not in the harmonic series are several requiring a tone-and-a-half shift (e.g., d♭' for both trumpets in C on f. 61). It is certain that Wesley did not write the part for high-pitched cornets, because twice in the final verse (pp. 93–94 [no folio numbers], and ff. 78v–79), the second trumpet part descends to the fundamental C, below the bass staff! In practice, however, the players could have played most of the *Ode* on their slide trumpets, switching to cornets for the unplayable notes; this custom was to become a common occurrence in the concert hall as it had in some of the opera houses.

The most important British composer of the mid-century, and one who begins to write for the slide trumpet in a featured role, is Sir William Sterndale Bennett (1816–1875). His youthful symphonies and overtures from the 1830s exhibit very conservative trumpet

---

[84]Samuel Sebastian Wesley, *Ode for the North London Working Mens' Industrial Exhibition*, words by W. H. Bellamy (1864) *Lcm*, MS 4034.

writing: no use of notes outside the harmonic series, limited range, and little use of out-of-tune harmonics. But his important Symphony in G Minor (1864–67) includes the heretofore rarely featured brass section alone in an extended section.[85] The first version of the work was in three movements, and was premiered at the concerts of the Philharmonic Society on 27 June 1864; three years later, Bennett added a slow *Romanza* before the last movement, to complete the final version of the symphony. The first, third, and fourth movements require no non-harmonic-series notes for trumpet.[86] The original Minuet and Trio (second movement), however, contains notes outside the harmonic series in the trio section, scored entirely for brass choir. The main theme of the trio is given to the first trumpet (Figure 34, p. 134).

Both the d' and f' would of course require a whole-tone extension of the slide, but these notes would have been playable on the E♭ crook. The trio is marked *pomposo*, and the tempo is lively, but not too fast. This is a good example of skilled writing for the slide trumpet; the non-harmonic-series notes lie well on the instrument, the

---

[85]William Sterndale Bennett, *Sinfonie G moll für grosses Orchester*, Op. 43 (Leipzig: Fr. Kistner, [1872]); see also facsimile repr. in *The Symphony, 1720–1840*, ed. Barry S. Brook, Series E, Vol. VII, ed. Nicholas Temperley (New York & London: Garland Publishing, Inc., 1982), 47–169.

[86]There is a curious *fortissimo* e♭" half-note in the first trumpet part (in D) of the *Romanza* on page 111 of the score. This is the only non-series note in either trumpet part in the entire movement. It would have been playable on the slide trumpet, but I think it is, in fact, a misprint, the horn staff and trumpet staff having been switched for this page only. On the following page the same melodic motive, which ends on the e♭ in question, is found on the horn staff, while the trumpets are given the same octave g's that are found on the horn staff on page 111. Throughout the movement the horns (also in D) are required to play that same e♭", while the trumpets never play above g'! But in editorial remarks to Garland's facsimile reprint, Nicholas Temperley writes that the composer corrected the proofs, and that "printing errors and inconsistencies have been corrected." If this is true, then perhaps Bennett was trying to create an echo effect by having the trumpet, then horn, play the motive. But the note is certainly inconsistent with the rest of the trumpet writing in this movement.

Figure 34: Sterndale Bennett, Symphony in G Minor (p. 84). By permission of the British Library. [e.59.d]

slide movement would have not have been a problem at the indicated tempo, and the classic natural trumpet sound would have blended well with the rest of the brass instruments. At the premieres of both versions of the symphony, the trumpeter responsible for playing the part would have been Harper Jr., who is said by many to have always used the slide trumpet unless the part was impossible to play on it.

Of the contemporary continental composers, Mendelssohn was still among the most regularly performed in England during the middle third of the century. Some of his works require the trumpeters not only to use the notes available to them on their slide trumpets, but to resort to cornets occasionally. An example is the "Scottish" Symphony, performed as early as 1842 at the Philharmonic concerts.[87] Only three notes outside the harmonic series for trumpets appear in the symphony: b', e♭'' and c♯'. Both of the former would have been playable on the slide trumpet, but the latter would have required a cornet for the extended passage between rehearsal mark M and the end of the first movement.[88] Another Mendelssohn work with non-harmonic-series notes for trumpet is the incidental music from *A Midsummer Night's Dream*, selections of which were performed for the first time at Philharmonic Society concerts in 1844.[89] Both the Scherzo and the "Wedding March," with the notes a' and b', were included in the performance.

Some of the more progressive—and controversial—continental composers were heard with increasing frequency in London during the middle of the century. Several works by Berlioz with cornet parts were performed at the Philharmonic concerts during this time, including the overture to *Benvenuto Cellini* in 1841, and in 1853 the *Roman Carnival Overture* and *Harold in Italy*. The two latter works

---

[87]Foster, *Philharmonic Society*, 173.

[88]Felix Mendelssohn, Symphony No. 3 in A Minor ("Scottish"), from *Felix Mendelssohn, Major Orchestral Works*, ed. Julius Rietz (New York: Dover Publications, Inc., 1975), 284–288.

[89]Foster, *Philharmonic Society*, 183 and 186.

were performed in a concert that Berlioz conducted. Schumann's works, although resisted at first, were beginning to be heard in London. His *Overture, Scherzo and Finale*, with parts for valved trumpet, was performed at a Philharmonic concert in 1853. For the 1855 season of the Philharmonic Society, Wagner was invited to be the conductor. He programmed only two of his own works, the overture to *Tannhäuser* and the Prelude and other selections from *Lohengrin*, but both were written for valved trumpet and contain many notes outside the harmonic series that could not have been played on the slide trumpet.

Works by these composers, however, were not performed often because they met with resistance by critics and patrons. Berlioz's Overture to *Benvenuto Cellini* was hissed by the audience in its 1841 performance.[90] A critic from the *Athenaeum* wrote that the 1853 performance of Schumann's *Overture, Scherzo and Finale* was "received with the almost dead silence of disapproval" and called it "a display of unattractive cacophony."[91] During Wagner's tenure with the Philharmonic Society in 1855, *The Musical World* called the music from *Lohengrin* "poison, rank poison" and "an incoherent mass of rubbish, with no more real pretension to be called music than the jangling and clashing of gongs, and other uneuphonius instruments."[92] Of his *Tannhäuser* Overture, the *Athenaeum* critic wrote that it "is one of the most curious pieces of patchwork ever passed off by self-delusion for a complete and significant creation. The instrumentation is ill-balanced, ineffective, thin and noisy."[93]

Late Nineteenth Century: Sullivan, Mackenzie, Parry, and Stanford

In the late 1860s and 1870s British composers began to write notes outside the harmonic series for trumpet with increasing fre-

---

[90]Elkin, *Royal Philharmonic*, 47.

[91]Quoted in Cox, *Recollections*, 272–273.

[92]Quoted in Foster, *Philharmonic Society*, 240.

[93]Ibid., 240.

quency. It is a paradox, though, that just as composers finally seem to have become aware of the capabilities of the slide trumpet, they began to write notes that the instrument could not play. There are many scores from this time that have parts that are, for the most part, idiomatically written for the slide trumpet, but always with some notes unplayable on that instrument. A possible reason is that the composers also became aware of the capabilities of the valved instruments that were just then beginning to encroach even upon the concert hall.

Arthur Sullivan's orchestral scores show an approach to trumpet scoring different from that in his operettas. Reflecting the general prejudice against cornets in the concert hall, Sullivan designates trumpets only in these scores. Two important works from 1866 that helped establish his reputation in the concert hall, the Overture in C ("In Memoriam") and the Symphony in E ("The Irish"), are scored for trumpets pitched in the keys of C, and C and E, respectively. The overture was premiered that year at the Norwich Festival, and subsequently performed at the Philharmonic Society concerts in 1870.[94] Near the beginning of the overture (rehearsal mark A) is a lyrical trumpet solo that is doubled by two horns and harmonized by clarinets and bassoons. Whether intended or not, the melody is beautifully written for the slide trumpet (Example 21 on p. 138).

The rest of the overture lies well for the slide trumpet, except for the f' played by the second trumpet in a series of fanfare-style octaves with the first trumpet (p. 11). Since this note, with the trumpet pitched in C, would have been difficult to play down to pitch, the player would most likely have used a cornet or valved trumpet to play the passage. Harper Jr. would probably have played his slide trumpet for the first trumpet parts in both performances of the overture; he was at the height of his career at the Philharmonic in the

---

[94]Arthur Sullivan, Overture in C ("In Memoriam") (London: Novello, Ewer and Co., [1885]).

Example 21: Arthur Sullivan, Overture in C ("In Memoriam") (pp. 3–4).

1860s and 1870s, and the principal player at all of the provincial festivals.[95]

Sullivan's other major work from 1866 is the "Irish" Symphony, premiered at the Crystal Palace.[96] With regard to trumpet scoring, this work is very similar to the Overture in C; it is idiomatically written for the slide trumpet except for only a few impossible notes. In the first movement are several examples of the low a—unplayable on a slide trumpet in any crooking. The final movement contains the full-tone-shift d' several times, but since it is always used as a short pickup note, it might have been playable.

Again, the only solution would have been for the player to pick up a cornet or valved trumpet for the passages requiring the low a. There is, however, some evidence to suggest that, at least in this orchestra, cornets were being used for all of the music performed. John

---

[95]His engagement book lists a Norwich Festival appearance in the fall of 1871. Harper Jr., Engagement Book, entry for 1871.

[96]Arthur Sullivan, Symphony in E ("The Irish") (London: Novello and Co., 1915).

Ella states that August Manns was conductor of the Crystal Palace orchestra at least by 1868,[97] and Ernest Walker, writing about the same orchestra in the 1880s, mentions that "for some reason that apparently no one ever succeeded in fathoming, Manns normally preferred to substitute cornets for trumpets...."[98] Yet we know from the Harper Jr. engagement book that he had been associated with the Crystal Palace orchestra since the Great Exhibition in 1851. Perhaps the situation required Harper to play "serious" concerts on trumpet, and cornet players (maybe even Harper himself, who also played the cornet and wrote an important tutor for that instrument) were engaged to play concerts of a more popular nature. At any rate, Sullivan's "Irish" Symphony could have been played mostly on slide trumpet, with cornet being required only for a few passages.

Sullivan's *Overture di Ballo*, premiered at the Birmingham Festival of 1870, shows that the composer was now thinking specifically of the valved trumpet in his orchestration; the designation in the score is "2 trumpets in E♭ (Valve)."[99] But much like the two previous works, the parts could have been played entirely on slide trumpet except for a lone c♯' in the second trumpet part (m. 651). Although Sullivan designated valved trumpets for this work, he clearly was not taking advantage of the full potential of that instrument, and most likely, Harper would have played this work on the slide trumpet except where impossible.

Many other works from the 1860s and 1870s feature trumpet scoring of a similar nature. Sir William Cusins (1833–1893), who was conductor of the Philharmonic Society from 1867 to 1883;[100] Ebenezer Prout (1835–1909), an important theorist and composition teacher;[101] and Sir Frederic Cowen (1852–1935), a Jamaican-born

---

[97]Ella, *Musical Sketches*, 324.

[98]Walker, "Orchestra," 12.

[99]Arthur Sullivan, *Overture di Ballo* (London: Novello, Ewer and Co., 1889).

[100]*Baker's*, 6th ed., s. v. "Cusins, Sir William George."

[101]*Baker's*, 6th ed., s. v. "Prout, Ebenezer."

composer who was also conductor of the Philharmonic Society concerts for several years in the late 1880s,[102] show the same tendency as Sullivan to write trumpet parts that, except for a few isolated passages, are playable on the slide trumpet. Others from this time exhibit an even more conservative approach to orchestration, the most eminent representative being George Macfarren. Much of the late music of this by now elder statesman of British music features trumpet parts that for the most part could have been played on natural trumpets. Very few notes outside the harmonic series for trumpets appear, and those that are could have been played on slide trumpets.

Other British composers of this time were clearly influenced by the orchestration practices of Berlioz. Examples include John Francis Barnett (1837–1916) and Sir Julius Benedict (1804–1885), who wrote symphonic works including parts for two trumpets and two cornets.[103] Benedict also wrote a symphony in 1873, but this work does not require cornets, and the trumpet parts, although they include many non-harmonic-series notes, are idiomatically written for the slide trumpet.[104]

In the 1880s British orchestral composers turned to valved trumpets and cornets more frequently. Not only were more and more non-harmonic-series notes written that were unplayable on the slide trumpet, but many trumpet parts included slurred passages and rapid passages with these notes; music that began to move beyond the technique of the slide trumpet. Some scores make the composer's choice clear. The pianist and composer Oliver A. King (1855–1923) wrote his only symphony in 1882; it was premiered at the Philhar-

---

[102]*Baker's*, 6th ed., s. v. "Cowen, Sir Frederic Hymen."

[103]John Francis Barnett, *The Ancient Mariner*, cantata (London: Novello, Ewer and Co., [1890?]), prem. 1867; and Julius Benedict, *Overture to Shakespeare's Play "The Tempest"* (London: Enoch and Sons, [1875?]), prem. 1872.

[104]Julius Benedict, *Symphony (in G-minor) for Grand Orchestra* (London: Stanley Lucas, Weber and Co., [1874]).

monic concerts in that year.[105] On the first page of the score under the designation "Tromba in C" is the additional designation "Cylinder" in parentheses. A year later, his overture *Among the Pines* won a composition prize offered by the Philharmonic Society and was premiered at the Society's concerts.[106] This score also calls for two "cylinder" trumpets. Both of these works, however, could have been played primarily—and the overture entirely—on slide trumpet because most of the numerous notes not in the harmonic series are playable on that instrument and the technique is not beyond that of Harper Jr. Harper, it should be remembered, did not completely retire from his playing career, including the Philharmonic, until 1885.

Conservative composers were still performed during the 1880s; Prout, for example, continued to write trumpet parts that could have been played on the slide trumpet. Indeed, Prout was a true friend of the instrument. In 1878 he published a primer on instrumentation, followed by a two-volume orchestration treatise in 1898. Both of these works tell us much about the treatment of the trumpet in England in those years. In the 1878 primer, Prout introduces the valved trumpet and admits that "many composers write exclusively for these instruments."[107] In the 1898 treatise, he acknowledges that the valved trumpet is "much more generally used than the slide trumpet,"[108] but Prout himself was careful to write idiomatically for the slide trumpet, as can be seen in his 1882 cantata *Alfred*, and his

[105]Oliver A. King, *Night: Symphony in F for Full Orchestra* (London: Novello, Ewer and Co., [1882]).

[106]Oliver A. King, *"Among the Pines": Concert-Overture for Full Orchestra* (London: Novello, Ewer and Co., [1884]).

[107]Ebenezer Prout, *Instrumentation*, No. 15, *Novello, Ewer and Co.'s Music Primers*, ed. Dr. Stainer (London: Novello, Ewer and Co., [1878]), 80.

[108]Ebenezer Prout, *The Orchestra*, Augener's Edition No. 9189 (London: Augener, 1898), 1: 203.

1885 Symphony No. 3 in F major.[109] In his treatise, he reproduces an excerpt from *Alfred* as an illustration of how to write for the slide trumpet (Example 22).

Example 22: Ebenezer Prout, *Alfred* (from Prout, *Orchestra*, 205–206).

Among the composers who wrote exclusively for the valved trumpet, the Scottish-born Sir Alexander Campbell Mackenzie (1847–1935) should be mentioned. Many of his trumpet parts contain rapid technical passages with notes outside the harmonic series that would have been extremely awkward, if not impossible, on the slide trumpet. An example is his *Rhapsodie Ecossaise* of 1880, in which many such passages can be found.[110] Further proof that Mackenzie was writing for valved trumpets can be found in his 1883 orchestral ballad *La Belle Dame sans Merci*.[111] Here the two trumpets in B♭ are given a key signature of one sharp; the work is in the key of

[109]Ebenezer Prout, *Triumphal March from the Cantata Alfred* (London: Augener and Co., [ca. 1885]); and Symphony No. 3 in F major (London: Novello, Ewer and Co., [ca. 1885]).

[110]Alexander Mackenzie, *Rhapsodie Ecossaise* (London: Neumeyer and Co., [1880]).

[111]Alexander Mackenzie, *La Belle Dame sans Merci* (London: Novello, Ewer and Co., [1884]).

F major. Of course, natural and slide trumpet parts had been written with crooking designations, but without key signatures, since the late eighteenth century. The very presence of a key signature in a trumpet part in the late nineteenth century is a clue that the valved trumpet was intended. Later Mackenzie works follow this pattern, with several pieces being scored for cornet.[112]

Many of the composers of the 1880s wrote their trumpet parts, like Mackenzie, with the valved trumpet in mind. But in practice, much of this music might have continued to be played on the slide trumpet, at least until the retirement of Harper Jr. An example is the passage for solo trumpet in F (Example 23) from the 1883 Symphony in F ("Cambridge") by Sir Hubert Parry (1848–1918).[113] After 1885, though, the great champion of the valved trumpet in F, Walter Morrow, would have no doubt played this, and most of the new orchestral music, on that instrument.

Finally, composers such as the Scottish-born Hamish McCunn (1868–1916) and the Irish-born Sir Charles Villiers Stanford (1852–1924) wrote music for which trumpeters had very little reason to

Example 23: Hubert Parry, Symphony in F ("Cambridge") (pp. 50–51).

---

[112]Mackenzie's *Burns: Second Scotch Rhapsody* (London: Novello, Ewer and Co., [1880]); and *Britannia: A Nautical Overture* (London: Joseph Williams, [1895]), prem. 1894, are both written for two "cornetti" in B♭.

[113]Sir Charles Hubert Hastings Parry, Symphony in F ("Cambridge") (London: Novello and Company, [1905]).

continue using their slide trumpets. A player of the caliber of Harper Jr. might have been able to play some of the more challenging passages in the works of these composers, but most of their music was premiered after Harper's retirement and during the time that Morrow was encouraging players to use the valved F trumpet. Thus a passage such as the one in Example 24, from Stanford's Symphony No. 3 in F Minor ("The Irish") (1887), could have been played by good slide trumpeters, but probably was not since Morrow was most likely involved in the performance. Passages such as the one in Example 25, however, were beyond the technique of the instrument, and provide evidence that the century-long reign of the slide trumpet had come to an end.

Example 24: Charles Villiers Stanford, Symphony No. 3 in F Minor ("The Irish") (p. 55).

As would be expected, music of the progressive continental composers was being more widely performed in England during this time. Schumann and Wagner continued to be played, although not without persistent controversy. The second and third symphonies of Schumann, both with notes outside the harmonic series unplayable on the slide trumpet, were performed at the Philharmonic concerts in 1864 and 1870 respectively, and his cello concerto, with its parts for *Ventil Trompete*, was played in 1892. Wagner's *Flying Dutchman* overture was performed in 1873, and the overture to *Die Meistersinger von Nürnberg* was played in 1876. Wagner's champion,

Example 25: Stanford, Symphony No. 3 in F Minor ("The Irish")
   (pp. 163–164).

Liszt, was beginning to be performed in London—for example, his symphonic poems *Tasso* in 1873 and *Hungaria* in 1882.[114] All of these works contain many non-harmonic-series notes, and many notes that the slide trumpet of the 1870s could not produce, especially low notes in the second trumpet parts, such as a and a♭.

The 1870s also brought first performances of the works of Brahms by the Philharmonic Society. 1873 saw a performance of *A*

---

[114]Foster, *Philharmonic Society*, 565.

German Requiem; the *Haydn Variations* (1875), and his Symphony
No. 1 (1877) were subsequently performed. These works, although
containing some notes outside the harmonic series, could have been
performed for the most part on slide trumpet. Likewise, the Grieg
Piano Concerto in A Minor, which was performed in 1877, could
have been managed mostly on the slide trumpet, despite numerous
non-harmonic-series notes.

The 1880s saw more continental music written for valved trumpet performed in London and, like the contemporary British music,
much of it was playable only on that instrument. The rest of Brahms'
symphonies, several of Dvorak's symphonies, Wagner's *Siegfried
Idyll*, and Tchaikovsky's Piano Concerto were all played in that decade at the concerts of the Philharmonic Society for the first time.
And the 1890s brought performances of the Dvorak "New World"
Symphony, the Saint-Saëns "Organ" Symphony and the fourth and
sixth symphonies of Tchaikovsky, although London premieres of the
music of Richard Strauss, perhaps the most progressive orchestrator
of the time, did not occur until the first decade of the twentieth century. The late-century London performances, however, of music of
other German, French, Russian, Bohemian and other composers
confirm that the time of the slide trumpet had passed, and the valved
trumpet was becoming entrenched in concert orchestras.

The Trumpet in the Concert Hall

The cornet and valved trumpet began to infiltrate the concert
hall in the middle third of the century. No British composers wrote
orchestral music for these instruments until the 1860s, but no doubt
some orchestral players (certainly not the Harpers) began to borrow
the more facile cornet from the opera house during this time. Foreign
influences were also felt. It has been noted earlier that Berlioz
brought his music, with cornet parts, to London in the 1850s. The
Dutch-born, Paris-trained composer Edouard Silas moved to Eng-

land,[115] also in the 1850s, and began writing orchestral music specifically calling for trumpets *à cylindres*, but it is not clear what instruments the players used for parts such as this. Silas' 1852 symphony, which was premiered in London in 1863, calls for valved trumpets, but there is nothing in the score, except for several low notes in the second trumpet part, that could not have been played by Harper Jr. on the slide trumpet.[116]

Of course, it must also be remembered that much of the repertory of the mid-to-late nineteenth-century concert orchestras consisted of older music. Beethoven, Mozart, Haydn, and Mendelssohn were still performed regularly, and the orchestral music of Schubert was just then being discovered in London.[117] The slide trumpet would have been used to perform all of this older music, even when newer works calling for valved instruments were performed on the same concerts.

When notes impossible on the slide trumpet were called for, did the players use cornets or valved trumpets? Evidence presented earlier from Walter Morrow suggests that valved trumpets were slow to be accepted in the British orchestras. Writing in 1894–5, Morrow discusses the subject in more detail:

> The cornet has an agreeable tone and is comparatively easy to manipulate. It very quickly became popular, and its popularity has not declined; on the contrary, it has caused the [natural] trumpet proper to become almost obsolete. Students perceived that showy results were easy of attainment and forsook the study of the trumpet. Experienced players of the older instrument, when they were called upon to play parts written for the valve trumpet, instead of adapting themselves to the valve trumpet resorted to the cornet. Consequently, the

---

[115]*New Grove* , s. v. "Silas, Edouard," by Christopher Senior.

[116]Edouard Silas, *1ère Symphonie dediée à Mr. Henri Broadwood* (London: Cramer, Beale and Wood, [1864]).

[117]Schubert's Symphony No. 8 ("Unfinished") was first performed at the Philharmonic concerts in 1867; the "Great" C Major Symphony in 1871. See Foster, *Philharmonic Society*, 594.

cornet has crushed the trumpet out of the orchestra altogether. One rarely hears the sound of a real trumpet now.[118]

Interestingly, the instrument cases used by professional players also tell us much about the kinds of instruments that were being used. John Webb has several trumpet cases in his collection, including a double case that carried an 1835 Köhler slide trumpet and a cornet. He writes:

> This [slide trumpet] player (in 1835) doubled on valved cornet. Another case in my collection contained a slide trumpet and keyed bugle, with all their accessories. Yet another, later, slide trumpet shared its case with a valved F trumpet, exemplifying the reluctance with which the valved trumpets, even at the end of the 19th century, were accepted by the ever-conservative British.[119]

Probably most of the orchestral players used cornets for those difficult notes and passages, and slide trumpets for everything else, but a few no doubt played the valved trumpet in order to retain some remnants of the classic trumpet sound. Valved trumpets, although not used with any frequency until much later, certainly were not unknown in England by mid-century. Indeed, there is evidence that Harper Sr. had been introduced to the valved trumpet as early as 1829 (see below: "Chamber Works with Trumpet"). Also, a display of some of the newest British musical instruments was included in the Great Exhibition of 1851; it is interesting that of all the soprano brass instruments exhibited, most were valved instruments, and the majority of these were cornets.[120] Three-valved trumpets in E♭ and F

---

[118]Morrow, "Trumpet," 139.

[119]Webb, "Slide Trumpet," 264.

[120]*Official Descriptive and Illustrated Catalogue of the Great Exhibition of the Works of Industry of all Nations, 1851* (London: W. Clowes and Sons, 1851), vol. 1, *Index and Introductory; Section I.–Raw Materials, Classes 1 to 4; Section II.– Machinery, Classes 5 to 10,* 468–471.

by Pace and Köhler were on display, however, while only one slide trumpet, a Köhler "Harper's Improved" model, was exhibited.

The fact that the slide trumpet was third in representation at the mid-century Great Exhibition is not surprising. In fact, the various quantities of the three types of brass instruments displayed is probably a good indicator of the numbers of those instruments being made and sold at the time. It must be remembered that only professional trumpeters would have regularly used slide trumpets, as well as the new valved trumpets. The most prevalent mass-marketed brass instrument was the cornet, which, of course, reflected its huge popularity in social, dance, and military music.

The final third of the nineteenth century saw these three different instruments competing for primacy in English orchestras. The slide trumpet held the upper hand, at least until the retirement of Harper Jr. The cornet, however, was quickly becoming more popular, despite the admonitions of the leading players; and it surpassed the slide trumpet as the preferred instrument of orchestral trumpeters after 1885, and perhaps even before Harper's retirement. Harper himself provided evidence that the cornet was overtaking the slide trumpet in general orchestral use as early as 1875, when his *School for the Trumpet* was published. Indeed, according to Harper, the tutor was partly "intended as a protest against the misappropriation of another instrument—good also in its kind and in its proper place—to parts designed for the Trumpet."[121] After describing, in the preface to his tutor, how the cornet makes it easier "to produce the harmonic notes," Harper gives the following insight into the prevalence of the cornet at that time:

> These facts make the former instrument [cornet] attractive to many persons, who wish to produce the loudest music with the least trouble, and who would never attempt to play on the latter [slide trumpet] because of its greater difficulties, notwithstanding its purity and fineness of tone. The flexibility and facility of the Cornet have tempted

---

[121]Harper Jr., *School*, Preface, p. 2.

some composers, at first of dance music only, but later of more pretentious works, to write for this to the exclusion of the Trumpet.

Certain orchestral directors, with more regard for economy than musical effect, think it expedient to engage Cornetists for waltzes and music of some latest composers, and leave the players to make the best their means allow of the Trumpet-parts in other works, by perverting them to the quality and capabilities of their instrument. This leads to the very little practise, approaching to total neglect, of the Trumpet, among musicians who regard personal convenience above art interest. Hence it is necessary to make a stand in favour of a noble instrument, to which many of the most delicate, as well as most majestic effects in music are due.[122]

When Walter Morrow became London's principal trumpeter, he also tried desperately to stem the tide of the cornet, but he knew that by then the slide trumpet was not the answer, and he instead became the leading advocate for the valved trumpet in F. His statement regarding the use of the cornet in the 1890s, which sounds very much like those of his mentor twenty years earlier, has been quoted above. Morrow's summation of his argument for the F trumpet is as follows: "A good trumpet player can always be a good cornet player; a good cornet player cannot play the trumpet without much practice. My advice to students is to practise the latter assiduously, it will be to their ultimate benefit."[123] With Morrow's promotion, therefore, the valved F trumpet, though never as dominant as the slide trumpet during its heyday, probably held the upper hand against the cornet in the London concert orchestras, but only in the last decade of the century.

British composers, as we have seen, did not for the most part take into account either the advantages or the limitations of the slide trumpet in orchestrating their scores. This is explained by the fact that, as soon as trumpet notes outside the harmonic series began to be written, notes impossible on the slide trumpet also were used.

---

[122]Ibid., Preface, pp. 1–2.

[123]Morrow, "Trumpet," 141.

Most composers, it seems, followed the advice of Ebenezer Prout, from his 1878 instrumentation primer. After listing the various types of trumpet then available, he recommends the following: "In writing, no account need be taken of the different varieties of mechanism."[124] Therefore in nineteenth-century British orchestras, as throughout the history of music, performers were challenged and pushed by composers, and were thus required to develop new techniques and to use whatever equipment was at their disposal in order to play the music written for them.

ENSEMBLE LITERATURE

The trumpet was rarely used in chamber ensembles of mixed instruments during the nineteenth century, due no doubt to the limitations of the harmonic series, and then to the compromised sound quality of the various chromatic instruments. Of course, the natural trumpet was still used for martial and ceremonial music in trumpet ensembles, and the slide trumpet was sometimes employed here as well. There is also some evidence that the slide trumpet was used, if sparingly, in the popular British brass bands. A contemporary portrait of the Distin Family Band, one of the pioneering ensembles of the brass band movement, shows one of the members holding a slide trumpet.[125]

In art music, however, it was not until the end of the century, when composers such as Strauss, Mahler, Debussy, and Elgar began treating the trumpet like other melodic instruments, that composers began to think of the trumpet as being appropriate for chamber music. It is not until that time, therefore, that we see the first flowering of serious brass ensemble literature, such as the quintets of Victor Ewald. There are, however, a few isolated earlier examples of en-

---

[124]Prout, *Instrumentation*, 80.

[125]See the reproduction in Baines, *Brass Instruments*, Plate XI. Also, a clock-spring slide trumpet with the name "J. Distin" engraved on a shield attached to the bell can be found in the Jack Coleman Collection, Trazana CA. Albert Rice, letter to the author, 1 January 1996.

semble writing for the trumpet, with several pieces most likely written for performance by Thomas Harper Sr. and his slide trumpet.

Chamber Works with Trumpet

The most important of the few nineteenth-century compositions in this category is surely the 1881 *Septet* for trumpet, strings, and piano by Camille Saint-Saëns, which was written for a valved trumpet in E♭. Fully half a century earlier, however, Johann Nepomuk Hummel published a septet for piano, flute, violin, clarinet, cello, bass, and trumpet, which he called the "Military" Septet. This work was written for a London performance in 1830 and for the city's leading instrumentalists; it was "Composed and Dedicated to Mrs. Lucy Anderson," an English pianist.[126] Thomas Harper Sr. performed the trumpet part in the premiere performance of the piece, which was declared to be "full of masterly writing" by a review in the *Harmonicon*.[127] The composition was also performed a year later at the first concert of the Philharmonic Society's season, with the same soloists.[128] The trumpet part, while challenging, remains totally within the harmonic series. It is unfortunate that Hummel, who wrote such a remarkable concerto for the keyed trumpet in his youth, did not take full advantage of this situation to write another fine chromatic trumpet part—this time for the slide trumpet.

It is possible, however, that the Philharmonic performance of Hummel's "Military" Septet was heard by another composer, who was then inspired to try the genre himself. Sigismund Ritter von Neukomm (1778–1858), born in Salzburg and a student of both Michael and Joseph Haydn, was at this time on an extended stay in

---

[126]Johann Nepomuk Hummel, "Military" Septet for the Pianoforte, Flute, Violin, Clarinet, Violincello, Trumpet and Double Bass (London: J. B. Cramer, Addison and Beale, [1830]), title page.

[127]*Harmonicon* (June 1830): 264.

[128]The Septet was performed at the 21 February 1831 concert. See Foster, *Philharmonic Society*, 106.

Britain.[129] His only symphony was performed at the Philharmonic concerts during the 1831 season, but there is some confusion as to the exact concert. Miles Birket Foster, in his *History of the Philharmonic Society*, lists the programs for every concert in the first one hundred years of the Society's existence, and he includes Neukomm's Symphony in E♭ in the listing of the third concert of the season, on 21 March.[130] But in the text, which gives the highlights of the 1831 season, Foster writes: "The Chevalier von Neukomm placed his Symphony in E♭ at the disposal of the Society, and it was performed in the 1st concert."[131] Of course, this was the same concert at which Hummel's "Military" Septet was performed; and, according to Rudolph Angermüller's catalogue of his works, Neu- komm wrote three similar septets in the next few years.[132]

Although Neukomm was not held in high regard by contemporary writers, his septet(s) received many more performances by the Philharmonic Society than did Hummel's "Military" Septet. Foster writes that although Neukomm was "destitute of anything that could be reckoned 'genius,' he must have been remarkably diligent, for his compositions number something like a thousand works."[133] Neukomm's contemporary, John Edmund Cox, was less complimentary:

---

[129]He was in England, with a short excursion to Ireland, from 30 September 1830 to 4 August 1832, save one short eleven-day trip to Paris in August of 1831. See Rudolph Angermüller, *Sigismund Neukomm: Werkverzeichnis, Autobiographie, Beziehung zu seinen Zeitgenossen* (Munich-Salzburg: Musikverlag Emil Katzbichler, 1977), 11–12.

[130]Foster, *Philharmonic Society*, 107.

[131]Ibid., 105.

[132]The three septets are No. 399 in E-flat major for flute, oboe, clarinet, bassoon, horn, trumpet and bass, composed in February of 1832 in London; No. 458 in E-flat major for flute, oboe, clarinet, bassoon, horn, trumpet and bass, dated 24 August 1834 in Cherbourg; and No. 517 in E-flat major for flute, two clarinets, bassoon, horn, trumpet, and bass, dated 28 March 1836 in London. See Angermüller, *Neukomm: Werkverzeichnis*, 273.

[133]Foster, *Philharmonic Society*, 105. Actually, Angermüller's catalogue lists over 1200 compositions by Neukomm. See Angermüller, *Neukomm: Werkverzeichnis*.

A composer of considerable pretension, but very ordinary capacity, about this time [1831-1832] pushed himself into notoriety; and having been warmly taken up by several musical enthusiasts, and pronounced by them to be a second Haydn or Mozart, managed to keep his name for a year or two before the public, but then wholly and helplessly died out of everybody's remembrance—the Chevalier Neukomm.[134]

Concerning a performance of one of his septets in the 1835 Philharmonic season, Cox writes: "In the second act, a septett by Neukomm, elicited some applause, but afforded nothing else than a fulfillment of the old proverb, *beaucoup de talent, pas de génie.*"[135]

At least one, and possibly two, of Neukomm's septets received performances at the concerts of the Philharmonic Society. In fact, five separate performances took place between 1832 and 1836.[136] In attempting to determine which of the septet(s) were performed at these concerts, instrumentation and dates must be considered. The first two of the septets are scored for flute, oboe, clarinet, bassoon, horn, trumpet, and double bass, while in the final septet a second clarinet is substituted for the oboe. Since all of the Philharmonic performances featured one oboe and one clarinet, instead of two clarinets, the third of the septets must not have been played. Furthermore, Angermüller's composition date of August 1834 rules out the second septet, at least for the first three performances (two in 1832 and one in May of 1834). The final two performances, in 1835

---

[134]Cox, *Recollections,* 1: 245.

[135]Ibid., 1: 330.

[136]The performances occurred on 12 March 1832 (second concert of the season), 18 June 1832 (eighth concert), 19 May 1834 (sixth concert), 27 April 1835 (fifth concert), and 23 May 1836 (seventh concert). The performances featured the following instrumentation and soloists: flute (Charles Nicholson), oboe (Grattan Cooke), clarinet (Thomas Willman), bassoon (John Mackintosh; 1836 performance with James Denman because of 1835 retirement of Mackintosh), horn (Edward Platt), trumpet (Thomas Harper Sr.), and bass (Domenico Dragonetti).

and 1836, could have been either of the first two Neukomm septets, Angermüller catalogue numbers 399 and 458. Foster's season summaries do not help with the mystery. His only mention of a Neukomm septet is the following, from the first performance of the 1832 season: "...the second concert, at which was...introduced Neukomm's Fantasia Concertante for Wood-Wind, Horn, Trumpet and Double-Bass; this work was so successful that it was repeated at the last concert of the season."[137]

It is most likely that the trumpet part to this septet, and the other Neukomm septets, was written for Thomas Harper Sr. and with his slide trumpet in mind. Convincing evidence that Neukomm knew Harper and was aware of his talent can be found in one of Neukomm's letters, housed in the British Library manuscripts department. The letter is dated 17 September 1829, and is addressed to an unidentified Englishman in Paris. After expressing the hope that the addressee will meet with Cherubini, Neukomm offers the following suggestion:

> It is possible that he [Cherubini] will forget to have you listen to the *trompette à pistons*, the one which is able to play all the tones, therefore I will urge you to become acquainted with this beautiful instrument that I would love to see in the hands of Mr. Harper. Please write to Mr. Dauverné, rue D'Anjou, Dauphine, #2; I implore you to simply ask him to show you for the first time this trumpet, he will do it with the greatest of pleasures.[138]

We know, of course, that Neukomm was not able to convince Harper to abandon his slide trumpet and adopt the new valved trumpet, but it is evident from the trumpet part of at least one of these septets that the slide trumpet, not the valved trumpet, was most likely intended, although the part could have also been played on the latter.

---

[137]Foster, *Philharmonic Society*, 110.

[138]Sigismund Neukomm, to unknown addressee, Paris, transl. Eduardo Aguilar, 17 September 1829, *Lbl*, Add. 33965, f. 282.

Example 26: Sigismund Neukomm, *Septetto*, trumpet part (mm. 84–87).

The first septet (Angermüller No. 399) was composed in London in February of 1832, and was the one performed in the Philharmonic performances of 1832 and May of 1834. A glance at the E♭ trumpet part of this work reveals idiomatic writing for the slide trumpet. The only non-harmonic-series notes employed are a' and b', the most commonly used notes requiring extension of the slide in all of the slide trumpet literature. The opening trumpet statement of the Finale, marked *Allegro Moderato*, is a good example (Example 26). Near the end of the Finale, we see some brilliant slide trumpet writ-

Example 27: Neukomm, *Septetto*, trumpet part (mm. 165–180).

Example 28: Neukomm, *Ottetto*, trumpet part (mm. 63–64).

ing, which reminds one of Hummel's keyed trumpet solo (Example 27).[139]

These septets are not the only chamber works with trumpet that Neukomm wrote during his years in England. Angermüller No. 421 is an octet in E♭ major, which features a popular English tune called "The Sea."[140] Written in Bridgehill, Belper (Derbyshire), it is scored for flute, oboe, clarinet, bassoon, horn, trumpet, cello, and double bass, and is dated 24 December 1832. Like the septet trumpet part, this one has many notes outside the harmonic series—including a', b' and e♭'—but all manageable by Harper on a slide trumpet. Neukomm even writes a chromatic *ad libitum* cadenza for the trumpet (Example 28), and also gives the instrument a prominent melodic role toward the end (Example 29, p. 158).[141] A nonet, also in E♭, is scored for flute, oboe, clarinet, bassoon, horn, trumpet, viola, cello, and double bass.[142] This work was written in Birmingham and dated 10 February 1836.[143] Again, in the trumpet part we find numerous

---

[139]Sigismund Neukomm, *Fantaisie Concertante for Trumpet, Horn, Flute, Clarionette, Oboe, Bassoon & Double Bass*, autograph score (February 1832), Angermüller No. 399.

[140]Angermüller, *Neukomm: Werkverzeichnis*, 108.

[141]Sigismund Neukomm, *Ottetto pour trompette, cor, flute, hautbois, clarinette, bassoon, violincello et contrebasse*, parts (24 December 1832), Angermüller No. 421.

[142]Sigismund Neukomm, *Nonetto for Trumpet, Horn, Flute, Oboe, Clarionet, Bassoon, Tenor, Violincello & Double Bass*, autograph score (10 February 1836), Angermüller No. 513.

[143]Angermüller, *Neukomm: Werkverzeichnis*, 117.

non-harmonic-series notes that would have playable on a slide trumpet. A solo passage is shown in Example 30.

According to Angermüller, Neukomm wrote three other works with trumpet in England. Two marches for brass band, with parts for keyed bugle, were written in Burton, Derbyshire, and Birmingham in 1832 and 1835, respectively.[144] Perhaps most intriguing of all is a septet entitled *Divertimento for Trumpet Solo, 2 Horns, and 3 Trombones*.[145] The composition was written in London and dated 31 October 1834.[146] The incipit provided in Angermüller's catalogue reveals

Example 29: Neukomm, *Ottetto*, trumpet part (mm. 138–163).

[144]Sigismund Neukomm, *March* (18 July 1832), Angermüller No. 416; and *A March & a Gallop March* (1 September 1835), Angermüller No. 496.

[145]Sigismund Neukomm, *Divertimento for Trumpet Solo, 2 Horns, and 3 Trombones* (31 October 1834), Angermüller No. 469.

[146]Angermüller, *Neukomm: Werkverzeichnis*, 113.

Example 30: Neukomm, *Nonetto*, trumpet part (mm. 288–303).

that this trumpet part, too, was probably written for slide trumpet (Example 31, p. 160).[147]

Although we are making a case here for the slide trumpet as the intended instrument in these chamber works—because of their genesis in England, Neukomm's likely acquaintance of Harper, and the inclusion of melodies by Neukomm in Harper's tutor—the reader should be reminded that all of these works could have been played on either the valved trumpet, cornet, or keyed trumpet.[148] No doubt Neukomm considered the marketability of these works elsewhere, for example in France with a player such as Dauverné using either a French-system slide trumpet, *cornet-à-pistons*, or valved trumpet.

---

[147]There is a short exercise in Harper Sr.'s tutor by the Chevalier Neukomm (Lesson No. 19 in E-flat). The melodic material is not from the trumpet parts of either the septet (No. 399), the octet, or the nonet. Perhaps this passage is from the Divertimento, or perhaps one of the other septets. According to Angermüller, these works are the only compositions for trumpet that Neukomm wrote in England. Incidentally, the same exercise is duplicated in Harper Jr.'s tutor (Exercise No. 81). See Harper Sr., *Instructions*, 25; and Harper Jr., *School*, 36.

[148]Neukomm wrote a keyed trumpet part in a Requiem for the Congress of Vienna in 1815; it was performed successfully by Anton Weidinger. See Dahlqvist, *Keyed Trumpet*, 17–19.

Example 31: Neukomm, *Divertimento*, incipit.

Trumpet Ensemble Literature

The ceremonial trumpet corps provided more of an opportunity than did mixed groups for small ensemble playing by trumpeters in the nineteenth century, and there is evidence that the slide trumpet, as well as the natural trumpet, was used in this way. The trumpet corps, a remnant of the Baroque era, was still much used in nineteenth-century England, a country steeped in ceremonial traditions. Both Harpers were involved, to some extent, with this type of playing. Harper Sr. joined a military band, the East India Volunteer Band, when he first came to London as a young man, and although he did not play with the band after 1804, he remained associated with the group, as inspector of musical instruments, until his death in 1853.[149] Harper Jr. held the post of trumpeter to the Lord Mayor "for nearly half-a-century," and in 1884 was appointed to the post of Sergeant Trumpeter to Queen Victoria, which he held until his death.[150]

The largely administrative post of Sergeant Trumpeter was already an ancient one at the time of Harper's appointment. The first Sergeant Trumpeter was Benedict Browne, who was appointed to the post in 1546,[151] and many of Britain's leading trumpeters throughout the years have held the position; John Shore and Valentine Snow are

---

[149]Sorenson and Webb, "The Harpers," 35–36, 41.

[150]"Obituary: Thomas John Harper," *Musical Times* 39 (1 October 1898): 681.

[151]Crispian Steele-Perkins, letter to the author, 7 September 1993.

two of the most famous that come to mind. The duties of the Sergeant Trumpeter are described by Steele-Perkins:

> The Post of Sargeant of the Trumpeters or Sargeant-Trumpeter was a lucrative, administrative non-playing one. *All* trumpet players had to apply for a license to perform in theatrical presentations and *all* military and naval trumpeters were appointed and licensed by the Sargeant-Trumpeter who accumulated such a huge salary from his commissions that the comparatively small fees for playing were not worth bothering with. I have estimated that the annual salary from the Royal Exchequer of £100 may have been at least trebled by various "perks."[152]

But did the Sergeant Trumpeter ever play the trumpet under the auspices of his title? In an 1848 book entitled *Sketches of Her Majesty's Household*, the post is discussed and it is revealed that at the time the salary was £100, "plus fees for performing at major state occasions."[153] Steele-Perkins, however, argues that performing did not necessarily go along with the job.

> His [Harper Jr.] playing had nothing to do with the ceremonial fanfaring...though like previous sargeants he may have been present bearing his mace of office and wearing a collar of silver...at important ceremonies. The sargeant-trumpeter played the trumpet no more than the President drives his own official car. Harper Junior's musical activities...were entirely his own recreational (albeit well paid) pastime."[154]

Although the position of Sergeant Trumpeter did not require Harper Jr. to perform, there is evidence from his engagement book that he either participated in ceremonial playing, served as a kind of impresario by hiring other ceremonial trumpeters, or simply at-

---

[152]Ibid.

[153]*Sketches of Her Majesty's Household: Interspersed with Historical Notes, Political Comments, And Critical Remarks,...* (London: William Strange, 1848), 76–78, quoted in Sorenson, "Harper, Sr.," 220.

[154]Steele-Perkins, letter, 7 September 1993.

tended important events. Many of these occasions, however, took place before his appointment as Sergeant Trumpeter: the christening of the Prince of Wales on 25 January 1842; the opening of the Great Exhibition in Hyde Park in May of 1851; the opening of the Crystal Palace on 10 June 1854; the Guildhall for an Emperor's visit on 19 April 1855; the marriage of the Princess Royal on 25 January 1858; the marriage of the Prince of Wales at Windsor Castle on 10 March 1863; the opening of the Royal College of Music on 7 May 1883; and a reception for the King of Denmark at the Guildhall in 1893.[155] It seems likely that Harper performed at some of these events, especially the civic ceremonies, perhaps, in the office of Trumpeter to the Lord Mayor.

At any rate, Harper Jr. left much trumpet ensemble music in both score and parts, and this legacy is preserved in the library of the Royal College of Music in London. Perhaps some of this music was used pedagogically, for his students at either the Royal Academy of Music, where he taught during his playing career, or the Royal College of Music, where he taught from 1884 to 1893.[156] But at least one flourish for four trumpets was intended for official ceremonial use. The manuscript title reads as follows: "Jubilee Flourish performed by The Queen's State Trumpeters in Westminster Abbey on June 21st 1887."[157] This is no doubt a fanfare that Harper, as Sergeant Trumpeter, composed for the Queen's Jubilee, which was then performed probably without his assistance.

Another manuscript, a small book of musical staff paper, contains sixteen folios, on which are written marches and flourishes for from two to four trumpets, and one with added trombone.[158] In addi-

---

[155]Harper Jr., Engagement Book.

[156]Sorenson and Webb, "The Harpers," 47.

[157]Thomas Harper Jr., "Trumpet Cadenza and Flourish," n. d., *Lcm*, MS 4078, f. 35.

[158]Thomas Harper Jr., "Marches, Flourishes, etc., for trumpets," n. d., *Lcm*, MS 4072.

tion, there is a box full of small cards on which are written the individual parts of trumpet fanfares and marches.[159] The cards are fairly durable; the staff paper seems to have been pasted onto hard paper. No doubt these cards were used for performances both inside and outside, and for many different kinds of weather and circumstances. Whether Harper participated in any performances of these trumpet ensembles is uncertain, but his authorship is beyond doubt: thus we must assume that he kept this music ready for any occasion, organized and perhaps rehearsed the musicians, and either participated occasionally or at least was present at the event with the mace and silver collar of the Sergeant Trumpeter.

The score booklet contains thirteen ensemble pieces, with the music on several folios being either simple sketches or crossed out entirely. The pieces are given the titles "March," "Flourish," and "Quick Step," and most of the works are restricted to notes of the harmonic series. Two, however, were definitely written for slide trumpets. An arrangement of *God Save the Queen* is scored for four trumpets (three in D and one in E) and one trombone.[160] As would be expected, this arrangement contains many notes outside the harmonic series. Another slide trumpet piece is *"The Grand March" for 4 Trumpets*, reproduced in Figure 35 (p. 164). The first and second parts are idiomatic for the slide trumpet; that is, they employ the easily-corrected out-of-tune eleventh partial, as well as a' and b'. In addition, f#' is used, mostly in passing situations, in the second part. It is almost certain that these parts were intended for slide trumpets, although natural trumpets could have been used for the lower parts; because of tradition (e.g., the hanging of banners from natural trum-

---

[159]Thomas Harper Jr., "A collection of Marches, Flourishes, etc., for trumpets, written on cards in separate parts," n. d., *Lcm*, MS 4074.

[160]Harper Jr., "Marches, Flourishes, etc.," ff. 7v–8. His father included an arrangement of *God Save the Queen*, for four trumpets in D, bass trombone, and kettledrums in D & A, in his tutor. The version in Harper Jr.'s score booklet may have been taken from, or perhaps based on, his father's arrangement. See Harper Sr., *Instructions*, 36.

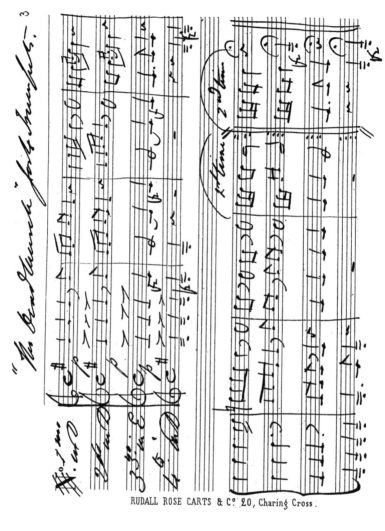

Figure 35: Thomas Harper Jr., *"The Grand March" for 4 Trumpets*. By permission of the Royal College of Music.

pet tubing), no doubt the sound and appearance of valved trumpets would have been frowned upon in ceremonial playing.

SOLO LITERATURE

The history of the trumpet as a solo instrument during the nineteenth century is a short one. The predominant solo brass instrument of the century was the cornet, but the literature written for it consists mostly of variations on popular tunes and opera arias, and dance music. In strict and conservative Victorian England this type of music was considered common and trivial, especially in the circles that cultivated orchestral music. The trumpet was accepted by this audience, but little solo literature was written for it. Tarr explains the situation:

> Although the valve mechanism was an essential improvement and had lasting effects on the technique of trumpet playing, oddly enough it brought no enlargement of the trumpet repertoire. On the contrary, the nineteenth century was an epoch in which the trumpet was employed chiefly as an orchestral instrument. This is...analogous to the situation of woodwind instruments. They too were mechanized in the nineteenth century, however they had already passed their heyday as solo instruments. For the brass as for the woodwind, one bought the full chromatic range (with uniform timbre on all notes) at the price of greater richness of sound. The leading composers wrote their famous concertos for string instruments and for the piano; not for wind instruments.[161]

The sound compromise was certainly true of valved trumpets, but it was not the case with the slide trumpet. Just as with the orchestral literature, however, English composers had a wonderful solo instrument at their disposal but, for the most part, did not take advantage of it.

Most writers agree that the slide trumpet was used for the purpose of performing solo trumpet parts from Handel's music that con-

---

[161]Tarr, *The Trumpet*, 162–163.

tinued to be in great demand throughout the nineteenth century. Proof that the instrument was used for other solo literature can be found in numerous concert programs stored in the Department of Portraits and Performance History at the Royal College of Music.[162] Furthermore, several compositions found in the British Library offer additional evidence not only that the slide trumpet was often used as a solo instrument, but that solo works were composed for it as well.

Solo Performances with Slide Trumpet

A 1935 letter to *The Times* from a descendant of the Harpers deals with, among other things, the solo performances of his for-bears. Thomas F. Harper, the descendant, writes that Harper Jr. "never resorted to a valve instrument (whose tone he considered in-ferior) in all his solo playing."[163] In truth, however, the Royal College of Music programs show that Harper Jr. had an active solo career performing not only on slide trumpet, but also on valved trumpet, cornet, and posthorn. These concert programs are bound in five vol-umes, and most feature Harper Jr. in provincial engagements only; there are no London programs in the collection. A substantial num-ber of these programs came to the Royal College of Music as a gift from the Harper family, but over the years several of the original volumes have disappeared; approximately one hundred programs are all that remain.[164]

These documents show the vast number of performances of Handel's oratorios, particularly *Messiah*, that were performed at pro-vincial festivals throughout the nineteenth century. In most of these *Messiah* performances, Harper Jr. was featured as soloist in "The

---

[162]Thomas Harper Jr., Concert Programs, 5 vols., *Lcm*, Department of Portraits and Performance History.

[163]Thomas F. Harper, "The Trumpets," letter to the editor, *The Times* (London), 25 January 1935, 10.

[164]Oliver Davies, Keeper of Portraits, Royal College of Music, conversation with the author, 10 June 1993.

Trumpet Shall Sound." Also included in the collection are many programs of variety festival concerts, seemingly built around Harper Jr. and several vocalists, as featured soloists. A concert given in the town of Coalbrookdale, under the auspices of the Literary and Scientific Institution in 1876, is typical. As can been seen from the reproductions in Figure 36 (p. 168) and Figure 37 (p. 169), Harper was featured, along with four vocalists, and played slide trumpet for a solo and for the obbligato in a soprano song. He also played an arrangement of *Ave Maria* on the valved trumpet, and ended the concert with a posthorn galop, his own work *Down the Road*.[165] The programs consistently distinguish "valve trumpet" from "trumpet," therefore we can assume that the latter designation refers to the slide instrument. Other instruments, such as *cornet à pistons* and posthorn, are similarly and consistently designated.

A further examination of the programs reveals that "The Trumpet Shall Sound" and "Let the Bright Seraphim" were staples of Harper's repertoire; many, many performances of these works took place throughout his career. Also, the same popular solos were used again and again in festival performances like the one at Coalbrookdale: the "Ave Maria" on valved trumpet; an unnamed cornet solo by Flotow; Harper's own *Solo à la polonaise*, presumably on slide trumpet; variations on themes from *Il Trovatore* on cornet; and many vocal solos with slide trumpet obbligato, such as Bishop's *Peace Inviting* and Arne's *The Soldier Tir'd*.[166] The last work, however, was

---

[165]The orchestral parts for this work were published in 1877, and can be found in the British Library, *Lbl*, f.415.c.(19.).

[166]Both of these works have been found in nineteenth-century publications in the British Library. They are piano/vocal arrangements, though, and have no separate trumpet parts. *Peace Inviting* has occasional *tromba* cues in the piano score, but *The Soldier Tir'd* does not, although there are several passages that would adapt well to the trumpet. See Henry R. Bishop, *Peace Inviting: Sung by Mr. Sims Reeves* (London: B. Williams, [1863]), *Lbl* H.1428.(21.); and Thomas Arne, *The Soldier Tir'd of Wars Alarms: Sung by Miss Stephens* (London: Goulding & D'Almaine, [1825?]), *Lbl* H.2826.b.(3.).

LITERARY AND SCIENTIFIC

INSTITUTION, COALBROOKDALE.

The Committee beg to announce that they have made arrangements with

MR. THOMAS HARPER

FOR AN EVENING

CONCERT

TO BE GIVEN

On Tuesday, February 8th, 1876.

Vocalists:

MADAME CLARA SUTER,

(Principal Soprano at the Sacred Harmonic Society, Exeter Hall, &c.)

MADAME ALICE BARNETT.

MR. WALLACE WELLS,

AND

MR. HENRY PYATT,

(Principal Basso Royal Albert Hall, and London Ballad Concerts.)

Instrumentalists:

MR. T. HARPER,

(Solo Trumpet)

AND

MR. ARTHUR H. JACKSON, R.A.M.

(Solo Pianoforte and Conductor.)

To commence at Half-past Seven p.m.

ADMISSION:

Reserved Front Seats, 3s.; Back Seats, 1s. 6d.

Tickets may be had of Mr. I. Dunbar, the Institute, where a Plan of the room may be seen and Seats secured.

The usual privilege to Members of Admission at Half-price will in this instance be withdrawn.

S. Slater, Steam Printing Works, Ironbridge.

Figure 36: Thomas Harper Jr., front page of concert program. By permission of the Royal College of Music.

168

PART I.

GLEE, "There is beauty on the mountain." ....Sir John Gosa.

DUET, "The sailor sighs." ....Balfe.
Madame ALICE BARNETT and Mr. WALLACE WELLS.

SONG, "It was a dream." ....Cowen.
Madame CLARA SUTER.

SONG, "Rocked in the cradle of the deep." ....J. P. Knight.
Mr. HENRY PYATT.

SONG, "The Maid of the Mill." ....**Hamilton Aïdé.**
Madame **ALICE BARNETT.**

SOLO à la polonaise ....TRUMPET.............**Harper.**
Mr. T. HARPER.

SONG, "The Red-Cross Banner." ....Knight.
Mr. WALLACE WELLS.

PART SONG, "All among the barley." ....Stirling.

PART II.

FANTASIE IMPROMPTU .....PIANOFORTE ....Chopin.
Mr. ARTHUR H. JACKSON.

DUET, "All's Well," ....Braham.
Mr. WALLACE WELLS and Mr. HENRY PYATT.

SONG, "Peace inviting." ....Sir H. Bishop.
Madame CLARA SUTER.
Trumpet obbligato, Mr. T. HARPER.

SONG, "The gallant cavalier." ....F. Kingsbury.
Mr. HENRY PYATT.

SONG, "Little Maid of Arcadie." ....Sullivan.
Madame ALICE BARNETT.

SOLO, VENTIL TRUMPET, "Ave Maria." ....Schubert.
Mr. T. HARPER.

SONG, "Tom Bowling." ....Dibdin.
Mr. WALLACE WELLS.

DUET, "Of Fairy Wand." ....(Maritana).......Wallace.
Madame CLARA SUTER and Mr. HENRY PYATT.

GLEE, "I love my love in the morning." ....Allen.

FINALE, New Galop..... "Down the Road."* ....Harper.
(Performed with great success at the Promenade Concerts, Covent Garden.)
Pianoforte, Mr. ARTHUR H. JACKSON.
Post Horn obbligato, Mr. T. HARPER.

Published by RUDALL and CARTE, 20, Charing Cross, London, and to
be had of all Musicsellers.

Figure 37: Thomas Harper Jr., concert program. By permission of the Royal College of Music.

listed in the programs alternately as a trumpet solo and as a vocal solo with trumpet obbligato. No doubt Harper arranged most of this music himself, as suggested by the existence of a Harper Jr. arrangement of Bishop's song *Thine For Ever*, for soprano and obbligato slide trumpet, in the British Library.[167]

Some of these arrangements performed by Harper Jr. were possibly handed down to him by his father. The Royal College of Music also has a well preserved concert bill promoting a series of concerts given by Paganini at the Theatre Royal, Covent Garden, in 1832.[168] One of the advertised concerts was held on 6 July, and included in the program was *The Soldier Tired*, sung by Miss Shirreff and with trumpet obbligato by "Mr. E. Harper." The "E" initial is obviously a mistake; the trumpeter for this performance is without question Harper Sr. who was at the peak of his career in the 1830s.[169] It is also very interesting that Walter Morrow seems to have carried on the tradition. A Morrow program from the 1894 Leyton festival is also found in the collection, and it indicates that he performed Harper's *Rondo à la polonaise* and *The Soldier Tired* as solos.[170]

What was the nature of the trumpet solos that the Harpers and others wrote themselves? Apparently none of these works survive, but a clue possibly relating to them exists in an autograph book[171] housed in the British Library and originally owned by Eliza Wesley, the illegitimate daughter of Samuel Wesley and sister of S. S.

---

[167]Sir Henry Rowley Bishop, *Thine For Ever: Arranged for Voice, Trumpet & Pianoforte by Thomas Harper* (London: Stanley Lucas, Weber and Co., [1873]), *Lbl* H.1428.b.(21.).

[168]Niccolò Paganini, Concert Bill, 1832, Department of Portraits and Performance History, *Lcm*.

[169]Perhaps the mistake resulted from confusion with Harper's oldest son Edmund, who was an important hornist. See Brown and Stratton, *British Musical Biography*, 184.

[170]Concert Programs, *Lcm*.

[171]Eliza Wesley, Autograph Book, n. d., *Lbl*, Add. 35026.

Wesley.[172] In this book are many autographs, musical and otherwise, of major nineteenth-century figures, including Charles Dickens, Henry Bishop, Michael Balfe, Jenny Lind, Mendelssohn, Meyerbeer, Spohr, Johann Strauss, Verdi, and Thomas Harper Sr. Many of the musicians wrote music—some one or two lines, and others much more elaborate—along with their autographs. Harper wrote a melody that is obviously meant for the slide trumpet.[173] This piece is, again, typical of slide trumpet repertoire in that a' and b' are the only non-harmonic-series notes used (Figure 38, p. 172). It is interesting that this same melody is reproduced in Harper's tutor.[174] This and other exercises provided in the tutors of both Harpers are fair indications of the type of solos they may have played. Indeed, some of the studies in Harper Jr.'s tutor are quite tuneful and might have been effective concert pieces if combined with skillful accompaniments.

Finally, there was the famous "Trumpet Battle" in New York City in 1834, between two immigrant trumpeters: John Norton, a slide trumpeter and colleague of Harper from England; and Alessandro Gambati, the Italian keyed trumpeter (mentioned above along with his brother) who earlier had a brief London career with that instrument, but who was by then playing a two-valved trumpet.[175] Each contestant had built his reputation by playing variations and other solos as intermission entertainment at various New York theaters and outdoor pleasure gardens, and each was promoted by rival New York newspapers. The final contest, however, was played on natural trumpets, in order to level the playing field between two performers of such diverse instruments. Norton was proclaimed the winner, as should have been expected; as a slide trumpet player, he

---

[172]Frederick George Edwards, "Wesley, Samuel (1766–1837)," *The Compact Edition of the Dictionary of National Biography* (London: Oxford University Press, 1975), 2: 2234.

[173]Thomas Harper, E. Wesley Autograph Book, f. 32v.

[174]Harper Sr., *Instructions*, 22.

[175]For a detailed description of the contest see Cynthia Hoover, "A Trumpet Battle at Nimblo's Pleasure Garden," *Musical Quarterly* 55 (July 1969): 384–395.

Figure 38: Thomas Harper Sr., melody from Eliza Wesley autograph book (f. 32v). By permission of the British Library. [Add. 35026]

would have had the advantage because his instrument was essentially a natural trumpet.

Trumpet Songs

The trumpet was frequently used as an obbligato instrument in opera and oratorio arias throughout Europe by the late Baroque.[176] David Fuller traces the development of the obbligato part:

> The archetype of the obbligato part is the instrumental solo which, with a basso continuo, constitutes the accompaniment of vast numbers of late Baroque arias. The roots of the instrumental obbligato to vocal music could be said to reach as far back as medieval polyphony, but the direct antecedents of the late Baroque phenomenon are to be found in the *concertato* style of the early 17th century. Schütz's *Benedicam Dominum in omni tempore* (*Symphoniae sacrae*, i, 1629) for soprano, tenor, bass, and continuo, with obbligato "cornetto, o violino" is an early example, and the trumpet arias in later 17th century opera carry on the development.[177]

In Italy the arias for soprano and trumpet of Scarlatti, and in Germany the trumpet obbligato parts in J. S. Bach's cantata arias, immediately come to mind. The country, however, that embraced the genre and cultivated the "Trumpet Song" for almost two hundred years was England.

The Early English Trumpet Song

The birth of the English "Trumpet Song" tradition happened in an amazing decade, the 1690s, which, as we have seen in Chapter One, also saw the flat trumpet evolve, flourish, and pass from favor.

---

[176]For an in-depth examination of trumpet obbligato in Baroque opera, see Peter Ciurczak, "The Trumpet in Baroque Opera: Its Use as a Solo, Obbligato, and Ensemble Instrument," *Journal of the International Trumpet Guild* 6 (October 1981): 2–17, 54–68; 7 (September 1982): 14–33.

[177]*New Grove*, s. v. "Obbligato," by David Fuller.

Smithers writes about this first flowering of art music for trumpet in England:

> As nearly as can be ascertained, Purcell is one of the earliest English
> composers to score for the Baroque trumpet. At any rate, there seem
> to be no earlier surviving manuscript or printed sources of seven-
> teenth-century English trumpet music before his "Birthday Song"
> (1690) for Queen Mary, *Arise my Muse* (Z 320). Purcell's older con-
> temporaries, Locke, Child, Humphrey and Blow, may have scored for
> the trumpet before 1690, but no music by these composers written
> before that date and indicating the use of trumpets appears to have
> survived.[178]

Downey has made a case for a pre-1690 English trumpet tradition in art music,[179] but many of his arguments have subsequently been challenged.[180] Until more evidence, in the form of extant music or documentary sources, surfaces, Smithers' statement must stand as correct.

A good introduction to early English trumpet songs can be found in a collection of Purcell's most popular theater music, *The Orpheus Britannicus*, which was first published three years after Purcell's death and again in a second edition in 1706.[181] The latter edition contains a total of eight trumpet songs, most for single trum-pet obbligato, but with two songs scored for two trumpets. Sir John Hawkins, in his 1776 history of music, mentions Purcell's trumpet music with reference to this collection:

---

[178]Smithers, *Baroque Trumpet*, 206.

[179]See Downey, "What Pepys Heard," 417–428.

[180]Pinnock and Wood, "A Counterblast," 436–443.

[181]The 1706 edition contains three more trumpet songs than the 1698 edition. See Henry Purcell, *Orpheus Britannicus. A Collection of all the Choicest Songs. For One, Two, and Three Voices, Compos'd by Mr. Henry Purcell. Together, With such Symphonies for Violins or Flutes, as were by Him design'd for any of them: and a Through–Bass to each Song; Figur'd for the Organ, Harpsichord, or Theorbo–Lute* (London: William Pearson, 1706).

Purcell was the first who composed songs with symphonies for that instrument; and that it is to be inferred from the many instances in the Orpheus Britannicus of songs so accompanied, that he had a great fondness for it...."[182]

A song from this collection to which Hawkins specifically refers is "Genius of England," a vocal duet with trumpet obbligato, originally written for the theater piece *Don Quixote*. The trumpet part, in C, is a demanding one, reaching c''' in rising scale passages three times near the end of the song; it was written for Purcell's friend and trumpeter John Shore. Burney, also writing in 1776, indicates that this song "was long the favourite song of our theatres, though its passages are more common and vulgar now, than those of any other of Purcell's capital songs."[183]

By the late eighteenth century the trumpet song had become a regular feature of British concert life. Several of Handel's many trumpet songs immediately entered the standard repertory of oratorio concerts; of course, "The Trumpet Shall Sound" was performed during each of the countless performances of *Messiah*, but "Let the Bright Seraphim," from *Samson*, was also regularly performed in performances of that oratorio, and in miscellaneous oratorio and vocal concerts.

Handel, however, was not the only composer in Britain to write mid-century trumpet songs that enjoyed enduring popularity. Thomas Arne (1710–1788), in his opera *Artaxerxes*, included a soprano aria, "The Soldier Tir'd," which quickly became a regular feature of miscellaneous vocal concerts. According to Roger Fiske, "...'The Soldier tir'd', is...enlivened with an obbligato trumpet part. It was often sung at concerts well into the next century, being regarded as a standard test of vocal agility."[184] Indeed, we know from the concert

---

[182]Sir John Hawkins, *A General History of the Science and Practice of Music* (London: Novello, 1853; repr., New York: Dover, 1963), 2: 752.

[183]Burney, *General History*, 2: 397.

[184]Fiske, *English Theatre Music*, 308.

programs of Harper Jr. that the song was performed with trumpet obbligato, and also as a trumpet solo, until the end of the nineteenth
century.

Late-Eighteenth-Century Operatic and
Vauxhall Trumpet Songs

The late eighteenth century saw the continued popularity of
trumpet songs in operas, with many new ones, such as those discussed in Chapter Two by William Shield, being composed. John
Thiessen has provided a description of the typical Shield trumpet
song, with its "motto" beginning:

> The trumpet plays a solo in the introduction, either at the beginning
> or several measures into the piece. The soloist usually picks up the
> trumpet's melodic motif, before developing the main melody further.
> Throughout the song, the trumpet responds to either direct or indirect
> textual allusion, playing short fanfare figures or more extended obbli-
> gato passages in the interludes. There is also a recurring pattern of
> trumpet and oboe obbligatos against a long held dominant in the
> voice, as well as cases where the trumpet is heard in extended duet
> passages with the voice. The songs often end with the trumpet play-
> ing a fanfare figure at the final cadence. The key of songs featuring
> the trumpet is primarily D major, although there are also many ex-
> amples in E♭ and C major as well.[185]

The venues of popular entertainment, such as the pleasure gardens, also provided a forum for the performance of trumpet songs.
Thomas Busby writes that Valentine Snow performed regularly at
Vauxhall Gardens, at the mid-century point, when vocal soloists were
first beginning to sing there.[186] This trend continued into the nineteenth century, as evidenced by the British Library's holdings of
volumes of music, both printed and manuscript, of songs written for

---

[185]Thiessen, "Late Eighteenth-Century Trumpet," 6.

[186]Thomas Busby, *Concert Room and Orchestra Anecdotes, of Music and Musicians,
Ancient and Modern* (London: Clementi & Co., 1825), 3: 3.

Figure 39: Anonymous, *When Briton's Silver Trumpet Sounds* (ca. 1775). By permission of the British Library. [G.312.(222.)]

Vauxhall performances by such composers as James Hook (1746–1827) and William Reeve (1757–1815). A search through any one of these volumes will turn up many pieces either labeled as trumpet songs, or with soloistic trumpet parts written in the scores.[187] An anonymous example from about 1775 can be seen in Figure 39 (p. 177).

There are no separate trumpet parts to these Vauxhall trumpet songs, although that the trumpet is featured as an obbligato instrument is evident from the occasional trumpet cue. The scores examined by this author restrict the trumpet to notes of the harmonic series, so the use of notes outside the series, and hence the use of the slide trumpet itself, must be left to speculation. The first page, including the trumpet introduction, of a song by Hook published in 1790, is reproduced in Figure 40. Of course, 1790 is the same season that Sarjant is thought to have played non-harmonic-series notes on a slide trumpet. Although harmonic-series notes only are called for in this song, it is interesting to speculate as to what Sarjant might have done if he played this obbligato part on a slide trumpet.

The only difference between typical operatic trumpet songs, as described by Thiessen, and these Vauxhall songs is that there is no evidence for trumpet-and-oboe duo-obbligatos. One of the Vauxhall songs examined by this author, however, was originally written for the opera house. William Reeve's song *Hark! The Trumpet Sounds Afar* includes a duo-obbligato, which, though not specifically labeled for trumpet and oboe, is nonetheless present over a sung dominant (Example 32, p. 180). Again, it is worth speculating about the in-

---

[187]Consider, for example, James Hook, *Hark, Hark the Dreadful Din of War: A favorite Trumpet Song, Sung by Miss Bertles at Vauxhall Gardens* (London: Preston, [1788?]), *Lbl* H.1651.a.(1.); James Hook, *The Solace of Life: A Favorite Trumpet Song, Sung by Mr. Duffey at Vauxhall* (London: Preston & Son, [1791?]), *Lbl* H.1651.b.(67.); William Reeve, *Love Sounds the Trumpet of Joy: A Favorite Trumpet Song, Sung with Unbounded Applause, by Miss Daniels, at Vauxhall Gardens* (London: Bland & Weller's, [1800?]), *Lbl* G.424.a.(25.); and William Reeve, *Hark! The Trumpet Sounds Afar: A favorite new Song, Sung by Mr. Bannister in "Hero and Leander"* (London: G. Goulding, [1787]), *Lbl* G.808.e.(40.).

Figure 40: James Hook, *Volunteer* (1790), first page. By permission of the British Library. [H.1651.a.(5.)]

Example 32: William Reeve, *Hark! The Trumpet Sounds Afar* (p. 2).

the   call   my bea - ting   bo - som warms   my

(trumpets)

bea-ting   bo-som   warms...

struments that might have been used in the performance of this passage. The published date of 1787 would place this song in the early years of the slide trumpet's existence. Could this duo-obbligato part have been played on slide trumpets, with the first player correcting the intonation of the eleventh partial and the second player using the slide to produce the non-harmonic-series note b' on a trumpet in D?

Handelian Trumpet Song Tradition
in the Nineteenth Century

The popularity of the trumpet song diminished only slightly at the beginning of the nineteenth century. It is true that with the decline of the clarino style of solo trumpet playing fewer new trumpet songs were being written, and it was not until Thomas Harper Sr.'s career was well established that trumpet songs began to be written again for him to play. Nothing could be done, however, to stem the popularity of the Handelian trumpet songs, performances of which continued without abatement.

It would be interesting to consider how these Baroque trumpet songs were adapted to nineteenth-century performance practice in general, and the slide trumpet in particular; and this is possible,

thanks to several duo-cadenzas written for "Let the Bright Seraphim," formerly in the possession of Thomas Harper Jr.[188] There are
nine cadenzas in two separate volumes of manuscript music by other
composers; eight in one and one in another. Each of these cadenzas
has been reproduced in Appendix A, by permission of the Royal
College of Music. The single cadenza is grouped with the previously
mentioned flourish by Harper Jr., written for Queen Victoria's Jubilee; the eight are numbered and each is identified with a certain soprano, with whom the aria was performed. It is unclear who wrote
them; the single cadenza is signed "T. H.," and underneath is the
following statement signed by an A. H. Follet [?]: "This is a copy of a
manuscript given to me by Mr. Thomas Harper in December
1894."[189] Presumably this single cadenza was written by Harper Jr.,
but the other eight could have been written by Harper Sr. An examination of the careers of these sopranos might solve the mystery.

The sopranos in question are Mrs. Salmon, Mrs. Dickens, Miss
Goodall, Clara Novello, Madam Grisi, Miss Paton, Miss Stephens,
Madam Carradore Allan, and Miss Birch. There is evidence that
Salmon and Dickens were performing professionally as early as
1806.[190] Miss Paton is said to have made her debut in 1822.[191] Carra-
dore Allan was performing as early as 1825, and died in 1865.[192]
Miss Stephens' performances are reviewed the *Harmonicon* in
1826.[193] The careers of Goodall, Grisi, and Novello came a bit later

---

[188]Thomas Harper Jr., "Trumpet Cadenza and Flourish," n. d., *Lcm*, MS 4078, f.
34; and "Cadenzas for Voice and Trumpet," n. d., *Lcm*, MS 4082, ff. 3–4v.

[189]Ibid., f. 34.

[190]Parke, *Musical Memoirs*, 2: 4.

[191]Cox, *Recollections*, 1: 68–69.

[192]Adam Carse, "The Choral Symphony in London," *Music and Letters* 32 (January
1951): 47; and Cox, *Recollections*, 1: 116.

[193]*Harmonicon* 4.37 (January 1826): 82; and 4.47 (November 1826): 219.

than the others, but they were in their primes before mid-century.[194] Because the careers of these sopranos flourished in the first half of the century, then, we must assume that Harper Sr. wrote the cadenzas, perhaps in collaboration with each of the sopranos.

In fact, some of the sopranos have an even more direct connection with Harper Sr. The *Harmonicon* reviewed provincial performances of "Let the Bright Seraphim" with Stephens and Harper in 1825 and 1826,[195] and Clara Novello appears with him in a famous drawing from an article about both performers in *Musical World* (Figure 41).[196] Harper, it seems, was sought after by many sopranos eager to perform with him. The same *Musical World* article says of Harper's popularity with the sopranos of the day, "Some two or three seasons ago, Mr. Harper announced a benefit concert, when he received upwards of a dozen offers from young ladies, to sing 'Let the bright Seraphim' to his trumpet accompaniment..."[197]

Some of these sopranos continued their "Seraphim" performances with Harper Jr. after the retirement of his father. There is a review of Harper Jr.'s performance of the work with Miss Birch in 1851,[198] and a notice of a performance by Clara Novello (with an unidentified trumpeter), at the Crystal Palace in 1859.[199] Presumably Harper Jr. used his father's cadenzas, particularly when performing with sopranos for whom the cadenzas originally were written.

---

[194]J. W. Davison, *Music during the Victorian Era from Mendelssohn to Wagner: being the Memoirs of J. W. Davison, Forty Years Music Critic of "The Times,"* comp. Henry Davison, (London: Wm. Reeves, 1912), 67, 87, 230–231.

[195]*Harmonicon* 3.34 (October 1825): 176; and 4.47 (November 1826): 219.

[196]"Orchestral Sketches: Clara Anastasia Novello; Thomas Harper," *Musical World* 2 (1836): ix–xi.

[197]Ibid., xi.

[198]"Sacred Harmonic Society," *The Times* (London), 12 March 1851, p. 8.

[199]Cox, *Recollections*, 2: 340.

" LET THE BRIGHT SERAPHIM."

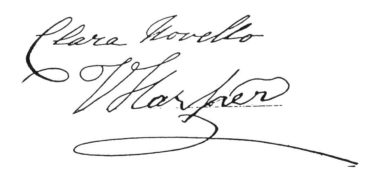

Figure 41: Thomas Harper Sr. and Clara Novello, from frontispiece of *Musical World* article (1836). By permission of the British Library.

The cadenza is invariably inserted into the aria at measure 52, on the first beat.[200] None of the cadenzas have text, but presumably each would have been sung to the syllable "trum-," with the penultimate cadenza note, either an eighth-note pickup or trilled note, sung to "-pets," and "blow" for the final cadence note on the third beat of measure 52. The cadenzas are idiomatic for the slide trumpet, with frequent use of the non-harmonic-series notes a' and b', and with a more chromatic version for performances with Miss Goodall, making use of a recurrent d♯". They show a great deal of virtuosity for both soprano and trumpeter.

These flashy cadenzas must have been popular with the audiences because the Harpers evidently used them time and again. But some critics were harsh, as can be seen in a review of an 1825 Yorkshire Festival performance with Harper and Stephens:

> "Let the Bright Seraphim," was sung by Miss Stephens, in her best style...—the trumpet, by Harper, more wonderful than ever. We are decidedly of opinion that this song is sung too quick. The slackening of the time when the trumpet answers to the words "their loud," and again at "uplifted," may be tolerated, but the starting off again at "Angel-trumpets blow," is quite ludicrous. The double cadence was a fine performance, but a gross absurdity.[201]

A review in *The Times* of an 1851 Sacred Harmonic Society performance of *Samson*, with Harper Jr. and Miss Birch, was even more scathing:

> Miss Birch sang all the *soprano* airs with great fluency and the best taste until "Let the bright seraphim," at the end of which she introduced a rambling and incoherent *cadenza a due*, with Mr. T. Harper's

---

[200]Or one measure before letter E in the Ode edition. See G. F. Handel, *Three Arias for Trumpet and Voice*, ed. James Ode (Nashville: The Brass Press, 1976).

[201]*Harmonicon* 3.34 (October 1825): 176.

trumpet, which was neither well executed nor in character with the music, and spoiled the effect of what was otherwise on both sides a dextrous piece of mechanical execution.[202]

Nineteenth-Century Trumpet Songs

The British Library contains at least three songs dating from the nineteenth century that were written for the slide trumpet.[203] One of these, *Thine For Ever*, by Henry Bishop, has long been known and accessible because it was arranged by Thomas Harper Jr. and listed under his name in *The Catalogue of Printed Music in the British Library to 1980*. The others have been rediscovered by means of digital search capabilities, which have only recently been made available through the release of the *Catalogue of Printed Music* on CD-ROM. *The Warrior's Triumph*, by Alfred Bennett (1805–1830),[204] and *The Trumpet on the Rhone*, by J. L. Hatton (1809–1886), are, like *Thine For Ever*, trumpet songs very much in the tradition of Purcell and Handel, but with a nineteenth-century aesthetic (Figure 42, p. 186, and Figure 43, p. 188). *Thine For Ever* and *The Trumpet on the Rhone* both have separate trumpet parts, in addition to piano/vocal scores. As mentioned, the former was arranged by Harper Jr., but the trumpet part of the latter was possibly written by the

---

[202]"Sacred Harmonic," 8.

[203]Alfred Bennett, *The Warrior's Triumph: Song with an Accompaniment for the Trumpet, Composed for and Sung by Sr. Sapio, to Whom it is Respectfully Dedicated by ALFRED BENNETT*, words by William Walter Tireman (London: S. Chappell, [1828]), *Lbl* h.1167.(3.); J. L. Hatton, *The Trumpet on the Rhone: Song, with Trumpet Obligato*, words by W. H. Bellamy (London: Addison, Hollier and Lucas [1860]), *Lbl* H.1492.b.2; and Sir Henry Rowley Bishop, *Thine For Ever: Arranged for Voice, Trumpet & Pianoforte by Thomas Harper* (London: Stanley Lucas, Weber and Co., [1873]), *Lbl* H.1428.b.(21.). *The Trumpet on the Rhone* also exists in a reprint, published in 1871 by B. Williams of London, *Lbl* H.210.b.(31.).

[204]A promising young composer and organist of New College, Oxford, whose career was cut short due to a fatal coach accident. See Brown and Stratton, "Bennett, Alfred William."

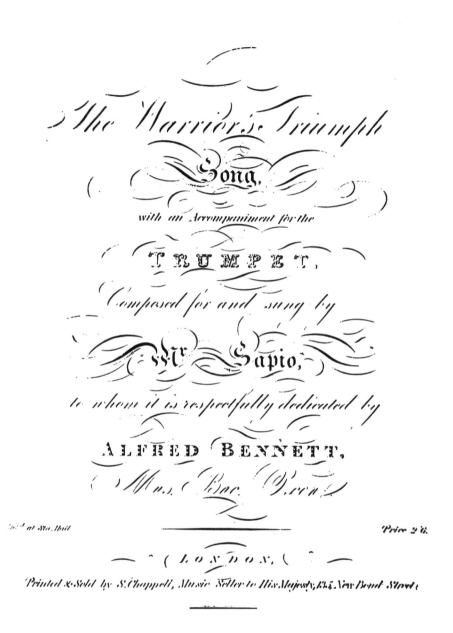

Figure 42: Alfred Bennett, *The Warrior's Triumph* (1828), title page.
By permission of the British Library. [h.1167.(3.)]

186

composer, as no arranger is listed. *The Warrior's Triumph* exists only in piano/vocal score, but with extensive trumpet cues.

The Warrior's Triumph, for tenor voice, was published in 1828, and the trumpet part was written for Thomas Harper Sr. On the first page of the music is the caption "The Warrior's Triumph, Accompanied on the Trumpet by Mr. Harper." Although the trumpet part is not as extensive as *Thine For Ever*, it is perhaps even more virtuosic. Examples of this virtuosity can be found in two passages: the introduction of the main theme by the solo trumpet (Example 33), and the ending duo-cadenza, where the trumpet plays parallel thirds above the tenor (Example 34, p. 189). This duo-cadenza, like the one in *Thine For Ever*, is reminiscent of the *Seraphim* cadenzas mentioned earlier, but more virtuosic. These passages from *The Warrior's Triumph* seem to confirm contemporary reports that Harper Sr. was the finest trumpeter of his time.

The Warrior's Triumph is in the key of D major and is in strophic form, with several introductory sections and a short coda following the cadenza. The non-harmonic-series notes included in the trumpet part are a' and b'. There are cues for a second trumpet

Example 33: Alfred Bennett, *The Warrior's Triumph*, trumpet part.

Figure 43: J. L. Hatton, *The Trumpet on the Rhone* (1860), title page.
By permission of the British Library. [H.210.b.(31.)]

Example 34: Bennett, *The Warrior's Triumph*, duo-cadenza.

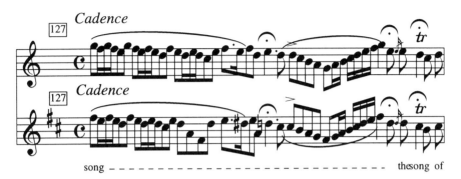

part for a single short passage (mm. 111–118); thus, it must be assumed that the second part is optional. If a second trumpeter is used, however, a slide trumpet is also appropriate for this part, since a note outside the harmonic series (c♯'') is included.

The Trumpet on the Rhone, also for high voice, has a trumpet part that might have been written for Harper Jr., but there is no dedication in the published score, as there was for *The Warrior's Triumph*. The music, however, was first published in 1860, during the reign of Harper Jr., and the trumpet part is definitely for slide trumpet, although there are fewer notes outside the harmonic series than in either of the other two trumpet songs. Included are two each of the a' and b', and one d'; the rest contains only harmonic series notes, although both natural and sharp versions of the eleventh partial are included. Neither is the trumpet part as virtuosic, as can be seen from the concluding section, which contains no duo-cadenza (Example 35, p. 190). The song is in D major, and is organized in two sections—an opening andante followed by an allegro.

Thine For Ever, also in D major, is another virtuosic trumpet song that was published in 1873, when Thomas Harper Jr., at age 57, was still very active professionally and involved in many solo performances throughout England and Scotland. It is very much a slide trumpet part: the only non-harmonic-series notes are a' and b', and these appear quite frequently (b' twenty-three times; a' ten times). While the title is not suggestive of traditional trumpet associations, the text does contain allusions to war and battle. The song is structured much like the trumpet songs of a century earlier: it be-

Example 35: J. L. Hatton, *The Trumpet on the Rhone*, trumpet part.

gins with a rather lengthy trumpet statement (of thirty-nine measures), followed by a soprano melody derived from the trumpet introduction, and ends following a lengthy and virtuosic duo-cadenza
(Example 36, p. 192).[205]

These three trumpet songs, along with the programs of Harper
Jr., are ample evidence that the slide trumpet was used as a solo
instrument, and not just for the continuing performances of Handel's
oratorios.[206] It is unlikely that these pieces are the only nineteenth-
century trumpet songs that still exist today. There are numerous
references, for example, to *Luther's Hymn*, for male vocalist and
trumpet obbligato, in various sources from the 1820s and 1830s.[207]
To date, this music has not been found nor has the work been
identified. *The Warrior's Triumph* and *The Trumpet on the Rhone*
were discovered only because the keyword "trumpet" was found in
the titles or subtitles in a digital catalogue search. The fact that some
known trumpet songs, such as *Luther's Hymn* and *Thine For Ever*,
lack the word "trumpet" on the title page leads one to suspect that
there are more of these works in the vast holdings of the British
Library, and indeed, in the holdings of other important libraries,
such as the Bodleian at Oxford, which lack the capability of CD-
ROM search.

We have seen from this discussion of literature that the slide
trumpet must have coexisted with other soprano brass instruments,
especially in the last half of the nineteenth century. But in order to
comprehend more fully the decline of the instrument, and conse-

---

[205] A compact disc recording of this piece has been made by soprano Deborah
Roberts, trumpeter Jonathan Impett, and pianist Paul Nicholson. Impett uses a
modern reproduction of a compression-spring slide trumpet by John Webb. It is a
copy of the T. Lloyd trumpet mentioned in Chapter Two. See The Clarion Ensemble, *Trumpet Collection*, Compact Disc CD-SAR 30, Amon Ra Records, 1987.

[206] For information on another slide trumpet solo, see Addendum, p. 214.

[207] See Parke, *Musical Memoirs*, 158; and Cox, *Recollections*, 1: 312.

quently the acceptance and eventual dominance of valved trumpets, we must consider documentary evidence from the final years of the slide trumpet.

Example 36: Bishop/Harper Jr., *Thine For Ever*, duo-cadenza.

Chapter Four: The Last Trumpet

Tutors, music, extant instruments, and writers such as Parke and Busby[1] reveal that the slide trumpet became the dominant English trumpet for all types of playing in the first half of the nineteenth century. A review of the literature shows that it began to be replaced first in the opera house, after the introduction of the cornet in the 1830s; but also that it coexisted in concert orchestras with the cornet, and later also with the valved trumpet, until the last decade of the century. Sybil Marcuse claims that even in the twentieth century the slide trumpet was occasionally used in the orchestra.[2] It has already been noted that the trumpet tutor by Hawkes and Son, which included a section devoted to the slide trumpet, was published in 1906 (see Figure 29 and related discussion in Chapter Two). As a solo instrument, too, it was used in the twentieth century as well, particularly in Handelian repertory. Victor Mahillon, writing in 1908, tells us that the slide trumpet "has remained in use even until our time. A few artists still use it in the performance of Haendel's oratorios."[3] These cases, however, were the exception. Morrow writes in 1894–5 that the slide trumpet "is rarely seen in an orchestra; about two players have an affection for it and like to use it in the old works, but it is looked upon with more curiosity than appreciation, and no composers trouble to write for it now."[4]

A survey of the new English music being performed in concert halls reveals that the slide trumpet could not have been used exclusively until the end of the century. We know, however, that much of the late-century orchestral repertory was older music playable on the slide trumpet. In order to understand fully the degree to which the slide trumpet was used during this time, therefore, we must turn to

---

[1]Parke, *Musical Memoirs;* and Busby, *Concert Room and Orchestra Anecdotes.*

[2]Marcuse, *Survey,* 807.

[3]Mahillon, *Dominant* 16 (September 1908): 19.

[4]Morrow, "Trumpet," 143.

other sources. Thomas Harper Jr. and Walter Morrow have been cited earlier, but they are not the only sources; many others offered their views on the state of the trumpet and trumpet playing, particularly in the last decade of the century. In this chapter, comments from contemporary sources will be considered in order to study the decline of the slide trumpet. Also, reasons will be explored for the century-long domination of the slide trumpet, and finally, some suggestions will be offered for modern use of the instrument.

THE SLIDE TRUMPET AT THE END OF THE CENTURY

The written sources are, at times, somewhat contradictory. We have seen that Harper Jr. complained about the growing use of the cornet in the orchestra in his 1875 tutor, and Morrow wrote that "one rarely hears the sound of a real trumpet" in 1894–5.[5] Henry Bassett, in an 1877 article in the *Proceedings of the Musical Association*, implied that the slide trumpet was in decline:

> By the invention of valves or pistons a so-called complete scale was obtained on all brass instruments, together with great facility of execution, and the old slide trumpet has been in consequence to a great extent superseded by trumpets and cornets with three valves: a fact which is, I believe, generally regretted by those who have given attention to the subject, as these instruments, besides being decidedly inferior in quality of tone, are most faulty in intonation.[6]

On the other hand, William Stone, in the 1889 first edition of George Grove's *A Dictionary of Music and Musicians*, wrote about the slide trumpet as if it were still the standard orchestral trumpet.[7] Much of the information for Stone's trumpet article, however, was obviously gleaned from Harper Jr.'s tutor, and may have been a bit behind the times. The Grove *Dictionary* was published over several

---

[5]Ibid., 139.

[6]Bassett, "Improvements," 140.

[7]Stone, "Trumpet," 180–183.

years, beginning in 1878, and while the fourth volume was published in 1889, the trumpet article could have been written much earlier.

The Slide Trumpet versus the Cornet

A major source for information about all types of late-century brass instruments and players is Algernon S. Rose's *Talks with Bandsmen.* Published in 1895, this book is a discourse on the various brass instruments in use at the time, and includes comments from other books, brass players, instrument makers, and others. Early in the book, Rose suggests that the slide trumpet is still widely used in orchestras, although not in the military:

> Of the chromatic trumpets, there is the orchestral instrument, furnished with a slide, with which I now have to deal, and there is the valve trumpet, that, owing to the greater facility with which it is played and learnt, has, in military bands, superseded the slide instrument.[8]

Unlike many contemporary writers, Rose does not defend the slide trumpet by criticizing the cornet. While admitting that the cornet has "less carrying power than the trumpet," he adds that "it is not my intention to decry the cornet.... It is a wonderful instrument and invaluable to boot."[9] After a page or more in support of the cornet, Rose offers a statement that gives one a good idea of the relative use of the slide trumpet versus the cornet in the 1890s: "Knowing how habitually the cornet is used in place of the trumpet, it seems indeed strange that composers still persist in writing for the almost obsolete instrument."[10]

Rose, however, also defends the slide trumpet; especially its sound quality:

---

[8]Algernon S. Rose, *Talks with Bandsmen: A Popular Handbook for Brass Instrumentalists* (London: William Rider and Son, [1895]), 92.

[9]Ibid., 93.

[10]Ibid., 187.

As with all natural instruments without valves, the tone of the slide trumpet is very brilliant and far-reaching. In its upper register, the tone of a single trumpet will penetrate through the combined force of an immense orchestra, as at the Handel Festivals at the Crystal Palace, or in several military bands massed together.[11]

He also writes extensively about the advantages and disadvantages of the instrument:

In orchestral music, slide trumpets were introduced to make possible a complete series of semi-tones. The slide of a brass instrument, which telescopes hermetically, so that no air can escape laterally, is a wonderful contrivance; and yet it has its detractors. The slide instrument is undoubtedly very difficult to play in a masterly manner, on account of the number of modulations contained in modern music, and especially marches; so there is a marked partiality for valve trumpets. Regarding the trumpet from a hyper critical standpoint, its detractors deny the perfection of the slide, by pointing out that, when the slide is extended, the air vibrates in two bores of different diameters, so that the purity of the tone is impaired. On the other hand, advocates of the slide contend that the heavy machinery of the valve-attachments must materially deaden the vibratile power in a piston instrument. On weighing, for instance, a cornet and its valves in their entirety, the scale shows that total to be 2 lbs 1 oz. Now, taking off the valve attachments and weighing the instrument separately, the result is 1 lb. 1 1/2 oz. This shows that the addition of three valves will weigh half as much as a whole instrument approximately the size of the trumpet."[12]

Later in his book, Rose offers an excellent discussion of the state of trumpet playing and trumpet players in the 1890s:

Although in our great orchestras "trumpet" players may be advertised in the programmes, in nine cases out of ten these musicians perform

[11]Ibid., 96.
[12]Ibid., 96–97.

their parts, in an excellent manner, not on the trumpet but on the cornet.... The fact is, musicians cannot get a living nowadays by playing the slide-trumpet. Cornet players, who have their instruments at their fingers' ends, find it easier to transpose trumpet parts than adapt their lip to a different *embouchure*, or their hands to another manner of manipulation. Thus one well-known trumpet-player usually transposes the first trumpet parts on to his cornet in a certain famous London orchestra, whilst another distinguished trumpeter, although he carries a valve trumpet with him to perhaps the most famous classical concerts there are in London, not infrequently uses— the cornet.... A delicious story to this effect is told about a well-known conductor who insisted on a trumpet being used instead of the cornet in the performance of a certain oratorio. Unfortunately, just before the most important passage for the trumpet occurred, the slide of the instrument stuck. There was, therefore, no alternative but to use the cornet, which was, of course, by the player's side. "Ah!" said the conductor, after the performance, "see how *much* better the real trumpet-tone sounds!" When the conductor insists upon the use of the trumpet by a player not in practice with it, the notes are generally spluttered. This may be regarded by some conductors with regret, inasmuch as the conical bore of a cornet produces a different tone-complexion to that of the cylindrical trumpet. At the same time a good cornet-player will frequently interpret the composer's intentions more intelligibly than will an indifferently played, cracky, and spluttering trumpet, which is harder to blow. Besides, why should pious writers on instrumentation simulate horror at the thought of replacing an inferior trumpet, with valves—which, by-the-bye, is never the same as a slide trumpet—by a *good* cornet in the orchestra?... On account of its form, the cornet truly lacks the excessive penetration and ring of the trumpet, and by reason of this shrillness, the three-valved trumpet crooked in E♭ or F, is lauded as a "magnificent instrument."[13]

Rose is not the only late-century writer to advocate the use of the cornet. The composer Frederick Corder (1852–1932) wrote an orchestration treatise in 1894; in it he reveals his low opinion of the

---

[13]Ibid., 179–180.

trumpet, and, although he agrees that the cornet tone is "less bright and piercing," he does not consider that problematic. He thinks "the vaunted brilliancy of the trumpet its most serious drawback, because it simply kills all the other instruments."[14] He further postulates his ideas about the trumpet:

> I desire here to record my emphatic opinion that the Trumpet in the orchestra is an almost unmitigated nuisance. In the small orchestra of Haydn and Mozart it obliterates everything else, and dare only be used here and there in the padding; in the modern orchestra it is useless because of its limited scale, while in the music of Bach and Handel it is a source of constant vexation of spirit.[15]

Corder continues by cautioning composers that they can write melodies for the trumpet, but it is "rather dangerous," and "most musical hearers are sorely offended at hearing on this instrument a melody which departs very markedly from the natural scale."[16] Corder concludes his discussion with a statement in support of the cornet:

> The Germans use chiefly the Valve trumpet in F; we in England write for the slide trumpet "crooked" in F, E, E♭, D, C or B♭—and very seldom get it. The student (except when writing examination papers) will do far better to write for the instrument upon which his music will probably be played, and this is the Cornet.[17]

However, Corder's concert overture *Prospero*, premiered at the Crystal Palace in 1885, was written for two "chromatic" trumpets in E; and although they are given little to do, they are obviously meant to be valved trumpets.[18]

---

[14]Frederick Corder, *The Orchestra and How to Write for It* (London: J. Curwen and Sons, 1894), 57.

[15]Ibid., 55.

[16]Ibid., 56.

[17]Ibid., 56–57.

[18]Frederick Corder, *Prospero: Concert Overture for full Orchestra* (London: Novello, Ewer and Co., [1888]).

Most writers, though, consistently argue against the use of the cornet in lieu of the slide trumpet. Ebenezer Prout's comments are typical:

> The tone of the cornet is absolutely devoid of the nobility of the trumpet, and, unless in the hands of a very good musician, readily becomes vulgar. It is, however, so much easier to play than the trumpet, that parts written for the latter instrument are very often performed on the cornet. In some cases, especially in the provincial orchestras, this may be a necessity, as it is not always possible to find trumpet players; but it is none the less a degradation of the music.[19]

In another source, Prout again lashes out against the cornet:

> The cornet is far easier to play than the trumpet, which is doubtless one reason why it so frequently replaces the latter instrument. Its tone is, however, much more coarse and vulgar; and it is far more fit for performance of dance-music, or of solos in operatic selections at promenade concerts than for classical compositions. Rapid passages can be executed upon it with ease; but in dignified and serious music it is entirely out of place.[20]

Prout's instrument of choice is the slide trumpet, and in 1898 he still prefers it to the cornet. Although he admits that it is "unfortunately falling into disuse," he claims that the slide trumpet is superior "as regards purity of intonation and quality of tone." Even with the limitations of its scale, Prout believes that "the instrument is most valuable. The quality of the tone is in no way affected by the slide, as it is by valves, while perfect intonation is possible for nearly every note...."[21]

The successors of Harper Jr. were Morrow and John Solomon (1856–1953), both of whom studied slide trumpet with Harper at the Royal Academy of Music. According to Baines and Tarr, Morrow

---

[19]Prout, *Orchestra*, 1: 286.

[20]Prout, *Instrumentation*, 105.

[21]Prout, *Orchestra*, 1: 203.

began his playing career in the early 1870s as a slide trumpet and
cornet player,[22] and Baines writes that Solomon "began playing principal trumpet (on the cornet, with occasional use of the slide trumpet) in the provinces in 1873 and in London (at St. James Hall) in
1876."[23] Baines adds that the study of the slide trumpet under Harper at the Royal Academy was "compulsory," but that Solomon,
"like the other pupils, regularly used the cornet on outside engagements of every kind."[24]

The Slide Trumpet, the Cornet, and the Valved Trumpet in F

Morrow joined the trumpet/cornet debate, but he advocated the
valved trumpet in F (Figure 44) as a replacement for the slide trumpet. His 1894 presentation to the Musical Association on this very
topic engendered many comments from those present in a general
discussion following the reading of his paper.[25] According to David
James Blaikley:

> It is regrettable that the trumpet is not more popular, but it is ex-
> ceedingly difficult to get men to take to it and keep to it. Bandsmen
> say it is all very well learning it, but later on they will be obliged to
> play the cornet if they consider pounds, shillings and pence, and so
> long as conductors will accept the cornet for the trumpet it will be
> used. The matter, I believe, is entirely in the hands of conductors.[26]

Dr. Charles Maclean rose to endorse Morrow's efforts in support
of the valved trumpet over the cornet, and offered the following explanation for the continued use of the cornet in the orchestra:

---

[22]*New Grove*, s. v. "Morrow," by Anthony Baines and Edward H. Tarr.

[23]*New Grove*, s. v. "Solomon, John," by Anthony Baines.

[24]Ibid.

[25]See Morrow, "Trumpet," 145–147.

[26]Ibid., 145.

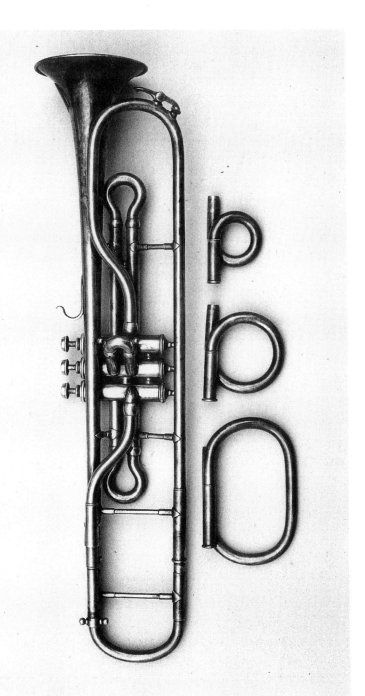

Figure 44: Mahillon, valved trumpet in F (ca. 1880). Courtesy of John Webb.

The cardinal point in the paper which has been read is the question of valve trumpet *versus* cornet-à-pistons in the English orchestras. The causes which have impeded the introduction of the former in this country are, I believe, these. In the first place, the slide trumpet (peculiar to England) took and occupied the ground in advance...the scale was still very defective. The slide trumpet was also, like the trombone, deficient in *legato*. Being thus a comparative failure the slide trumpet fell out of use, and the circumstance generally made trumpets unpopular, and confirmed the use of the cornet-à-pistons in English orchestras. The second cause has been that, as stated in the lecture, the cornet-à-pistons is an easy instrument to play. The third cause has been that the specimens here available of the valve trumpet have been mostly military band instruments in which the mouthpiece and bore have departed from the true trumpet character; however, as correct orchestral trumpets are now readily procurable, this consideration ought not to operate.

...speaking generally, the use of the valve trumpet is now universal on the Continent, with a G standard for France and an F standard for other countries. It is in England alone that this instrument is in the position of asking leave to come in. The present state of the case is, as remarked by the lecturer—namely, that our conductors have only to insist upon the trumpet being used and it would be used. I rose mainly because I wished to point out that the lecturer is a practical pioneer in what is really an important matter, and that he deserves much support.[27]

Not all writers, however, followed Morrow's lead and supported the valved trumpet in F as the necessary replacement for the slide trumpet. Rose, as we have seen, was an advocate of the cornet, and was not a fan of the valved trumpet. Rose compares the slide and valved trumpet in the following statement, although he is incorrect in his placement of this slide trumpet during the late Baroque:

The regrettable "passing away" of the thrilling *slide* trumpet—an instrument considered essential in the palmy days of Handel and Bach—invests the valve trumpet, perhaps, with unusual interest. It is, of course, easier to play and to write for than the slide trumpet.

---

[27]Ibid., 146–147.

Nevertheless, it scarcely possesses the distinctive tone of the slide. Being a cylindrical instrument, it may truly infuse a different tone-colour into a Brass Band of saxhorns. Yet it is an usurper. No more need therefore be said of it than of that worse abomination—the valved trombone.[28]

In the mid-1890s, therefore, there is no doubt that the slide trumpet was no longer in general use, although there were still some who stubbornly resisted the change. Written sources, such as Morrow's paper and others, consistently imply, though, that the valved trumpet was not the instrument that players turned to when the slide trumpet was deemed inadequate. The cornet was used most often for these parts until Morrow began to encourage use of the valved trumpet in F; according to Baines and Tarr, the valved trumpet "was hardly known in England" when Morrow became London's principal trumpeter. They also suggest that this trend away from the combined use of the slide trumpet and cornet toward the F trumpet did not last long. They write that the use of the valved trumpet in F lasted "roughly from 1898 to 1905, by which time the modern B♭ trumpet had arrived in England."[29]

The Introduction of the B♭ Trumpet

Morrow resisted not only the use of the cornet in the orchestra, but also the new, short B♭ trumpet. His complaint about this instrument was that it had the same length of tubing as the B♭ cornet, and although more cylindrical than the cornet, it did not retain the classic sound of the long trumpet; according to Morrow, only the F valved trumpet fulfilled this requirement. The F trumpet, though, like the slide trumpet, had its difficulties, especially in the upper register. John Solomon, consulted in 1935, remembered the slide trumpet as being "not well adapted for the production of the highest

---

[28]Rose, *Talks with Bandsmen*, 219–220.

[29]*New Grove*, s. v. "Morrow," by Baines and Tarr.

notes."[30] Indeed, Solomon was the player who advocated, and eventually brought about the general acceptance of, the B♭ trumpet. A younger contemporary of Morrow, he eventually succeeded the older man as principal London trumpeter upon the latter's retirement around 1902,[31] and was one of the founding members of the London Symphony Orchestra several years later.[32] According to Baines, Solomon "eventually persuaded him [Morrow] to use it [the B♭ trumpet] and thereby avoid most of the missed notes which not infrequently marred Morrow's performances on the F."[33]

The B♭ trumpet, often called the "trumpetina" in England during this time, was introduced to that country in the late 1880s. It had been widely adopted first in Germany in the 1870s, but was not used in England with any regularity until the first decade of the twentieth century. The general acceptance of the B♭ trumpet there was encouraged not only by Solomon, but also by Ernest Hall (1890–1984), who was a student of Morrow and Solomon, and a teacher of many of today's leading British trumpeters.[34] One of his students, Steele-Perkins, relates the following story: Hall "played only B♭ trumpet as do *all* leading British orchestral players still.... [Hall] was told by Solomon to 'throw away' his 'F' when he studied with him prior to joining the LSO in 1912."[35]

Morrow, however, did not accept the short trumpet; he continued to consider it a disguised cornet:

[30]W. F. H. Blandford, "The Bach Trumpet," *Monthly Musical Record* 65 (1935): 97.

[31]Birkemeier, "F Trumpet," 40.

[32]*Grove's Dictionary of Music and Musicians*, 5th ed., s. v. "Solomon, John," by Anthony Baines.

[33]*Grove's Dictionary*, 5th ed., s. v. "Morrow, Walter," by Anthony Baines.

[34]Tarr, *The Trumpet*, 170–171.

[35]Steele-Perkins, letter to the author, 13 February 1994.

Feeling some qualms of conscience that the cornet does not look well in a symphony orchestra, or in the performance of an oratorio, they have adopted what is called a "trumpetina"—a sweet name. This is an instrument of the exact dimensions of a cornet—that is to say, a tube fifty-four inches long; but instead of having four bends, it has only two, and thus has something of the appearance of the trumpet, but is in reality only a cornet. It is excused by saying that it has a *trumpet bore*, but even this cannot make a short tube give a tone equal to the longer.... It is a veritable jackdaw in peacock's feathers. A deception. Do not use it or countenance it. The cornet is an honest instrument, the other is not. Get an F valve trumpet and a slide trumpet, and practise them.[36]

Morrow was still not satisfied with the sound of the short B♭ trumpet when teaching at the Royal College of Music in the first two decades of the twentieth century, and continued to encourage the use of the long F trumpet. In order to provide study material for his students, Morrow revised and adapted tutors for the F trumpet. In his 1907 edition of *Julius Kosleck's School for the Trumpet*, Morrow writes:

It is hoped that this book will encourage the study of the real Trumpet, as distinct from the Cornet à pistons, which frequently replaces the Trumpet; but as regards beauty of tone, inadequately. Small Trumpets in B♭ are also frequently used. These however are no better, if so good as the Cornet in tone; but as they are made to *look* long, they are often mistaken for the real thing.

A student will find the trumpet in F a very interesting instrument; and once he gains proficiency will discard the Trumpets in B♭.[37]

Even Morrow, however, finally conceded the demise of the long F trumpet in the 1910s, and stopped requiring his students at the

---

[36]Morrow, "Trumpet," 140.

[37]Walter Morrow, ed., *Julius Kosleck's School for the Trumpet: Revised and Adapted to the Study of the Trumpet-à-Pistons in F as Used in the Orchestras of England and America* (London: Breitkopf & Härtel, 1907), iv.

Royal College to learn it. According to Richard Birkemeier, one of the main influences in this decision was Morrow's student Ernest Hall, although Hall himself is reported to have played the F trumpet in the orchestra occasionally, and as late as 1926.[38] Birkemeier has also found that many of the players who switched from F to B♭ trumpet in the first decade of the twentieth century, actually had their F trumpets cut down to B♭. It is interesting that this situation parallels that of one hundred years before; in that earlier age of change players cut down their long C and D natural trumpets to F, and added slides.

REASONS FOR SLIDE TRUMPET PRIMACY IN ENGLAND

Why did the slide trumpet dominate English trumpet playing in the nineteenth century? Why did it take so long for the valved trumpet finally to gain general acceptance, when it had done so in Germany more than fifty years earlier? There are several reasons for this, but one of the most important considerations must be the traditionally conservative nature of the British. Christopher Monk characterizes this conservatism as a "lingering pride in dying traditions," and writes that the "slide trumpet preserved the best qualities of the natural trumpet in a time of transition, reducing its defects to a minimum."[39] The British, at least in the nineteenth century, were not quick to embrace the newest trends in this transitional time in music.

Most of nineteenth-century Europe was basking in the prosperity of the industrial revolution, but Britain was the most important and wealthy of the industrial powers. In much of Europe, however, and especially in England, the birthplace of the revolution, the strains of development were beginning to show: the growth of London

---

[38]Birkemeier, "F Trumpet," 43–45.

[39]Christopher W. Monk, "The Older Brass Instruments: Cornett, Trombone, and Trumpet," *Musical Instruments Through the Ages,* 2nd ed., ed. Anthony Baines (New York: Walker and Co., 1976), 262–263.

alone, between 1800 and 1850, was almost overwhelming. "Conscious of being propelled into the future, Europe began to take a long and wistful look at the past and embarked on a series of revivals."[40] In Britain, architects designed the neo-Gothic Parliament Building, which was built at mid-century, and artists such as Constable painted nature scenes of landscapes and quaint villages. Likewise, British composers were conservative in their musical language, retaining the simpler styles of past generations. British composers were also conservative in their demands on the musicians; we have already seen that British trumpet parts are not nearly as formidable as contemporary continental trumpet music.

Many writers place much of the blame for this conservatism on Handel and his ascendancy to the musical throne of Britain.[41] Nicholas Temperley sums up the arguments of these writers, "who give the impression that English composers did nothing but mimic Handel until Mendelssohn's appearance, and that they then did nothing but mimic Mendelssohn."[42] Handel was certainly a towering figure that had much musical influence on his society—and on future generations, but Temperley thinks that Handel's influence has been greatly exaggerated; he argues that, except in oratorio, the styles of Haydn and Mozart were much more influential.[43]

Whether because of tradition, a longing for simpler times, or the influence of Handel and/or Mozart, a conservative trend was reflected in English composers and in the music they wrote. It is interesting to note that in the same years that certain continental composers were considering new sounds and roles for soprano brass

---

[40]Bruce Cole and Adelheid M. Gealt, *Art of the Western World: from Ancient Greece to Post-Modernism* (Summit Books: New York, 1989), 231.

[41]See for example J. A. Fuller Maitland, *English Music in the XIXth Century* (London: G. Richards, 1902); and Ernest Walker, *A History of Music in England*, 2nd. ed. (London: Oxford University Press, 1931).

[42]Nicholas Temperley, "Handel's Influence on English Music," *The Monthly Musical Record* 90 (1960): 164.

[43]Ibid., 168–174.

instruments, English composers were for the most part content to
write trumpet parts that were little changed from previous generations. Fourteen short years before Berlioz' *Symphonie fantastique*,
with its parts for *cornet-à-pistons*, John Marsh's orchestration treatise
was published; and although parts of this treatise have been quoted
above, it would be beneficial to repeat one telling passage:

> In orchestra music I cannot help thinking the present natural com-
> pass [of the natural trumpet] sufficient. For the trumpet and kettle-
> drums form, as it were, a *corps de reserve*, to augment the band and
> produce a grand fortissimo by way of contrast now and then; and
> therefore it is enough, if they are brought into action at those times,
> when the original key, or that next related to it is preserved, there
> being plenty of instruments without them for the purpose of modu-
> lating into others.[44]

Another result of this conservatism was the strict and rigid
class structure of Victorian society. Although cornets eventually replaced the slide trumpet in English orchestras after the retirement of
Harper Jr., we have seen that there was much resistance to the former instrument. Its sound quality was partly to blame, but social
reasons also came into play. The cornet was first associated with
dance bands and brass bands; both of these types of ensembles were
looked down upon by the higher classes as being pastimes of the
working classes. Thus the sound of the cornet was associated with
the audience and given the labels "vulgar," "unrefined," "coarse,"
and "crude." This attitude can be seen in nineteenth-century English tutors; cornet instruction was at a very basic level compared
with the trumpet. It seems that the cornet player's understanding of
music was assumed to be elementary, almost to the point of musical
illiteracy. This prejudice can also be seen in instrument quality. A
catalogue of 1887 indicates that Higham of Manchester made brass
instruments in three different classes: 2nd class; 1st class; and
"Superior Class." All cornets, and even a three-valved trumpet in F,

were available in all three classes. The slide trumpet with a full set of crooks, however (listed as "Trumpet Chromatic"), was made only in first-class (£6. 6s.) and superior-class (£8. 8s.) versions.[45] No doubt these negative stereotypes accompanied the cornet when it began to be used in orchestras, resulting in the overwhelming outcry against it.

The strict moral code of Victorian society also kept much of the more progressive music out of London. This was a society that shunned the newest continental trends and mistrusted foreigners with questionable moral character, such as Liszt and Wagner. Unfortunately, foreigners such as Liszt and Wagner were the very ones who were composing the new music that required completely chromatic trumpets. According to Joel Sachs:

> London's response to Liszt, Berlioz, Chopin and Schumann was fraught with mistrust of the continental avant garde. Romanticism and such innovations as chromatic harmony and programme music were regarded as symptoms of degeneracy. As a result, the Romantic movement passed London by.[46]

Resistance to change by the trumpeters themselves was no doubt partly the reason for the domination of the slide trumpet. Tarr gives this explanation for the reluctance to change to valved trumpets:

> While the Baroque trumpeter had needed to co-ordinate only lips and tongue, trumpeters with the new valved instrument had to reconcile three elements one with another: lips, tongue and fingers. One can easily imagine that because of the convenience and retention of tradition, and probably also because of the defects of the first valved in-

---

[45] *Joseph Higham, Wholesale Brass Musical Instrument Manufacturer, to the Trade and for Export, to the Army, Navy, Volunteers, &c.,* illustrated catalogue (Strangeways, Manchester: January 1887).

[46] J. Sachs, "Professionalization of Music," 231.

struments, there was much opposition to the new instrument, especially from the older players.[47]

Another reason given by Tarr for the primacy of the slide trumpet is the strong influence of the Harpers.[48] It is amazing that this father and son dominated English trumpet playing for almost three-quarters of the century. The slide trumpet was, of course, favored by both, but commercial interests must also be considered. Both made minor improvements to the instrument and both had business arrangements with instrument makers for the manufacture of slide trumpets bearing their names. As late as 1895, ten years after his retirement and only three years before his death, Harper Jr. was still peddling his trumpet. In a letter to an unknown addressee who evidently asked him to evaluate a particular trumpet, Harper replied:

> I know nothing of the Orchestral Trumpet you mention but most probably it is a valve instrument & consequently not equal to the Slide Trumpet. I [played?] for many years, *"Harper's Improved" Slide Trumpet* manufactured by Kohler & Son Victoria St Westminster, & should you wish to learn a similar one I will guarantee you get a first class Trumpet [three words indecipherable]. The slide is far superior to the valve.[49]

Of course, the sound of the slide trumpet is the reason given time and again in contemporary sources for its primacy. Both Harpers, Morrow, critics, composers, and authors of orchestration treatises all decried the sound of the cornet, and even the valved trumpet in F, in comparison with the pure, brilliant sound of the slide trumpet. Many explanations were offered; Dauverné's is typical:

> The [valved trumpet] has only the advantage of being easier and faster in rapid passages, be they diatonic or chromatic; but the exces-

---

[47]Tarr, *The Trumpet,* 157–58.

[48]Ibid., 151–152.

[49]Thomas Harper Jr. to unknown addressee, 2 April 1895, Lcm, MS 4071, p. 2.

sively rapid oscillation of the pistons produces a confusion of sounds. The breaking up of the continuity of the inner wall of the resonant tube weakens the sound and at the same time makes the piston trumpet lose that clear and silvery sound which is possessed by all natural and slide trumpets to various degrees.[50]

Whether it was due to a real deterioration of sound quality caused by the valves, or the connection with lower-class music, the cornet, and, by association the valved trumpet, was shunned in England while the slide trumpet was accepted.

MODERN USES FOR THE SLIDE TRUMPET

Does the slide trumpet have a future? Peter Barton thinks not: "In these revivalist days, it seems unlikely that the slide trumpet will appear with any frequency in the interests of so-called 'authentic performances,' unless perhaps in a recreation of the 'Vauxhall Gardens' or similar concerts."[51] Indeed, if there is any interest in reviving pleasure garden music or sentimental Victorian parlor songs, then there is solo literature available for the slide trumpet. Three such pieces are described in this book. And, as previously mentioned, more of these works with slide trumpet obbligato probably remain to be found.

In addition, there is a controversial trend in historical performance for which the slide trumpet might offer some solution. For years, period orchestras have performed and recorded eighteenth-century music either on period instruments or copies thereof. In most cases copies of old natural trumpets have included finger holes to correct the tuning of difficult harmonics and make the instruments easier to play. This practice is, of course, anachronistic; not "authentic" at all. The only trumpet with such holes known to exist

---

[50]Dauverné, *Méthode*, 243 (page reference is to translation).

[51]Barton, "Woodham-Rodenbostel," 119.

before the nineteenth century was the 1787 "Harmonic Trumpet" of William Shaw—probably the only instrument of its kind and used very little, if at all.

Of course, use of the slide trumpet for seventeenth- and eighteenth-century music would also be anachronistic (with the exception of the limited flat trumpet repertory), but, in a sense, less so than trumpets with finger holes. At least there is a strong tradition of playing Baroque music on the slide trumpet throughout the nineteenth century. And although this author hesitates to suggest the replacement of one anachronism with another, the slide trumpet would certainly satisfy the desires of period conductors and record producers for correct intonation as well or better than natural trumpets with finger holes. Moreover, recreations of late-eighteenth- and nineteenth-century London performances of Beethoven, Mozart, Haydn, or Mendelssohn would be well-served by using slide trumpets. In June of 1993, the Hanover Band recreated an 1841 Leipzig Gewandhaus concert in a London performance, using nineteenth-century performance practices and authentic instruments, or modern reproductions.[52] In similar fashion, early-nineteenth-century Philharmonic Society concerts could be recreated, with trumpeters playing slide trumpets. Finally, slide trumpets clearly would be appropriate for authentic performances of English orchestral music up to and including some of the music of Bennett, Sullivan, Parry, and Stanford.

THE LAST TRUMPET

The slide trumpet was the last of the trumpets with the natural trumpet sound. The addition of valves and subsequent shortening of the tubing considerably changed the classic trumpet timbre. The adoption of shorter, valved trumpets was inevitable, though, because of the demands of the music. The slide trumpet could no longer

---

[52]The Hanover Band at Queen Elizabeth Hall, London, 10 June 1993. Recreation of Leipzig Gewandhaus concert of 6 December 1841, consisting of works by Schumann, Mendelssohn, Mozart, and Liszt.

compete in an increasingly chromatic musical environment. Also, both the slide trumpet and the valved trumpet in F were difficult instruments to play in the upper register, and the new music at the turn of the twentieth century was again challenging this register. W. F. H. Blandford sums up the dilemma for the trumpeter:

> That fault [wrong notes], to which ancient audiences must have been more or less inured, must today be avoided at all hazards: fifty people can tell whether a trumpet is playing the wrong notes for one who knows that the tone is not classically correct.[53]

As more and more cornets and short trumpets were used, audiences, and even the players themselves, gradually lost the sound of the old trumpet, and resistance to the newer instruments faded. Christopher Monk has succinctly summarized the legacy of the slide trumpet: "Only when the tone and style of the natural trumpet were finally abandoned, the slide trumpet lost its place.... One can best regard it as the last of the old instruments rather than the first of the new."[54]

---

[53]Blandford, "Bach Trumpet," 100.

[54]Monk, "Older Brass Instruments," 262.

Addendum

Just before going to press, this author obtained copies of two significant sources previously unknown to him: a tutor and a solo for slide trumpet. The first of these is a twenty-four page tutor for slide trumpet by John Norton (see p. 171 and Appendix B). It was published in London, where Norton was Professor of Trumpet at the Royal Academy of Music, before his move to the United States in 1827; thus it predates the tutor of Harper Sr., first published in 1835. In comparison with Harper's tutor, Norton's provides more basic musical instruction, but offers no advice on holding position, slide movement, or articulation. Moreover, his scale for slide trumpet allows only for half-tone shifts from harmonic-series notes. Study material includes two pages of basic trumpet "Lessons," twelve progressive duets, and four difficult studies, "written expressly for the purpose of making the pupil familiar with the use of the slide" ("Studio No. 4" is included in the tutor of Harper Jr.; see *School for the Trumpet*, p. 40, Exercise 86). A portrait of Norton appears on the last page. See John T. Norton, *Preceptor for the Trumpet, in which the Various Scales of that Instrument together with the use of the Chromatic Slide are fully explained* (London: T. Percival, [before 1827]).

J. H. Walch composed an extensive solo work for slide trumpet and military band which was published in Leipzig. The composition consists of an adagio introduction, a theme and six variations ("Allegretto con Variazione"), another theme with five variations ("Andantino con Variazione"), a "Tempo di Polacca," and a final allegro in duple meter. The solo D♭ trumpet part, labeled *Tromba obligato in Des,* begins in the written key of C and concludes in the written key of G. A performance of the entire work would require about fifteen minutes. This is a virtuoso work for slide trumpet with all of the customary non-series notes: b' and a' both appear in excess of 100 times; other non-harmonics, such as d♯", c♯", f♯', d♯', and b, are used as well. No date appears on the title page, but the presence of a part for serpent suggests the work was composed at or before mid-century. The allegretto theme and its first, second, and fourth variations were included as etude material in Harper Jr.'s *School for the Trumpet* (p. 31, Exercise No. 74). See J. H. Walch, *Potpourri pour Musique militaire pour Trompette obligeé, Clarinette en Es, 3 Clarinettes en B, 2 Cors, Flûte, 2 Bassons, et Serpent, 2 Trompettes, 2 Trombones, et Tambour grand, composeé par J. H. Walch* (Leipzig: Bureau de Musique de C. F. Peters, n.d.).

Appendix A: Nine "Seraphim" Cadenzas

Cadenza   "Let the bright Seraphim"

T. H.

No 1   *As Sung by Mrs Salmon and Mrs Dickens*

* This note was written as an A in the manuscript.

No 2   *As Sung by Miss Goodall*

* Fermata omitted in manuscript.

No 3   As Sung by Miss Paton

No 4   As Sung by Miss Stephens

No 5   As Sung by Madam Caradore Allan

No 6   As Sung by Miss Birch

* In the manuscript, the quarter rest is positioned at the beginning of this measure in the voice staff.

No 7   As Sung by Miss Clara Novello

No 8   As Sung by Madam Grisi

Appendix B: A Chronological Checklist of British Trumpeters During the Time of the Slide Trumpet (ca. 1780–1900)

SOURCES

The following sources have been used to prepare this checklist. The abbreviations identify specific sources used for information on each trumpeter. See bibliography for complete references.

BaT   Baines and Tarr, "John Solomon," *New Grove.*

Bir   Birkemeier, "The F Trumpet…," *Brass Bulletin.*

BrS   Brown and Stratton, *British Musical Biography…*

Bur   Burney, *An Account of the Musical Performances…*

CaJ   Carse, *The Life of Jullien…*

CaO   Carse, *The Orchestra from Beethoven…*

Cox   Cox, *Musical Recollections…*

Cud   Cudworth, "The Vauxhall Lists," *Galpin Society Journal.*

Fos   Foster, *History of the Philharmonic Society…*

Ha1   *Harmonicon* 1: 10 (October 1823).

Ha3   *Harmonicon* 3: 34 (October 1825).

Ha4   *Harmonicon* 4: 47 (November 1826).

Har   Harper Jr., Engagement Book.

Hig   Highfill, Burnim, and Langhans, *A Biographical Dictionary…*

Hoo   Hoover, "A Trumpet Battle…," *Musical Quarterly.*

Kel   Kelly, *Reminiscences…*

Lan   Langwill, *An Index of Musical Wind-Instrument Makers*, 5th ed.

McG   Alexander McGrattan, information supplied through personal cor-
        respondence.

MT   *Musical Times* 3: 66 (1 November 1849): 230.

Par   Parke, *Musical Memoirs...*

RSM   Matthews, compiler, *The Royal Society of Musicians...*

Sor   Sorenson, "Thomas Harper, Sr...."

SoW   Sorenson and Webb, "The Harpers...," *Galpin Society Journal.*

St-P   Crispian Steele-Perkins, information provided through personal
        correspondence.

Tar   Tarr, *The Trumpet.*

Tim   *The Times* of London.

Wat   Waterhouse, *The New Langwill Index.*

BRITISH TRUMPETERS FROM 1780 TO 1900

James Sarjant (d. 1798)   trumpet

Opera; Covent Garden oratorios; Ancient Music concerts; soloist 1784
    Handel Commemoration and subsequent Handel memorial concerts;
    Vauxhall concerts as first trumpeter and soloist; numerous benefits;
    played at ceremony awarding doctorate to Haydn at Oxford; played
    chromatic trumpet solos at Vauxhall 1790–91; first known notice is
    1774 performance of trumpet concerto at Haymarket. Shown in Thomas
    Rowlandson drawing of Vauxhall orchestra (versions in Yale Center for
    British Art and Victoria and Albert Museum; 1785 engraving of same
    reproduced in *Hig*, vol. 3). Joined RSM in 1769.   *RSM, Hig, Par, Cud*

Christian Nicolai (ca. 1726–99)   trumpet
Covent Garden band; Vauxhall Gardens; St. Paul's benefit concerts in
    1789–90; Handel concerts from 1784–1790. Joined RSM in 1762.
                                                              RSM, Hig

William Jenkins (before 1740–ca. 1799) trumpet

Trumpeter in the King's Musicke ca. 1750; member of Drury Lane band in 1760s and 1770s; Handel Memorial concerts from 1784 to 1790; member of city waits; last known notice is 1789 St. Paul's benefit concert. Nicknamed "Fat Jenkins." Joined RSM in 1755. *RSM, Hig, Par*

William Jones (fl. 1760s–90s) trumpet

Drury Lane band from late 1780s; possibly Covent Garden band from late 1760s; performed in Handel concerts from 1784–90. Joined RSM in 1770. *RSM, Hig*

Edward Marley (before 1750–ca. 1796) trumpet

Possibly member of the King's Musicke as early as 1759; Handel concerts from 1784–90; St. Paul's benefit concerts in 1785. Joined RSM in 1771. *RSM, Hig*

Thomas Attwood (1737–after 1817) trumpet, horn, and viola

Opera; Ancient Music concerts; many benefits; trumpet section of 1784 Handel Commemoration and subsequent Handel concerts through 1790; His Majesty's Band of Musicians. Is reported to have played billiards with young Mozart during latter's visit to London. Joined RSM in 1782. *RSM, Hig, Bur, St-P*

Thomas Hill (ca. 1747–before March 1799) trumpet and horn

Probably member of theatre band in York and performed horn concerto there at benefit concert in 1782; performed in Handel concerts 1784–90; played trumpet in benefits at St. Paul's in early 1790s. Joined RSM in 1785. *RSM, Hig*

Robert Green (b. ca. 1758) viola, trumpet, and violin

Member Drury Lane band playing viola and trumpet in late 1770s and early 1780s. Possibly featured in engraving by Van Assen (published 1804 by J. Parry) of two itinerant musicians. Joined RSM in 1780. *RSM, Hig*

Mr. Willman of Limerick (fl. late-18th century)   trumpet

Son of immigrant German military bandmaster; lived in Limerick, Ireland; brother of Willman, principal clarinet at King's Theatre; according to Michael Kelly, "the finest trumpet player I ever heard in any country," and "his execution on the instrument almost baffled belief...." *BrS, Kel*

William Napier of Edinburgh (fl. 1790s)   trumpet

Perhaps most important trumpeter in Edinburgh in late-18th century. A William Napier listed as "trumpet maker to the Board of Ordnance [of British Army]" in 1800 by Waterhouse; possibly same person? *McG, Wat*

Hezekiah Cantelo (before 1760–1811)   trumpet, bassoon, oboe, and flageolet

Drury Lane band from at least 1785 to 1807; Vauxhall Gardens; first Regiment of Foot Guards; Handel Memorial concerts from 1784–90; Covent Garden oratorio concerts in late 1790s. Active professionally in Bath as early as 1770s, in London in late 1770s. Joined RSM in 1785. *RSM, Hig*

Richard Vinicombe (before 1760–after 1786)   trumpet

One of principal trumpeters in 1784 Handel Commemoration; also performed in Handel Memorial concerts in 1785–86. Joined RSM in 1771. *RSM*

Laserre Purney (ca. 1765–1802)   trumpet, clarinet, violin, and viola

Played trumpet in first Troop of Life Guards; performed (probably not trumpet) in 1784 Handel Commemoration; performed in Handel festivals and oratorio concerts from 1787 through 1790s; trumpet at St. Paul's benefit concerts in 1790s. Joined RSM in 1788.   *RSM, Hig*

James Abington (d. 1806)   trumpet and vocalist

Member of the King's Trumpeters; performed trumpet concerto as early as 1752 in benefit concert at Hampstead; sang in 1784 Handel Commemoration. Married actress Francis Barton, but "proved an embarrassment" and "she paid him a fixed yearly sum to live apart from her." Brother of Leonard and Joseph Jr., also trumpeters, and son of Joseph Sr., founding member of Royal Society of Musicians.   *Hig*

Joseph Woodham (1767–1841)   all strings, horn, trombone, and trumpet

Not primarily a trumpeter. Played double bass in Covent Garden band more than 40 years; also Sadler's Wells, Covent Garden oratorio concerts, and concerts at Free Masons Hall. Possible relation to watchmaker Richard Woodham, inventor of slide trumpet clock-spring?

RSM, BrS

Johann Georg Schmidt (1775–ca. 1822)   trumpet, clarinet, and violin

Opera; Surrey Theatre; Oratorios; benefit concerts; principal trumpet of Prince Regent's band from about 1800; performed trumpet concerto at Vauxhall Gardens in 1807; performed *Messiah* and "Seraphim" with Miss Stephens at 1819 Edinburgh festival. According to Carse, principal London trumpeter in 1818. Joined RSM in 1811.

RSM, McG, CaO, Par

Mr. Libe (fl. 1810s)   trumpet

Listed as second to Schmidt in King's Theatre band in 1818.   *CaO*

Thomas Smith (1776–after 1813)   trumpet, violin, and viola

Covent Garden oratorio concerts; Royal Circus. Joined RSM in 1801, but expelled after 1813 "for non payment."   *RSM*

John Christian Rost (1776–1836)   trumpet, trombone, horn, violin, and viola

Covent Garden and Haymarket Theatres. Joined RSM in 1821.   *RSM*

George Adams (1777–1810)   violin, viola, 'cello, horn, and trumpet

Not primarily a trumpeter. St. Paul's benefit concert on violin in 1799; the same on trumpet in 1800. According to RSM documents "has many engagements...." Joined RSM in 1798.   *RSM, Hig*

John Flack (d. before March 1813)   violin, trombone, and trumpet

Often confused with John Caspar Flack, his father (who played horn and trombone). Drury Lane opera and oratorios; 1794 Three Choirs Festival on trombone; several Three Choirs Festival appearances on trumpet and trombone 1784–1803, but not clear whether father or son; debut as violin soloist in 1785 *Messiah* concert at Drury Lane.   *RSM, Hig*

Robert Thomson (d. 1823)   trumpet, oboe, and clarinet

Trumpet player in second Troop of Life Guards; Handel Memorial concerts
from 1784 to 1790. Joined RSM in 1780.   *RSM*

Cotton Reeve (1777–1845)   violin and trumpet

Not primarily a trumpeter. Violin at Italian Opera and Vauxhall Gardens;
leader of band at Covent Garden 1819–20. Joined RSM in 1798.
                                                              RSM, Hig

John Hyde (fl. 1780s–1820s)   trumpet, violin, and impresario

Drury Lane and King's Theatre bands; trumpeter to Duke of York; 1793
Canterbury Festival; several Handel Memorial and *Messiah* concerts in
1790s; performed "Seraphim" and trumpet concertos in benefit concerts
in 1800; several Birmingham Festivals from 1802; performed
"Seraphim" with Mrs. Salmon at 1815 Edinburgh festival; performance
of *Dettingen Te Deum* with Harper at provincial festival in 1817 (or
son?); performance with Harper at 1823 York Festival (or son?). Initial
developer of and performer on slide trumpet. Published trumpet tutor in
1799, with slide trumpet instruction. Proprietor of Hyde's Rooms concert venue from 1800.   *Hig, McG, Par, Tim, Cox, BrS, CaO, Tar*

Henry Hyde (ca. 1792–after October 1853)   trumpet, pianoforte,
                                                              and violin

Philharmonic Society concerts; Ancient concerts; Theatre Royal band. According to RSM application documents "served an apprenticeship to his
Father for Seven Years." Joined RSM in 1815.   *RSM*

William Hyde (fl. 1810s)   trumpet

Described by Carse as having succeeded his father as principal trumpet.
Orchestra listing (no source given by Carse) from 1817 as principal to
Schmidt's second.   *CaO*

James Hyde (fl. 1810s and 1820s)   trumpet and composer

Son of John Hyde; performer on trumpet and composer of popular ballads
who settled in Manchester. Performed in 1811 Birmingham Festival
band. A second Hyde, from Manchester, is listed in trumpet section of
1823 Yorkshire Festival along with Harper, Hyde, and Norton (this
Hyde or perhaps Henry Hyde?).   *BrS, Hal*

Mr. Anson of Manchester (fl. 1820s) trumpet

Listed in section for 1823 Yorkshire Festival with Harper, two Hydes, Norton, and Farrer of York. *Hal*

Mr. Farrer of York (fl. 1820s) trumpet

Listed in section for 1823 Yorkshire Festival with Harper, two Hydes, Norton and Anson of Manchester. *Hal*

James Napier of Edinburgh (fl. 1820s) trumpet

Appointed trumpeter in ordinary in Scotland at death of his father, William Napier, in 1823; it is not known if James Napier was a trumpet soloist. Brother of Maxwell Napier? *McG*

Maxwell Napier of Edinburgh (fl. 1820s and 1830s) trumpet

Performed "Seraphim" with Miss Noel at Edinburgh subscription concert in 1825; listed as second in trumpet section to Harper for performance of *Dettingen Te Deum* at 1825 Yorkshire Music Festival; possible performance of "Seraphim" with Clara Novello in Edinburgh in 1836. Appointed trumpeter in ordinary in Scotland in 1825. *Ha3, McG*

Thomas Wallis Jr. (1778–before August 1838) trumpet and horn

First trumpet at Covent Garden and Little Theatre, Haymarket in 1808; first trumpet in Covent Garden band in 1818; Covent Garden oratorio concerts. Father of Thomas Samuel Wallis Jr. Joined RSM in 1808. *RSM, CaO*

Gambati Brothers (fl. early-19th century) keyed trumpets

Originally from Italy, played a RAM concert in 1826 at Hanover Square with Harper and Norton; "temporarily displaced" Harper and Irwin at King's Theatre in 1829, received bad reviews. Alessandro Gambati lost famous trumpet battle to John Norton in New York in 1834. *CaO, Hoo*

Thomas Harper Sr. (1786–1853) trumpet, horn, keyed bugle, and cornet

Premier British trumpeter in first half of nineteenth century. Trumpet and horn in Drury Lane and Adelphi Theatre bands from about 1806; later English Opera at Haymarket; Lyceum Theatre; King's Theatre; Ancient concerts; Jullien Promenade concerts; Philharmonic Society concerts; all major provincial festivals, many solo performances of Handel and others on slide trumpet; played in orchestra that performed at Weber's funeral. Professor of Trumpet at RAM at least from 1829 to 1845. Published slide trumpet tutor in 1836–37. Joined RSM in 1815.

RSM, Cox, CaJ, Sor, SoW

John Rae (1787–1841)   horn, trumpet, violin, and viola

First horn at Surrey Theatre in 1817, but also performed on trumpet. Joined RSM in 1817.   *RSM*

George Macfarlane (1805–1866)   trumpet, cornopean, bugle, horn, and violin

First trumpet at Drury Lane before 1834; bandmaster, Duke of Devonshire's private band. "Macfarlane's Improved" cornopeans made by Köhler. Published cornopean tutor in 1860. Joined RSM in 1834.

RSM, BrS, Lan

Thomas Samuel Wallis Jr. (1809–ca. 1864)   trumpet, pianoforte, and organ

Haymarket and Adelphi theatres in 1831; organist at Saint Mary's Chapel in Lambeth. Son of Thomas Wallis Jr. Joined RSM in 1831.   *RSM*

John Polglaze (fl. early-19th century)   trumpet

Second to Thomas Wallis in 1818 Covent Garden band.   *CaO*

John Norton (before 1810–1868)   trumpet and keyed bugle

Opera; Philharmonic Society concerts; York Festival with Hyde (?) and Harper in 1823; Birmingham Festival with Harper and Irving (Irwin?) in 1826; second to Harper in 1826 RAM concert in section with Gambatis. Emigrated to America in 1827. Chestnut Street Theatre in Philadelphia from 1827; St. Charles Theatre in New Orleans in 1835; many solo performances of Handel on slide trumpet. Won famous trumpet battle in 1834 in New York against Alessandro Gambati. Professor of Trumpet at RAM before 1827.   *Tar, Ha4, Hoo, CaO*

John Bernard Irwin (1806–ca. 1891)   trumpet

Italian and English operas; Ancient concerts; Philharmonic Society concerts; possibly played in 1826 Birmingham Festival in trumpet section with Harper and Norton but listed as Irving(?); second to Harper in

1832 and 1839 King's Theatre band; 1839 Ancient concerts; 1837 and 1842 Philharmonic concerts. Joined RSM in 1830. *RSM, Ha4, Cox, CaO*

William Huntington Handley (1815–before July 1896)   trumpet and cornet

Member of Her Majesty's Band of the Coldstream; first trumpet at Drury Lane and English Opera House in 1839; second to Harper at Covent Garden in 1847. Joined RSM in 1839.   *RSM, CaO*

Charles Emile Laurent Jr. (1819–1857)   cornet and trumpet
Third in trumpet section with Harper and Irwin at Her Majesty's Theatre in 1839; conductor at Royal Adelaide Gallery in the Strand in 1849. According to RSM documents was "teacher and performer on the cornet-à-pistons." Joined RSM in 1849.   *RSM, CaO*

Thomas Harper Jr. (1816–1898)   trumpet, cornet, violin, and pianoforte
Principal British trumpeter in second half of nineteenth century. Cornet and violin at Her Majesty's Theatre from late 1830s; later first trumpet at Opera Buffa, Her Majesty's Theatre, Covent Garden, Ancient concerts, Philharmonic Society concerts, New Philharmonic concerts, Sacred Harmonic Society concerts, Crystal Palace concerts, Vauxhall concerts, and all important provincial festivals. Many solo performances of Handel and important solo recitalist. Professor of Trumpet at RAM, and at RCM after his retirement from playing in 1885. Published slide trumpet and cornet tutors, cornet arrangements of popular melodies, and arrangement of Bishop's *Thine For Ever*, for soprano and trumpet obbligato. Appointed Sergeant Trumpeter to Queen Victoria in 1884; awarded Jubilee medal by Queen Victoria in 1897. Joined RSM in 1838.   *RSM, Sor, SoW, Har*

Mr. Ellwood (fl. mid-19th century)   trumpet
Performed "Seraphim" with Mrs. Sunderland in 1849.   *MT*

Mr. Zeiss (fl. mid-19th century)   trumpet
Imported from Brussels to play first trumpet at Her Majesty's Theatre when major instrumentalists, including Harper, singers, and conductor left for new Covent Garden Italian Opera company in 1848. Listed as principal at Grand National Concerts at Her Majesty's Theatre in 1850.   CaO

Mr. Maffei (fl. mid-19th century)   trumpet

Listed as second to Zeiss at Her Majesty's Theatre in 1848.   *CaO*

W. Davis (fl. mid-19th century)   trumpet

Listed as second to Koenig at 1847 Jullien Opera Concerts conducted by
  Berlioz at Drury Lane; second to Zeiss at Her Majesty's Theatre in
  1849; second to Zeiss at Grand National Concerts in 1850.   *CaO*

Mr. Koenig (fl. mid-19th century)   cornet and trumpet

Leading cornet soloist; first trumpet (cornet) for 1847 Jullien Opera Concerts conducted by Berlioz at Drury Lane; many cornet solo performances at Crystal Palace and other promenade concerts.   *CaO*

William Ellis (fl. late-19th century)   trumpet

Listed as soloist in performance of "Seraphim" with soprano Lillian
  Nordica at Philharmonic Society concerts in March 1887.   *Fos*

Walter Morrow (1850–1937)   trumpet

Foremost British trumpeter after retirement of Harper Jr. in 1885. Philharmonic Society concerts; Royal Albert Hall concerts; Richter concerts; Royal Choral Society concerts; Queen's Hall orchestras; other
  promenade concerts; all important provincial festivals. Professor of
  Trumpet at Guildhall School of Music from 1882; Professor of Trumpet
  at RCM from 1894. Published tutors revised for valved trumpet in F.
  Joined RSM in 1887.   *RSM, BrS, Bir*

Joseph Freeman (1855–1933)   trumpet

Principal Trumpet in many concerts in the Midlands; solo trumpet in Birmingham Festival and Halford Concerts; solo cornet in Harrogate Orchestra in 1904. Grandfather of R. Walton (first Principal Trumpet of
  Royal Philharmonic at its formation by Sir Thomas Beecham).   *St-P*

John Solomon (1856–1953)   trumpet

Contemporary of Morrow and succeeded him as principal British trumpeter
  after Morrow's retirement ca. 1902. Globe Theatre; Bach Society concerts; first trumpet at Henry Wood's Promenade Concerts in 1895; provincial festivals. One of founders of and first principal trumpet in
  London Symphony Orchestra. Published B-flat trumpet tutor. Joined
  RSM in 1880.   *RSM, BaT*

Appendix C: A Checklist of English Slide Trumpet Makers

The following information was gleaned from Lyndesay G. Langwill, *An Index of Musical Wind-Instrument Makers*, 5th ed.; William Waterhouse, *The New Langwill Index*; *New Grove*, s. v. "Slide Trumpet," by Edward H. Tarr; information provided by Crispian Steele-Perkins; personal correspondence; and museum catalogues (listed in the Bibliography).

NATURAL TRUMPETS CONVERTED TO SLIDE TRUMPET

Astor London

Natural trumpet converted to clock-spring model at *US-MA-Boston* (attributed to Astor by Bessaraboff due to engraving "I.A." on bell, but may have been only owned by Astor; Peter Barton thinks the bell is not original; maker now listed as unknown).

John Harris London

Harris was son-in-law of William Bull, famous maker of English Baroque trumpets. Steele-Perkins notes that Harris took over business of father-in-law in 1709/10 at Bull's retirement. Natural trumpets converted to clock-spring slide trumpets in *GB-Oxford* (#x70; Figure 13) and *GB-London-RCM* (#189)—both owned by Harper Jr.

George Henry Rodenbostel London

Natural trumpet converted to slide trumpet, with clock-spring mechanism added by Richard Woodham—the "Woodham-Rodenbostel slide trumpet" (see *Galpin Society Journal* article by Peter Barton and Figure 14). The instrument is currently owned by Brian Galpin. Langwill also lists horns, hunting horns, and natural trumpets.

George Smith Birmingham

Natural trumpet converted to slide trumpet, possibly by Smith apprentice Gisborne, in private collection of Michael Muskett of England (see Gisborne below). Firm also made cornopeans and keyed bugles.

Ulyate   London

Natural trumpet converted to slide trumpet by Ulyate (may have been made by Ulyate) in *US-CA-Claremont* (#B66). Langwill (5th ed.) also lists a six-key keyed bugle; Waterhouse lists a *demi-lune* horn.

Richard Woodham   London

Watchmaker who became brass instrument maker in 1780. Made (invented?) clock-spring for Rodenbostel converted slide trumpet in collaboration with trumpeter John Hyde (Figure 14); connection with Samuel Keat, who is supposed to have worked with Woodham and succeeded him at his death in 1797. Related to Joseph Woodham, double bass player and trumpeter?

ENGLISH SLIDE TRUMPET MAKERS

Mary Arnold   London

Firm established in 1837 as "John Charles and Mary Arnold." Listed from 1844 to 1847 as "Mrs. M. A. Arnold." Clock-spring slide trumpet in private collection of William Scarlett of Chicago.

Besson   London

London branch of famous Parisian instrument makers produced many different woodwind and brass instruments. Elastic-cord slide trumpet (Serial No. 7) from ca. 1862–1889 in private collection of Crispian Steele-Perkins. Elastic-cord slide trumpet with inscription "F. Besson" from ca. 1880 in private collection of John Webb (Figure 20).

Boosey and Sons   London

"Ortho-Chromatic" slide trumpet (Figure 24). Other slide trumpets advertised in catalogs.

Clementi and Co.   London

"Harper's Improved" clock-spring slide trumpet in *GB-Oxford* (#x7; Figure 16). Firm made full range of woodwinds, brasses and pianos, and published music.

Collard and Collard London

Successors to Clementi and Co. Made pianos, brass instruments, and woodwinds.

Courtois Paris

Royal Society of Musicians owns an elastic-cord/expansion-spring model from ca. 1880. It was owned and played by Joseph Freeman, and donated by his grandson R. Walton of Sussex (first principal trumpet of Royal Philharmonic; later BBC Symphony).

William Duncan Cubitt London

Elastic-cord slide trumpet in private collection of Crispian Steele-Perkins. According to Waterhouse, Cubitt was a dealer who had instruments made to his specifications and then sold them with his dealer mark. Steele-Perkins claims Cubitt was dealer for Higham of Birmingham. For further information on this practice, see Herbert Heyde, "Makers' Marks on Wind Instruments," trans. William Waterhouse, in *New Langwill*, xiii–xxviii.

Richard Curtis Edinburgh

Could Curtis have supplied the mysterious slide crook (see Chapter 2)? According to Waterhouse, an advertisement from 1798 claims that "he makes and sells...sliding horns and sliding crooks for tuning...."

Richard Curtis Glasgow

Son of Edinburgh Curtis, or perhaps same firm, but two shops? Also made keyed trumpets. Regent's Bugle in *GB-Brighton* (#5773/37).

D'Almaine and Co. London

More than likely a dealer who only supplied slide trumpets.

Richard Garrett London

Slide trumpet in *B-Brussels* (#1255). Firm also made woodwinds, and keyed and military bugles.

Alfred W. Gilmer   Birmingham

Elastic-cord slide trumpet in *A-Kremsmünster* (#297). Firm listed in *New Langwill* only as "Dealer," on evidence that Gilmer may have bought unmarked instruments from maker and added own dealer mark.

Gisborne   Birmingham

Steele-Perkins believes Gisborne was converter of a George Smith trumpet, due to style of workmanship and the fact that Gisborne apprenticed under Smith; trumpet is currently in private collection of Michael Muskett of England. Firm also made cornopeans, saxhorns, and keyed bugles.

James Goodison   London

Clock-spring slide trumpets in *GB-Edinburgh* (#3288) and *GB-London-RCM* (#326). Langwill (5th ed.) also lists slide trumpets in *F-Paris* (#656) and *B-Brussels* (#3157). Clock-spring model with four crooks, from ca. 1830, in private collection of Jeffrey Nussbaum of New York.

William Grayson   London

Clock-spring slide trumpet in private collection of Jeremy Montagu (can be viewed at *GB-Oxford*). Compression-spring short model in *US-SD-Vermillion* (#423; Figure 22). Firm also made cornopeans, cornets, and keyed bugles.

Hawkes   London

Firm established in 1860 by William Henry Hawkes, who was state trumpeter to Queen Victoria. Elastic-cord slide trumpet (Serial No. 14573) in *US-MA-Cambridge* (#258; Figure 21). Elastic-cord model, named "Excelsior," listed in 1983 catalog of Bingham antique dealer. Expansion-spring model with original case, mouthpiece, and crooks in private collection of Henry Meredith of Arva, Ontario.

Joseph Higham   Manchester

Expansion-spring model in *GB-Edinburgh* (#3215). 1862 clock-spring slide trumpet in private collection of Frank Tomes of Wimbledon. Firm also made keyed bugles, ophicleides, flugelhorns, brass clarinets, cornets, and trombones.

Keat London

Samuel Keat was apprentice to Richard Woodham and inherited Woodham's firm at his death in 1795 (1797?); Keat's sons George and Henry joined father and eventually inherited business. Langwill (5th ed.) lists six silver trumpets in Tower of London, posthorns, trombones, and coach horns. Keat's name inscribed on spring box of short model by Power, which was in possession of Harper Jr. at his death. According to Steele-Perkins, Keat's firm "supplied the clock-spring mechanism 'to the trade' for 50 years."

Key London

Instruments made by Samuel Keat and son George were supplied to Key under terms of an exclusive agreement that commenced in 1825.

Köhler London

More surviving slide trumpets by Köhler than any other maker (see Figures 17 and 19). "Harper's Improved" clock-spring models in *GB-Edinburgh* (#2975) and Royal Military College of Music, Kneller Hall, London. "Harper's Improved" expansion-spring/elastic-band models in *GB-Edinburgh* (#2977), *GB-London-RCM* (#252), *GB-Oxford* (#76), *GB-London-H* (#71), *US-CA-Claremont* (#B67), *US-NY-New York* (#89.4.2533), and *US-SD-Vermillion* (#420). Slide trumpets found in continental museums include *B-Brussels* (#1254) and *F-Paris* (#657). An interesting Köhler can be viewed at *GB-London-H*: item no. 147, originally a clock-spring model, was converted to spiral spring, and a single detachable valve was added later.

T. Lloyd Handsworth

Compression-spring slide trumpet in private collection of John Webb.

Pace London

Clock-spring models in *GB-London-H* (#229), *US-DC-Washington-S* (#76.25), and in private collection of Richard Levine of Upper Saddle River, NJ; compression-spring model in *US-SD-Vermillion* (#418; Figure 18). Langwill (5th ed.) also lists keyed bugles, valve trumpets, cornopeans, cornets, bassoons, and ophicleides.

Thomas Percival   London

Business partner of John Köhler, nephew of firm's founder, from about
1811; when John Augustus Köhler took over father's business in 1834,
Percival became independent and remained at St. James's Street loca-
tion. Firm made natural trumpets, horns, keyed bugles, keyed trumpets,
and serpents. Blandford claims Percival made the "Regent's Bugle" (see
Chapter 2), but specimen at *GB-Brighton* was made by Richard Curtis
of Glasgow.

James Power   Dublin and London

Short model slide trumpet with clock-spring by Keat, owned by Joseph
Wheeler in 1966 and described by him in *Galpin Society Journal* article. Firm also made oboes, flageolets, bass horns, keyed bugles, and instruments for the military.

Robinson, Bussell and Co.   Dublin

A solid silver slide trumpet from 1840 listed in 1983 catalog of Bingham
antique dealer; asking price was £6000. Firm made many types of
woodwind and brass instruments.

William Sandbach   London

Langwill lists clock-spring slide trumpet formerly in private collection of
Reginald Morley-Pegge. Also listed are natural trumpets, keyed trum-
pets, keyed bugles, horns, and basshorns. Clock-spring slide trumpet by
Sandbach & Wyatt in private collection of Henry Meredith of Arva,
Ontario.

Adolphe Sax   Paris

According to Tarr, Sax manufactured an English-system slide trumpet, but
with a single clock-spring return mechanism. An example is in the Ber-
noulli collection at the Historisches Museum in Basle, Switzerland.

William Wyatt   London

Maker of patent full chromatic slide trumpet. Slide trumpets in *GB-
London-H* (#73) and *B-Brussels* (#3156), and in private collections of
John Webb (Wyatt No. 6) and Crispian Steele-Perkins (Wyatt No. 7).

Bibliography

WRITTEN SOURCES

Advertisement of benefit concert by John Hyde. *The Times* (London), 24 May 1800, 1.

Advertisement of concerts by Anton Weidinger. *The Times* (London), 7 March 1803, 1.

Altenburg, Detlef. *Untersuchungen zur Geschichte der Trompete im Zeitalter der Clarinblaskunst (1500–1800)*. 3 vols. Regensburg: Gustav Bosse, 1973.

Altenburg, Johann Ernst. *Essay on an Introduction to the Heroic and Musical Trumpeters' and Kettledrummers' Art*. Transl. Edward H. Tarr. Nashville: Brass Press, 1974.

Angermüller, Rudolph. *Sigismund Neukomm: Werkverzeichnis, Autobiographie, Beziehung zu seinen Zeitgenossen*. Munich-Salzburg: Musikverlag Emil Katzbichler, 1977.

Anzenberger, Friedrich. "The Earliest French Tutor for Slide Trumpet." *Historic Brass Society Journal* 4 (1992): 106–111.

Baillie, Laureen, ed. *The Catalogue of Printed Music in the British Library to 1980*. 62 vols. London: K. G. Saur Ltd., 1983.

Baines, Anthony. *Brass Instruments: Their History and Development*. London: Faber & Faber, 1976; reprint, New York: Dover Publications, 1993.

_____. *European and American Musical Instruments*. New York: The Viking Press, 1966.

_____. "James Talbot's Manuscript (Christ Church Library Music MS 1187)." *Galpin Society Journal* 1(1948): 9–26.

_____. "Two Cassel Inventories." *Galpin Society Journal* 4 (1951): 30–38.

Barclay, Robert, and Robert North. *A Step-by-Step Guide to the Construction of a Slide Trumpet in C*. Ed. Timothy J. McGee. The Toronto Consort Workshop Series; Manual #7. Scarborough, Ontario: Consort Enterprises, 1978.

Bargans [*sic*], Karl. "On the Trumpet, as at Present Employed in the Orchestra; with a retrospective View of the Earlier Methods of using it." *Harmonicon*, January 1830, 23–25.

Barton, Peter. "The Woodham-Rodenbostel Slide Trumpet and Others, Employing the 'Clock-Spring' Mechanism." *Galpin Society Journal* 42 (1989): 112–120.

Bassett, Henry. "On Improvements in the Trumpet." *Proceedings of the Musical Association* 3 (1877): 140–144.

Bate, Philip. *The Trumpet and Trombone*. 2nd ed. London: Ernest Benn, 1978.

Bennett, Joseph. *Forty Years of Music, 1865–1905*. London: Methuen & Co., 1908.

Berlioz, Hector. *Memoirs of Hector Berlioz, Member of the French Institute: including his travels in Italy, Germany, Russia and England 1803–1865*. Transl. and ed. David Cairns. New York: Alfred A. Knopf, 1969.

_____. *A Treatise on Modern Instrumentation and Orchestration*. Transl. Mary Cowden Clarke. Ed. and rev. Joseph Bennett. London: Novello and Co. Ltd., 1904.

Bessaraboff, Nicholas. *Ancient European Musical Instruments*. Cambridge, MA: Harvard Univ. Press, 1941.

Birkemeier, Richard P. "The F Trumpet and its last Virtuoso, Walter Morrow." *Brass Bulletin* 65 (1989): 34–45.

_____. "The History and Music of the Orchestral Trumpet of the Nineteenth Century." *Journal of the International Trumpet Guild* 9.3 (1985): 23–39; 9.4 (1985): 13–27.

_____. "The Orchestral Trumpet of the Nineteenth Century: an historical and acoustical survey." D.M.A. thesis, Northwestern University, 1984.

Blaikley, D. J. "Trumpet." *A Dictionary of Music and Musicians.* Ed. J. A. Fuller Maitland. London: Macmillan, 1911.

Blandford, W. F. H. "The 'Bach Trumpet'." *Monthly Musical Record* 65 (1935): 49–51, 73–76, 97–100.

_____. "The Regent's Bugle." *The Musical Times,* 1 May 1925, 442–443; 1 June 1925, 539; 1 August 1925, 733–734.

Brown, Howard Mayer, and Stanley Sadie, eds. *Performance Practice: Music after 1600.* The New Grove Handbooks in Music. London: Macmillan, 1989.

Brown, James D., and Stephen S. Stratton. *British Musical Biography: A Dictionary of Musical Artists, Authors and Composers, born in Britain and its Colonies.* London: William Reeves, 1897; reprint, New York: Da Capo Press, 1971.

Budds, M. J. "Music at the Court of Queen Victoria: A Study of Music in the Life of the Queen and her Participation in the Musical Life of her Time." Ph.D. diss., University of Iowa, 1987.

Burkart, Richard. "The Trumpet in England in the Seventeenth Century with Emphasis on its Treatment in the Works of Henry Purcell and a Biography of the Shore Family of Trumpeters." D.M.A. diss., University of Wisconsin, 1972.

Burney, Charles. *An Account of the Musical Performances in Westminster Abbey and The Pantheon, May 26th, 27th, 29th; and June the 3d, and 5th, 1784 in Commemoration of Handel.* London: Printed for the Benefit of the Musical Fund, 1785.

_____. *A General History of Music from the Earliest Ages to the Present Period.* 2 vols. With critical and historical notes by Frank Mercer. London: 1776–1782; reprint, New York: Harcourt, Brace and Co., 1935.

Busby, Thomas. *Concert Room and Orchestra Anecdotes, of Music and Musicians, Ancient and Modern.* 3 vols. London: Clementi & Co., 1825.

_____. *A Dictionary of Music, Theoretical and Practical.* 5th ed. London: Sir Richard Phillips and Co., 1823.

Byrne, Maurice. "The Goldsmith-Trumpet-Makers of the British Isles." *Galpin Society Journal* 19 (1966): 71.

_____. "William Bull, John Stevenson and the Harris Family." *Galpin Society Journal* 45 (1992): 67–77.

Carse, Adam. "Beethoven's Trumpet Parts." *The Musical Times* 94 (1953): 32.

_____. *Catalogue of the Adam Carse Collection of Old Musical Wind Instruments.* London: London County Council, 1951.

_____. "The Choral Symphony in London." *Music and Letters* 32 (January 1951): 47–58.

_____. *The History of Orchestration.* London: Kegan Paul, Trench, Trubner & Co., 1925; reprint, New York: Dover Publications, 1964.

_____. *The Life of Jullien: Adventurer, Showman-Conductor and Establisher of the Promenade Concerts in England, Together with a History of those Concerts up to 1895.* Cambridge: W. Heffer & Sons, 1951.

_____. *Musical Wind Instruments.* London: Macmillan, 1939; reprint, New York: Da Capo Press, 1965.

_____. *The Orchestra From Beethoven to Berlioz: A History of the Orchestra in the First Half of the 19th century, and of the Development of Orchestral Baton-Conducting.* New York: Broude Brothers, 1949.

_____. *Practical Hints on Orchestration.* Augener's Edition No. 10093. London: Augener, [1919].

Chan, Mary, and Jamie C. Kassler, eds. *Roger North's CURSORY NOTES OF MUSICKE (c. 1698–c. 1703): A Physical, Psychological and Critical Theory.* Kensington, Australia: Unisearch Ltd., 1986.

Chouquet, Gustave. *Le Musée du Conservatoire National de Musique: Catalogue descriptif et raisonné.* Paris: Librairie de Firmin-Didot et Cie., 1884.

Ciurczak, Peter. "The Trumpet in Baroque Opera: Its Use as a Solo, Obbligato, and Ensemble Instrument." *Journal of the International Trumpet Guild* 6 (October 1981): 2–17, 54–68; 7 (September 1982): 14–33.

Claggett, Charles. *Claggett's Method of Constructing and Tuning Musical Instruments.* A specification, dated 15 September 1788. No. 1664. London: George Edward Eyre and William Spottiswoode, 1856.

_____. *Musical Phaenomena, founded on Unanswerable Facts; and a proof that Musical Instruments have been hitherto fabricated on the most uncertain, therefore the most improper materials; No. 1: The Aiuton, and the Chromatic Trumpets and the French Horns, capable of fine tune and regular harmony in all the keys in use, minor as well as major.* London: printed for the author and sold at the Musical Museum, 1793.

Coerne, Louis Adolphe. *The Evolution of Modern Orchestration.* New York: Macmillan, 1908; reprint, New York: AMS Press, 1979.

Cole, Bruce, and Adelheid M. Gealt. *Art of the Western World: From Ancient Greece to Post-Modernism.* New York: Summit Books, 1989.

Corder, Frederick. *The Orchestra and How to Write for It.* London: J. Curwen & Sons, 1894.

Cox, John Edmunds. *Musical Recollections of the Last Half-Century.* 2 vols. London: Tinsley Brothers, 1872.

Cudworth, Charles. "The Vauxhall 'Lists'." *Galpin Society Journal* 20 (1967): 24–42.

Dahlqvist, Reine. "Gottfried Reiche's Instrument: A Problem of Classification." *Historic Brass Society Journal* 5 (1993): 174–191.

_____. *The Keyed Trumpet and its Greatest Virtuoso, Anton Weidinger.* Nashville: Brass Press, 1975.

_____. "Pitches of German, French, and English Trumpets in the 17th and 18th Centuries." *Historic Brass Society Journal* 5 (1993): 29–41.

Dauverné, François Georges Auguste. *Méthode pour la trompette.* Paris: Brandus, Dufour et Cie, 1857. Transl. as "Method for Trumpet," by Gaetan Chenier, Ruby Miller Orval, Rebecca Pike, and Jeffrey Snedeker in *Historic Brass Society Journal* 3 (1991): 179–261.

Davey, Henry. *History of English Music.* 2nd. ed. London: J. Curwen & Sons, 1921; reprint, New York: Da Capo Press, 1969.

Davison, Henry, comp. *Music during the Victorian Era From Mendelssohn to Wagner: Being the Memoirs of J. W. Davison, Forty Years Music Critic of "The Times."* London: Wm. Reeves, 1912.

A Dictionary of Music and Musicians (A. D. 1450–1889) by Eminent Writers, English and Foreign. Ed. George Grove. London: Macmillan, 1878–1889. S. v. "Harper, Thomas," by William H. Husk.

_____. S. v. "Shore, John," by William H. Husk.

_____. S. v. "Trumpet," by William H. Stone.

_____. Appendix. Ed. J. A. Fuller Maitland. S. v. "Trumpet," by A. J. Hipkins.

Downey, Peter. "The Renaissance Slide Trumpet, Fact or Fiction." *Early Music* 12.1 (1984): 26–33.

_____. "What Samuel Pepys Heard on 3 February 1661: English Trumpet Style under the Later Stuart Monarchs." *Early Music* 18.3 (1990): 417–428.

Dudgeon, Ralph T. *The Keyed Bugle.* Metuchen, NJ: Scarecrow Press, 1993.

_____. "The Keyed Bugle, Its History, Literature and Technique." Ph.D. diss., University of California at San Diego, 1980.

Duffin, Ross W. "The *trompette des menestrels* in the 15th-century alta capella." *Early Music* 17.3 (1989): 397–402.

Edwards, Frederick George. "Wesley, Samuel (1766–1837)," *The Compact Edition of the Dictionary of National Biography.* London: Oxford University Press, 1975.

Ehrlich, Cyril. *The Music Profession in Britain since the Eighteenth Century: A Social History.* Oxford: Clarendon Press, 1985.

Elkin, Robert. *Royal Philharmonic: The Annals of the Royal Philharmonic Society.* London: Rider & Co., 1946.

Ella, John. *Musical Sketches, Abroad, and at Home.* London: Longmans & Co., 1869.

Fasman, Mark J. *Brass Bibliography: Sources on the History, Literature, Pedagogy, Performance, and Acoustics of Brass Instruments.* Bloomington: Indiana University Press, 1990.

Fiske, Roger. *English Theatre Music in the Eighteenth Century.* 2nd ed. Oxford: Oxford University Press, 1986.

Forsyth, Cecil. *Orchestration.* 2nd ed. New York: Macmillan, 1936.

Foster, Myles Birket. *History of the Philharmonic Society of London 1813– 1912: A Record of a Hundred Years' Work in the Cause of Music.* London: John Lane, 1912.

Galpin, Francis W. *Old English Instruments of Music: Their History and Character.* 3rd. ed. London: Methuen & Co. Ltd., 1932.

Ganz, A. W. *Berlioz in London.* London: Quality Press Ltd., 1950.

Gardiner, William. *Music and Friends; or, Pleasant Recollections of a Dilettante.* 3 vols. London: Longman, Orme, Brown, and Longman, 1838 and 1853.

Gardner, Ned. "In Search of the Renaissance Slide Trumpet." *Journal of the International Trumpet Guild* 12.2 (1987): 4–9.

Geiringer, Karl. *Musical Instruments: Their History in Western Culture from the Stone Age to the Present Day.* Transl. Bernard Miall. Ed. W. F. H. Blandford. London: George Allen & Unwin, Ltd., 1943.

Good, Edwin M. *The Eddy Collection of Musical Instruments: A Checklist.* Berkeley: Fallen Leaf Press, 1985.

Grove's Dictionary of Music and Musicians. 5th ed. Ed. Eric Blom. London: Macmillan, 1954. S. v. "Morrow, Walter," by Anthony Baines.

_____. S. v. "Solomon, John," by Anthony Baines.

Halfpenny, Eric. "Musicians at James II's Coronation." *Music and Letters* 32.2 (1951): 103–114.

_____. "William Shaw's 'Harmonic Trumpet'." *Galpin Society Journal* 13 (1960): 7–13.

Harley, John. "Music at the English Court in the Eighteenth and Nineteenth Centuries." *Music and Letters* 50 (1969): 332–351.

Harper, Thomas. *Instructions for the Trumpet, With the use of the Chromatic Slide, Also the Russian Valve Trumpet, the Cornet à Pistons or small Stop Trumpet, and the Keyed Bugle, In which the Rudiments of Music and the Various Scales, Are clearly explained in a Series of Examples, Preludes, Lessons, Solos, Duets, &c for each Instrument.* London: Published by the Author, 1837; facsimile reprint, Homer, NY: Spring Tree Enterprises, 1988.

Harper, Thomas, and John Köhler. Contract. 1833. *Lcm*, MS 4071.

Harper, Thomas F. "The Trumpets." Letters to the Editor. *The Times*, 25 January 1935, 10.

Harper Jr., Thomas John. Concert Programs. 5 vols. Department of Portraits and Performance History, *Lcm*.

_____. Engagement Book. 1838–1897. *Lcm*, MS 4073.

_____. *Harper's School for the Trumpet: Containing (in addition to the usual Instructions) a full description of the Instrument, Observations on the use of the Slide and on the mode of writing music for the Trumpet, also several remarks connected with the Art of playing the Instrument, and 100 Progressive Exercises.* London: Rudall, Carte & Co., [1875].

_____, London, to unknown addressee, 1 March 1894. *Lcm*, MS 4071.

Harrison, Frank Ll. "Tradition and Innovation in Instrumental Usage 1100–1450." In *Aspects of Medieval and Renaissance Music: A Birthday Offering to Gustave Reese*, ed. Jan LaRue, 319–335. New York: Norton, 1966.

Hawkins, Sir John. *A General History of the Science and Practice of Music.* 2 vols. London: Novello, 1853; reprint, New York: Dover, 1963.

Herbert, Trevor. "The Sackbut in England in the 17th and 18th Centuries." *Early Music* 18.4 (1990): 609–616.

Heyde, Herbert. Catalogue notes. Vermillion, SD: The Shrine to Music Museum, December 1992.

Highfill Jr., Philip H., K. A. Burnim, and E. A. Langhans. *A Biographical Dictionary of Actors, Actresses, Musicians, Dancers, Managers & Other Stage Personnel in London, 1660–1800*. Carbondale: Southern Illinois University Press, 1973–.

Hogarth, George. "Musical Instruments: The Trumpet, Trombone, Serpent and Ophicleide." *Music World* 4 (17 February 1837): 129–132.

Hogwood, Christopher. "The London Pleasure Gardens." In *Favourite Songs Sung at Vauxhall Gardens*, by Johann Christian Bach. Series F, Volume I, *Music for London Entertainment, 1600–1800*. Tunbridge Wells: Richard Macnutt, 1985.

Holloway, William Wood. "Martin Agricola's *Musica instrumentalis deudsch*: A Translation." Ph.D. diss., North Texas State University, 1972.

Holman, Peter. "English trumpets—a response." *Early Music* 19.3 (1991): 443.

Hoover, Cynthia Adams. "The Slide Trumpet of the Nineteenth Century." *Brass Quarterly* 4 (1962–63): 159–178.

———. "A Trumpet Battle at Nimblo's Pleasure Garden." *Musical Quarterly* 55 (July, 1969): 384–395.

Hueffer, Francis. *Half a Century of Music in England: 1837–1887*. London: Chapman & Hall, 1889.

Hughes-Hughes, Augustus. *Catalogue of Manuscript Music in the British Museum*. 3 vols. London: The Trustees of the British Museum, 1965.

Hyde, John. A *New and Compleat Preceptor for the Trumpet and Bugle Horn, With the Whole of the Cavalry Duty as approved of and ordered by his Royal Highness the Duke of York, Commander in Chief*. London: Printed and to be had of the Author, [1799].

Joseph Higham, Wholesale Brass Musical Instrument Manufacturer, to the Trade and for Export, to the Army, Navy, Volunteers, &c. Illustrated Catalogue. Strangeways, Manchester: Higham, January 1887.

Kelly, Michael. *Reminiscences of Michael Kelly, of the King's Theatre, and Theatre Royal Drury Lane, including a Period of Nearly Half a Century; with Original Anecdotes of Many Distinguished Persons, Political, Literary, and Musical.* 2 vols. London: Henry Colburn, 1826.

Klein, Hermann. *Thirty Years of Musical Life in London: 1870–1900.* New York: The Century Co., 1903.

Kosleck, Julius. *Julius Kosleck's School for the Trumpet: Revised and adapted to the study of the Trumpet-à-pistons in F as used in the orchestras of England and America.* Revised by Walter Morrow. London: Breitkopf & Härtel, 1907.

Koury, Daniel J. *Orchestral Performance Practices in the Nineteenth Century: Size, Proportions, and Seating.* Ann Arbor: UMI Research Press, 1986.

Krickeberg, Dieter, and Wolfgang Rauch. *Katalog der Blechblasinstrumente: Polsterzungeninstrumente.* Berlin: Staatliches Institut für Musikforschung, 1976.

Langwill, Lyndesay G. *An Index of Musical Wind-Instrument Makers.* 5th ed. Edinburgh: Lyndesay G. Langwill, 1977.

Lebrecht, Norman. *Music in London.* London: Aurum Press, 1992.

Lewis, H. M. "Extra-harmonic Trumpet Tones in the Baroque Era—Natural Trumpet vs. Tromba da Tirarsi." *Journal of the International Trumpet Guild* 5 (1980): 39–45.

Mackerness, Eric D. *A Social History of English Music.* London: Routledge and Kegan Paul, 1964.

Mahillon, Victor Charles. *Catalogue descriptif et analytique du Musée Instrumental du Conservatoire Royal de Musique de Bruxelles.* 2nd ed. Vol. 2. Brussels: 1906; reprint, Brussels: Les Amis de la Musique, 1978.

_____. *Les Instruments à Vent.* Vol. 3, *La trompette; Son Histoire, Sa Théorie, Sa Construction.* Brussels: Mahillon & Co., 1907.

_____. "The Trumpet—its History—its Theory—its Construction." Transl. Major F. A. Mahan. *Dominant* 16.7–9 (September–November 1908): 17–19; 15–17; 17–19.

Maitland, J. A. Fuller. *English Music in the XIXth Century*. London: G. Richards, 1902.

Marcuse, Sibyl. *Musical Instruments: A Comprehensive Dictionary*. New York: Norton, 1975.

_____. *A Survey of Musical Instruments*. London: David & Charles, Ltd., 1975.

Marsh, John. "Hints to Young Composers of Instrumental Music." *Galpin Society Journal* 18 (March 1965): 57–71.

Matthew, James E. "The Antient Concerts, 1776–1848." *Proceedings of the Musical Association* 33 (1906–7): 55–79.

Matthews, Betty, compiler. *The Royal Society of Musicians of Great Britain List of Members 1738–1984*. London: The Royal Society of Musicians, 1985.

Monk, Christopher. "Christopher Monk and the 'flat trumpet'." *Historic Brass Society Journal* 1 (1989): 121–122.

_____. "The Older Brass Instruments: Cornett, Trombone, and Trumpet." In *Musical Instruments Through the Ages*, ed. Anthony Baines, 259–262. 2nd ed. New York: Walker and Co., 1976.

Montagu, Jeremy. *The World of Baroque and Classical Musical Instruments*. Newton Abbot: David and Charles, 1979.

_____. *The World of Medieval and Renaissance Musical Instruments*. Newton Abbot: David and Charles, 1976.

_____. *The World of Romantic and Modern Musical Instruments*. Woodstock, NY: The Overlook Press, 1981.

Morley-Pegge, Reginald. "The Regent's Bugle." *Galpin Society Journal* 9 (June 1956): 91–96.

Morrow, Walter. "The Trumpet as an Orchestral Instrument." *Proceedings of the Musical Association* 21 (1895): 133–147.

Myers, Arnold, ed. *Historic Musical Instruments in the Edinburgh University Collection.* Vol. 2, Part H, Fascicle iii: *Trumpets and Trombones.* Edinburgh: Edinburgh University Collection of Historic Musical Instruments, 1993.

Myers, Herbert W. "Slide Trumpet Madness: Fact or Fiction?" *Early Music* 17.3 (1989): 382–389.

Naylor, Tom L. *The Trumpet and Trombone in Graphic Arts: 1500–1800.* Nashville: The Brass Press, 1979.

Nettel, Reginald. *The Orchestra in England: A Social History.* London: Jonathan Cape, 1946.

Neukomm, Sigismund, Paris, to unknown addressee, 17 September 1829. Transl. Eduardo Aguilar. *Lbl*, Add. 33965, f. 282.

The New Grove Dictionary of Music and Musicians. Ed. Stanley Sadie. London: Macmillan, 1980. S. v. "Bishop, Sir Henry R(owley)," by Nicholas Temperley.

_____. S. v. "England: Art Music," by Jack Westrup.

_____. S. v. "Hall, (Alexander) Ernest," by Edward H. Tarr.

_____. S. v. "Harper," by William H. Husk and Edward H. Tarr.

_____. S. v. "London: Concert Life—Choirs and Choral Societies, Concert Organizations and Concert Rooms and Halls," by Henry Raynor.

_____. S. v. "London: Concert Life—Festivals," by William H. Husk and Watkins Shaw.

_____. S. v. "London: Concert Life—Orchestras," by Noël Goodwin.

_____. S. v. "London: Education—Conservatories," by Bernarr Rainbow.

_____. S. v. "Morrow, Walter," by Anthony Baines and Edward H. Tarr.

_____. S. v. "Obbligato," by David Fuller.

_____. S. v. "Reiche, Gottfried," by Edward H. Tarr.

_____. S. v. "Shore," by Don L. Smithers.

_____. S. v. "Silas, Edouard," by Christopher Senior.

_____. S. v. "Snow, Valentine," by William H. Husk and Edward H. Tarr.

_____. S. v. "Solomon, John," by Anthony Baines and Edward H. Tarr.

The New Grove Dictionary of Musical Instruments. Ed. Stanley Sadie. London: Macmillan, 1984. S. v. "Collections," by Laurence Libin.

_____. S. v. "Flat Trumpet," by Edward H. Tarr.

_____. S. v. "Invention," by Niall O'Loughlin.

_____. S. v. "Slide Trumpet," by Edward H. Tarr.

_____. S. v. "Trumpet," by Edward H. Tarr.

_____. S. v. "Tuning Slide," by Howard Mayer Brown.

Norton, John T. *Preceptor for the Trumpet, in which the Various Scales of that Instrument together with the use of the Chromatic Slide are fully explained*. London: T. Percival, [before 1827].

Official Descriptive and Illustrated Catalogue of the Great Exhibition of the Works of Industry of all Nations, 1851. Vol. 1, *Index and Introductory; Section I.—Raw Materials, Classes 1 to 4; Section II.—Machinery, Classes 5 to 10*. London: W. Clowes and Sons, 1851.

"Orchestral Sketches: Clara Anastasia Novello; Thomas Harper." *Musical World* 2 (1836): ix–xi.

Parke, William Thomas. *Musical Memoirs; comprising an Account of the General State of Music in England from the First Commemoration of Handel, in 1784, to the Year 1830*. London: Henry Colburn and Richard Bentley, 1830; reprint, New York: Da Capo Press, 1970.

Peyser, Joan, ed. *The Orchestra: Origins and Transformations*. New York: Charles Scribner's Sons, 1986.

Phillips, Henry. *Musical and Personal Recollections during Half a Century*. 2 vols. London: Charles J. Skeet, 1864.

Pinnock, Andrew. "A Wider Role for the Flat Trumpet." *Galpin Society Journal* 42 (1989): 105–111.

Pinnock, Andrew, and Bruce Wood. "A Counterblast on English trumpets." *Early Music* 19.3 (1991): 436–443.

Pirie, Peter J. *The English Musical Renaissance*. London: Victor Gollancz Ltd., 1979.

Polk, Keith. "The Trombone, the Slide Trumpet and the Ensemble Tradition of the Early Renaissance." *Early Music* 17.3 (1989): 389–397.

Prout, Ebenezer. *Instrumentation*. Novello, Ewer and Co.'s Music Primers No. 15. Ed. Dr. Stainer. London: Novello, Ewer and Co., [1878].

————. *The Orchestra*. Vol. 1. Augener's Edition No. 9189. London: Augener, 1898.

Ridley, E. A. K. *The Royal College of Music Museum of Instruments Catalogue*. Part I, *European Wind Instruments*. London: The Royal College of Music, 1982.

Rose, Algernon S. *Talks with Bandsmen: a Popular Handbook for Brass Instrumentalists*. London: William Rider and Son, [1895].

Rycroft, David. "Flat Trumpet Facts and Figures." *Galpin Society Journal* 42 (1989): 134–142.

Sachs, Curt. "Chromatic Trumpets in the Renaissance." *Musical Quarterly* 36 (1950): 62–66.

Sachs, Joel. "London: the Professionalization of Music." In *The Early Romantic Era Between Revolutions: 1789 and 1848*. Ed. Alexander Ringer. Englewood Cliffs, NJ: Prentice Hall, 1991.

"Sacred Harmonic Society." *The Times*, 12 March 1851, 8.

Sainsbury, John, ed. "Hyde." *A Dictionary of Musicians from the Earliest Times*. London: 1825; reprint, New York: Da Capo Press, 1966.

Sandor, Edward P. "Development and Use of the Chromatic Trumpet in the Nineteenth-Century Orchestra." *NACWPI Journal* 33.4 (1985): 4–12.

Schneider, Wilhelm. *Historisch-technische Beschreibung der musikalischen Instrumente*. Leipzig: T. Hennings, 1834.

Scholes, Percy A. *The Mirror of Music, 1844–1944: A Century of Musical Life in Britain as Reflected in the Pages of the "Musical Times."* 2 vols. London: Oxford University Press, 1947.

Shaw, George Bernard. *London Music in 1888–89: As Heard by Corno di Bassetto (Later Known as Bernard Shaw) with some Further Autobiographical Particulars.* New York: Dodd, Mead & Co., 1937.

_____. *Music in London, 1890–94.* 3 vols. London: Constable & Co. Ltd., 1932.

Skei, Allen B. *Woodwind, Brass and Percussion Instruments of the Orchestra: A Bibliographic Guide.* Garland Reference Library of the Humanities, Vol. 458. New York: Garland, 1985.

Smithers, Don L. "Mozart's Orchestral Brass." *Early Music* 20.2 (1992): 254–265.

_____. *The Music and History of the Baroque Trumpet before 1721.* 2nd. ed. Carbondale: Southern Illinois University Press, 1988.

Sorenson, Scott P. "Printed Trumpet Instruction to 1835." *Journal of the International Trumpet Guild* 12.1 (1987): 4–14.

_____. "Thomas Harper, Sr. (1786–1853): Trumpet Virtuoso and Pedagogue." Ph.D. diss., University of Minnesota, 1987.

Sorenson, Scott, and John Webb. "The Harpers and the Trumpet." *Galpin Society Journal* 39 (1986): 35–57.

Spohr, Louis. *The Musical Journeys of Louis Spohr.* Transl. and ed. Henry Pleasants. Norman: University of Oklahoma Press, 1961.

Squire, W. Barclay. "Purcell's Music for the Funeral of Queen Mary II." *Sammelbände der Internationalen Musik-Gesellschaft* 4.2 (1903): 225–233.

Steele-Perkins, Crispian. "Practical Observations on Natural, Slide and Flat Trumpets." *Galpin Society Journal* 42 (1989): 122–127.

Sundelin, Augustin. *Die Instrumentirung für sämmtliche Militär-Musik-Chöre, ober Nachweisungen über alle bei denselben gebräuchliche Instrumente, um dafür wirkungsvoll und ausführbar componiren zu sönnen.* Berlin: Wagenführ's Buch- und Musik-handlung, 1828.

Tarr, Edward H. "The Romantic Trumpet." *Historic Brass Society Journal* 5 (1993): 213–261.

_____. *The Trumpet.* Transl. S. E. Plank and Edward H. Tarr. Bern: Hallwag AG, 1977; English transl., Portland: Amadeus Press, 1988.

Temperley, Nicholas. "Domestic Music in England, 1800–1860." *Proceedings of the Royal Musical Association* 85 (1958–59): 31–47.

_____. "Handel's Influence on English Music." *Monthly Musical Record* 90 (1960): 163–175.

_____. Introduction to *The Overture in England, 1800–1840*. Series E, Vol. 6. *The Symphony, 1720–1840*. Ed. Barry S. Brook. New York: Garland, 1984.

_____. "Mendelssohn's Influence on English Music." *Music and Letters* 43 (1962): 224–233.

_____. "Mozart's Influence on English Music." *Music and Letters* 42 (1961): 307–318.

_____, ed. *Lost Chord: Essays on Victorian Music*. Bloomington: Indiana University Press, 1989.

_____, ed. *The Romantic Age: 1800–1914*. London: Athlone Press Ltd., 1981.

Thiessen, John C. "The Late Eighteenth-Century Trumpet in England: A Reconstruction of Repertory." M.M. thesis, King's College, University of London, 1990.

Tomes, Frank. "Flat Trumpet Experiments." *Galpin Society Journal* 43 (1990): 164–175.

The Trumpet: Valve and Slide. Hawkes and Son's Simplicity Instruction Books. London: Hawkes and Son, 1906.

Unwin, Robert. "'An English Writer on Music': James Talbot 1664–1708." *Galpin Society Journal* 40 (December 1987): 53–72.

Vernon. "Musical Obituary." [Harper, Sr.] *Musical Times* 5.105 (1 February 1853): 133–134.

Virdung, Sebastian. *Musica Getutscht*. Documenta Musicologica, Erste Reihe: Druckschriften-Faksimiles XXXI. Ed. Klaus Wolfgang Niemöller. Basle, 1511; facsimile reprint, Kassel: Bärenreiter, 1970.

Walker, Ernest. *A History of Music in England*. 2nd. ed. London: Oxford University Press, 1931.

_____. "An Orchestra of Fifty Years Ago." *Monthly Musical Record* 61 (January 1951): 11–12.

Waterhouse, William. *The New Langwill Index: A Dictionary of Musical Wind-Instrument Makers and Inventors*. London: Tony Bingham, 1993.

Webb, John. "Designs for Brass in the Public Record Office." *Galpin Society Journal* 38 (1985): 48–54.

_____. "The English Slide Trumpet." *Historic Brass Society Journal* 5 (1993): 262–279.

_____. "The Flat Trumpet In Perspective." *Galpin Society Journal* 46 (March 1993): 154–160.

Wesley, Eliza. Autograph Book. *Lbl*, Add. 35026.

Wheeler, Joseph. "New Light on the 'Regent's Bugle'; with some notes on the Keyed Bugle." *Galpin Society Journal* 19 (April 1966): 65–70.

White, Eric Walter, compiler. *A Register of First Performances of English Operas and Semi-Operas from the 16th Century to 1980*. London: The Society for Theatre Research, 1983.

Young, Percy. *A History of British Music*. New York: Norton, 1967.

MUSICAL SOURCES

Arne, Thomas. *The Soldier Tir'd of Wars Alarms: Sung by Miss Stephens*. London: Goulding & D'Almaine, [1825?].

Balfe, Michael. *The Armourer of Nantes*. Score. 1863. *Lbl*, Add. 29363–4.

_____. *Bianca, the Bravo's Bride*, Overture and Introduction to Act I. Score. 1860. *Lbl*, Egerton 2740 (ff. 224–257v) and Add. 29356.

_____. *Blanche de Nevers*, Introductory Prelude. Score. 1862. *Lbl*, Add. 29361.

_____. *The Bohemian Girl*. Score. 1843. *Lbl*, Add. 29335.

_____. *The Bondman*, Overture. Score. 1847. *Lbl*, Add. 29346.

_____. *Catherine Grey*, Overture. Score. 1837. *Lbl*, Add. 29329.

_____. *The Daughter of St. Mark*, Overture. Score. 1845. *Lbl*, Egerton 2740 (ff. 258–298v).

_____. *Diadeste, or, The Veiled Lady*, Overture. Score. 1838. *Lbl*, Add. 29333.

_____. *The Enchantress*, Overture. Score. 1845. *Lbl*, Add. 29344.

_____. *Falstaff*, Overture. Score. 1838. *Lbl*, Egerton 2740 (ff. 40–73v).

_____. *Falstaff*. Score. 1838. *Lbl*, Add. 29334.

_____. *Joan of Arc*, Overture. Score. 1837. *Lbl*, Add. 29331.

_____. *The Maid of Artois*. Score. 1836. *Lbl*, Add. 29327–8.

_____. *The Maid of Honour*. Score. 1847. *Lbl*, Add. 29348–9.

_____. *The Puritan's Daughter*, Opening Scene. Score. 1861. *Lbl*, Add. 29358.

_____. *The Rose of Castille*. Score. 1857. *Lbl*, Add. 29352–3.

_____. *Satanella, or, The Power of Love*, Preludio. Score. 1858. *Lbl*, Add. 29354.

_____. *The Sicilian Bride*. Score. 1852. *Lbl*, Add. 29350–1.

_____. *The Siege of Rochelle*. Score. 1835. *Lbl*, Add. 29325.

Barnett, John Francis. *The Ancient Mariner* [cantata]. Poem by S. T. Coleridge. London & New York: Novello, Ewer and Co., [1890?].

Benedict, Julius. *The Octoroon Overture*. London: Boosey and Sons, [1873].

_____. *Overture to Shakespeare's Play 'The Tempest'*, Op. 77. London: Enoch and Sons, [1875?].

_____. *Symphony (in G Minor) for Grand Orchestra*, Op. 101. London: Stanley Lucas, Weber & Co., [1874].

Bennett, Alfred. *The Warrior's Triumph: Song with an Accompaniment for the Trumpet, Composed for and sung by Sr. Sapio, to whom it is respectfully dedicated*. Words by William Walter Tireman. London: S. Chappell, [1828].

Bennett, William Sterndale. *Fantasie-Ouverture zu Thomas Moore's "Paradies und Peri" für grosses Orchester*, Op. 42. Leipzig: Fr. Kistner, [1868].

_____. *Die Najaden Ouverture für grosses Orchester*, Op. 15. Leipzig: Fr. Kistner, [1845?].

_____. *Overture zu Lord Byron's Dichtung Parisina*, Op. 3. Leipzig: Fr. Kistner, [1875?].

_____. *Sinfonie G moll für grosses Orchester*, Op. 43. Leipzig: Fr. Kistner, [1872].

_____. Symphony in A Major. In *The Symphony 1720–1840: A Comprehensive Collection of Full Scores in Sixty Volumes*. Ed. Barry S. Brook. Series E: Great Britain, Vol. VII. Ed. Nicholas Temperley. New York & London: Garland, 1982–1984.

_____. Symphony in G Minor. In *The Symphony 1720–1840: A Comprehensive Collection of Full Scores in Sixty Volumes*. Ed. Barry S. Brook. Series E: Great Britain, Vol. VII. Ed. Nicholas Temperley. New York & London: Garland, 1982–1984.

_____. *Die Waldnymphe: Ouverture für grosses Orchester*, Op. 20. Leipzig: Fr. Kistner, [1850?].

Bishop, Henry Rowley. *Aladdin*. Score. 1826. *Lbl*, Add. 36957.

_____. *Clari, or, The Maid of Milan*. Parts. 1823. *Lbl*, Add. 36574.

_____. *The Coronation of Charles the 10th*, Overture. Score. 1825. *Lbl*, Add. 33570 (ff. 139–171).

_____. *Edward the Black Prince*, Opening Scene. Score. 1828. *Lbl*, Add. 27722.

_____. *Englishmen in India*, Overture. Score. 1827. *Lbl*, Add. 27720.

_____. *For England, Ho!*, Overture. Score. 1813. *Lbl*, Add. 27704.

_____. Grand Sinfonia in C. Score. 1805. *Lbl*, Add. 34725 (ff. 37–149).

_____. *Guy Mannering*, Overture. London: Lafleur and Son, [1873].

_____. *The Heart of Mid-Lothian*, Overture. Score. 1819. *Lbl*, Add. 27711 (ff. 70–86v).

_____. *The Heir of Vironi; or Honesty the best Policy*, Overture. Score. 1817. *Lbl*, Add. 27707.

_____. *The Humourous Lieutenant; or Alexander's Successors*, Overture. Score. 1817. *Lbl*, Add. 27710.

_____. *The Knight of Snowdoun*. Score. 1811. *Lbl*, Add. 36940.

_____. *The Law of Java*. Score. 1822. *Lbl*, Add. 36955.

_____. *Love in a Tub: a Pastoral Ballet*. Score. 1808. *Lbl*, Add. 32461.

_____. *Manfred*, opening scene. Score. 1834. *Lbl*, Add. 27727.

_____. *The Maniac, or The Swiss Banditti*, Overture. Score. 1810. *Lbl*, Add. 36938.

_____. *A Midsummer Night's Dream*, Overture. Score. 1816. *Lbl*, Add. 36944.

_____. *The Miller and his Men*, Overture. Score. 1813. *Lbl*, Add. 27703.

_____. *Peace Inviting: Sung by Mr. Sims Reeves*. London: B. Williams, [1863].

_____. *The Romance of a Day!* Score. 1831. *Lbl*, Add. 36959.

_____. *Rural Felicity*. Score. 1834. *Lbl*, Add. 27728.

_____. *The Slave*, Overture. Score. 1816. *Lbl*, Add. 36947.

_____. *Thine For Ever: Arranged for Voice, Trumpet & Pianoforte by Thomas Harper*. London: Stanley Lucas, Weber and Co., [1873].

_____. *The Vintagers*, Overture. Score. 1809. *Lbl*, Add. 27702.

_____. *Waterloo* [cantata]. Score. 1826. *Lbl*, Add. 33570 (ff. 184–216).

_____. *Who Wants a Wife, or The Law of the Land*. Score. 1816. *Lbl*, Add. 36946.

_____. *Yelva*, Overture. 1829. In *The Symphony 1720–1840: A Comprehensive Collection of Full Scores in Sixty Volumes*. Ed. Barry S. Brook. Series E: Great Britain, Vol. VI. Ed. Nicholas Temperley. New York & London: Garland, 1982–1984.

Bishop, Henry Rowley, arr. *The Coronation in Shakspea's* [sic] *Play Henry the Fourth 2nd Part* [pastiche]. Score. 1821. *Lbl*, Add. 33570 (ff. 95–183v).

Cherubini, Luigi. "Concert-Ouverture." Ed. Friedrich Grützmacher. Leipzig: C.F. Kahnt Nachfolger, [1892].

_____. *Sinfonia in Re Maggiore*. Ed. Adriano Lualdi. Milan: Edizioni Suvini Zeboni, 1950.

Clementi, Muzio. *Ouverture in Do Maggiore*. Milan: Edizioni Suvini Zerboni, 1978.

_____. *Ouverture in Re Maggiore*. Ed. Pietro Spada. Milan: Edizioni Suvini Zerboni, 1978.

_____. *Sinfonia N. 1 in Do maggiore*. Milan: Edizioni Suvini Zerboni, 1976.

_____. *Sinfonia N. 2 in Re maggiore*. Milan: Edizioni Suvini Zerboni, 1978.

_____. Symphony No. 2 in D Major. In *The Symphony 1720–1840: A Comprehensive Collection of Full Scores in Sixty Volumes*. Ed. Barry S. Brook. Series E: Great Britain, Vols. IV/V. Ed. John Walter Hill. New York & London: Garland, 1982–1984.

_____. *Sinfonia N. 3 in Sol maggiore* ["Great National Symphony"]. Ed. Pietro Spada. Milan: Edizioni Suvini Zerboni, 1977.

_____. *Sinfonia N. 4 in Re maggiore*. Milan: Edizioni Suvini Zerboni, 1975.

Cliffe, Frederic. Symphony in C Minor. London & New York: Novello, Ewer & Co., [1890].

Corder, Frederick. *Prospero:* Concert Overture for full Orchestra. London & New York: Novello, Ewer & Co., [1888].

Cowen, Frederic Hymen. *Symphonie in C-moll ("Scandinavische") für Orchester*. Vienna: Albert J. Gutmann, [1888].

_____. Symphony No. 4 "The Welsh" in B flat Minor for Orchestra. London & New York: Novello, Ewer & Co., [1885].

Crotch, William. Overture (in A). Score. 1795. *Lbl*, Add. 30393 (ff. 1–30).

_____. Overture (in G). Score. 1815. *Lbl*, Add. 30393 (ff. 64–94).

_____. Sinfonia (in E♭). Score. 1817. *Lbl*, Add. 30394.

_____. Sinfonia (in F). Score. 1814. *Lbl*, Add. 30393 (ff. 31–63b).

Cusins, William George. *Concert Overture No. 1 Les Travailleurs de la Mer (after Victor Hugo)*. London: Stanley Lucas, Weber & Co., [1875?].

_____. *Love's labour's lost: Concert-Overture (No. II) (after Shakespeare)*. London: Stanley Lucas, Weber & Co., [1875?].

Fane, John (Lord Bughersh). Sinfonia No. 3 (in D). *Lbl*, Add. 33315.

German, Edward. Bourée and Gigue, from the music to Shakespeare's *Much Ado About Nothing*. London: Novello and Company, 1902.

_____. *Coronation March and Hymn*. London: Novello & Co., 1911.

_____. *Masque*, from the music to Shakespeare's *As You Like It*. London: Novello and Company, 1902.

_____. Overture to Shakespeare's *Richard III*. London: Novello and Company, [1902].

_____. Prelude to Shakespeare's *Romeo and Juliet*. London: Novello and Company, 1902.

_____. Symphony #2 ("Norwich"). London: Novello & Co., [1931].

_____. *Valse Gracieuse* from the Orchestral Suite in D Minor. London: Novello and Company, 1902.

Handel, George Frederic. *Admeto*. Kalmus Miniature Scores #1253. Leipzig: Kalmus, 1877; reprint, Melville, NY: Belwin Mills, n. d.

_____. "Let the Bright Seraphim." In *Three Arias for Trumpet and Voice*. Transc. James Ode. Nashville: The Brass Press, 1976.

_____. *A Song to the March in Scipio*. [London]: [1730].

Harper, Thomas. "Melody in C." In Eliza Wesley Autograph Book. *Lbl*, Add. 35026, f. 32v.

Harper Jr., Thomas John. "Cadenzas for Voice and Trumpet." *Lcm*, MS 4082, ff. 3–4v.

_____. "A Collection of Marches, Flourishes, etc., for trumpets, written on cards in separate parts." *Lcm*, MS 4074.

_____. "Marches, Flourishes, etc., for trumpets." *Lcm*, MS 4072.

_____. "Trumpet Cadenza and Flourish." *Lcm*, MS 4078, f. 34.

Hatton, J. L. *The Trumpet on the Rhone: Song, with Trumpet Obligato.* Words by W. H. Bellamy. London: Addison, Hollier and Lucas, [1860].

Hook, James. *Hark, Hark the Dreadful Din of War: A favorite Trumpet Song, Sung by Miss Bertles at Vauxhall Gardens.* London: Preston, [1788?].

_____. *The Solace of Life: A Favorite Trumpet Song, Sung by Mr. Duffey at Vauxhall.* London: Preston & Son, [1791?].

_____. *Volunteer: A favorite Song Sung by Mr. Incledon with the utmost applause at Vauxhall.* London: Preston and Son, [1790].

King, Oliver A. *Among the Pines:* Concert-Overture for full Orchestra, Op. 36. London: Novello, Ewer & Co., [1884].

_____. *Night:* Symphony in F for Full Orchestra, Op. 22. London: Novello, Ewer & Co., [1882].

MacCunn, Hamish. *The Dowie Dens o' Yarrow:* Ballad-Overture, Op. 6. London: Augener & Co., [1891].

_____. *Highland Memories:* Suite of 3 Scottish Scenes for Orchestra, Op. 30. London: Augener & Co., [1897].

_____. *The Land of the Mountain and the Flood:* Concert Overture, Op. 3. London & New York: Novello, Ewer and Co., [1889].

_____. *The Ship o' the Fiend:* Orchestral Ballad, Op. 5. London: Augener & Co., [1890].

Macfarren, George Alexander. *Chevy Chase Overture*. Score. 1836. *Cfm*, MS 1061.

_____. *Don Carlos*, Overture. Parts and score. 1842. *Cfm*, MS 1064–65.

_____. *Don Quixote Overture*. Score. 1846. *Cfm*, MS 1066.

_____. *Hamlet*, Overture. Score. 1856. *Cfm*, MS 1016.

_____. *Idyll in Memory of Sterndale Bennett*. Score. 1875. *Cfm*, MS 1154.

_____. *Kenilworth*, Overture. Score. 1880. *Cfm*, MS 1073.

_____. *King Charles II*, Overture. Score. 1849. *Cfm*, MS 1077.

_____. *The Lady of the Lake* [cantata]. Score. *Lbl*, Add. 50773A, B.

_____. Overture in E♭. Score. 1832. *Cfm*, MS 1024.

_____. *Robin Hood*, Overture. Score. 1860. *Cfm*, MS 1086.

_____. *Romeo and Juliet*, Overture. Parts and score. 1836. *Cfm*, MS 1084.

_____. *She Stoops to Conquer*. Score. 1864. *Cfm*, MS 1087.

_____. *St. John the Baptist* [oratorio]. London: Stanley Lucas, Weber & Co., [1876].

_____. Symphony No. 2 in D Minor. Score. 1831. *Cfm*, MS 1017.

_____. Symphony No. 3 in E Minor. Score. 1832. *Cfm*, MS 1018.

_____. Symphony No. 4 in F Minor. Score. 1833. *Cfm*, MS 1019.

_____. Symphony No. 5 in A Minor. Score. 1835. *Cfm*, MS 1020.

_____. Symphony No. 6 in B♭. Score. 1836. *Cfm*, MS 1021.

_____. Symphony No. 7 in C♯ Minor. Parts and score. 1839–40. *Cfm*, MS 1022.

_____. Symphony No. 8 in D ("Thalchen"). Parts and score. 1845. *Cfm*, MS 1023.

_____. Symphony No. 9 in E Minor. Parts and score. 1874. *Cfm*, MS 1025–26.

Mackenzie, Alexander Campbell. *Ballet Music and Rustic March*, from the opera *Columba*, Op. 28. London: Novello, Ewer & Co., [1884].

_____. *La Belle Dame sans Merci:* Ballad for Orchestra, Op. 29. London & New York: Novello, Ewer & Co., [1884].

_____. *Britannia: A Nautical Overture*, Op. 52. London: Joseph Williams, [1895].

_____. *Burns: Second Scotch Rhapsody*, Op. 24. London: Novello, Ewer & Co., [1880].

_____. Concerto for the Violin, Op. 32. London & New York: Novello, Ewer & Co., [1885].

_____. *Courante* from *Ravenswood (The Bride of Lammermoor)*. London: Novello & Co., [1899].

_____. *From the North: (Three Scottish Pieces)*, Op. 53. London: Joseph Williams, [1895].

_____. *Overture and Three Dances*, from *The Little Minister*. London & New York: Novello, Ewer & Co., 1897.

_____. *Overture to Shakespeare's Comedy Twelfth Night*, Op. 40. London & New York: Novello, Ewer and Co., 1888.

_____. *Rhapsodie Ecossaise*, Op. 21. London: Neumeyer & Co., [1880].

_____. *Schottisches Concert für Pianoforte mit Begleitung des Orchesters*, Op. 55. Leipzig: Fr. Kistner, 1899.

Mendelssohn, Felix. *The Hebrides Overture ("Fingal's Cave")*, Op. 26. In *Felix Mendelssohn Major Orchestral Works*. Ed. Julius Rietz. New York: Dover Publications, 1975.

_____. Symphony No. 3 in A Minor ("Scottish"). In *Felix Mendelssohn Major Orchestral Works*. Ed. Julius Rietz. New York: Dover Publications, 1975.

Moscheles, Ignaz. *No. 2 Grosses Concert in Es-dur für das Pianoforte*. Vienna: Tobias Haslinger, [ca. 1825].

_____. Third Grand Concerto for the Piano Forte. London: Chappell & Co., [1825?].

Neukomm, Sigismund. *Fantaisie Concertante for Trumpet, Horn, Flute, Clarionette, Oboe, Bassoon & Double Bass.* Angermüller No. 399. Score. February 1832.

_____. *Nonetto for Trumpet, Horn, Flute, Oboe, Clarionet, Bassoon, Tenor, Violincello & Double Bass.* Angermüller No. 513. Score. 10 February 1836.

_____. *Ottetto pour trompette, cor, flute, hautbois, clarinette, bassoon, violincello et contrebasse.* Angermüller No. 421. Parts. 24 December 1832.

Parry, Charles Hubert Hastings. *Overture to An Unwritten Tragedy.* London: Novello and Company, [1906].

_____. *Symphonic Variations for Full Orchestra.* London & New York: Novello, Ewer and Co., [1898].

_____. Symphony in C ("The English"). London: Novello and Company, 1907.

_____. Symphony in F ("Cambridge"). London: Novello and Company, [1905].

Potter, Philip Cipriani Hambly. Overtura [in E]. Score. 1848. *Lbl*, LOAN 4/837.

_____. Overture (in E). Score. 1815. *Lbl*, LOAN 4/837.

_____. Overture to Shakespeare's Play *Antony & Cleopatra*. Score. 1835. *Lbl*, LOAN 4/839.

_____. Overture to Shakespeare's Play *Cymbeline*. Score. 1836. *Lbl*, LOAN 4/838.

_____. Overture to *The Tempest*. Score. 1837. *Lbl*, LOAN 4/840.

_____. Sinfonia [in B♭]. Score. 1821. *Lbl*, LOAN 4/377.

_____. Sinfonia (in C Minor). Score. 1826. *Lbl*, Add. 31783 (ff. 1–55).

_____. Sinfonia in C Minor. Score. 1834. *Lbl*, LOAN 4/375.

_____. Sinfonia (in C Minor). Parts. 1847. *Lbl*, Add. 31790–91.

_____. Sinfonia (in D). Score. 1833. *Lbl*, LOAN 4/379.

_____. Sinfonia (in D Major). Score. 1834. *Lbl*, LOAN 4/376.

_____. Sinfonia in G Minor (No. 1). Score. [before 1826]. *Lbl*, LOAN 4/378.

_____. Sinfonia No. 7 (in F). Score. 1826. *Lbl*, Add. 31783 (ff. 56–125).

_____. Sinfonia No. 8 (in E♭). Score. 1828. *Lbl*, Add. 31783 (ff. 126–148).

_____. Sinfonia (No. 10) [in G Minor]. Score. 1832. *Lbl*, LOAN 4/374.

_____. Sinfonie in E♭. Score. 1846. *Lbl*, Add. 31788–89.

Prout, Ebenezer. Concerto in E Minor for Organ & Orchestra, Op. 5. London: Augener & Co., [1886].

_____. Minuet and Trio for Orchestra, Op. 14. London: Augener & Co., [1881].

_____. *Suite de Ballet*, Op. 28. London: Augener and Co., [1892].

_____. Symphony No. 3 in F Major, Op. 22. London & New York: Novello, Ewer & Co., [1885?].

_____. *Triumphal March*, from the Cantata *Alfred*. London: Augener & Co., [ca. 1885].

Purcell, Daniel. "Symphony of Flat Trumpets," from *The Island Princess*. In *Music for London Entertainment, 1600–1800*. Series C, Vol. II. Facsimile reprint of *Lbl* Add. 15318, f.39. Tunbridge Wells: Richard Macnutt, 1985.

Purcell, Henry. *Orpheus Britannicus. A Collection of all the Choicest Songs. For One, Two, and Three Voices, Compos'd by Mr. Henry Purcell. Together, With such Symphonies for Violins or Flutes, as were by Him design'd for any of them: and a Through-Bass to each Song; Figur'd for the Organ, Harpsichord, or Theorbo-Lute*. London: William Pearson, 1706.

Reeve, William. *Hark! The Trumpet Sounds Afar: A Favorite New Song, Sung by Mr. Bannister in "Hero and Leander."* London: G. Goulding, [1787].

―――. *Love Sounds the Trumpet of Joy: A Favorite Trumpet Song, Sung with Unbounded Applause, by Miss Daniels, at Vauxhall Gardens.* London: Bland & Weller's, [1800?].

Silas, Edouard. *1ère Symphonie dedièe à Mr. Henri Broadwood*, Op. 19. London: Cramer, Beale & Wood, [1864].

Stanford, Charles Villiers. *Flourish of Trumpets for the Imperial Coronation Durbar held at Delhi January 1st 1903.* London: Houghton & Co., 1902.

―――. *Phaudrig Crohoore: Choral Ballad*, Op. 62. London: Boosey & Co., 1896.

―――. *Prelude to the Oedipus Rex of Sophocles*, Op. 29. London: Novello, Ewer & Co., [1888].

―――. Requiem for Solos, Chorus and Orchestra, Op. 63. London and New York: Boosey & Co., 1897.

―――. Symphony in F Minor ("The Irish"), Op. 28. London: Novello, Ewer and Co., 1887.

―――. Symphony No. 4 in F Major, Op. 31. London & New York: Novello, Ewer and Co., [1891].

―――. Symphony No. 5 in D Major ("L'Allegro ed il Pensieroso"), Op. 56. London: Stainer & Bell, 1923.

―――. *Suite of Ancient Dances*, Op. 58. London: Boosey & Co., 1895.

Sullivan, Arthur Seymour. *The Gondoliers.* Libretto by W. S. Gilbert. Score. n.d. *Lbl*, Add. 53779.

―――. *H.M.S. Pinafore ("Amor An Bord").* Braunschweig: Henry Litolff's Verlag, [ca. 1890].

―――. *Ivanhoe.* Libretto by Julian Sturgis. London: Chappell & Co., [1891].

―――. *Macbeth Overture.* London: Chappell & Co., [1893].

_____. *The Mikado*. Libretto by W. S. Gilbert. Introduction by Gordon Jacob. Farnborough, Hants.: Gregg International Publishers, 1968.

_____. *The Music to Shakespeare's Play The Tempest*, Op. 1. London & New York: Novello, Ewer and Co., 1891.

_____. *Overture di Ballo*. London & New York: Novello, Ewer and Co., 1889.

_____. *Overture in C (In Memoriam)*. London & New York: Novello, Ewer & Co., [1885].

_____. *Patience*. Score. n.d. *Lbl*, Add. 53778.

_____. Symphony in E ("The Irish"). London: Novello and Company, 1915.

Thomson, John. *Hermann, or, the Broken Spear*, Overture. In *The Symphony 1720–1840: A Comprehensive Collection of Full Scores in Sixty Volumes*. Ed. Barry S. Brook. Series E: Great Britain, Vol. VI. Ed. Nicholas Temperley. New York & London: Garland, 1982–1984.

_____. *The Shadow on the Wall*, Overture. 1835. In *The Symphony 1720–1840: A Comprehensive Collection of Full Scores in Sixty Volumes*. Ed. Barry S. Brook. Series E: Great Britain, Vol. VI. Ed. Nicholas Temperley. New York & London: Garland, 1982–1984.

Walch, J. H. *Potpourri pour Musique militaire pour Trompette obligeé, Clarinette en Es, 3 Clarinettes en B, 2 Cors, Flûte, 2 Bassons, et Serpent, 2 Trompettes, 2 Trombones, et Tambour grand, composeé par J. H. Walch*. Leipzig: Bureau de Musique de C. F. Peters, n.d.

Wallace, Vincent. *Lurline*, Overture. London: J. R. Lafleur & Son, [1887].

Weber, Carl Maria von. *Oberon*. Score. 1826. *Lbl*, Add. 27746–48.

Wesley, Samuel. Overture in E. [ca. 1834]. *Lbl*, Add. 35010 (ff. 39–100).

Wesley, Samuel Sebastian. *Ode for the North London Working Men's Industrial Exhibition*. Words by W. H. Bellamy. Score. 1864. *Lcm*, MS 4034.

_____. Symphony in C Minor. In *The Symphony 1720–1840: A Compre-hensive Collection of Full Scores in Sixty Volumes*. Ed. Barry S. Brook. Series E: Great Britain, Vol. III. Ed. John I. Schwartz. New York & London: Garland, 1982–1984.

_____. *The Wilderness* [anthem]. Score. 1852. *Lcm*, MS 4030.

When Briton's Silver Trumpet Sounds: Sung by Mrs. Wright at Vauxhall. [London]: [1775?].

SLIDE TRUMPET DISCOGRAPHY

The Clarion Ensemble: Deborah Roberts, soprano; Jonathan Impett, trum-pet; and Paul Nicholson, piano. *Trumpet Collection.* Compact Disc CD-SAR 30. Amon Ra Records, 1987.

Crispian Steele-Perkins, trumpet, and *Tafelmusik*, conducted by Jeanne Lamon. *Music for Trumpet and Orchestra.* Compact Disc SK 53365. Sony Classical, 1993.

Index